THE
ICON

THE
ICON

A NOVEL

NEIL OLSON

HarperCollinsPublishers

HarperCollins books may be purchased for educational, business, or sales pro-
motional use. For information, please write: Special Markets Department,
HarperCollins Publishers Inc., 10 East 53rd Street, New York, NY 10022.

FIRST EDITION

Designed by Jaime Putorti

Printed on acid-free paper

Library of Congress Cataloging-in-Publication Data

Olson, Neil.
      The icon: a novel/by Neil Olson.—1st ed.
        p. cm.
      ISBN 0-06-074838-9
      1. Icons—Collectors and collecting—Fiction. 2. New York (N.Y.)—
Fiction. 3. Greece—Fiction. I. Title

      PS3615.L735I23 2005
      813'6—dc22   2004054227

05 06 07 08 09   ❖/RRD   10 9 8 7 6 5 4 3 2 1

For Caroline

What *is* God and eternal life in Paradise? Paradise is this fire, and God is this dance, and they last not just a moment but forever and ever.

—Nikos Kazantzakis, *The Fratricides*

ACKNOWLEDGMENTS

My agent, Sloan Harris, provided countless insights into the troubles that beset earlier versions of this work, and proved himself the embodiment of patience, perseverance, and good humor. Dan Conaway, my editor, left no line unturned in his effort to make the novel all that it could be, and has a grasp of storytelling magic that is a gift to any writer. Jill Schwartzman, Kristin Ventry, Sandy Hodgman, and Liz Farrell have all gone above and beyond the call of duty.

The many people whose close reads and thoughtful advice were invaluable include Katharine Cluverius, Jesse Dorris, Jake Morrissey, Mary Ann Naples, Marcia Olson, Rose Olson, and Olga Vezeris. I'm grateful to Cameron Olson for supplying critical information about military history, and to Sean Hemingway for a backstage look at the Metropolitan Museum. Vasili Andreopoulos' memories of the German occupation of his village in Kozani were among the first inspirations for this work. And the support shown to all my writing endeavors by my entire family, including Brad, Laura, and Big Neil, has been faith-sustaining.

I am deeply indebted to the works of countless authors, among them Helen C. Evans, Dan Hofstadter, John Lowden, John Julius Norwich, David Talbot Rice, Steven Runciman, C. M.

Woodhouse, and especially Mark Mazower. Any errors or deliberate departures from fact for dramatic purposes are upon my head, of course.

Greatest thanks and deepest love go to Caroline Sutton, who was my first reader, editor, sounding board, provider of names and colors, and comic relief—and who got me up at six o'clock every morning.

THE
ICON

F rom the summit of the high hill called Adelphos, above the
wind-bent cedars that shrouded the caves, he could see the
Pindos Mountains rise like a gray cloud to the east, could see
brown ridges march north toward Konitza and the Albanian bor-
der, could almost imagine he saw the sun glint off of the Ionian
Sea to the west. And below, steep green valleys and rocky villages, marked out by tall stone church towers. The hill was a
place Captain Elias had gone often as a child, when he would
conjure a life beyond these mountain walls: in Athens, to the
south; or across the sea in America, where his uncle had gone. He
might be a soldier, doctor, traveling musician, or spy—the role
did not greatly matter; every dream was a dream of escape. In
none of those dreams did he ever imagine returning to these
hills, a hunted man in his own country.

It was after midnight when Father Mikalis arrived at the Cave
of Constantine. Though his visits to the guerrillas had been rare
of late, he knew where to find them. Elias, who seldom slept anymore, summoned the young priest to his lantern-lit circle in the
back. The captain had warned Mikalis weeks before that the Ger-

mans were watching him more closely, so all the men understood that his present visit must be of great urgency.

"Bless us, Father."

Dirty hands grasped gently at the flowing black cassock as it passed, beseeching pardon for things they had done and would continue to do, to the Germans and their countrymen alike, in the days to come. Like children, thought Elias, watching his men. Crude and murderous until the stern father was before them, then meek and repentant. It was not the young cleric they saw now but God himself, the first touch of the mighty one in months for some, and the cave's darkness only heightened the effect. Whispered blessings were returned to them, but the words did not reach Elias, and he was content with that. He alone was not surprised to see the priest.

"Welcome, Father," the captain said as Mikalis' long, handsome face appeared out of the shadows. "Come for a sermon, or a drink?"

"Don't be foolish. With news."

Elias noted once more how much age, bred of three years' hard experience, had settled in the lines of the priest's face. In truth, there had always been something old about Mikalis, something unconnected to earthly experience, an ancient spirit that showed itself at odd moments in the center of those dark eyes. Elias had seen it when they were both children. There was still a young man's eagerness, a young man's sense of mission. Mikalis had witnessed atrocities, had given absolution for those same atrocities, had never lost hope. That required a certain kind of strength, the captain conceded, a kind he himself did not possess. And yet, the priest had never committed a violent act, had never driven the life out of a fellow man with his own hands. Surely that had to make all the difference. Priests should be murderers. How else could they understand?

"Tell me your news," Elias said at last.

"The Germans will burn the village tomorrow."

In the shadows, Spiro cursed, but the others were silent.

The captain considered, not for the first time, how to respond. It was important that he seem to take the threat seriously, yet he must be circumspect, keep Mikalis talking. Above all, keep him here.

"Who told you?"

"What does it matter who? What's to be done?"

"It matters a great deal. Certain names would convince me that it's true, others that it is not."

"Four trucks full of soldiers arrived a few hours ago. You must have seen them."

"We did."

"Forty or fifty men. They're here for some purpose."

"Looking for us, maybe," someone wondered.

"No," Elias said. "Too few of them for that. They don't come into the hills with less than a battalion now."

"Since we blew up the fuel depot," added Spiro.

"You're proud of that raid?" asked the priest. "They shot forty-three men in the square of Prasinohorion the next day."

"I know it," the captain answered.

"Forty Greeks for one German. You think that's a good trade?"

"One German and a fuel depot. The fuel was the point; I wouldn't have killed anyone if I could have avoided it. Worse is coming. In the Peloponnisos they're attacking armed convoys, in daylight, killing dozens of Germans."

Elias was aware of the envy in his tone. If he only had the communist guerrillas' numbers and resources, he wouldn't have to play the dirty games his superiors dreamed up.

"I'm sure that makes your English friends happy," the priest said scornfully, "but it's just getting a lot of simple people killed."

"It's a war, Mikalis; more will die."

"Many will die tomorrow if you don't help. The old men will try to defend their houses."

"That would be stupid," snapped Elias, "but look, you have it wrong. They *will* burn the village, they'll burn all the villages, whether we fight them or lie down, but they won't do it until they withdraw from the region. And that time is not yet come."

"The English tell you this?"

"It's how they do things. Meantime, we've conducted no operations near here. They have no reason to burn the place. Otherwise, they would already be at it."

They stared at each other across the lamplight, two young men, neither yet twenty-five, forced into parts intended for more experienced souls. Mikalis had returned from the seminary three years earlier, days before the Germans arrived, to assist the ailing Father Pantelis. Six months later he was burying the old priest and assuming his duties. Disruptions from the war kept the local bishop from assigning a new priest, and Mikalis, who had grown up in the village of Katarini, became its spiritual shepherd at the age of twenty-one. Elias had been at the military academy when war broke out. He was an artillery observer when the army routed the Italians, but had been back in Athens when the Germans launched "Marita," a whirlwind assault that enveloped and shattered the Greek army within days. As the government packed up and sailed to Crete, he rode a horse north to help organize the resistance in these hills. The old men are weak, his grandmother had told him before he left Athens, all the good men are dead.

"People are starving down there," the priest insisted.

"I know that, too."

"Of course you know, your men have taken everything. These people have given their food, their sons, their lives for you. What are you prepared to do for them?"

"Not waste their sacrifice."

"Nothing, then."

"I have only twenty men here."

"Where are the rest? Every boy in the four villages has gone to join you, if only to get something to eat. You should have twice that many."

"They're on an operation."

"Without you?"

"Who told you the Germans would burn the village?"

The priest shook his head in disgust.

"All you want is that name. If he's wrong, shoot him as an agitator. If he's right, shoot him as a collaborator. Either way you'll do nothing."

The fact that the truth was more damning than the priest's

insinuations did not prevent the words from stinging. Before Elias had taken over this group of *andartes*—a motley assortment of republican and royalist-minded farmers and ex-soldiers—they had spent more time fighting the local communist guerrilla band than either faction had spent fighting the Germans. It had taken the British commandos to halfway reconcile the feuding parties and direct their actions in any meaningful way. Despite a deep suspicion of the foreigners, and his shame at the necessity of being instructed by them, Elias had to concede that he had learned much from the Englishmen. How to plant explosives. How to kill silently. How to work side by side with men who might, on another day, be your enemies. Perhaps he had learned some lessons too well. He had seen how much stronger and better organized the communists were; now the Italians had surrendered, and it was only a matter of time before the Germans withdrew. He could no longer ignore the warnings of his superiors regarding where the long-term threat to the country lay. Thus the present, hateful subterfuge.

"Captain." Kosta's voice reached them from the mouth of the cave, in a tone demanding attention. Elias, Mikalis, and a few others shuffled through the darkness, gathering their old, battered rifles as they went. "Above, Leftheris has seen something."

The cave entrance was screened by a short stand of cedar, but the ledge above commanded a view of the entire valley. Leftheris grabbed the captain's sleeve as he came up, and pointed toward a low hilltop a kilometer or so away. Elias recognized the black silhouette of the church tower against the indigo sky, then saw the odd, multihued flickering of light below. Flames, seen through the rose window. Something had gone wrong.

"Looks like they got started early," said Kosta, "and with your church, Father."

"Quiet, you ass," said Spiro.

Elias grabbed Mikalis' shoulder, even as the priest began to struggle down the slope.

"There's no point. The whole thing will be on fire before you get there."

"The Holy Mother," whispered Mikalis, and several of the men crossed themselves in the darkness. Most had not known until that moment that their protectress was still in the church, hidden behind a false wall. In his mind's eye, Elias saw candlelight on gold leaf, saw the sad black eyes burning out of the wood as the object was brought forth, saw a church full of strong, cynical men fall to their knees in reverent silence. Saw even the Snake hypnotized by its beauty. Love of the icon could undo all his plans.

"Where is it?" Leftheris asked. "Will someone down there retrieve it?"

"No—no one else knows where it is."

"What do we do?"

"Leave it," the captain pronounced, but they were all speaking at once now. The fire had not been part of the plan, but it would hide the icon's disappearance, assuming the Prince had been quick enough to get it out first.

"Listen to me," Mikalis broke in. "If we can't put out the flames, at least I can save the Holy Mother. Let me go."

"We all go," said Spiro.

"No," Elias commanded, but he could feel the men balking at his resistance. They seldom disobeyed orders, and never contradicted him to his face, but he was fighting a higher power here and risked losing control. Besides, something had gone wrong, and he should see what could be salvaged. He took the priest by the shoulders and pushed him in the direction of Leftheris.

"Keep hold of this one," he told the sentry. "Kosta, Spiro, come with me."

"But how will we find the Mother without him?"

"I know where it is."

The priest's objections pursued them briefly down the rugged hillside, then all was silence. Trees loomed and disappeared in the dark; they crossed a low stone wall. There was no clear path from the cave to the church, but each man knew the way easily, even on a moonless night. Elias could hear old Spiro's labored footfalls behind him, but Kosta was impossible to pinpoint, though the boy was just yards away. Everyone had said Elias was mad to take Kosta under his tutelage, but he had known better. Few men could be trained to move silently, convey complicated messages in code, kill without hesitation. It had been strange for Elias to be teaching these skills so soon after learning them himself, but Kosta had proved an apt pupil. It was always the outcasts who were the best at the game.

Stamatis Mavroudas was Katarini's leading merchant, a black-marketeer and suspected collaborator with the Germans, and so his son Kosta, while tolerated for his good humor, was trusted by no one. That meant nothing to Elias; insurgency work was full of compromises. And the boy had taken to him quickly, all the more so since the father had virtually disowned him: what idiocy, to join the guerrillas when there was money to be made from this war. Now it was rare to see Kosta and the captain apart. Elias wondered at the cost to the young man. Cut off from his family, with no real friends, Kosta seemed unmoved by the occasional deaths of comrades, and a little too eager for the kill when the time came. Yet he was completely dependable, able to execute the most difficult tasks with speed and creativity. Elias could have used ten more men like him.

In a short time they ascended the slope below the church, and crawled on hands and knees until they could crouch behind the north wall of the front courtyard. The old stone edifice was lit from within, wild, jumping flames playing against the sooty stained glass. The crack of burning timber was audible, and the cool air stank of smoke. Across the courtyard a dozen German soldiers milled about, some still strapping on helmets and checking rifles, seemingly having arrived only minutes before the guerrillas, and so far unaware of them. An officer was backing out of the church entry, from which black smoke billowed. Probably Müller, the SS man, thought Elias, but it was hard to tell in the strange light. There was nothing in the officer's hands, no treasure taken from within. Had he arrived too late?

The captain swore silently. The plan was turning to shit. It had been a miserable scheme from the start; damn the Snake for talking him into it.

"Spiro, go and see if the crypt entry is clear."

The old *andarte* slipped away silently.

Now the German officer—definitely Müller, the Prince as they called him—was moving off, around the south side of the church, and most of the soldiers followed. A glance passed between Kosta and the captain, and the younger man looked away quickly. Was he ashamed of his commander, ashamed of his own knowledge? Kosta was the only other person besides the Snake and Müller to know the captain's plan, and had run messages between various parties when Elias needed to be elsewhere. Was the secret proving too great for him?

There was a commotion of snapping branches from the base of the hill behind them, and the two guerrillas swung their rifles up to fire.

"Hold," said the captain.

Mikalis emerged from the trees and came recklessly up the slope, Leftheris on his heels. Kosta slid down the incline and yanked the priest to the ground.

"I'm sorry," whispered Leftheris, unable to look the captain in the eye. "He said I would be damned if I didn't let him go."

Elias did not waste time berating his man, but looked hard at the priest.

"Threatening damnation to get your way. You surprise me, Father."

"Brother, let me get into that church."

"See those soldiers?"

"They won't shoot me."

"The fire is in the front, you can't get in."

"Then let us try the back. Or the crypt."

As if in answer, Spiro reappeared at the captain's shoulder.

"The crypt is no good. Too many Germans that way."

"Then we try the back," Mikalis insisted. "There are trees, they won't see us."

Again, the men were eager, and the captain could not justify inaction. Nor could he trust the errant priest to anyone else.

"Stay by me. On my left, and just behind me, understand?"

"Yes."

They skirted the tree line to the north and came up on the rear of the old stone structure, where the cleric's private entry lay in shadow. The fire had indeed started in front, but they could chart its progress through the tall, murky windows, and it seemed that the better part of the interior was now in flames.

"It's too late," Leftheris said mournfully.

"No." The priest began to force his way past the captain, who seized him.

"Leftheris is right."

"Let me at least try. The icon . . ."

"Is wood and paint, Mikalis. Let it go."

The long face thrust itself at Elias, forehead to forehead, whispering.

"You're wrong. There is more to it than you see."

"What?"

"But even if you were right, faith may invest objects with power. The Mother has cured the ill here for centuries; it means everything to these people."

The captain could not respond at once. The cult of the icon had always seemed an old woman's obsession to him, something his father had scorned, as he scorned all religion, something the young people of the local villages would surely grow up to reject, or ignore. Elias was no communist, but he was a man with his eye on the wider world, where science trumped superstition, where worship of the Mother of God did not guide men's actions. Athens had given him a taste of that world, but perhaps he had been there too long. Or perhaps he'd done wrong to return here. His young fighters trusted priests even less then he did, yet in moments of fear they turned not to each other, like their brothers with the communists, but to God, and to *Panayía*, the forgiving Mother. How had it happened? If the priests and old women had no hold over them, from where had this belief emerged? Where had Mikalis, whose own father was utterly godless, found his faith? And how could Elias look such faith in the eye after setting such mischief in motion?

"Listen to me."

There was nothing to say. His words would have hung unfinished in any case, but at that moment the captain noticed shadows on the far side of the church, moving among the graves. Müller and six or eight soldiers, looking for the rear entrance.

They had gone the long way around but would be upon the *andartes* in moments. Distracted, Elias loosened his grip fractionally. It was enough; the priest was gone from beneath his hands, leaping the broken wall and racing up the remaining slope for the dark portal. The captain froze, unable to call out. The Germans apparently recognized the black cassock and did not shoot, but one soldier darted forward to intercept the cleric.

"Halt, halt."

A rifle boomed to the captain's left—Spiro's old Männlicher—and the soldier sat heavily, listed sideways to the ground. A moment later shots came from the other side, springing hot chips from the stone wall, and the guerrillas ducked their heads as the Germans sought cover. Mikalis stumbled over the fallen soldier but righted himself and disappeared into the entry.

Elias, calmed by the eruption of fighting, found his voice and commanded his men to spread out along the wall and shoot as fast as they could reload. Accuracy was not important. The crosses and narrow tablets gave the Germans no refuge; their only real cover was the corner of the church—and since only one or two men at a time could fire from that position, the guerrillas might keep them pinned briefly, while disguising their own paltry numbers. It would be four against fifty once the rest of the Germans arrived, presumably in minutes, but perhaps the priest would emerge before that.

Then a second figure was leaping the wall and making for the door. Black shirt and kerchief, running low and swift. Kosta. What the hell was the boy up to? He had no love for priests or icons, but so be it: the action was undertaken. Reloading the Enfield was too slow; the captain tossed the rifle aside, drew his pistol, and fired blindly at the shadows, wasting precious ammunition. Spiro and Leftheris picked up their fire as well, and Kosta raced through the doorway.

Captain Elias bent to reload his hot pistol and consider his position. A bad business, no helping that now. Spiro should not have shot but must have thought Mikalis was in danger. The dead German would cost the village dearly unless Elias could put it right with Müller. Müller, with whom he was now exchanging hostile fire, never a good place from which to negotiate. To hell with it all. If he had the men the Snake had taken to retrieve the weapons, he would scrap the whole dirty plan and kill as many Germans as he could. If. No, this was a foolish action, thoughtlessly undertaken, his own fault.

Never mind. From the woods to the north, almost behind them, he could just discern the sound of creaking rifle straps. From the lane behind the church, clattering boot heels. They would be encircled in minutes.

"Withdraw."

He scrambled along the wall to Leftheris and Spiro, and when they would not listen he knocked their rifle barrels up and forcibly pushed them toward the wood line.

"Withdraw, damn you. Not the cave, the old monastery." An eight-kilometer trek, hard on old Spiro, but the Germans would not pursue them so far in the dark, and they must by no means expose the cave.

Slowly, the men obeyed, disappearing into the trees, leaving the captain alone. He rushed back along the broken wall and slipped over it at a point closer to the front of the church, out of sight, he hoped. A heavy machine gun suddenly opened up from the graveyard, spraying the position were Elias and his men had been half a minute before. On his belly, he arrived at the church wall and slid upright against it. The tall stained-glass window above him had already shattered from the heat. Kerchief against his face, Elias peered in. The fire was nearly out in the front—having consumed everything there—but still in full fury near the back. The altar and ancient iconostasis were lost in smoke. Venerable wooden pews were skeletal beneath fiery cowls, roof timbers exploded above. The church was old, much of it contents centuries older, and even the godless captain felt the loss. He could not see the place where the icon was hidden, and there was no sign of any man.

He ducked down again. There were voices and rushing feet in the woods below. A lantern swung wildly. They would be up the slope any moment, finding only their fellow Germans in the graveyard beyond. With any luck the bastards would shoot each other. Elias dropped to his stomach and crawled back toward the front of the church.

The few soldiers who had been left in the courtyard had abandoned it, presumably to join the encircling troops. That left the front entrance clear, if the men inside had been able to fight through the flames to get to it. The crypt passage still seemed the most likely route, though. At a safe distance from the enemy, the captain reentered the woods, where he quickly stashed his rifle and bandoleer inside a split tree trunk. Then he tucked the pistol under his loose vest. Anyone with a good eye and a little bit of light to work with could spot him as an *andarte,* but it would have to do. He must make his way into the village. Already the wheels of his mind were turning with the night's terrible possibilities. He had three places to search, four men to find, and some hard questions to answer. Then he had to make things right with the Prince.

By morning everything would be clearer, though certain questions would persist for a lifetime. Six weeks later, upon their retreat from the region, the Germans would burn the village of Katarini to the ground.

PART
ONE

1

The blue sky that had oppressed him for days was gone, replaced by a solid wedge of leaden gray and the sound of rain in the courtyard. He could still make out the towering brown mass that formed the rear of an old hotel, but the wet leaves and branches of the giant plane tree were now beyond his failing sight. The nurse constantly assured him that the tree was still there, and he would accept her word. It had, after all, been there forty years and more, long before he'd moved into these haunted chambers. It would be there after he was gone. This was reassuring.

He had become grateful for the ordinary things that could be maintained in this thoughtless city. It was no longer necessary for these things to last indefinitely. A few more years would do, perhaps less. Better not to think too much about that, his granddaughter kept telling him. Absurd. It was *all* that he could think about; it was the only thing that made sense to think about. His wife and son were already gone before him. He spoke to no one but the nurse and the girl, when she made time for him, when she wasn't in London, or California, spending his money. He could picture her now, perusing the walls of some slick Santa Monica gallery, striding about in the track-lit backroom, making hasty decisions she could repent at leisure. A Hockney or Thiebaud being wrapped for packing, or else some new, even less talented artist she had just discovered. Abominable. Why had she inherited his interest but not his taste? Where did she put all the pieces she bought? She must have filled the walls of all her flats by now. It couldn't be that she was hanging them on the walls around him, taunting his advancing blindness? No, he didn't think she hated him that much, but he would ask the nurse just the same. Of course, he wouldn't know if she was telling him the truth. After all, she was stealing his books. That was all right; she could have them.

Books had been his solace since childhood. They were an older and, he could now see, a far better love than the paintings, which had become a sad obsession, a bright flame burning up the middle decades of his life. The books never disappointed him. He didn't worry about getting first editions, though he probably had many. He didn't try to keep them pristine, never treated them as objects of art. They were for reading, preferably over and over again. Most of his books had seen hard duty, were well and proudly worn. He wanted what was in them. Not knowledge so much, or wisdom—every fool chasing wisdom in books, dear God, what idiocy. Stories, which was to say, the chaos of life made coherent, this is what compelled him. Lies, his father had called the novels he read as a boy. Yes, but what beautiful lies, what useful lies in a world of hard, unrevealing truth. Even the biographies, memoirs, essays: Boswell, Augustine, Montaigne, all liars. Who cared? They got at something that was real.

Could it be that he had gone to the paintings, sixty, seventy years ago, with similar expectations, similar needs? He could no longer remember, but it seemed likely. Somehow the values assigned by the world, by men like his father, the wealthy pack that plucked and hoarded, had clouded his mind. He became very good at the acquisition game, ceasing to wonder why he played. He had so many stories, which he remembered telling and retelling with pride, at the clubs in Zurich, or here in New York,

tales of triumph, getting this painting from that one, or snatching
it out from under the nose of that other one, his vanquished
opponents sometimes sitting at the same table with him, laughing with him. The dilettante, the banker who could outduel the
craftiest dealers. And the stories were always about the deals,
never about the paintings.

Yet surely that wasn't right. That was an oversimplification.
Club talk had no bearing on his private impulses; the two were
unrelated. He had loved the works he had collected, of course he
had. There was no other explanation for the choices he had made.
Love, not greed, had compelled the decisions that hounded his
conscience. It was the only logical explanation. It was his only
hope for forgiveness, that he had acted out of love.

He pressed the familiar button on the arm of the chair and
sensed the bell ringing in the nurse's quarters below. She might at
least tell him which volumes she was taking, but that would be a
confession, of course. How to let her know that he didn't mind?
He could even direct her to which titles might best suit her limited
intelligence. As long as she was reading them, or giving them to
friends. God, what if she were selling them? That would be hateful. No, if she were selling them she would have to be stopped.

The books. He could no longer see the words well enough to
read, not even in the large-print editions. His granddaughter
used to read to him, poetry mostly. She had a mannered delivery,
but he suffered it to hear her beautiful voice, to hear her say anything at all. Recently, all he heard was the distraction in her tone,
the moment's hesitation when he asked her to read him this or
that passage, and so he told her to stop. She protested, but he
understood that she was relieved. Anyway, he seldom saw her
anymore. Something had changed, she could no longer be the
same old girl with him. The nurse was a miserable reader; only
the Bible inspired her. He tried the books on tape, but it was
impossible, some heinous actor's interpretation of a text he
couldn't even grasp. So, no more books. It was the heaviest blow
he'd suffered since his son's death, a killing blow he suspected.
And the girl wondered why he obsessed about the end! What else
was there?

He pressed the button again but the woman was suddenly there before him, blocking the light from the window, her face in shadow. She was clever that way.

"I'm right here, Mr. Kessler."

"I can see that." How long had she been there, reading the thoughts on his face? Or worse, reading his lips? He had acquired the habit of speaking his inner musings aloud, or so a few people had told him.

"Do you want something to eat? You haven't eaten today."

Always with the food. He understood that these basic activities went neglected without her reminders, but he still resented the nagging. He must seize control of the conversation, command her, or else suffer an endless series of questions about his diet, digestion, hygiene. But her name wavered before him uncertainly.

"Do you want me to have André make you something? Some oatmeal, or a sandwich?"

"Diana." There it was. Like the huntress, or the dead princess. Must use her name when he thought of her, stop leaning on lazy terms like "the nurse." "Diana, I want to go to the chapel."

He heard her sigh, ignored it. Her manipulations did not move him; he knew what he wanted. Contemplation, not food. She worked for him, damn it. He sat quietly, not repeating the request, determined not to sound desperate. Then she was behind him, and they were moving. In theory, he could do this for himself. The chair was motorized, and he'd had the lift installed years ago, after he had taken that fall down the narrow stairs. With his vision going, however, simple negotiations around the furniture had become perilous, and he was terrified of having a seizure on the lift, unable to call for help, dying alone in the tall, mechanized coffin. They might not find him for hours.

The lift door rolled shut, and Kessler clutched his armrests as they descended. He had never learned to like this contraption, but it had allowed him to move freely about his home, rather than become a one-floor recluse, with all of the limitations of mind and spirit that entailed. Truthfully, most days he did not feel like stirring from his bed, but something always drove him to move, cover ground, breathe fresh air. Sometimes he would even go to the park, if he was able to persuade the girl—no, use her name. Christiana. Chris to her school chums, such a bland, American name. Ana to him. He had felt so painfully close to the child before Richard died, and she to him, it seemed. Visiting often, accompanying him on his daily walk, an honor he had accorded none before her. Going to all the museums and galleries, speaking about art, German expressionism, surrealism. She was so curious about everything.

Then the newspaper stories surfaced, dirty deals during the war. His name wasn't mentioned, of course, but his bank was, and he had been rather highly placed. Awkward questions arose within the family, seldom voiced but always present. And then his first serious illness, the errand undertaken by his son, which ended in his death. Her mother forbade Ana's visits after that. Nobody told him this, but he knew it must be so. Richard's wife hated him, blamed him for Richard's death, as he blamed himself. After her schooling ended, Ana sought him out again, and they had a few wonderful years. He'd made his last trip to London with her, set her up with dealers and gallery owners, made purchases for her growing collection. Somewhere between his first stroke and her short, unfortunate marriage, Ana stopped seeing him so often. There were plenty of good reasons why, but he suspected the girl had simply grown weary of his dark moods, his feebleness of mind and body. She hadn't grown tired of his money, that was certain. It was the last hold he had upon her.

They maneuvered through the dim ground floor of the brownstone until they reached a pointed archway in back. Diana would not enter. That was fine with him. He had ceased wondering whether she was offended by his eclectic religious tastes, was simply spooked by the place, or had somehow intuited that it had been paid for in blood. It didn't matter. Long his private preserve, the chapel had come to feel like more than that, a place apart from the rest of the world, a place no one else *could* enter, even had anyone wanted to. In fact, he could not remember when the chapel had seen another soul besides himself. Diana's footsteps retreated. He gripped the motor controls and rolled through the archway.

The place had once been a sort of solarium, decades ago, but he had seen right away how to utilize it. The walls were reinforced, a domed oval ceiling stuck on, more Byzantine than Western. The six stained-glass windows came from a bombed-out church in Alsace. There were a dozen wooden panels from Hungary, depicting the stations of the cross. Also, some blackened, ornate candelabra from Italy, though he seldom lit candles in here. None of these objects was terribly valuable, not by the standards of his other possessions, but they all pleased and eased him in a way that other work could not.

On the far wall, lit softly from above and serving as altarpiece, was the Byzantine panel. Older by a thousand years than anything else in the room, his greatest treasure, though it had failed him in nearly every way. The Virgin's face and hands had faded long before he had taken possession of the work. Now, except for those dark eyes, she had become indiscernible to his failing vision, creating the impression of a deep maroon robe wrapped about some spectral being. Not what the maker intended, but quite effective. Kessler wheeled himself the length of the chamber to sit before it.

Müller had never meant to give this one up. Safekeeping only, but when the situation became hopeless in '45, he'd needed money to get out. Money, a Swiss identity, safe passage, Kessler had arranged it all. His own funds, not the bank's. It was far from the only treasure to pass through his hands, and the bank or its managers had kept many when the owners vanished into the cauldron of war, but this was the only one that he had taken for himself. Contrary to the snide insinuations that he knew circulated about him, he had purchased all the other items in this room and in the rooms beyond after the war, legally and aboveboard. True, he'd had the upper hand over emotionally shattered churchmen and penniless aristocrats, whose temporary need outweighed their devotion to art. He wasn't proud of that, but business transactions were never made at equal odds. Someone always had the advantage, and it might as well have been someone like him, who would properly revere the work.

No one knew the icon's true history; at least it had never

reached Kessler's ears. Some said it had been in that village church for centuries. Others, that it had been owned by a long succession of despots, Greek and Muslim, priests, thieves, from Ali Pasha all the way back to the last Byzantine emperor, Constantine XI Palaiologos. It had almost certainly been made in Constantinople, long before the fall, even before the first iconoclasm. Shrouded in rumor, impregnated with mystery.

His blurred vision blurred even further, a dampness in his eyes. Not piety, or God's grace, but simple fear moved him to tears. Fear of his impending end and what waited beyond, sorrow at all that was lost, loved ones, friends, a world that he understood, his youth and vigor, his sight and sense, all lost, irretrievable. He closed his eyes. Prayer was, as always, impossible. He was not such a fool as to ask anything of heaven, even an explanation, so what should he pray for, and to whom? Contemplation was the best he could offer, a meditation on his past and his sins, and before him the Virgin, most forgiving of those heavenly rulers, to witness his soul laid bare, to grant, if she saw fit, the mercy for which he could not ask. It was a pathetic act, like crying in the corner until mother came, rather than confessing his misdeeds to father, but it was all he was capable of. Heaven must meet him halfway, or leave him below.

He had nearly confessed to Ana, in the grip of one of his fevers. The weight of his guilt over Richard was terrible; it bore down on the whole length and breadth of his life, crushing everything. There was no one to tell, and no hope of comfort from that direction even if he did. What had he actually said to the girl? He couldn't remember, but it could not have been much; she had never spoken of it afterward. Yet there was that drawing back on her part. Is that when it had happened? Again, he could not remember. All recent experience had become indistinct. His powers of recall were fragmenting, the wrong shards always stabbing to the surface—a first, unrequited love he'd forgotten for seventy years, random childhood terrors, the looming figure of his father, that sour grimace just before he struck. His mother, whose face he could no longer conjure up, just the softness of her hands, her voice.

He might have slept; it was unclear. When he opened his eyes again the room seemed darker, and the icon glowed with a radiance he knew from descriptions but had never yet seen. A smile forced the stiff muscles of his face, and he felt a presence behind him. That was not a new or even an unexpected sensation, but it was rare, only the third or fourth time he'd experienced it, and in combination with the odd glow around the painting, it must portend something. His scalp tingled, and he would swear he felt heat in all his extremities, even his feet, strangers these ten years. He maneuvered the controls with his right hand and the chair turned ninety degrees, so that he faced the gold-and-red window depicting Christ with the cross upon his shoulder. The shadows in the chapel had grown deeper, but light still seeped through the archway from the hall beyond, and interrupting that weak light, at the farthest edge of his peripheral vision, was a figure.

The old Greek priest, whom Kessler allowed to see the work years before, had told him that the magic had gone out of it. Of course, he didn't call it magic. Energy, perhaps, or spirit, yes, the spirit had gone out of it, the old fraud announced, close enough to kiss the paint, gray head shaking. Apparently, he had known the icon before the war, had prayed before it in the sacred stone church of that little village in Epiros. He had recognized it as being far older than the locals guessed and possessed of powers older still, had sensed—how had he described it?—a living presence in the wood. Despite himself, Kessler had felt his breath catch at that description. Gone, the priest insisted, dismissing the spell he had cast in an instant. Something had happened, some desecration, some strange devaluation, perhaps stemming from the icon's removal from its native soil—those damn Greeks. Whatever the case, the magic was gone. The work's value was now strictly artistic, granting, of course, the power of art to inspire the faithful.

Kessler had suspected some attempt to delegitimize the icon in his eyes and compel him to part with it. Nevertheless, it had wounded him, so deeply that he was not even able to think about the encounter for a long time afterward. Perhaps on some level he came to believe what the old man had said. Yet things had happened, things written of in the past that found a place in his life, bracing up his ever-shaky faith. He had lived long, too long, maybe, yet he had outlived countless dangers, illnesses, injuries. Longevity was one of the powers attributed to the icon. Stories existed of men who owned it, or dedicated their worship to it, living 120 years, fathering children in their eighties. In Kessler's case, long life had seemed a kind of mockery. He'd defeated illness but had never been completely free of it. There had been only the one child, the son whom he had lost. What was the purpose, the gain of such an old age?

At some point it had occurred to him that his reward might come in the next world, not this one, and that proved a difficult change in thinking. Because he was not sure he believed in a next world, was not even sure he believed in the Almighty. It was conceivable to him that there was such an entity, and such a place, but one did not arrive there without a deep, abiding faith. No hellfire was necessary for the rest. The contemplation of a black abyss, utter nothingness, was more than sufficiently terrifying. Then he had begun to see Her. And what unexpected joy that had caused. And fear, too, for she would not be there without a purpose, but he was hopeful that she intended him some good. She had ever been the source of mercy in all the tales that he knew, and if she could not save his enfeebled body, perhaps she could save that thing that was more important, if it was real: his soul. He thought of all these things in a moment as the figure hovered at the edge of his vision, waiting. Shame overwhelmed him, suddenly, sickeningly. Belief came from the heart, not the eyes. He had no right to demand proof, he, the worst sinner on earth. And yet, had it not been so with Paul? With all the disciples? And countless others since. Might not the eyes persuade the heart? Who was he to decide?

He had never yet been able to face the figure. Having tried the first time it appeared to him, years before, and been met with an empty doorway, he'd decided the time was not right. Since then, he had been content simply to sense the presence near him. More content, he suspected, than he would have been with the actual laying on of sight, for there would be a reason for it when that time came, and his craven heart feared the reason. But this was wrong, he must steel himself; he could not escape his fate, only face it bravely and with an open heart. He had never been brave about anything in his life; now was the time. She was forgiveness. His fingers hovered over the chair controls.

She was forgiveness. Like his mother, who had protected him from his father. A dark study, rain-soaked gusts outside the window, the man in his familiar suit, his familiar smell, tobacco and shaving cream, taller than God, the smile of a fiend, the heavy hand falling over and over again. He hated his father, a mortal sin; he was damned. Fresh tears rushed to his blind eyes. He shook his head. No, she would understand, she was forgiveness. He hesitated.

What if he were completely mistaken? If what he felt was simply Diana standing there, unwilling to enter his sanctum, waiting for him to finish his prayers to false gods? What if his doubting intellect had been right the whole time? Father, Son, and Holy Spirit, Mother Mercy, all spinning away from him into the void, a fantasy, no salvation. Mother, wife, and betrayed son all spinning away, no reunion, no forgiveness. The hand fell again and again. All his life he'd feared punishment for his wrongs. Here, at the end, he feared judgment far less than its absence. If the end was the absolute end? He could not accept it.

Enough. His vision swam. The rain had increased to a roar. Enough, be a man, look. His numb fingertips manipulated the controls and the chair made a quarter turn toward the archway.

Intense, cramping pain in his chest and down his arm collapsed his mental processes for a moment. He either could not see or could not understand what he was seeing, and the small part of his consciousness that was neither afraid nor in pain was able to look on this condition with curiosity. Then something in his head popped and the pain diffused, though his heart still felt like a clenched fist, and his vision was too silky to make out anything. The figure had remained in the doorway, but he had not been able to really see it before his eyes failed. No, be true, he had seen it for a moment. A man, not a woman. Neither his father nor his son, but a young man, lean and bearded, face half discolored, the eyes wide with fear or rapture. Not anger; Kessler did not think it was anger. A man, not a woman. The Son, not the Mother, dear God help him, the heavier judge. He felt his useless torso slumping forward as the figure approached. The stilled terror within him leaped up once more, then was transformed in an instant into something else, a new emotion, hard to encompass. Sadness, perhaps, broad and profound, but that too was transitory, for sadness melted into wonder, wonder into understanding, then all was light.

2

Andreas clutched the narrow armrests and prayed for the earth to leap up and catch him. The plane seemed to have dropped out from underneath, sucking his internal organs along with it and leaving the empty shell of his body floating in the ether. Yet when he opened his eyes he found himself intact, still squeezed into the cramped coach seat, the aisle to his right, the fat, constantly shifting businessman to his left. A world of trouble awaited, and he could have used the disconnected hours above the Atlantic to compose his mind, but he had found concentration impossible. It had been years since he'd flown, and he was distressed to learn how fully age had caught up with him. His ears rang, his neck ached, his legs were cold. He could no longer filter distractions. No matter. He would not truly know the situation until he was on the ground, and anyway, he often functioned better on instinct.

The plane dipped again, and Jamaica Bay loomed up below. Twenty seconds later they touched down at JFK. The businessman smiled at Andreas.

"Welcome to Gomorrah."

•   •   •

His suitcase was the first out of the chute—an omen, surely. He
retrieved it from the carousel and went to look for Matthew at
the arrival area, eyes casually searching every face for potential
mischief. Old habits. He had long ago ceased to be worth anyone's troubling over.

"Father?"

He turned, despite his caution; the voice was so clearly
directed at him. Three meters distant, a young man, square-
faced, powerful. The cheap dress jacket fit awkwardly, and
Andreas sensed more than saw a concealed weapon.

"Andreas Spyridis," the younger man said, more uncertainly.

Would it be now? How many moments like this had there
been in the last fifty years, when he had to wonder if some old
debt had caught up with him? His body tensed but his mind was
calm, ready for whatever would happen.

"I am Spyridis."

"Mr. Dragoumis sends me to meet you."

Andreas uncoiled partway. He doubted that Fotis would have
him shot at the airport.

"What's your name?"

It was always the last question they expected, these couriers.
It was important to surprise them, and to show no surprise on
your own part. He had not told Dragoumis he was coming, but
that was no matter. Fotis simply knew things.

"Nicholas. I work for Mr. Dragoumis, he waits for you now."
Serviceable English. Neither man was speaking his native
tongue, though Andreas could not quite catch the other's inflec-
tion. Not Greek, but a language he knew. "I am to bring you
directly. For dinner."

"I'm supposed to meet someone."

"Mr. Dragoumis has telephoned your grandson. He will also
be there."

Russian, almost certainly.

"I see. Well, it seems everything is arranged."

Nicholas nodded eagerly.

"Follow me please."

A huge jet roared overhead as they made their way across the parking lot to a big blue sedan; American, of course. Nicholas held open the right rear door, but Andreas hesitated.

"I would prefer to ride in front."

The Russian scowled. The request clearly offended his sense of professionalism, but he closed the rear door firmly and opened the passenger side. Andreas removed his gray fedora and slid carefully into the deep, comfortable leather seat. Queens always depressed him. The thick tangle of highways, warehouses, and tenements; cars rotting into the broken pavement. Only the season improved the ride, with the dirty slush or poisonous smog of previous visits replaced by clean air and banks of yellow forsythia, pressing through chain-link fences up and down the blocks of brick row houses.

"You live around here?" Andreas asked.

"Further out. Little Odessa, they call it."

"You like this country?"

Nicholas shrugged. "Better than where I come from."

"How long have you been here?"

"Two years."

"You learned English before you came?"

"A little. Mostly here."

"You speak Greek?"

"Not so good." He swung onto Astoria Boulevard. "Not really. No."

"Mr. Dragoumis likes it better if you don't speak Greek, yes?"

Nicholas conceded a brief smile.

They turned onto Twenty-first Street, then a quick left and the car pulled up before a white clapboard house. The place was unremarkable, but for the profusion of rosebushes in the narrow strip of soil in front. The house appeared small, though in fact it ran quite deeply back from the street. A warehouse bracketed the building on one side, a semi-famous restaurant on the other. Fotis owned both. Andreas had been here before. He examined the roses, not even in bud yet, then followed Nicholas up the concrete steps into the house. A barrel-chested man came out of the parlor and met them in the narrow hall, crowding Andreas against the wall. The younger men exchanged a few words in their native tongue, then the new man led Andreas down the dim corridor. Black beard, black eyes, full of suppressed violence. There would be no pleasant conversation with this one. A soft knock at the door, a word, and they were in the study, Fotis' inner sanctum. The man himself, gray as a ghost and sporting a huge white mustache, stood to greet them, covering the plush oriental carpet in great strides. The effort cost him, Andreas could see at once.

"My friend," Fotis said with real warmth, "my old, dear friend." They squeezed hands, rights over lefts, shaking their intertwined fists like happy children, like palsied old men. Andreas was always surprised by the affection he received from his old boss, ally, adversary. There was dampness in the corner of Fotis' eyes, and he grinned a huge smile of expensive false teeth, looking his comrade up and down. Then his face turned stern, and he swiveled a fierce gaze on the young Russian. "You donkey, you couldn't take his coat?"

Blackbeard murmured an apology and helped Andreas out of the heavy gray fabric. Fotis appraised the black suit and white shirt buttoned to the collar, and laughed, a short, barking exhalation.

"You look like a priest."

"Your man seemed to think I was one."

"Well, no wonder, dressed like that. Sit, sit. Coffee? Cognac?"

"Just water."

Without instruction, Blackbeard slipped out the rear door of the study. Fotis clasped his hands before him and leaned back in the creaking chair, a satisfied look on his face. Andreas took him in properly now. An elaborate maroon smoking jacket, stitched with abstract designs, hiding his too-lean frame. Slippers on his long feet, a box of Turkish cigarettes on the table by his elbow. Behind him, a stack of large, framed canvases leaned face-away against the wall. In fact, there appeared to be more paintings hanging about the room than Andreas had remembered previously, and despite the poor light and his imperfect knowledge of art, he guessed that some were quite valuable. A winter landscape. A small, very old-looking religious work, the Annunciation or some such. Gold leaf from what could only be an

Orthodox icon threw reflected light from a dark corner. His old friend had many identities, many roles he liked to play. Fotis the spy, Fotis the exiled politician, Fotis the respectable businessman. Now it appeared to be Fotis the collector.

"How was your flight?" Dragoumis asked, switching from English to their native tongue.

Andreas shrugged. "I'm here."

"It's hard on old men, and you are younger than me. Even once a year I find too much now. I may not see Greece this spring."

"Oh, I think you will go."

Blackbeard returned with a glass of tepid water, which was how Andreas preferred it.

"That is all, Anton," said Fotis, and the young Russian left the room again.

"How is the restaurant?" Andreas asked.

"The restaurant," the other groaned. "Quite successful. We have our loyal customers, you know, from the neighborhood, and now we are getting young people from Manhattan. Apparently, we have been written up somewhere as the best Greek food in Astoria."

"Congratulations."

Fotis waved a hand. "What the hell do those people know about food? Anyway, I am not involved much with the restaurant these days."

"No?"

"I have an excellent manager, who doesn't even steal. And I have other concerns."

It was an invitation, but Andreas was not interested. He knew about his friend's various activities, and if there were some new ones, it was no matter. Ambition did not impress him, nor even audacity in the pursuit of it. There was a sort of sad desperation in Fotis' extralegal dealings—the desperation of a dying man trying to stave off fate with accomplishment.

"My son is ill," Andreas said.

Fotis looked at him hard, sympathy vying with annoyance at the change in subject.

"I know."

Of course he knew. Matthew, Andreas' grandson, was also
Fotis' godson. Irini, Matthew's mother, was Fotis' niece. The two
old men were hopelessly entangled. There was no chance of
escaping each other.

"Matthew tells me that it's bad," Andreas went on, needing to
speak. "Alekos is not responding to the treatment."

"Maybe he needs better doctors."

"They are supposed to be the best at that place. Mount Sinai."

"There are better ones in Boston. But then, science can only
do so much."

"We do not have such illnesses in my family."

"You must have faith."

Was it a taunt? Spoken with such gentleness, it was more
likely an old man's forgetfulness.

"I do not think I am likely to acquire it so late in life."

Fotis stared at him, unreadable, the ever-present jade worry
beads clacking in his hand.

"My poor Andreou."

They sat in silence for a minute or two, comfortable with it.
Andreas sipped his water and finally decided to indulge the other
man.

"Some of these paintings are new."

Fotis' eyes lit up. "I have become more involved in collecting
the last few years," he said eagerly. "I think it is my true calling."

"Ah."

"Never mind that, I know what you're thinking. Only a fool
would collect art for money. Too unstable. I enjoy it. I enjoy pursuing my own peculiar tastes, and I enjoy being surrounded by
beautiful things."

"This landscape?"

Fotis shifted to look. "Dutch. A student of Bruegel, I'm told.
Beautiful, yes?"

"Very beautiful. And I see you have an icon."

"A few of them. Not very old, or valuable. They have been
greatly overproduced in recent centuries. This one is Russian."

"You would like to collect some authentic Byzantine exam-
ples, no doubt."

Dragoumis turned back around, a smile both cold and satisfied on his long, regal face.

"There is no real trade in Byzantine icons. Not enough of them in private hands. It's all museums and churches, so it is hard to set a price. Their true value is spiritual." Fotis the pious.

"Of course."

"You know that Kessler is dead."

Andreas sighed. It had occurred to him from the start that Kessler and the icon were behind this forced visit.

"I had heard."

"Keeping up those contacts. Good."

Andreas shrugged. Why bother saying he'd read it in the *New York Times*? Fotis assumed that all information must come through intelligence channels. Let him think that Andreas was still plugged into the network.

"So," Fotis continued, "what does our fine government of Greece think of this development?"

"What should they think? All they would know of Kessler is what you told them."

"You believe so? In that case the file is empty, because I told them absolutely nothing about Kessler. Why would I?"

"Neither did I. Perhaps they have other sources. You won't learn anything from me."

They became quiet again. Andreas wondered where the bathroom was.

"The granddaughter is executor." Dragoumis slid a long brown cigarette from the pack and lit it. "She is looking to have the whole collection appraised."

"Have you offered your services?"

Fotis laughed, blowing swirling orbs of smoke.

"I'm a small-time collector. I assumed she would go to one of the auction houses."

"Logical."

"But it seems she has loftier goals. Her lawyer has been speaking to some of the major museums. I can see it now, the Kessler Wing of the Metropolitan."

Andreas' radar began sounding.

"Why the Metropolitan?"

"Just an example, but it's the most obvious choice. Kessler concentrated on medieval. There aren't many places in this country that could do justice to that. None of the other New York museums."

"Why New York? Why not Europe?"

"Perhaps they will try Europe. New York was his home, though. Bad history across the Atlantic. The Swiss wouldn't touch him. Probably not the Germans, either. Anyway, you'll never guess whom the Met is sending over to look at a few things."

He did not have to guess.

"Your grandson," Fotis continued. "The world is small, my friend, no?"

Andreas managed not to show alarm, but he was unnerved. Dragoumis was older, sicker, self-deluding, but here was why he had always been better at these games. He was relentless, and he constantly found new ways to unbalance you.

"Fotis," he said quietly, without either threat or plea, "leave Matthew out of this."

"My dearest Andreou, what have I to do with it? You think they consult me?"

"How do you know about it?"

"Matthew told me. Look now, the chief medievalist is an old man, not young and handsome like our boy. Byzantine is his specialty; that's your doing, not mine. All those years taking him to churches and museums. Of course they would send Matthew. The girl will love him, the museum will get the icon, and our boy gets the credit. Where is the harm?"

"No harm. If that is all there is to the story."

"Truthfully? I begin to wonder." The old man waved his cigarette around casually. "Because here you are."

"My son is ill."

"Your son has been ill for months. Kessler died ten days ago."

Andreas leaned back in his chair, desperately wanting to be out of this place, to be anywhere else but in the lair of this sad, scheming creature. "You have lived too long, Foti, you see plots everywhere. I came to see my son, no other reason." He stood. "Have your man take me to my hotel. I can never find a taxi in this neighborhood."

Dragoumis stubbed out his cigarette and looked up at his old friend with large, watery eyes, seemingly on the verge of tears. As if he were the injured party! Despite himself, Andreas almost clapped his hands at the performance. Fotis the wronged.

"I have offended you, I am sorry. Please, sit. Please, my friend, let us not part in anger."

Andreas sat, but his mind was made up to go.

"I withdraw my question," Fotis continued. "If I have expressed doubts, there are reasons. I must trust that you too have reasons for not sharing your plans with me. Now that you understand Matthew is involved, you may adjust your actions in a way that will not direct harm to his interests."

"What the hell is it that you think I'm up to? You think the Greek government wants that icon? You think they would send me to get it?"

"What have you heard of Müller?"

Now Müller. The man was shameless.

"Only that he's dead."

"Really. I have heard that he is here, in New York."

Andreas shifted uneasily in his chair, willing himself not to respond, but failing. "From whom?"

"An unreliable source, I admit. Still, another thing I thought you should know. It would make sense that he would come. You never believed that he was dead."

"I don't want to discuss Müller. I need to see Alex."

"Yes. I have been to the hospital twice. He refused to see me the first time."

"I am sorry to hear it."

"But not surprised. He may resist seeing you also. Are you prepared for that?"

Prepared for it. How did one prepare for rejection from an ill son, a possibly dying son? Andreas had lived through many terrible things, but he could imagine nothing worse than such a rejection, and would not let his mind dwell on it.

"With Matthew's support, I hope to overcome resistance."

"Excellent. Look now, let us forget this gloomy talk for an hour. Come into the parlor and have a cognac with me."

"I should see Alekos immediately."

"Visiting hours are late. We'll all go, after we eat."

"No, I will go with Matthew."

"Of course. He is joining us for dinner. Then you will both go to see Alex."

The schemer had thought of everything. Anyway, the food would be good, and Matthew's company would make the evening tolerable. Andreas did not drink, but he would have a cognac with Fotis. It seemed like just what he needed.

"You have the good Metaxa?"

"Better. Remy Martin XO."

3

The night before, Matthew had the dream again. A painting vanished, a masterpiece of the collection which he was expected to find, but he couldn't remember what it looked like. A group stood before the empty wall, declaiming the lost portrait's beauty, the lips, the eyes, the otherworldly flesh tones, and he tried to build an image in his mind, but it shifted, eluded him, like faces do in dreams. The museum he knew so well became an impenetrable maze, with no Ariadne to help him. Darkness came down. Strange sounds distracted. The search went before and behind, he chased, he was pursued. In a dim basement chamber he saw what must be the image on the far wall, but the path was uncertain, no course took him directly there. No help, he was alone. And then not alone, as a terrible presence filled his consciousness. He always woke then.

They drove in silence, Matthew at the wheel of his colleague Carol's borrowed Taurus, Andreas settled deeply into the passenger seat. The life had gone out of the old man as soon as they stepped through Fotis' front door into the cool evening air, and it became clear that the animation he had shown over dinner was an act, for Fotis' benefit. They were always performing for each other. Coming off the Triboro Bridge, Matthew paid the toll and accelerated away, glancing at his grandfather. Hat and collar obscured his face, and shadow alternated with pink streetlight across the barely visible features. Matthew had seen Andreas in Athens two years before and been struck once again by how little he aged. Still sharp-eyed, clear-minded, grip like a vise. At seventy-seven he could have passed for a vigorous sixty. This night he seemed old, stoop-shouldered and shuffling. His eyes wandered, as did his mind. Of course, it could be fatigue from the flight.

The car shaped the looping entry to the FDR Drive, and Matthew turned off almost immediately on 116th Street. Shouts and the metallic bang of a backboard reached them from a dimly lit basketball court. Tall brick projects rose up around them.

"This is Harlem?" Andreas asked.

"Spanish Harlem, I guess."

"It's ugly."

"Yeah, well."

"This is an ugly city."

"So is Athens."

"A strange comparison. Have I offended your local pride?"

"Modern cities are ugly. New York has some beautiful places."

"Athens has history."

"Too much history."

"It's true. It's true that the Greeks are undermined by their history; it is a common phenomenon in Europe. Americans are more willing to attempt things. This is their strength, but it also leads them into much foolishness. They change friends constantly, abandon old allies. This is why the world distrusts America."

Matthew had heard it all before but was pleased to have the old man sounding like himself.

"What is the latest news?" Andreas asked.

The looming black monolith of Mount Sinai appeared on the left, checkered with tiny squares of light. Heaviness fell upon Matthew at the sight of it, dulling his mind like an anesthetic.

"Apparently his blood cell count is stable, but they don't know why, and it could drop again any time. The infusions don't seem to do much good anymore."

"So they cannot help him?"

Matthew balked, rolled his shoulders. One could go day to day without ever asking that question. His mother never wanted to know the long-term prognosis. She simply prayed to God the Father, Christos, *Panayitsa,* the whole useless crew. Yet it was a fair question, and the father of his father had every right to ask.

"They've made some progress, but the toll on his body has been pretty heavy. After every one of those treatments he's just . . . I'm beginning to wonder if it's worth it."

"They should send him home. A man should be at home to face a thing like this."

"It's not that simple, *Papou.*" The sharpness in his voice surprised him. "We can't give up on him improving. And I'm not even sure he's strong enough to go home. Mamá would have to do everything for him, which she would try to do, but she's a wreck right now herself."

Andreas patted his shoulder.

"Do not think too much about things before it is time to face them."

At that hour upper Fifth Avenue was nearly empty, and they were able to park near the hospital entrance. The long, tangled branches of elm trees swayed overhead, softly clacking. Andreas looked up at them for a few moments. Then Matthew took his arm and they went in together.

They had shaved the beard, but a heavy stubble had grown back. Where there had once been thick waves of black hair, only a thin gray buzz cut remained. His cheeks were sunken, and the body beneath the sheets seemed to have lost a good deal of mass. To say that Andreas did not recognize his son would be wrong. The forehead, long nose, sullen mouth, the small scar on the chin remained instantly familiar, but the general alteration of the body was terrible. What, fifty-three now? His ancestors had lived well into their nineties, as Andreas grimly expected to do. The son should not precede the father.

The old man stood rooted in the doorway. Had Alekos been awake, Andreas would have strode purposefully into the room, giving nothing away; but since the boy slept, he allowed himself a little time. He had not watched his son sleep since he was a child. He had not seen Alekos at all in five years. That last visit they had put some of the past bitterness behind them, reached some understanding common to their shared sadness. Yet a truce was not a friendship. They had not made the effort to know each other years before, and it was impossible to bridge the distance all at once. With the ocean between them, they had grown apart once more. Perhaps there had been another revelation of past shame, from Fotis, or from Irini, the wife. Perhaps it was simply old hurts that had been picked at again and festered.

Matthew went around the bed and stood by the window. Andreas could not see what the boy saw, but he knew from the turns they had taken that he faced east, toward the river. From the back, his grandson—broad shoulders, round head, black hair—looked like his father. The resemblance was otherwise slight, nor did Matthew particularly look like his mother. His grandmother, Andreas thought, not for the first time: *my wife.* The boy looked just like dear, dead Maria.

"*Babás.*" A dry whisper from the bed. The old man turned to face the narrow-eyed gaze of his son. Had he been awake all along?

"*Ne,*" Andreas answered. He did not trust himself to move swiftly, so he shuffled like an invalid to the bed.

Alex tried to pull himself up. Desperate to help, the old man hesitated for fear of a rebuke. Matthew came over instead, dragging his father upright. Andreas quickly rearranged the flattened pillows, and Matthew set Alex back against them. The sick man pointed to a cup on the bedside table, and Matthew filled it with water from a white plastic pitcher. Alekos took it with a steady hand and sipped slowly without looking at them, in no hurry to speak further. Andreas' legs trembled, but he would not sit.

"How is that silent sister of mine?" Alex finally asked, in English, for Matthew's sake, though the boy's Greek was good.

"Well. The children keep her busy, you know, and the husband is no help."

"Always defending her." But Alex smiled, a tiny lift at the corners of his mouth.

"When I am with her, I defend you." And then, as an afterthought: "She will be coming to see you soon."

"Yes, as soon as you report on my condition. I have no doubt they will all be at my bedside, with holy water and a priest. I will count on you to keep the priest away." Andreas knew better than to answer, and Alex looked to his own son. "You picked him up at the airport?"

"Fotis did," Matthew responded.

"Of course. The conspirators."

"He sends his best."

"You must send mine back, at the next planning session."

Matthew laughed. "What are we planning?"

"God knows," Alex rasped. "Ask your *Papou.*"

"He sent a man to get me at the airport," Andreas said. "I was not expecting him. I haven't seen Fotis in years."

"How was today?" Matthew asked quietly.

His father's hand flipped palm up, then palm under, a gesture both of the others recognized.

"The same. They did some tests. They say I may go home soon. *Babás,* sit down."

Andreas nearly fell into the hard chair. He unbuttoned his coat and put his hat in his lap.

"That's great news," Matthew answered. "So your blood looks better?"

"A little. It's not worse, anyway."

"But in that case, shouldn't they go on with the therapy? How do they know it won't continue to improve?"

"It might. They tell me it might, but they don't believe it, and I don't believe them." Alex spoke without anger. Profound weariness seemed to be the controlling tone in his voice. "Anyway, I can't take any more of the therapy now. I need a rest. I can't rest in this place."

"Of course not," Andreas insisted. "You should be home."

"Well now. I think you may be the one who needs a rest, old man. You look worse than me."

Andreas could only manage to stare at his son, as at a car wreck, unable to take his eyes away, aware of all the naked emotions on his face but unable to hide them.

"I am well. It's the airplane. I have never gotten used to them."

The look on Alekos' face was more gentle than Andreas had seen since his son was a child, and the past overtook him just then in a numbing wave. He reached to unbutton his coat and realized he had already done so; he unbuttoned the collar of his priestly white shirt instead.

"Matthew, get your *Papou* some water," Alex commanded.

"No," Andreas said. "We passed a coffee machine in the hall, you remember?"

"You sure you want coffee this late?" The boy's concern was kindly, but anger rose in Andreas instantly.

"You think I'm some old woman? I will get it myself."

"No, it's all right."

"Black, no sugar," Alex said from the bed.

"Yes," Andreas agreed, "your father knows. Thank you, my boy."

Then Matthew was gone, they were alone together, and Andreas no longer knew why he had schemed for this chance, what he had intended to say.

"Fotis told me you would not see him at first." He spoke Greek now.

"Are you surprised?"

"So much time has passed. Why do you cling to your anger?"

"Do you think these things go away because time has passed? You would like to think that, wouldn't you? That there is some clock on your sins, and when so much time elapses . . ."

"We were not discussing my sins." Andreas heard the hardness come into his voice, despite himself.

"No? What were we discussing? My mind wanders, you see."

"Your happiness."

"My happiness, yes. Always a great concern of yours. Anyway, I saw him, so why hound me?"

"Rini made you."

"I became too tired to fight about it, just like I am too tired to fight with you now."

"I don't want to fight. I am grateful to you for seeing me."

Alekos seemed almost shocked, or played well at it.

"You're my father. You're family."

"Fotis is family."

"Fotis is a *relation*. You are blood. Anyway, what am I going to say to Matthew, 'Tell your grandfather to wait in the hall'?"

"Once you might have done that."

"I had strength then."

"So is that the reason I am here? For Matthew's sake?"

"You know, this isn't about you, old man. This is not about your forgiveness. This is about me. You came, God knows why. I don't want to know your other reasons. You're here. It's right that you should be. Leave it alone now, don't ask for anything else."

Alex slumped back on his pillows. Fool, Andreas scolded himself, stupid ass, exhausting him this way. Leave it alone, indeed.

"Fotis is involving him in something," Alex said. "About that damn icon. You know about it?"

"I learned about it today."

"You're not involved?"

"No."

"How the hell would I know if that's true?"

"It's true."

"Keep him out of it. Leave my son alone. Tell the schemer to leave my son alone."

"It's for the museum. There is no harm in it that I can see."

"You think Fotis hasn't arranged it somehow? The man has his fingers in everything."

"I do not see where the gain is for him. The museum getting the icon would be the end of his hopes for it."

"How can we know if it is that simple? Who told you about Matthew's involvement?"

"Fotis."

"And how did it seem to him? How did he feel about it?"

Alex had a scientist's mind, untrained in the ways of deliberate misdirection. This was no doubt one reason that he resented his father and uncle: not just because duplicity was so much a part of their lives, but because he himself was so easy to dupe.

"Pleased," Andreas answered.

"I am not a spy, of course, but when that man is pleased about something, I worry. Keep my boy out of it."

"It's for his work." Work was the closest thing to sacred to Andreas.

They heard Matthew's voice in the corridor, speaking quietly to the nurse. Alex leaned forward again, straining.

"At least speak to him. Tell him the history."

Andreas' mouth was dry. How much of the history did Alex know? Who told him? Not Fotis. Maria? Himself, some forgotten evening long ago? His son was staring hard at him.

"No, you can't do that, can you? Just tell him to stay out of it, then. Do that for me. He won't listen to his father, but he will listen to you."

"I'm not so sure."

Matthew walked back into the room.

"Will you do that for me, old man?"

A dozen calculations collided in Andreas' brain, all of them unsolvable with his son's face looking at him that way.

"I will speak to him."

Matthew touched his shoulder, and when Andreas turned the boy handed him the paper cup of coffee. The old man's stomach lurched, and sourness crawled up his throat. He placed the cup on the arm of his chair with his hand around it, warming his stiff fingers.

"Your *Papou* has worn me out," Alex announced. "You'll have to leave soon."

"We'll come back tomorrow."

"Your mother will be here tomorrow. She'll get some straight answers. Who knows, maybe the next time you see me I'll be at home."

"That would be wonderful."

Andreas rose then, too quickly, and touched the edge of the mattress to steady himself.

"I'm worried about you, *Babás*." Alekos' voice was quiet. Andreas grabbed his son's hand with sudden force and squeezed it. The face remained neutral but the hand squeezed back. The old man found his balance and straightened.

"I am the only one here who does not need any worrying over."

"I should have called the hotel," Andreas said at last. "I hope they have held the room."

Matthew accelerated down the empty avenue.

"It's absurd for you to stay in a hotel when Ma is all alone in that big house. She would be happy to have you."

"She would not refuse me, but it would be awkward."

"So you could stay with me. It's not a big apartment, but there's room. You would be a lot closer to the hospital."

"You will have to trust that I prefer it this way. Now please tell me what the nurse said."

"You never miss a thing, do you?" The light stopped them at Eighty-sixth street. "No prognosis, you have to speak to a doctor for that. She did confirm that they'll probably send him home soon. She also warned that he might be right back there in a week."

That must be avoided, Andreas thought, but it would be Alekos' decision.

They were moving again, past the massive, spotlighted edifice of the Metropolitan Museum, columned and crenellated, bleached stone and huge, colorful banners. Matthew's museum.

"We must get him some morphine," Andreas said.

"They'll give him something, I'm sure. He hasn't been in a lot of pain so far."

"That may not last, and we cannot count on the compassion of doctors. I mean that we must procure some morphine ourselves. In case of need." He felt the words sink in during the silence that followed.

"Fotis could get it," Matthew said.

"No doubt. We will ask him, if we have no other alternative."

"You don't like asking him for favors."

"We have a complicated relationship, your godfather and I. I try to make distinctions between business and friendship. No such distinctions exist for him."

"You know Dad doesn't like him."

"I'm sure your father's feelings are also complicated. I think he mostly mistrusts him. He feels Fotis may try to involve you in one of his schemes."

They turned east on Seventy-second street. Matthew did not respond right away, but Andreas waited him out.

"I don't think Fotis is doing so much scheming these days," the younger man finally said. "He's feeling his mortality. He wants to do the things that give him pleasure, wants to be with his family, which is basically us. I don't think he's looking to stir up trouble."

"Perhaps not." He must be careful; the boy was very close to his godfather. "Trouble has a way of finding Fotis, however."

Matthew smiled at that.

"He says the exact same thing about you."

"Yes? Well, I won't deny it. We have both had difficulty avoiding trouble. We sought it out so often as young men that it has become friendly with us. I tell you, though, I was always the amateur. Fotis was the expert."

Matthew's face was hard to read. Confusion or annoyance sat on his forehead and in the muscles around the eyes, or perhaps he was just concentrating on the right turn onto Lexington Avenue. They were close to the hotel now.

"It will be on the left," Andreas said. "A little further on."

"Where do you find these places?"

"Friends recommend them."

"They must be poor recommendations, since you never stay in the same place twice."

"Just another habit of mine. Right there, I think. The green awning." Andreas shifted in the seat to observe Matthew as they pulled into an open curb space before what appeared a pleasant old second-rate establishment. "I hope I have not offended you.

You know I am fond of your godfather, but I say that with a full knowledge of who he is. He is not an easy man to understand. It would be better for you, and better for your father's peace of mind, if you did not become involved in any business arrangement with Fotis. Not even an exchange of favors."

Matthew was silent, staring out the windshield. He would never be uncivil, but this talk had made him uncomfortable. Matters might have progressed further than Andreas had anticipated. He would have to speak more openly, but not now.

"Are you free anytime this week, my boy? Tomorrow, even?"

"Tomorrow is tough. I'll call you when I see how things are shaping up."

"Very well."

"Come on, let's get you checked in."

4

In the beginning was the word. In the end, words weren't worth much. At the church services he surreptitiously attended, Matthew quickly lost the thread of the words spoken, sung, lost his grip on the Greek language, found it transformed into pure music, pure sound. Sound mixed with the smell of incense, the glint of pale lamps off gold leaf, the dark eyes of saints in the iconostasis. Some days it was enough to invoke a sort of trance, which was soothing to the soul or at least the psyche. Was it faith? He knew that if he followed the words, if he attempted the journey in any sort of intellectual manner, it all felt ridiculous. He had to let himself go. His former girlfriend Robin, a lapsed Catholic, had experienced the same phenomenon. Christ Hypnotist, she called it.

In Greece, in his grandfather's village, an old priest had shown Matthew a poor black-and-white photograph of the Holy Mother of Katarini, taken before the war, before its disappearance. His godfather's descriptions, the text he had read in a handful of books, words, had all been rendered pointless by a single glance at a sixty-year-old, five-by-seven image. In an instant, he had understood everything. The longing, the hope, the despair, all present in the swirl of deep gray color, in those black eyes. Now, if his godfather was right, he was mere minutes from seeing the real thing. And words would fail once more.

The brownstone looked like several others on the street, except for the iron bars on the windows and the discreet surveillance camera by the door. The buzzer made no noise audible from the outside, but Matthew waited. His attention was focused on the grill of the speaker when the door swung open.

She wasn't the maid, that was certain. Early thirties, attractive, dark blond hair, circles under her pale blue eyes, an expensively casual beige suit. The granddaughter. She seemed startled to see him but spoke his name.

"Mr. Spear?"

"Yes. Ms. Kessler."

"That's right. You look surprised to see me."

"I was going to say the same thing."

She laughed, a short, uninhibited burst of sound.

"Come in." He stepped into the cramped entry and stood very close to her while she continued to speak. "Preconceptions are funny. Who were you expecting?"

"I don't know, a maid, I guess."

"No maid."

A dark, wood-paneled library stood immediately to the right of the entry, but the rest of the place was remarkably light. He followed her down a narrow corridor of warm wood and white paint. Framed prints covered the walls, maps of medieval cities; the dead man's taste, no doubt. She hadn't yet put her own touches on the place, he noted, then realized he didn't have a clue what her own tastes might be. As Robin would have told him, he was trying to construct a personality without yet knowing the person. It was a bad habit of his.

"The cook is deaf, and he's not here now. I let the nurse go after my grandfather died, so it's just me. Would you like coffee?"

The kitchen was bright, the windows admitting as much light as the massive plane tree in the courtyard would allow. Matthew hesitated. This was his first solo house call, and he wasn't certain of protocol.

"Only if you're having some."

"Any excuse for a cup of coffee. Please sit down."

Into two blue china mugs she poured stale coffee—he could smell it—from a cheap plastic coffeemaker on the counter.

"Milk, sugar?"

"Black is fine."

"I'm glad you said that, because there is no milk and I don't know where the sugar is."

He took a sip and set the mug aside. No one in his family would serve coffee like that to his worst enemy. What was it with rich people and food?

"So who were you expecting," he asked.

"Oh, I don't know."

"Tweed jacket? Gray hair and spectacles?"

"That's right. Maybe a pipe."

"Not on the job. Don't want to get smoke on those delicate surfaces."

"Of course. I was really just expecting someone older."

"I'm working on it, every day."

She laughed again, and he realized that he was going to have to resist the impulse to keep making her do that.

"Have you been with the museum long?"

"Three years. Not long. You can be there ten years and still be the new guy."

"But you're a curator?"

"Assistant curator."

"That's impressive for someone as young as you, isn't it?"

He understood now. This wasn't small talk, he was being interviewed. Was he equal to the job of assessing her grandfather's work?

"Not really. They needed someone who knew Eastern Orthodox art, and that's been my primary focus. I was at the Byzantine Museum in Athens for two years before this."

"Interesting." She seemed to tire quickly of her own questioning. "This coffee is terrible, I'll make some fresh."

"I've had plenty this morning."

"You want to get to work and I'm dragging my feet."

"There's no rush." He had to be careful. "It's not an easy matter, exposing work that has a strong emotional connection to a complete stranger. It's one thing to contemplate parting with it, another to watch some so-called expert sizing it up, reducing it to a piece of commerce."

"Is that what you do, Mr. Spear?"

"I hope not. I was trying to see it from your side."

"You're very understanding. You must do this a lot."

"No, actually."

"The thing is, the icon is downstairs in this sort of chapel my grandfather built. It's a very private place. No one went in there but him."

"I see. Well, we, or you, could take it out of there and I could examine it up here. The light would probably be better, anyway."

"Sorry, I hadn't even thought about the light. I can't imagine seeing it any kind of way but the way it is now, in that strange room. I guess that's why I haven't moved it."

"Now you've made me curious."

"I'm making too much of it. It's just a little chapel, an old man's indulgence. I mean, who builds a chapel in their home anymore?"

"Your grandfather was obviously a medievalist at heart."

"Yes, he was."

"May I see it?"

She looked at him blankly for a moment. She was tired, sleep-deprived probably, fully formed thoughts coming slowly to her upper consciousness.

"The chapel? Absolutely, I want you to. Then we can take the icon someplace with better lighting, so you can examine it properly."

"Great."

"OK." She stood up, paused again. "I guess what I'm trying to explain is that this wasn't a valuable artwork to my grandfather. It was a sacred object, to be worshiped."

Matthew felt a tingling in the back of his skull, and an impulse, contrary to his nature, to reveal something of himself.

"That was its original purpose," he said quietly. "That's why it was created."

They were the right words. She seemed calmed, though she continued to stand there.

"It's odd. He was raised Catholic, but he preferred Orthodox art. It's as if his aesthetic tastes led him into a different kind of religious belief. Which might make you doubt his sincerity, except I think all art, even secular art, was spiritual to him."

He smiled, aware that no response was necessary.

"I hope," she said hesitantly, "that religious talk isn't offensive to you."

"Not at all. My family is Greek, religion is in the blood."

"I should have known that. My lawyer knows your godfather, or something?"

"That's right."

"Then Spear is . . . ?"

"Spyridis. My grandfather still hasn't forgiven my father for that."

"Right." She sat again, yet he sensed forward progress. "So you're Greek Orthodox?"

"Yes, I mean, so far as I'm anything. My father isn't religious, and I had only limited exposure to religion growing up."

"And your mother?"

"She's a believer, mostly, she and my godfather. Worry beads and calendars of the saints and all that. They took us to church at Easter, made sure we knew what it was about."

"'Us' is . . . ?"

"Me and my sister."

"Is your sister religious?"

Where the hell was she going with this?

"No. She has my father's scientific mind."

"And are you of the scientific or spiritual mind-set, Mr. Spear?"

"I try to blend the two. My training is scientific, but there's no real understanding of this kind of work without comprehending the religious purpose."

"What a careful answer."

"I write them down on my sleeve for quick reference."

"In case you get grilled by some rude creature like me," she laughed. "I'm sorry, I'm just trying to get to know you better. And I guess I'm stalling."

"If you're not comfortable doing this now, we can make another appointment. I confess I'd be disappointed, but—"

"No, it's fine. You are being incredibly patient."

"Please call me Matthew, by the way."

"Matthew. Good. I usually answer to Chris."

"Usually, huh?"

"Usually."

"Is that what I should call you?"

He could take her long stare so many ways that he decided to ignore it. She carried both mugs to the sink and stood for awhile with her back to him.

"No, I guess not. Call me Ana."

"Ana. All right."

"Follow me, Matthew."

The chamber was not large, maybe twenty feet deep by twelve wide, the darkness within accentuated by the brightness elsewhere in the house. The only illumination came from scattered streaks of blue, red, and yellow light from six small stained-glass windows. Matthew could make out a bench, candelabra, square panels on the walls. Details were visible on several of the near panels, figures in a crowd scene, a leaning cross against a gray-blue sky. Of the larger panel, directly opposite the arched entry, he could make out no details until his companion turned a dial in the room behind, and the Holy Mother of Katarini slowly emerged from darkness.

The icon, about twenty-four by thirty inches, was badly chipped and at first glance appeared nearly abstract: a luminous gold field with a maroon wedge emerging from the bottom and covering most of the panel. The wedge soon revealed itself as a robe wrapped about the torso and head of a woman. Her forearms were raised before her chest, her long hands raised in prayerful supplication. The shape of her hood could be made out clearly, but the details of her face were murky. Except for the eyes. The eyes drew you in, and Matthew realized that he had walked more than halfway across the chamber without any awareness of moving. Not even the photograph had prepared him for these eyes floating within that cowl. Large, dark brown almost to black, and almond-shaped, in the favored Eastern style. Penetrating, all-knowing, forgiving, or rather ready to forgive, but requiring something of you first. Matthew held the gaze as long as he could and then had to look away.

"Are you OK?" She spoke softly behind him.

"Yes."

"They get to you, don't they? The eyes. I can never look at them for long."

"They're very expressive."

"A little frightening, I think. Beautiful, but judgmental. The way religion feels when you're young."

"I suppose religion was a much more primal experience when this was painted."

"I think of all those Renaissance masterpieces." She was beside him now, speaking quietly, almost into his ear. "Aesthetically, they're flawless. Mary is always serene. Yet there's something so much more powerful, or vital, about this. She looks menacing. Godly. Not that Mary is a god, technically."

"To the Greeks she is."

"I'm sorry, I'm babbling. I'd blame the coffee, but the truth is I get nervous standing here."

"Guilty conscience?"

"Could be. I just find the work very unsettling. My grandfather could sit in front of it for hours, I don't know how." He felt her breath on his neck as she exhaled deeply, calming herself. "He died in here, actually."

"Really."

"Simultaneous heart attack and stroke. Diana, his nurse, found him just exactly where you're standing."

He resisted the impulse to move.

"No wonder it bothers you."

"So is it good work, Matthew?" she asked.

"It's a shame about the damage, though it only seems to add to the mystique. I'd say it's excellent work, and very old. Possibly pre-iconoclastic, which would make it quite rare. I'll know better when I look at it more closely."

"I guess we should take it off the wall."

"I'll do it, if you like. I'm experienced at handling these things."

She pulled her hair back with both hands and nodded.

"It probably violates the insurance policy, but I would prefer that. We just need to turn off the alarm."

"How do we do that?"

"I'm not exactly sure. Come help me figure it out."

Andreas had left a message for Morrison in Washington the night before, and the agency man had called him back at the hotel the next morning.

"What brings you to the States, my friend?"

"My son is ill."

"Sorry to hear that."

No doubt he was, but the tone of voice made it clear that he had more pressing business than chatting with a retired Greek operative. Andreas could picture the man, trim, regulation hair and that shifting, nervous gaze, determined to miss nothing while missing everything. Impatience. That was the reason, despite all its resources, that American intelligence was always getting things wrong. They were good at reading satellite photos, but not at reading faces. They could not gauge the mood of a people, or even a single man.

"I have a request," Andreas continued. "It is a rather delicate matter."

"I'm sure this line is secure."

"I would prefer to meet. I believe you are here in New York?"

"Why do you say that?'

"A guess." One had to become good at guessing when one had no resources. "You often come here. Besides, there are no secure lines in Washington."

Morrison laughed. "Probably true. OK, but it has to be brief, and it has to be soon. Like right now, this morning."

"That suits me well."

Morrison chose a generic coffee shop near Herald Square, the kind of place he always preferred. The man had an encyclopedic knowledge of every faceless, tasteless eatery in every northeastern American city. Morrison's predecessor, Bill Barber, had taken Andreas to wonderful restaurants where they ate, drank, told stories, and traded information almost incidentally, as if none of it were about business. But Barber hadn't been much for protocol, and Andreas had been useful then.

He arrived early and chose a booth in back, too near the hot, musty stink of the deep-fryer. Morrison arrived a few minutes later in his trademark blue suit and gray raincoat, the uniform, though today it was appropriate to the weather—windy, and threatening rain.

"You look well."

"I look terrible, and so do you," Andreas shot back, as much to unsettle the man as to state the truth. It had been years since they had last met, and the years had not been kind to Morrison. He had gotten heavy; gone gray at the temples; and his gaze no longer darted so much but had a set, glazed cast about it. Perhaps there had been some unpleasant fieldwork. Perhaps family. Andreas could empathize, but the other man was certain not to speak of whatever it was.

"I'm OK, not enough sleep is all. I am sorry about your boy. Alex, right?"

"You went to the trouble of checking my file. I am honored."

"Jesus, Andy, I happened to remember. You always insult people you need favors from?"

"Yes, it's a Greek custom. We hate to be in anyone's debt, so we offend them right at the start to let them know they do not own us."

Morrison shook his head, appeased or amused.

"Is that true?"

"No. I am an uncivilized old man, my apologies. Yes, Alex."

"What's wrong with him?"

"A blood disorder. You would know the name if I could remember it. Such illnesses are rare in my family, but for one so young . . . I do not understand."

"There's no understanding these things. God works in mysterious ways, the shit."

Andreas decided that he liked this older, crankier version of Morrison better than the insolently confident fellow he'd known before. A weary, bleached-blond waitress took silent but visible offense at their order of coffee, and the agency man felt compelled to add eggs and toast.

"Haven't had breakfast."

"You should always eat breakfast, Robert."

"I know, my wife tells me every day."

"Personally, I would not eat breakfast here, but I am very careful about food."

"I wasn't actually planning on it."

"She intimidated you. She is Peloponnesian, that one, fierce. The cook also, not a very clean-looking fellow. And the Mexican dishwasher has a cold. No, I would not eat here."

"I'll have an orange juice to kill the germs."

"Orange juice. Have garlic."

"In my eggs?"

"Better than in your coffee. I'm looking for a man."

"Official business?"

"I have no official business any longer. This is, as you say, a favor. I want to know if this man entered the country in the last two weeks. Probably somewhere in the New York region, though possibly farther away. I can give you all of his known aliases."

"That's too wide a net. Point of origin?"

"South America. Argentina, but it's likely he would pass through another country first."

"So he knows what he's doing."

"Yes, but I believe he may have lowered his guard in this instance. He will not expect to be tracked, and he will be in a hurry."

"Physical description?"

"Medium height, blue eyes. Older, in his eighties."

"This guy wouldn't be German by any chance? Dead for about thirty years?"

Andreas leaned back against the creaking imitation leather, disappointed by this development. He had counted on Morrison's relative youth to keep him in the dark.

"We never spoke of this before."

"Come on, Andy," laughed the government man, "it was your obsession. It's all in your file. But the guy is supposed to be dead."

"They showed me a grave. A wooden cross and some turned earth behind the last house he owned. I never saw a body."

"This was Argentinean intelligence?"

"The grave was fresh. No more than a day or two old. They could have dug it an hour before I came up the hill."

"People do just die, my friend. A lot of those old Nazis managed to die a natural death."

"It was too convenient. They were protecting him. They still are, I'm sure. Maybe you are, too."

"Me?" Morrison smiled innocently.

"The fine organization you work for. It's interesting that my hunt for Müller is so detailed in my file, when I could get no help from you people at the time."

"Resources were thin. He was small-time, a major or a colonel, I think. Not even a general, let alone some architect of the Reich. You needed the Israelis."

"He was small-time for them, also. They did give me a few leads in the end. That was how I found the house."

"But the Argentineans intercepted you."

"As soon as I stepped off the bus in a nearby village. They knew exactly who I was. They were polite, said that there had been a development which would please me. Took me up the hill to the house. Showed me the grave."

"It does sound awfully tidy."

"Will you help me, Robert?"

Morrison stuck a fork into the hefty pile of eggs just placed before him. Then paused, looking perplexed, or perhaps nauseated.

"It's sticky."

"Send it back."

"The situation is sticky. If there was some reason we didn't help you back then, I don't know what it was, and I don't feel like blundering into it now."

"All these years later, what can it matter? Indulge an old man."

"There's no upside to this. If he's dead, I've wasted my time. If he's alive, and I put you on to him, things could get ugly. I can't have you terminating this guy on American soil."

"Who said anything about that?"

"Isn't that what you were aiming for back then? Why else do you want to find him?"

"I have questions. More important, I must keep an eye on him to protect others."

"You think he means to try something? I've got to know about that if you do."

"I have no idea what he intends. Understand, Robert," and Andreas leaned across the chipped Formica, fixing the other man in his unblinking gaze, "all you can tell me is that he entered the country. I will still have to find him, which will likely prove impossible, but at least I will be on my guard. You will be protecting *me* with this information. Do you see?"

"I see that you're a smooth-talking old bastard."

"Have me watched."

"Can't afford that."

Andreas reached into his coat and removed a slip of paper, which he placed on the table. Morrison studied it a moment, chewing his toast.

"The aliases?"

"As many as I know of."

"He could have come up with twenty more in the last thirty years."

"True. But without someone hunting him, I doubt he would bother. It's troublesome work, creating identities. Anyway, at least one of these was used within the last ten years, in eastern Europe. I've marked it. Of course, it may not have been him."

This was becoming too much information for the agency man,

who had come to the great metropolis with other priorities and now shifted restlessly in his seat. Andreas was content. It was best that the tired bureaucrat remember as little of this conversation as possible.

"If I pick this up," said Morrison, nodding at the paper, "it doesn't mean I'm committing to anything. I may do the search and still decide to do nothing. You might not hear from me."

"I understand."

The younger man sighed and slipped his wallet from his suit jacket, sliding out a twenty as he slid the white scrap of paper in.

"Unless this guy is on a watch list, it's very unlikely I'll find him. Don't call me about this. I'll call your hotel if I have anything to report."

"You never let me pay."

"It's my country. You can buy me dinner in Athens."

"You always say that, but you never come."

"One of these days."

5

Fotis was on his usual bench, turned three-quarters from the sun, gray overcoat and fedora, white mustache like a beacon. Bright pink patches stood out on his prominent cheekbones, and he stared distractedly into space while feeding bits of soft pretzel to a flock of pigeons at his feet. Fotis occupied such a powerful place in his imagination that Matthew was constantly surprised to see what an old and delicate-looking man his godfather had become. And why not? He was pushing ninety. Yet there was more than age at work, some deeper change was under way that came clear only from weekly contact. Fotis was ill. The old charmer—or schemer, as Alekos always called him—would never let on, but he was not well, and his illness was bound to add a sense of urgency to all his latest efforts. Matthew sat.

"*Kaliméra, Theio.*"

Fotis turned slowly and smiled at him.

"It *is* a good morning. I can feel the sun. I think we have survived another winter."

"Winter was over weeks ago."

"You can never be certain. March is the worst month. It tempts you with warmth and flowers, then buries you in snow. April is better; I think we are safe now. How is your father?"

"Improved. They may send him home."

"Excellent. And how was it between him and your grandfather?"

"Not bad. A little tense. They sent me out of the room at one point, so I don't know everything that happened, but they seemed to be communicating when I got back."

Fotis shook his head. "Poor man."

"How are you?"

"The same, always the same." He patted his godson's knee. "That is my secret. Let us walk."

They went north, the sun at their backs. The wide path through the zoo grounds was full of shrieking children, and Matthew gripped his godfather's arm protectively. Fotis smiled benevolently at the zigzagging horde, taking an old man's delight in their youthful energy, even when a small boy collided with him. They watched the seals on their rock island, and caught a glimpse of the polar bear doing lazy laps in his pool.

"Has the deal gone through on the house?" Matthew asked. Fotis had described a place in Armonk he was going to buy, and on a lark Matthew and Robin, who had grown up there, drove around the town until they found it. Just a few weeks back, days before she ended things.

"The house." Fotis seemed surprised. "I did not remember mentioning the house to you. No, I have decided not to purchase it after all. Too great an indulgence."

This was curious. His godfather had seemed extremely excited about the house when they last discussed it, and Matthew had the impression the deal was virtually done. Another of the old man's little mysteries. Meanwhile, he realized it was up to him to raise the subject that was on both their minds.

"I saw the Kessler icon yesterday."

"Tell me."

"It's wonderful. I mean, it's suffered a lot of wear, but there is something very powerful about it. Very moving."

"So, you would say its value is more spiritual than artistic?"

"Not necessarily. I mean, value to whom?"

"Precisely." The older man paused before taking on a long, sloping incline in the path. "Will you recommend purchasing the work to your superiors?"

"My department chief needs to see it, probably the director. The decision will get made at a higher level."

"Come now, you have no influence at all?"

"I am the Byzantine specialist, I'm sure they'll give me a voice. For its age alone we should buy it, and it's also a great work of art. It could be the crown jewel of the new galleries."

"Certainly."

"But there are so many agendas. The museum can't buy everything it should."

"You would like for them to acquire it."

"Speaking selfishly, I'd like to have it around, to be able to study it whenever I wanted. We don't have a lot of icons, none like this one."

"There are none like it, I would guess. But will it go on a wall for all to see, or will it sit in a case in your wonderful temperature-controlled basement, for only scholars' eyes?"

"That's a concern, I confess."

"I sensed as much. You're a very conscientious boy. Now," he took Matthew's arm and began walking again, "tell me about the icon itself."

Matthew described the work while they proceeded, past a lush slope of yellow daffodils and white narcissi, through a small field of fruit trees, fat with just-splitting buds. He attempted to keep his language technical, yet feared that too much of his emotional response to the image showed through. It seemed impossible to use the academic voice, to keep that professional distance when speaking or even thinking of this particular piece, and he had yet to address with himself what that might mean. The older man listened quietly, his face neutral, until they paused at the Seventy-second Street crosswalk.

"Marvelous. I would very much like to see it again one day."

"I'm sure that can be arranged, wherever it ends up."

Fotis looked at him with damp eyes, which may just have been from the wind.

"I knew you were the right one to look at that icon."

"I should thank you for putting in a word with their lawyer. It was a nice coincidence that you knew him."

"We are in the same club, but it's nonsense to thank me. The museum would have sent you in any case."

"Maybe the family wouldn't have thought of the museum if you hadn't mentioned it. Whatever happens now, I've been able to see it, so I'm satisfied."

"I am told that you made a very favorable impression upon Ms. Kessler."

"The lawyer told you that?"

"Why should it be a secret? In fact, she may want you to come back and do a second examination. For herself this time."

Matthew shrugged uncomfortably.

"That really wouldn't be kosher while the museum is considering."

They crossed the road and started down the steep, looping path to the boat pond.

"Unless I am mistaken, it is she and not the museum who will decide the work's fate."

"Of course."

"And she will need help with that decision. She trusts you already."

"It's awkward."

"You are assuming that you will be placed in a position contrary to your conscience. There is another way to look at the matter. Ms. Kessler may need to be *told* what to do."

"I don't know that I understand you."

"You do not, yet."

They said no more before they reached the bottom of the path. Fotis gripped his arm more tightly, and Matthew realized that his godfather had a pained look on his face, physical pain, possibly quite acute. The jaw clenched and the eyes closed, and Fotis swayed a moment, breathing deeply through his nose.

"*Theio,* are you OK?"

Equanimity returned to the old man's face after several moments.

"The air is lovely today, is it not, my boy?"

"Do you want to sit?"

"A few minutes, perhaps."

They shuffled to a bench set back from the water's edge, a little past where the hawk watchers huddled about their telescopes. Fotis sat heavily. Concerned as he was, Matthew said nothing more. This was not the first time he'd seen these symptoms, and questions would only make the old man retreat. His pain was his own, as jealously guarded as his other secrets. The pond's surface was a dark glass, reflecting a shadowland version of the brick boathouse across the way. Behind that, tall trees, just touched with lime green, soared up well past the level of the street behind them, and above the trees the square stone towers of Fifth Avenue were bathed in yellow-white light.

"Can I get you anything?" Matthew asked, but Fotis waved him off.

"Fate is a peculiar thing. We believe that we command our own lives, but events will occur, again and again, which lead us in a certain direction. Do you not find this to be true? We can resist. We can go along, pretending we are still in control. Or, we can try to determine what fate wants of us, and help to make it happen."

"I'm not much of a believer in fate."

"That is because you are young. One must believe in one's own power at your age. In another time, however, the young sought advice from the old. The old were understood to hold wisdom from experience. This is no longer the way."

Matthew took the hint and shut up.

"You have said some interesting things today," Fotis went on. "It is possible that your unconscious already perceives a dilemma which your conscious mind has not grasped, because a choice has not yet been put before you. So. I was contacted a few days ago by a highly placed official of the Greek church. Regarding the icon. They are very much determined to acquire the work, and they want help from me in the matter."

A rush of anxiety coursed through the younger man. He sat

forward on the bench, both disbelieving and struck by a strange sense that he had expected something very like this.

"Why would the church contact you? How do they even know about the icon?"

"The church has many resources, and I have many friends within the church. They place a high value upon recovering stolen art treasures, especially those of great religious significance and power. Kessler's ownership of the icon was not a secret."

"You only conjecture that it's stolen."

"No," the old man countered instantly, then seemed to restrain himself. "You must have seen documents from the lawyer. What do they say of its provenance?"

"It's more or less in line with the work you and I have discussed."

"The Holy Mother of Katarini."

"They don't use that name, but it's an obvious match. Pre-iconoclastic, original source unknown. The last few centuries in a church in Epiros."

"And how did it come to be in Kessler's possession?"

"He claimed to have purchased it from a fellow Swiss businessman."

"So that fellow is the thief. Or the one before him. What does it matter? Somewhere along the line it was stolen. What Greek would have willingly parted with it?"

"Maybe one who needed money after the war."

"It was taken *during* the war, I tell you. The Germans took it with them when they left."

Now we've arrived at it, Matthew thought. His godfather had been hinting about something for weeks.

"How do you know that?"

Fotis sighed, smoothing his hands out across his gray pleated pants.

"Very well. Very well, I told you I had seen the work before."

"Yes. That's how we got talking about it in the first place."

"I didn't tell you everything. It was during the war that I saw it, in that church in your grandfather's village. It was your *Papou*, in fact, who arranged for me to see it. I have never forgotten that time. Less than an hour, but I was completely possessed by its beauty, by the power emanating from within it. You know I was with the guerrillas. I was in charge of the resistance in that area, and I sent a man to get the icon from that church. Before the Germans took it, or burned the place without knowing what it was. They burned so many villages, churches and all."

The old man paused, lost in a vision of houses aflame. Matthew watched the men who watched the birds. He sensed that this story would end up troubling him, and not just because the museum would never touch stolen work. The information, which he was hungry to learn, would come at the price of his neutrality. Every word got him deeper into whatever it was his godfather had planned. Yet how could he resist? These old guys gave up their secrets so infrequently.

"What happened?"

"Yes, what. I'm still not sure. The man I sent was my best man. *To Fithee* we called him. We all went by different names, so the Germans could not get information about our brothers, or our families. It must sound foolish to you now."

"*To Fithee.* The serpent."

"The Snake, if you like. Because he was so good at slipping into and out of places. And for other reasons. He had his own ideas of how best to do things, but I trusted him."

"And he failed."

"No, he succeeded. Too well. He understood the icon's value even better than I did, and he decided to take it at all costs." Fotis wet his lips with his tongue. "He killed a priest."

Matthew sat back on the bench. This was uglier than he would have guessed.

"Why?"

"I speak too quickly. I do not know for certain that he did it. The priest intervened somehow, and he died."

"What happened to the icon?"

"The church was burned, by the Germans, I think, though he might have done that also. At the time, I assumed the icon burned with it. Later I learned that my man had given it to a German officer."

"Given it?"

"Traded it, for guns and ammunition. To fight the communists. Once we knew the Germans were beaten, that became the priority. So you see, he was not being a thief, but a patriot. For all I know, he was under orders from someone above me."

Matthew tapped his feet to drive out the chill, as well as quell his agitation. The icon was suddenly marred, as if blood had been flicked across its surface. He would not be able to see it in the same way. Fotis seemed to read his thoughts.

"Many have killed for this work, and others like it, over the years. It should not surprise you, my boy. Or are you shocked to find blood on your godfather's hands?"

"You didn't send him to kill the priest."

"No. But I commanded him, controlled him, I thought. He had his own game; everyone did. It's a sad story. I am sorry to upset you. You would like to see the work in a purely artistic way, but since you are a kind of historian, I thought you should know."

"This wasn't a history lesson. You were talking about the Greek church, remember?"

"Indeed. My only point was this. We've discussed the minor importance the work would have to your museum. You know, or you should know, the value the icon had, not only as a source of faith, but as a source of healing, in the old country. This would seem to me sufficient reason to return it there. If not, well, then you have my sorry tale of its theft, and at what cost in blood. Can there be any doubt after that as to what the correct course should be?"

"So you want me to tell Ms. Kessler to donate the work to the Greek church?"

Fotis' eyes widened. "I see, you are afraid of defrauding her. No, the church is quite willing to pay. Of course, they might win the work in a lawsuit, but proving the theft and tracing the crooked path of ownership could take years, and cost as much in lawyers as it would take to buy the piece in the first place. They will make her an offer, perhaps not as much as she wants, but a fair offer, I have no doubt. And she is rich, so I would not be overly concerned about that."

"But you want me to talk her into it."

"To advise her, let her know your own heart on the matter. The rest will follow."

Matthew rose slowly, resisting the urge to swear, kick the bench, simply walk away. Instead he just stood there beside the shrunken old man.

"What are you up to?"

"What have I to do with it, my child? The situation is what it is. Fate chooses her own weapons."

Weapons, not tools, Matthew mused. He tried to think of himself as a weapon of fate. What a joke.

"Fate didn't bring me into this. You did."

"Am I not also an instrument? You were meant to be involved."

"That's a simple formula for justifying any damn thing you like, isn't it? That must make life very easy."

In fact, Fotis' life had been anything but easy, and Matthew did not hope to either understand or undermine his philosophy. Yet his godfather seemed unperturbed, serene; infuriatingly so.

"It is called faith, and it is available to anyone. You need not be your father's son."

"What the hell does that mean?"

"Nothing, my boy. It was a foolish thing to say. I apologize."

They had both misspoken, and silence followed. Matthew walked the pond's edge. The water was clear, springtime-fresh, with no dead leaves or debris. He could see the worn concrete shelf, then the bottom. This was Matthew's backyard, this whole section of park south of the museum to Seventy-second Street, the place he came to walk off stress, absorb a loss, get his head together. This was the very spot he would have chosen to contemplate the troubling revelation now before him. Yet here he was, and there was no comfort. He watched the still water and the vibrant spring light, smelled the damp earth, without emotion, without any reaction at all. An invisible screen seemed to have gone up between himself and the world. He would like to blame it on the conversation with Fotis, but that wasn't right. Had the feeling not been with him for the last two days, only now crystallizing? Could he not place it almost to the moment he stood before the icon, the dark eyes holding him, Ana Kessler's words, her breath, in his ear? And since then work, conversation, the necessary chores of life hummed like one long, dull interruption until he could think about the icon again, talk about it, see it. He wandered back to Fotis. The older man seemed far away in thought until Matthew began to sit.

"No, time to walk again. I have kept you too long. Help me up."

They continued north along the narrow path to the bridge below Cedar Hill, at ease once more in their manner, if not their minds. Matthew waited for a continued assault, but his companion was quiet, attention directed inward. Suppressing new pain, perhaps, or focusing his energy to finish the walk. Bright strips on the ceiling lit the short tunnel. A heap of clothing against the wall became, on closer inspection, a homeless man, sleeping or expired.

"If the church were to get it," Matthew began in mid-thought, "where would they put it?"

"We have not spoken in that sort of detail. I cannot ask them such things unless I am ready to support them if the answer is agreeable. And I cannot support them at all without you. So tell me what answer would make you happy."

"I'd just want to be sure it wasn't going to end up in a vault, or on some bishop's wall. That it would be somewhere the public could see it."

"Then we make that a condition of our involvement."

"I don't see how we can set conditions. I don't intend to talk Ms. Kessler into anything."

"But if she asks your advice, you will give it?"

"I have to think about all this."

"That is the wise course."

Dogs frolicked with their masters on the wide, sloping hillside above. To the north, through trees and across the Seventy-ninth Street transverse rose the massive concrete and glass south wall of the museum. A path bisected the one they were on, running up Cedar Hill to their left and out to Fifth Avenue on their right. Fotis would take this path to where his driver—one of the Russians, Anton or Nicholas—waited on the avenue. Obeying some unspoken rule, Matthew never accompanied him to the car, but did watch to see that he made it safely to the street.

"I will leave you to your work." Fotis took both of the younger man's hands in his own. "Do not let your thoughts be troubled. The correct decision will come to you if your mind is at peace. God keep you, my boy."

"Take care, *Theio.*"

A squeeze of fingers and the old man was off, slow but steady in his gait, never looking back. Matthew stood fixed in that little intersection until long after his godfather was out sight.

Jan placed the guidebook, open to the section on Central Park, facedown on the bench and waited for the old man to pass by. The younger one still stood there, fifty meters away, looking in his direction. Unlikely that he had noticed anything, Jan decided, merely making sure the old fellow was all right. He reached into his pocket and put his hand around the cool metal object, slipped it out carefully. One shot would do it, but two or three were protocol, in the back of the skull and between and just below the shoulder blades. That is, if this were a gun and not a cell phone.

Of course this was a terrible spot, far too many people and no cover. One of the three short tunnels they had passed through would be a better choice, especially if it were a rainy or cloudy day, a good bet in April in New York. But he might have to take out the younger one as well. Better still would be between the car and the house out in Queens. Well, best to have several options. He could inform del Carros that it would be no problem. The dealer would assume he was being nonchalant, having already pronounced the Greek a difficult target, but in truth Jan anticipated little trouble, even with the Russian bodyguards. He wouldn't mind adding them in; he hated Russians.

No messages. He put the phone away and picked up the guidebook again. Over 300 species of birds seen in the park every year, including the green heron and scarlet tanager. Amazing. Jan shook his head in wonder at the natural world.

6

Dust motes hung in the white shafts of light between the stacks, and Matthew had to work hard not to become hypnotized, not to let his imagination run wild with the strange reports on the pages before him. Down the hall in his office the red message light blinked on his telephone—the idiot lawyer for that potential donor in Chicago, no doubt. Memos from Nevins, the chief curator, from Carol and the planning committee, the director, Legal, all crowded his e-mail inbox, but Matthew was ignoring them. He was holed up instead in the department library, with the old volumes that held the few fragments of available knowledge on the Kessler icon.

An Internet search revealed nothing on so obscure a subject. There was nothing dependable from Byzantine sources, either, no way to trace the icon back to its place and moment of creation. The only clues were to be found in the image itself. The bottom of the work was so damaged that he hadn't been able to tell for certain whether there might once have been a depiction of the Christ child there, to whom Mary's badly chipped hands should be directing the viewer. This would place the image squarely in the *hodegetria* style, "She who shows the way," one of the most favored and oldest iconic traditions, based on an original painted by Saint Luke himself, according to popular myth. But the placement of the hands and the half turn to the right of the entire figure—more likely to direct the viewer's attention *outside* the frame—seemed to place the image more in the *hagiasoritissa* tradition. This series was associated with the relic of Mary's hood or sash, brought back from the Holy Land by Saint Helena in the fourth century and placed in a reliquary, above which the prototype of this image would have hung.

There were some arguments against this identification. The Katarini icon looked the viewer dead in the eye, instead of following the hand gestures to the right, where an icon of Jesus would generally accompany it. However, Matthew knew other images in the tradition which also broke that rule. A bigger stumbling block was that the style hadn't really become popular until the mid-tenth century, and the Katarini icon was certainly older than that, maybe much older. Yet who was to say the style hadn't existed earlier? Perhaps previous versions had all been destroyed in the iconoclasm of the eighth century. Indeed, Matthew thought, allowing the long-suppressed conjecture which had been building within him all morning to come forward, who was to say this image was not the long-lost prototype itself? The first of its kind, the inspiration for all that followed?

A shiver passed through his arms as the notion seized him. He fought this sudden agitation, assuring himself that the religious significance of such a find meant little to him. It would, though, mean a great deal to others, like the church officials who had contacted Fotis. Even as an art historical identification it would be impressive indeed—career-making, perhaps. Alas, unless further evidence came to light from some hidden source, it would remain forever a theory. Meantime, if he would never know for certain from where the Holy Mother had sprung, or how it made its eventual way to Epiros, at least he could review the traces of evidence regarding its time there.

The catalogs of the great art critics of centuries past had little room for Eastern Orthodox, and when it was included, it was always the same handful of icons: the sixth-century Peter, Mary, and Christ Pantokrator at Saint Catherine's in Sinai; some later pieces of Theophanes and Rublev in Russia; the Vladimir Virgin; a few others. Considering its placement in the rugged hills of Greece, not to mention the vast number of works in that country claiming special spiritual status, the Katarini Holy Mother's becoming known at all had to count as nearly miraculous. The first mention Matthew could discover was from the English adventurer Thomas Hall, who traveled all over Greece and Turkey in the 1780s. Hall's highly fanciful travelogues included, among many unlikely reports, one of the "Holy Mother of Epiros" (as if there were only one Holy Mother icon in the whole region), described as "more scratched wood than paint, except for the very lovely face of the Virgin" and as "curing blindness in true-hearted souls at a touch of its worn wood, but striking blind those of an evil or avaricious nature." This followed the story of the levitating monks of Metéora and directly preceded that of the miraculous vision of Christ in the peasant wife's washcloth. Matthew always had a good laugh reading Hall.

Lord Byron, on his first, nonfatal sojourn in Greece in 1809, made mention of a miraculous Holy Mother icon possessed by the Muslim tyrant Ali Pasha, who was already old but vigorous in mind and body, and would remain so until his death at the hands his Turkish overlords in 1822. Again, the description was very close to the Katarini icon, and Byron reported a strange golden aura about the work. Matthew shook his head. If I drank as much as you, Georgie boy, he thought, I'd see auras around paintings too.

The last volume on the table, however, was the one that troubled him most. Johann Mayer-Goff was a traveler of the late nineteenth century and a self-trained specialist on Orthodox art. The German was a sober, stolid, even somewhat boring writer, at least in translation, not given to hyperbole or floating monks. He was the first to name the village of Katarini as the residence of the icon, and he had attended the feast of the Annunciation in that same old church which Fotis' man burned down sixty years later. The day was rainy, Mayer-Goff wrote, and only candlelight illuminated the dank stone sanctuary:

*The icon was brought forth from its place of hiding and posi-
tioned near the altar. The peasant women wept in their seats, until
they fell into the aisle and approached the Mother of God upon
their knees, caressing the wood with their gnarled hands. One
among them, who had not walked unaided in many years, stood
suddenly upon shaking feet and praised Heaven. At the last, a
blind old shepherd with an angry face was led forward by a young
man and a girl, who seemed to pull him against his will. When his
hand was placed against the forehead of the All-Holy, he cried out
once and fixed his eyes upon the nearest candle flame, then upon all
of us in the congregation. It was made clear from his movements
that he could see us, and with another cry he fell upon the stone
floor and wept like child. I saw this with my own eyes.*

Matthew began to see dark spots on the page and realized that
he had not taken a breath in many moments. Inhaling deeply, he
then exhaled an embarrassed laugh. Get a grip on yourself,
buddy.

"There you are."

He looked up to see his older colleague Carol Voss standing
before the table, and slapped shut the volume of Mayer-Goff as if
he'd been caught by his mother reading *Penthouse*.

"Here I am, indeed."

"Not answering your e-mails," she scolded gently, her green
eyes behind large glasses looking him over carefully. Carol was a
mentor of sorts, his only close friend at the museum, and there
was little he could keep from her.

"It's not just yours I'm ignoring, if that makes you feel better."

"This about the Kessler icon?" she waved at the books on the
table.

"Yes."

"Checking provenance?"

"More or less. It's sketchy."

"Are we serious about this?" she asked skeptically.

"Are you pretending that I would know that better than you,
Ms. Finger-on-the-Director's-pulse?"

She laughed. "I haven't a clue. Nevins seems excited."

"Yeah, but he's up at the Cloisters every day. I don't even know if he's spoken to Fearless Leader."

"Speak to him yourself."

"We don't have that kind of relationship."

"You seem worried," she said, out of nowhere. "Are there ownership issues?"

"Maybe," he conceded, in a barely audible tone.

"Have we filed with the Art Loss Register?"

"Not yet. We need to be a little more certain we want it, right? Besides, if there's a theft involved, it isn't going to show up there. It would be older."

The phrase "wartime loot" hung in the air between them, unspoken. Carol clearly thought of saying more, and Matthew found himself wishing she would, wishing for someone upon whom to unburden himself. She squeezed his shoulder instead.

"Good luck, kiddo. Tell me if you want help. And Matthew, I know this is a fantastic piece and all, but it's just one piece. It's not your whole life."

Calling Benny Ezraki was a long shot. The card with the message service number was years old, and Andreas did not know if Benny was alive, much less still in the business of finding people, but he was unquestionably the right man for the job if he would take it. There was no recorded voice, just a tone. Andreas left his name and the hotel number, and ten minutes later his old Israeli contact called back. Andreas could stop by his new office, if he liked, but he might not approve of it. The old man knew he was being baited but agreed to go there anyway.

The name on the door was for a travel agency, and indeed the posters of Turkey and Egypt on the walls and the efficient young women with their headsets seemed to confer legitimacy. But that was only the first floor. The second, reached by a long stairway, consisted of narrow corridors and closed doors, and the barely dressed, boldly casual women smoking in the small lounge completed the picture. They all smiled at Andreas and pointed to the office in back.

Benny met him with a bear hug, which seamlessly segued into

a frisk. Habit, he apologized. The wily Greek Jew still looked younger than his age, which must be late fifties, though he seemed a little beaten down and tired. The beard was graying faster then the hair, the huge shoulders were more hunched, the pouches beneath the gentle brown eyes were more pronounced. The office had a view of the alley, a large computer monitor on the table, and a Pissarro calendar on the wall. The light was poor, and the cramped space was shrouded in blue cigarette smoke.

"Did you really expect me to be shocked by this place?"

"I was hoping so; you Athenians are all prudes. But I forget you are a man of the world."

"This is your new business?"

The big man sucked on a cigarette as if his life depended upon it, blew smoke just to the left of Andreas' face. He seldom smiled, even when he was kidding around.

"Always the same business. Travel, marketing, whores, it's all about information. I don't know why I didn't think of this years ago. You wouldn't believe the kinds of things these girls find out."

Andreas, a connoisseur of human nature, found it very easy to believe.

"Are they safe?"

"A doctor checks them every month. You want to try one?"

"That is not what I'm asking."

"I don't give them sensitive stuff. Mostly names. Send them around to the hotels whose databases we can't hack. But they always come back with stories. You know, blackmail is not my thing, but if it were I could make a fortune."

"You're too casual for that kind of work; you would get yourself killed."

"Maybe you're right."

"Can we speak freely? Is the Israeli ambassador in the next room?"

"We get very little traffic in here," Benny replied, the battered ergonomic chair groaning beneath his shifting weight. "Mostly we send out. Like Chinese food. This isn't a bordello."

"No?"

"No, we're an escort service. These aren't even the prime girls."

"Not so loud."

"The prime girls wait at home for the phone to ring. We screen it, make sure it's safe, get the credit card number, send them out."

"All in the name of information."

"That's my business."

"Excellent. I'm looking for someone."

Benny twisted awkwardly to reach the ashtray on his cluttered desk, mashed out one Gauloises, and immediately lit another. "Aren't you retired?"

"For years."

"But never completely, right?"

"I kept my hand in for a while. Until the idiots brought Papandreou back. That was the end."

"Papandreou, Mitsotakis, not much to choose from there. This new one seems like a decent fellow. Now our Israeli politicians—"

"We're not discussing politicians, Benny." Andreas sensed a brush-off in the other man's tone. "This is unofficial business. A favor. I'm reduced to asking favors these days. You can refuse after you hear what it is, but please let us not talk politics. That's for old men in cafés."

"Why would I refuse you?"

"Because there is nothing in it for you. Except my gratitude."

"And gratitude is such a small thing these days? I think I can judge best what is in my own interests."

Andreas pursed his lips and nodded. He'd hit the correct spot, but he must not push it.

"Years ago you helped me with something."

"God defend us, are you chasing Nazis again?"

"The same one."

"He's dead."

"No, he's here."

Benny looked at him hard. "You are certain?"

"Yes."

This was risky. He had only Fotis' word about Müller, which he would never normally trust uncorroborated. Yet his instinct told him it must be so, had been telling him since before he left

Greece. If he was wrong, it was a cruel trick. Benny's parents had been taken in the Salonika deportation in 1943 and died at Auschwitz. Müller may or may not have been involved, but he was a German officer in Salonika at the time, and that had been good enough for Benny thirty years before. He had been the one Mossad analyst to throw Andreas some leads, and the two had played straight with each other since then. They were both, by nature, careful about facts, and Andreas did not say he was certain of a thing unless he was.

"But you don't know exactly where he is."

"That's what I need you to tell me."

"Then how do you know he's here?"

"I have been informed."

"A dependable source, I hope."

"I'll pay you. So you're not wasting your time."

"Been hoarding your drachmas? Well, when a Greek agrees to pay, he must be pretty certain. But then it's not a favor."

"We can dispense with favors. Or you can refuse me, but don't toy with an old man."

Benny put up his hands in surrender, leaned over to get another cigarette, then realized he hadn't finished the one in the ashtray. He was more agitated than he would let on.

"Müller. You know how much trouble you got me into over that business?"

"How could I not, after all the times you told me? But you work for yourself now."

"Which means I have fewer resources than I used to."

"But better technology."

"This," Benny waved at the monitor, "this won't help us with Müller. I don't see him making it easy on us, staying at a big hotel."

"Why not? No one has looked for him in years. A private citizen, traveling under an alias, where better to hide but in a crowded hotel?"

The other man considered this. "You may be right. In my experience, however, people's behavior doesn't change. They may vary a pattern, but the pattern is discernible. Those old Nazis don't stay at hotels."

"Where do they stay?"

"Private homes, if they have those connections. In which case we'll never find him. I haven't looked for one of these guys for a while, and never in this country, but there used to be two small inns, run by elderly German ladies, very discreet. One in Brooklyn, which may be gone now; and one in the Village. That's where I would start."

"And will you?"

"I have some conditions."

Andreas sighed. He would rather have paid a king's ransom than have someone else set conditions, but Benny was a peer and couldn't be treated like some low-clearance freelancer.

"Yes?"

"What are your intentions when you find him?"

"That is a question, not a condition."

"One flows from the other. I need to know." Benny sized him up unblinkingly, while Andreas took longer to form a response than was wise. "My friend," the younger man pressed, leaning forward in his chair, "do you even know what your intentions are?"

"I have questions for him, if he can be made to answer them. It is also important that I monitor his actions."

"You once had bolder plans than that."

"I was younger. He is not responsible for your parents, Benny, he was only there to steal. That is all he has ever been about."

"That may be true, but it doesn't forgive his actions. I've seen his signature on arrest orders. He participated. Then there's your story, that would be reason enough."

"Reason for what? Tell me your damn conditions."

From the window came the faraway wail of sirens. In a room close by a woman laughed. Andreas felt pinned to his chair by age and fatigue.

"I don't want your money, first off. We do this together, or I don't involve myself. I find him, we pay him a visit. He's bound to be more responsive to your questions with me there."

"And then?"

Benny shrugged.

"Assuming the circumstances allow it, we get rid if him."

7

I made fresh coffee this time."

She was used to conveying calm self-assurance, Matthew could tell, but her fidgeting about the counters bespoke nervousness. Was he the cause? Why should he be? More likely the messy details of her grandfather's estate, which he had taken another afternoon away from his busy office to help her confront. He'd walked along the reservoir, barely aware of the brisk wind, the waning gold light on the water, the joggers' dirty looks as they darted around him on the narrow path. His senses blunted by images in his mind: a blind shepherd suddenly beholding a candle's flame; black-shrouded widows on callused, broken knees, baring their grief to the Mother, walking away cleansed; a dark chamber full of weary, resigned supplicants made one, made whole, if only for a little while, by a touch, a glance. Faces like his grandfather's, his aunts' and cousins', faces like his own. Mayer-Goff's words echoed in his skull: *I saw this with my own eyes.* He barely remembered to leave the park at Ninetieth Street, good shoes muddied by the horse trail, his pace and heartbeat quickening in a disquieting fashion the moment the Kessler brownstone came into view.

"Thanks," he said, "that wasn't necessary."

"It's not Greek coffee, of course. I'm not sure how to make that."

"You need the right grounds, like espresso. Better just to go someplace where they make it well."

"And do you know the right place?"

Ana carried two mugs to the table and sat across from him. Her face still appeared drawn, yet there was something strong in her, beneath the weariness. She wore it well.

"I know a few."

He was so certain that she would ask where those places were, ask him if he would take her to them sometime, that he was faintly embarrassed when she did not.

"Thanks for coming by," she said, staring into her coffee, her tone businesslike. "I know I only lured you with the chance to see the icon again, but the price you have to pay is talking some things through with me. Informally. I understand your allegiance is to the Met."

"I'd be happy to be of use."

"Can you tell me how serious the museum is?"

"We're interested, no question. I'm not sure yet how deep the interest goes."

"You mean it depends on the price."

"That's a factor, of course. The chief curator of my department needs to see the work. The director as well."

"Then I won't be negotiating with you?"

"I'll be involved, but this will get done above my head."

"What a shame," she said flatly. "We get along so well."

He laughed nervously. She was so direct in her approach, yet so quicksilver in her moods, that he had no idea what to make of her.

"You could insist upon it. People do things like that. We had one eccentric old lady who would only speak to our junior legal counsel, because he went to her dead husband's alma mater."

"That's brilliant."

"The director didn't think so."

"Shall I do that? Would it help your career?"

"You know," he said carefully, "you should probably leave the negotiating to your lawyer."

"My lawyer. He's a tricky guy, my lawyer. He may rob both sides blind."

"Shouldn't you have a lawyer you trust?"

"Oh, I guess I trust him." She averted her eyes to the table before taking a sip from the mug. "He's been taking care of Kessler business for thirty years, knows all the secrets. I couldn't get rid of him if I wanted to."

"Do you have a price in mind?"

"He does. Sounds high to me, but if the piece is as rare as you say, maybe not. I wish I could ask you what was fair."

"I wish I could tell you. Fair is what the market will bear."

"But we're not testing the market."

"I can't believe your lawyer wouldn't put out feelers."

"You think we should be fishing around?"

"It would be a natural thing to do."

"Talk to those pimps at the auction houses?" She spoke sharply. "They'll promise the sun, moon, and stars."

"They might get them."

"What are you telling me, Matthew? That I should go to some rich private collector?"

Her stare was intense, and he found himself struggling with his unease, compelled by an impolitic honesty.

"Actually, I think that would be a terrible idea. Not for you, necessarily."

"Don't waffle."

"It's just, the thought of that work being locked away from the world, stuck up on someone's wall . . ."

"Like it is now," she pressed.

He exhaled slowly. "Yes. Like it is now. It would be a sad choice. It should be where a lot of people can see it."

"A museum."

"A museum would be the most obvious call."

"But will a museum give it the attention it deserves?"

Fotis' question again, and Matthew had no better answer for it this time.

"You can attach conditions to the sale. It's done all the time."

Ana shook her head. "My lawyer says we don't have leverage with just the one painting. If I were donating the whole collection I could make demands. Or if it were a Picasso or a Rembrandt, maybe. Tell me if I'm wrong here."

"You're probably right." He shrugged. "It's still worth discussing."

"Does it annoy you that Byzantine doesn't get treated with the same respect as the Old Masters, or the Impressionists, or all of that popular stuff?"

"You know, I never considered popularity when I got into the field. I just studied what interested me, fool that I was."

"But it *must* piss you off. The people who made this icon, it was like life and death for them, right? They held these things up before their armies when they went into battle. They died to defend them. Did anyone ever die over a Renoir?"

She was leaning over the table, eyes wide, hand gesturing fiercely. He wanted to laugh at the ridiculousness of her argument, but it was impossible. She was so sincere, so fully present in her emotions that it was he who felt ridiculous, made small by his own restraint.

"That's true, except that it was really about religion. They killed and died over what the icon represented, not over its beauty."

Ana sat back, nodding slowly at his words, or in acceptance of some new thought.

"That is what it comes down to, isn't it? You can't take religion out of the equation."

She went to the counter, retrieved the coffeepot, and topped off their mugs, though neither had drunk much. The suit was gone today, she wore faded blue jeans and a white shirt, and he found himself distracted by the long arc of her leg in the tight fabric as she returned the pot to the counter. She remained there a few moments, her back to him.

"So Matthew, since we won't be negotiating directly, I want to ask your advice about something. I know you'll be straight with me."

"I'll try."

She came to the table and sat down again, watching his eyes as she spoke. "Somebody from the Greek church called Wallace, my lawyer. They want the icon."

He had guessed it before she spoke. Fotis was here before him, forcing the issue.

"The Greek church in Greece?"

"I'm not certain. The guy who called was an American priest, but it was on behalf of the church over there. I'm not really sure of the distinction."

"It's murky even to them."

"Apparently, they hinted pretty heavily that the work was stolen from Greece, years ago."

She was staring at him so hard that he felt implicated in the crime. This was clearly what she had wanted to talk about all along.

"Were you surprised to hear that?"

She sipped, not breaking eye contact. "No."

"Are they offering to pay?"

"They didn't float numbers, but yes, they'll pay."

"Where was it left?"

"Nowhere. We're supposed to get back to them."

"And what advice do you need from me?"

Finally she wavered, looked away.

"I'm just curious what you thought of the idea. I mean, I'm not seriously considering it."

"Why not?"

"You think I should?"

"Stop throwing all these questions back at me, and think about what you want." He had barely raised his voice, but she seemed stung. "Listen, Ana, there is no 'should' about any of this. I'm simply curious why you wouldn't consider the church a viable option."

"It's a new idea to me, that's all. I understand about dealers, collectors, museums. Then it's just about the art. This is bringing a whole new element into it. They want the icon for totally differ-ent reasons. I have no way of comparing the two things."

His thoughts were pulled in all directions: Fotis' plans, his own desires, what he should tell her, and when—he could not bring it all together.

"I guess one way to judge would be to think about who will get to see the work in each case, and what each group would get out of that experience. You need more information."

"But does that even matter? Let's say the icon *was* stolen. Doesn't it belong to them? And couldn't they make serious trouble for me or for the museum?"

He had been intentionally evading the issue, but there was no way around it. The mere whisper of "stolen Nazi loot" by the Greeks would cause the museum to drop its interest in a moment. There wouldn't even have to be evidence.

"Are those the arguments the church rep made to your lawyer?"

"They were more subtle, I'm sure, but he understood. And he made sure that I did too."

"What is he recommending?"

"He's not one to be intimidated, Wallace. As far as I know, the museum is still the first option, but he wouldn't have even mentioned the church if he didn't expect me to consider it."

"Well," Matthew struggled for words. "This is interesting."

"Is it? I find it rather nerve-racking, myself."

"You must be more undecided than you first let on."

"I go back and forth." She ran a hand through her hair. "No choice seems like the right one. My lawyer gives me this maddening, contradictory advice in his completely neutral tone, and all you can do is ask questions."

"At least he's getting paid. My advice is free."

"You want me to pay you?"

"I'm asking questions that I think are going to help you know your own mind. I'm not in a position to tell you what to do."

"Right now, I'd like someone to tell me."

"I strongly suspect that if someone tried you would resist strenuously."

She rewarded him with her first smile of the day.

"Do I seem that contrary?"

He leaned back in his chair and returned the smile. "It's what I would do."

"Really? Is there stubbornness lurking beneath that smooth exterior, Mr. Spear?"

"So I'm told," he said to the rust-colored floor tiles. Best to get off that topic quickly. "Have you considered simply holding on to it?"

"The thing is, some of this stuff has to go. Despite how careful my grandfather was, there are estate taxes, other expenses. Pretty hefty ones."

"Why the icon? There's plenty of other work, isn't there?"

"The modern I want to keep, that's my thing. Of the older work, the icon is the most valuable piece."

"Maybe that's all the more reason to hold on to it."

She placed both hands firmly on the table.

"OK, you want the truth?"

"Please."

"The thing gives me the creeps, it always has. I know, it's just paint, but it feels as though there's something more, something lurking inside. Then there's my grandfather dying in front of it. I want it gone. So, I've said it. Now you can be disgusted with me."

"Hardly. All it means is that the work is affecting you. Maybe not in the way the creator would have wanted, but nevertheless."

She was pensive for a moment, then broke into another smile.

"You mean the artist. Not the Creator."

He blushed for no reason.

"That's right. The little guy, not the big guy."

"I'm sorry, I'm punchy. I need a break from this." She checked her watch. "God, it's late. You didn't need to go back to your office?"

"I'm done for the day."

"Is there someplace you're supposed to be?"

"No," but he sensed the kiss-off and got to his feet. "Just some reading to catch up on."

He went to the sink to wash out his mug, childishly annoyed about being denied another look at the icon. This obsessiveness wasn't like him, and he felt unnerved. The visit had been about what she needed, not about him.

"Leave that, I'll do it."

"No problem." He put the damp mug on the counter.

"I was wondering if you want to have dinner. If you're not too busy."

Matthew shook his head at his own stupidity. When had he become this slow? Why was he misreading her, making things harder?

"It's a nice idea."

She was gazing at him serenely, and he waited for an excuse to roll off his lips. It was a terrible idea, in fact. There was this business matter between them, and she was an odd woman in a vulnerable place. Despite his sympathy for her, and even his fascination, he was made constantly uneasy in her presence. The hundred-year-old German grandfather clock in the dining room intruded a deep, resonant ticking into the expanding silence.

"I promise not to talk about the icon," she added, and he thought about the walk home, past the dry cleaners and Chinese restaurants to his empty apartment, while whatever lame excuse he concocted echoed around in this old brownstone, and she sat at the table drinking coffee all night.

"OK," Matthew said. "Sure, I'd love to. Where shall we go?"

As it turned out, they didn't go anywhere. Ana thought they could throw something together, the only difficulties being that there was little food in the house and that she didn't cook. She did know the wine cellar, however, and went to retrieve a bottle while Matthew chopped mushrooms and whisked four eggs with a little cold water. Sliced apple, some parmesan, and in minutes he created a perfect omelet, which they ate with toasted bagels and a 1984 Châteaux Margaux.

"This is the wrong wine," Ana said.

"Not if you like it."

"Do you?"

"Very much, not that I'm an authority. Too much retsina forced on me at a young age."

"Retsina," she groaned. "My God, that stuff is poison."

"This is where I'm supposed to say—with my chin in the air, like this—that you haven't had the good stuff. 'That export retsina, *Theomou, scatá!*'"

"That's good, you look like somebody."

"Marlon Brando."

"I was going to say Mussolini."

"Gee, thanks. The truth is, all retsina tastes like tree sap to me. Greek food, French wine." He swirled the dark liquid in his glass. The cooking had eased some of his tension. "Everybody, do what they're good at."

She stuffed a forkful of omelet into her mouth, as if she hadn't seen food in days.

"Do all Greek men know how to cook?"

"It's an omelet, Ana. Any single guy can make one, it hardly qualifies as cooking."

"To you. In this kitchen it's the height of culinary achievement."

"I'm honored."

"Can I ask a rude question?"

"Why start looking for permission now?"

"Why *are* you single?"

"Well, how do I answer that? Fate? I could ask you the same question."

"We'll get to me." She adjusted her wineglass on the table, minutely, precisely, as if it were an important engineering project. "So you're not involved?"

"I didn't say that."

"You can make a last-minute dinner date without having to answer to anyone."

"Maybe my girlfriend is out of town."

"Why make me guess?"

"All right," he conceded with a tight smile, "you're correct. I am currently unentangled."

"Now how can that be? A handsome, intelligent guy like yourself."

She said it casually, as if he must be used to such compliments, but Matthew felt his face flush once more. Maybe it was just the wine.

"This city is full of handsome, intelligent, lonely people," he answered carefully. "It's not such a mystery. Anyway, I just split with somebody I was with for a long time."

"Whose doing was that?"

"Her doing. My fault."

"Why your fault?"

"It was the Mussolini imitation, drove her nuts."

"Come on."

"Too many questions, Ana."

"Sorry." Her fork went down with a clatter. Her plate was empty.

"Looks as if somebody hasn't been eating."

"I forget, isn't that pathetic? I'm a grown woman, but I forget to eat. When I'm in Santa Monica I have friends I always see for meals. Here, it's more free-form. Actually, I used to have dinner with my grandfather a lot, before he became really ill."

"Don't tell me I'm sitting in his chair."

"Eat in the kitchen, my grandfather? We always sat in that gloomy dining room, even when it was just the two of us. I don't think he knew what the kitchen looked like."

"Who did the cooking?"

"André. A sweet old guy, who I think I need to let go."

"Maybe you should keep him," Matthew noted, pointing to her empty plate.

"He's almost eighty and wants to retire. I've already dumped Diana, that pain in the ass."

"She was the nurse?"

"Thought she owned the place. My grandfather was sure she was stealing. I don't know about that, but there was no reason to keep her. Gave her a nice severance and a good recommendation."

"And you're left with no one to take care of you."

"And no one to take care of. I am also, how did you say it? Unentangled?"

"Here's to that." They toasted with their half-empty glasses, crystal pinging against crystal. "Do you prefer it that way?" The wine was loosening his normally careful tongue.

She stared off into space, seeming to consider the matter. "Not really. No."

"All that jetting around the world makes it hard to maintain a relationship?"

"I never thought so, but it was definitely a problem for my ex-husband."

"The plot thickens." He refilled their glasses, working hard to keep his hand steady, making sure to give her more. Two of his fingertips were stained red from the wine. "What's the story with that?"

"Not much of a story. Married at twenty-four, divorced at twenty-eight. No kids, thank God. He was a painter, turned commodities trader. Not a bad guy, just immature and stupid. Almost as immature and stupid as I was. Tell you what."

"What?"

"You did such a great job with dinner, why don't you make the coffee?"

It surprised him how comfortable he felt in her kitchen. Perhaps because it wasn't really hers, but her grandfather's, or not even his, but old André's. And kitchens were familiar. His family was always in the kitchen, his father doing as much of the cooking as his mother, holding forth on some complex scientific theorem, his sister arguing. Robin and he spent a lot of time in the kitchen as well, touching as they slipped past each other going to the stove, cabinet, freezer. Though constantly together, they had separate apartments, and he was always aware of being at her place, on her turf, not his own—except for her kitchen, which felt somehow connected to his, a seamless parallel space passing from West to East Side. He recalled her stinging reply when he once admitted this strange theory to her: he loved her kitchen because that was where the front door was. It wasn't a long way from that comment to the end of their relationship.

"My grandfather loved good coffee," she said to his back. "He couldn't really drink it anymore the last few years."

"Which explains this cheapo coffeemaker. Who bought this, Diana?"

"Actually, I did."

"Sorry." He really shouldn't drink socially.

"I like good coffee too, but I can't be bothered with the effort. Turkish coffee, that's what he liked. Middle Eastern food, Orthodox religion. I think he hated being born Swiss."

"Did he join the Orthodox church?"

"No. He sort of drifted away from Catholicism, tried a bit of everything—I mean, of the Old Testament choices. He didn't do Buddhism. Eastern Orthodox art seemed to speak to him, and that's what pushed him in that direction. I don't think he even went to church."

"So it was more a personal spirituality."

"I guess. To tell you the truth, I don't really know how religious, or spiritual, he was. Sometimes he seemed intensely so. Other times, it just felt like superstition. I guess it all feels like superstition to me." She was quiet long enough that he wondered if he was expected to respond. "One thing I can tell you, though," she said finally, "he worshiped that icon."

Matthew came back to the table as the coffeemaker finished burbling. "So can I ask *you* a rude question?"

"Fair is fair."

"If he worshiped it, like you say, why did he leave no directions for its disposal?"

She looked perplexed. "He left all that to me."

"In most cases, with a collection like this, there are specific instructions about what should be done. Usually these things are worked out in detail with museums and galleries, long before the person dies. You must know all that. Did the will say anything?"

"There were instructions, but they weren't specific. A lot of latitude was built in for me to do what I wanted, add to my collection, sell to cover expenses. He had no relationship with museums. He knew very few people by the end of his life. And he never mentioned the icon."

"Do you find that odd?"

"I did," she nodded. "Then Wallace suggested that maybe the

icon was too personal to him, that he simply couldn't deal with the idea of being separated from it, even in death."

Matthew stifled a skeptical laugh. It had a ring of truth, after all.

"Mr. Wallace is a psychiatrist too, huh? Didn't he draw up the will?"

"The primary will. Notes on the paintings were appended to my grandfather's copy, in a safe, here. He didn't believe in safe-deposit boxes. I guess that came from being a banker. At one point some pieces were left to Swiss museums, but those were crossed out. Wallace pressed him to come up with a plan, but he just wouldn't deal with it. I think he believed he would live forever."

"He did pretty well. Ninety-seven years old, the obituary said."

"And very sharp of mind, right up until the last year or two. He had a bunch of illnesses and injuries in his eighties and nineties, all of which he bounced back from. I think the blindness really broke his spirit."

"He was blind?"

"Almost. The last several years, his vision started to go. It was devastating for him. That's when the other things, the arthritis and the weak heart, got the better of him." Ana caught his eyes lingering on her a little too long. "That coffee is ready."

The last thing either of them needed was more coffee, but it gave Matthew something to do, and he sensed that she took some comfort from his serving her.

"Wow, this is strong," she said.

"Don't drink it."

"I'm up all night anyway, might as well be alert."

"This has been very tough on you."

"Mostly it's the responsibility. There's a lot to handle with the estate. I snipe at Wallace, but I'd be lost without him."

"There's no one else, no brothers or sisters, uncles, cousins?"

"My dad was an only child, and he's gone. I'm his only child, so it's just me on the Kessler side. There's my mother, but she's no help. She and my grandfather hated each other. Well, she hated him, anyway."

"That's too bad." There was a story there, Matthew figured, but it was her business whether she felt like telling it. "You were close to him, right?"

"Off and on. Less so in recent years. Too much traveling."

"You enjoy it."

"Buying and selling art is what I do, for myself and a few friendly clients. I have to travel. But I do love it, it's true. I keep waiting for the settling-down urge to hit me. You must travel a lot, also."

"I lived in Greece, went to Turkey a few times. Ravenna, Venice, great Byzantine stuff there. Otherwise, I never go anywhere. Hate to fly."

"Most people do," Ana agreed. "I sleep like a baby right through turbulence. Must come from my dad owning a jet. I was always flying off with him someplace from the time I was, like, ten."

"Was he in the art trade too?"

"The family curse," she said, sadly, leaning back in her chair. "Actually, he was a banker, like my grandfather. But he dabbled in art, especially when the old guy stopped being able to travel. In fact, he died on a business trip for my grandfather."

Matthew wondered what to ask. She glanced over at him and he merely nodded.

"Plane crashed," she went on. "Nobody knows why. Mechanical failure, I guess. He was a good pilot."

"He was flying himself?"

"Oh, yeah, he loved to fly. But the circumstances were kind of awful. He and my mother were supposed to take a trip, about the same time that my grandfather was supposed to go to South America and see this painting. Another icon, actually. I guess the icon was being auctioned, or there was another bidder or something. Anyway, he got sick and persuaded my father to go in his place. So my dad flew down to check it out. And his plane crashed into a mountain in Venezuela, coming back. Took them days to find the wreckage and there was so little left they couldn't figure out what happened. They think he was too low and hit the mountain in a fog bank, but we'll never really know."

He waited a few moments to see if she would say more, then found his voice again.

"When did this happen?"

"Fifteen years ago. I was in high school."

"That's a terrible story. I'm sorry, Ana."

She shrugged. "History."

"It must have wrecked your grandfather."

"He was never the same. And my mother still hasn't forgiven him."

"Well. That's unfair, but understandable, I guess. Given the circumstances."

"I went through a period of blaming him, but it was no good. My dad could have said no. He loved that kind of thing, jetting off on a lark. You can't live in fear of what might go wrong."

"Maybe she'll forgive him now that he's dead."

Ana scoffed. "Mother's not big on forgiveness. She hasn't forgiven me for reestablishing a relationship with him, and I'm her only damn child."

He glanced at the clock above the refrigerator for the first time since arriving. It was late, after eleven.

"Doesn't look like you're going to get that reading done," she said.

"It'll wait."

"Thank you for dinner. And for talking to me."

"I don't know that I said anything useful."

"You listen, you ask good questions. And I find your voice soothing."

"Almost puts you to sleep," he countered, needing to make light of her words.

"Anything that puts me to sleep these days should not be disparaged." She stood abruptly and stretched, rolled her neck about gently. "Come on, let's make good on our deal."

Matthew followed her down the old, looping staircase, his steps uncertain, his suppressed excitement leaping up again with distressing intensity. She fumbled for the lights in the small antechamber, and then they passed through the narrow arch. The chapel was smaller than he remembered, claustrophobic. He made a show of examining the panels from eastern Europe, stations of the cross, but his eyes were drawn inexorably back to the icon. The colors, subtle to begin with, appeared to shift about. The cloak was maroon, mauve, bloodred; the luminosity seemed to come from a place below the surface. Focusing on details usually helped, but the closer he got, the harder objective observation became. He grew agitated. One of the Virgin's hands seemed to move, and he closed his eyes and stepped back.

"I'm not sure it's good for you to be in here," Ana said quietly.

"Don't read your own discomfort into other people's reactions."

"I'm not. I'm looking at you, and you seem very uneasy."

He shifted to avoid her gaze, then took a deep breath.

"Just tired. I should get going."

In fact, he had no real desire to leave, but he was troubled by her attention, by her seeming need to get under the lid of his emotions.

"All right," she answered.

He closed his eyes once more to compose himself. Then felt her hand on his shoulder, her lips on his, softly, gone again in a moment. She stepped back, the contact brief enough to have been only friendly if he saw fit to leave it at that. They faced each other for half a minute, enveloped by the warm light, the near walls. Ana tried to wait him out, but couldn't.

"You're not used to doing the work, are you? Things just come to you."

"I'm sorry," but it sounded less like the confused response he'd intended, and more like the apology it was. "Mostly, things just go away from me."

"Poor boy."

She turned to the door, but he reached out and gripped her shoulder. She turned back and kissed him again, more forcefully, and this time he took the hint.

8

He was supposed to wait on the sidewalk for the black sedan to come rolling down Seventy-ninth Street, but it was a cold day, and Matthew sat in the coffee shop instead. The big glass windows commanded a view of the intersection, busy with vehicular and human traffic, shoppers and museumgoers, marching beneath the little sign that proclaimed this stretch Patriarch Dimitrious Way. The Greek consulate was just down the street.

His concentration was shot—lack of sleep and a not altogether unpleasant state of agitation. Without warning, his mind shifted back a few hours to the warmth of her bed, the unexpected heat of her body. She had been so ready for him that a simple touch had been enough, and he had continued to touch her, in various ways, for some time, totally consumed with pleasing. He didn't make a conscious decision to stay, simply found himself there in the gray predawn, her weight upon him before he knew where he was. Half-asleep, they rediscovered their rhythm and proceeded in a steady, dreamlike fashion, Ana laughing in embarrassment at her own pleasure, thighs spasming against his hips, her whole body responding to his every motion. He had held her for a long time, not speaking, smelling her hair, her skin, his mind and muscles relaxing for what seemed like the first time in weeks. A blessedly uncomplicated sense of how right they had felt together still possessed him.

Over breakfast, they talked about the icon again, and she seemed to come to a decision. Matthew encouraged her not to make up her mind too quickly, but he had not been displeased. At the door, she wouldn't let him go.

"This was reckless," she'd said, squeezing his hand. "We hardly know each other."

"Knowing takes time. We haven't done too badly."

"I don't even know how old you are."

"Does it matter?"

"No."

"OK, I'm fourteen," he confessed. "Really, I've been shaving since I was eleven."

Ana smiled, but her mind had already moved to something else.

"You wouldn't marry her. That was the problem, wasn't it?" Her words carried such certainty that he'd felt no need to respond. "That doesn't make it your fault, Matthew. Just a decision."

"I'm thirty."

She'd made a show of being chagrined, but she couldn't be that much older. Obviously used to being surrounded by older men. Eventually he had broken free and escaped into the frigid morning, but he could picture her still at the half-open door, in a gray cashmere robe, hair askew, blue eyes tracking him down the stairs, seeing him, knowing him in some deep and unsettling way.

There was a draft in the shop, and Matthew wrapped his hands around the porcelain coffee mug. When he looked up again Fotis was there on the sidewalk, just beside the bus shelter. The old man pretended to look around, but Matthew was certain he had spotted him there in the window before ever leaving his car. He stood, and Fotis looked directly at him, gestured for him to stay put.

"Am I late?"

"No, I just didn't want to stand in the cold."

"We must get you a warmer coat. Why don't we forget the walk and stay here?"

"Sure." He hung his godfather's coat and squeezed into the second chair across the table. It was a slow day, and the waiter was hovering instantly.

"This is the place with the good rice pudding?" Fotis asked.

"Best in New York," Matthew confirmed.

"Two of those."

The waiter slid the eight feet back behind the counter. Three of them worked in that small space, banging dishes, shouting at each other in some hybrid of Greek and Spanish.

"Now," Fotis leaned across the table, "what is so urgent that it could not wait?"

"I would have told you on the phone."

"These conversations are better had in person."

Matthew tapped the speckled Formica table. He needed to pin the old bastard down.

"I'm pretty sure Ms. Kessler wants to make a deal with the church."

The older man nodded slowly.

"This is excellent. You have done a good thing, my boy."

"I didn't do anything, except talk to her."

"Did I not say that would be all that was required?"

"Anyway, I thought it would please you."

"But not you, I fear."

Matthew shrugged as the desserts were placed before them. Fotis began eating immediately.

"I think it's the right choice," the younger man continued, "but I can't help feeling that I've been dishonest. She doesn't know anything about your connection with the church."

"What is there to know? They asked for my help, it has proved unnecessary."

"I thought I would tell her. About them talking to you, and you talking to me."

Fotis continued eating methodically, pudding sticking to his huge mustache.

"You say she came to the decision on her own. If you tell her these things, you tell her to doubt her decision."

"Maybe she should doubt it."

The old man glanced up at him. "Why?"

"Because another buyer might pay her more. And a museum would be accountable for what it did with the work. Who knows what these Greeks will do?"

"Demand to know."

"I've told you, I can't demand anything."

"Advise her. You've done well so far."

"And why should I undermine my own museum's interests?"

"That is a different issue."

"I'm denying myself the chance to have this work at my fingertips, to examine it at length, any time I want. That's a very appealing idea to me."

"And that is a different issue still." Fotis paused to chew as two large women with several colorful shopping bags each bustled into the tiny shop, gabbling in some Scandinavian tongue. "Now we have the girl, the museum, and yourself. Who comes first?"

"It's Ana's icon."

Matthew hadn't meant to use her first name, but if the old fox noticed, he did not let on.

"Very good. She has taxes to pay, I understand, but her financial situation is sound. She has no real money needs. She may well have spiritual ones."

"That's not for us to conjecture about."

"Her grandfather built a chapel to contain the icon." The old man's bushy eyebrows rose meaningfully. "Mother of God, what could be a clearer sign of his intentions than that? What could better honor his feelings for the work than giving it to the church? So there is the girl. The museum, truly, I must tell you that I don't give a damn about them one way or another. Your loyalty is admirable, of course, but it is a big, rich institution which has no need of your protection. Eat your pudding."

Matthew wasn't hungry, but dutifully took a bite.

"As for what you need," Fotis continued, the long spoon clattering in his empty dessert glass, "that concerns me greatly." He wiped his face carefully and turned his eyes to the street. Always on the lookout, thought Matthew. For what? "The church will want to secure the icon before the girl has second thoughts, but they will not be able to take immediate possession. They have not made arrangements for transport, or for what happens to it over there. I can provide them with a neutral location to store it for a few weeks, insurance coverage, security. I do it for my own work anyway. And you may examine it during that time, whenever you wish."

"There are companies that specialize in the storage and transportation of art. I could even recommend a few. I can't believe they would leave that to you."

"I tell you I can arrange it."

Matthew squeezed his forehead. He needed sleep, needed to think clearly.

"Have you already arranged it? How deeply are you in with these people?"

"There have been discussions. Nothing has been agreed, but they will do as I suggest. I contribute generously to several of their causes, and unlike you, I am not ashamed to apply leverage. Anyway, they prefer to deal with countrymen, you know the Greeks."

"And you're doing this for what reason?"

"You don't believe it's for the church?" Fotis smiled at him. "Suspicious boy. Very well, say that it is for myself. There is little in life that would please me more than returning the icon to Greece, and having a few precious days alone with it before that."

"I see."

"And you know, there is another person who might benefit." Fotis eyed him keenly, but Matthew was unwilling to play. "Your father will be released from the hospital shortly."

"My father?" A cold panic turned the pudding to lead in his stomach.

"Yes."

"He's not much for art. Or religion."

"If you would remember what you have read, you would

understand that faith is not always necessary for healing. It is in the general nature of the miraculous. Doubters are critical to any religion. Their resistance defines faith, and it usually says something about their hearts. The truly godless never bother to think about the matter. Your father's scorn says something different to me from what he intends."

"I'm sure he'd be very interested to hear that," Matthew snapped, anger rising at Fotis' daring to bring his father into this, even as the old man's words stirred other, more elusive feelings.

"I would not be foolish enough to say it to him, and I trust that you will have the wisdom not to mention any of this. He will come to my home for a visit when he is out of the hospital. The icon will be there. The rest will be in God's hands."

"In God's hands?" Matthew could barely contain himself. Private musings had leaped from his mind, from the old dusty pages in the library to his godfather's lips. His own scorn died on his tongue, killed by some stronger emotion. Fear? Was it fear lurking beneath the cover of his righteous rage, and what should he be frightened off? "You honestly think that icon will miraculously cure him?"

"I expect nothing. I would not deny him the opportunity to derive some good from it. Why would you?"

"And for that ridiculous reason I'm not supposed to tell Ana Kessler the truth?"

"There is nothing useful you are keeping from her. And there are *many* reasons why you should allow the matter to take its course. Must we review them again? Do you need more?"

Matthew's anger reached some critical mass and converted itself into paralyzing self-disgust. A man who knew his mind would do what he had to, would not sit here debating.

"Do you think the girl is telling you everything?" Fotis continued.

"What do you mean?"

"Only that she may have secrets of her own."

"Like what?"

"I do not claim to know, but it is a strange and secretive family, from what little I understand. She has not hesitated to turn you to her own purposes, make you her personal adviser."

"I've done that willingly."

"It always feels that way with a woman, yes?"

"I don't like your insinuations."

"I withdraw them. You need no self-serving reasons to do what is right."

"How do either of us know what that is?"

"You will do what is right because you are a good man. You do not require the spur of familial guilt and obligation."

"Familial guilt," spat Matthew. "You mean your guilt."

"Are we not family? But that is not what I meant. The responsibility lies closer still."

"Please don't be mysterious, *Theio*. Say what you're going to say."

Fotis' eyes were suddenly damp, and his face seemed to droop with his mustache.

"I did not want to speak of this. I break a trust by doing so. Do you understand me? *To Fithee*. The Snake."

"The one who killed the priest."

Fotis reached one long, shaking hand across the table and caught Matthew's sleeve.

"We cannot know that he *did* kill him. He was doing what he felt was right, remember that."

"Tell me."

"Your *Papou*." And he withdrew the hand, looked away. Matthew simply stared.

"*Papou* was the Snake."

Fotis only nodded, back bent, hat falling over his eyes. Diminished. Matthew allowed any expressions of shock or denial to pass through his mind unspoken. Indeed, the longer he sat there, made mute by the terrible questions in his mouth, the more they tasted like truth. Had he thought about it before now, he might have guessed. Perhaps he had, perhaps that explained his present restraint. Killers grew into kindly old men. He knew his grandfather had an ugly past. His father had told him more than once that the man had done things of which he was now ashamed, things which haunted him. Certainly, there were circumstances that might explain what happened, yet Matthew had the feeling he would never learn what they were. He could fish for answers, but he would have to be careful, have to keep his own secrets from Andreas until he knew more. Even now, all these years later, it was clear that his grandfather was up to something here, something more than visiting his son in the hospital. He was hardly ever at the hotel when Matthew called, would not discuss whom he was seeing or why. Could it be about the icon?

"And if I ask him about this, he'll confirm it?"

Fotis looked shocked.

"My goodness, child, what could he say to such a thing? He might speak true, he might invent a lie, I don't know. More than likely, he will say nothing, but I think it would break his heart if he found out that you knew. I pray you will not mention it."

In the silence that followed, the waiter laid a check on the table. When Fotis did not immediately reach for it, Matthew knew the old man was shaken. He took the check himself, idly folding it several times.

"Damn it, *Theio*. I wish I didn't know this."

Andreas, in the backseat with Matthew, fought the drowsiness that always hit him in an overheated car. The smooth driving of his granddaughter Mary, the scientist in training, did not aid his efforts. He had never known a woman to drive so well. In the passenger seat, Alekos was still and pale, but his eyes blazed with new life as he looked out on the wet spring woods. He had not expected to see this place again, thought Andreas; he is wondering if this is the last time he will see it.

I have missed his whole life, the old man pondered. When Alex was a boy, Andreas had been constantly away on one awful piece of business or another. Serving his country. Errands for some bloody-minded brute, or worse, some arrogant idealist, soon corrupted. Forced retirements when governments changed, the chance to lead a normal life thrown away when he was called back to serve the next fool as he'd served the last. It might take months, but eventually they all understood how much they needed men like him. Irreplaceable men, who knew all the secrets. Why did he go back, once, twice, how many times? Because it was all he knew? He could have learned something else. He could have been a man of business. Why did he allow himself to stay in that terrible game, where nobody won, where keeping the idiots in power was the only goal? On good days, he understood the need; there were real enemies. But then there were all those men broken in body and spirit for harmless beliefs. Men not so different from himself.

Before long Alekos was off to school in America, where he fell in love, and never returned home. Which was just as well, given what Greece became in those years. But the familial bonds were strained, and Maria's death seemed to snap them. Andreas suspected some loose words from Fotis, either to Alekos or to his hard-hearted niece Irini, Alekos' wife. There was no other way that his son could have learned certain things, things he would have been better off not knowing. God only knew what Fotis' goal had been. To drive a wedge between father and son? If he had planned to step in and play surrogate father, that plan had failed. He alienated himself from the boy as well. The evil stories had bred others in Alekos' mind, until he had come to see plots everywhere. Yet that explanation felt like letting Andreas out of his share in the blame. His absence, his actions, had somehow poisoned his child's mind, made him turn a cold, scientific eye on life, which he found wanting in every regard.

Or perhaps he was being unfair to both of them. Every father wounded his son, it was almost a duty. A man needed to make his own way, and had not Alekos done that? His cynical, aggrieved manner aside, he had found a wife, made two beautiful children, been successful in his career. The price was the rejection of his old life, his old country, his father. It was fair. It may not have been necessary, but it was fair.

The house, a modest stone structure in this town of great brick mansions, appeared behind a stand of hemlock. Alex refused the wheelchair, and with his son and daughter supporting him, walked up the front steps under his own power. Inside, Irini helped him to his study, where he would rest until he could manage the stairs. Andreas was shown to a chair near a warm radiator, but when the others retreated to the kitchen, he joined them.

"He looks good," Mary said. "I mean, he looks happy to be home."

"God willing, we can keep him here," said Irini, whisking an egg furiously. She alone seemed capable of action. *"Babas,* do you want some water?"

"Make your soup, I will get it."

But Mary jumped up, which was just as well, since he did not know where to find the glasses. He'd been in this house only twice before and felt as if he were visiting distant relatives. It intensified his sadness, but he attempted to shut that out and gratefully accepted the glass of water from his granddaughter. Mary still had a girl's face, but she was twenty-seven and not yet married. Too beautiful, the old man surmised; too many choices.

"Thank you, child."

"Can I hang up your coat?"

"In a little bit."

"Mom, I'm putting up the heat, *Papou*'s cold."

"Please, I am well," Andreas protested. Most old men of his country expected this sort of fussing, but he found it humiliating. He could not sit like a pasha, waited upon. He asked for what he needed, or got it himself. Otherwise, he preferred to be invisible. "See to your father."

"There's nothing I can do for him." The girl looked stricken.

"Here, sit by me."

He squeezed Mary's hand and stroked her hair. Matthew gazed at them across the table. Trouble swirled behind that brow. They had not yet had a real talk, though Andreas had been here nearly a week. Besides long stretches at the hospital, they had not seen each other. The boy was busy, but the time must be found. There was no question that his common sense could be trusted; it was more a case of saving him the mental turmoil which the old schemer's machinations—assuming Aleko was right about that—might cause. A steadying hand was in order.

"Maria." Irini was pouring the frothy soup into a bowl, then

squeezing lemon furiously, filling the kitchen with its sharp odor. "Get a tray table and set it up by your father."

Mary leaped up again, and both women headed down the hall to the study. The two men were left alone in the suddenly quiet kitchen, and the distance between them was palpable.

"Listen for screams and breaking china," said Matthew.

"I think your father will take his medicine."

"That's right, *avgolemono* soup cures cancer."

Andreas nodded. "It's possible."

"I'm sorry we haven't seen each other. This has been a crazier week than I expected."

"I have kept myself busy, but it would be good to share some time. Alone, not here."

"Will you stay tonight?"

"If your mother asks."

"She doesn't ask because she assumes you will."

Andreas waved off the subject. "Tell me how your work is going."

"Hectic." Matthew put his feet up on a chair. He looked tired. "I'm clearing rights on some paintings for a new show. And I've been out a couple of days, doing research and making house calls."

"This is about the Greek icon?"

"Much of it, yes."

"And is the museum going to buy it?"

"To tell the truth," Matthew answered, pausing for some internal discussion, "that's looking doubtful."

"Really? Why should that be?"

"The seller has gotten cold feet. Also, the museum has gotten nervous. Seems the icon may be stolen property." The boy was staring at him hard. What did he know? Something, of course, but probably not much. "I guess that doesn't surprise you to hear."

"You know I grew up in that village, before I went to Athens. I was there during the war."

"It was taken by the Germans," Matthew added pointedly.

"That's right."

"And someone was killed trying to stop that."

"How much has Fotis told you?"

The younger man's prosecutorial style faltered.

"Almost nothing. Just what I've said."

Was it right to finally speak of it? Would there be relief, or just more pain? Could he do it to the boy? Could he do it, again, to himself?

"Truly, what have you been told?"

"Nothing. I want you to tell me. I want to hear it from you."

There was no noise from the study. It was as if the other three had vanished. The old man looked at the framed pencil sketch on the wall behind the boy, Alekos' face in profile, done by Matthew at age fourteen. Highly skilled work. He is fumbling in the dark, Andreas thought, he doesn't really know anything. Someone had let a loose word slip and the boy is pressing the case. I'm not the first he has asked, which means he's had no satisfaction else-where. He thought of the promise he and Fotis had made each other years before. Did he still owe that silence after all that had happened since then? Was there a way to speak to Matthew of this without breaking that bond?

"I am sorry," he said finally. "It is one of those foolish situa-tions where if you do not know, I cannot tell you. It is a trust between your godfather and myself."

Voices were suddenly raised in the study. Matthew's expres-sion grew distracted. Either he was letting the matter go, or he was casting about in his mind for a different approach. Then foot-steps in the hall, and both men looked up. A bewildered and defeated-looking Irini stood in the doorway.

"He threw me out. Do you believe that?" Matthew pulled out a chair, but she would not sit, just leaned against her son. "He can't bear to have me help him."

"You were probably trying too hard."

"I just wanted to make sure he actually ate it."

"What, were you trying to spoon-feed him?"

"He was spilling it all over."

"You've got to let him do things for himself. He doesn't want to feel like an invalid."

She sat, shaking her head, palms placed flat on the table, eyes on the large rain-spattered window. Then her gaze shifted to Andreas.

"You're staying with us tonight?"

He shrugged.

"No?" Her voice was hard. "You're going to make my daughter drive you into the city in the rain and dark, you selfish old man?"

He was taken aback by her fierceness, even as he recognized the need. This was not the passive, manipulative creature who had married his son thirty years ago. She had grown tough, and he was proud of her for it.

"I would never ask such a thing. I will stay, if you will have me."

"You are very welcome here," she answered softly. "You've always been welcome."

Let's not go into all that, he thought.

"I'm sorry to interrupt your talk," she continued. Neither man responded. "I don't know what all of you have been whispering about this week, and I don't care. But there will be no secret discussions, no arguments, no terrible stories while you're in this house. I won't have Alex being upset, or anyone upset around him. Do you both understand me?"

She looked to Andreas first, and he nodded. Matthew followed suit.

"Good. I need your help, boys. Matthew, go sit with your father. *Babas*, you go put your feet on the sofa, I'll wake you in half an hour."

They both moved to comply with her wishes.

She kissed him there in the doorway, for all the world to see, and Matthew found he didn't care. He could barely remember walking here, had found himself almost unconsciously carried to her doorstep. The impulse had been visceral, intense, *go to her*, his body knowing what was good for him better than his mind. Ana pulled him in the door and held him for many long, comforting moments.

"Your father's home?"

"Yes. We brought him home yesterday."

"Are you OK with that?" She stood back, her knowing gaze upon him once more, reading his doubts. "Is that good?"

"It is." He seemed to discern the truth of it there on the spot. The hell with more treatment, home and family were what was needed. Care. Hope. Faith. "It's good." He smiled at her as if it were her doing. "We'll see how it goes from here."

When she did nothing further, he started down the hall toward the kitchen, his mind already seeing the stairs beyond, the small chamber and that other woman who was the third part of this triangle. Ana took his arm and pulled him the other way, toward the stairs going up.

"No, no icon today. Just you and me."

He let her lead him up the stairs, his legs willing but his muscles clenched, while his heart began to race. Weird fears hounded him once more. He wanted to be up here, with her. He wanted to be down below, with it. She couldn't really mean to keep him from it. The idea angered him, and the anger shamed him. He strained to control his emotions as Ana stripped her clothes off, slowly, methodically. It was no good. She saw everything, he could tell.

"I want this to be about us, Matthew. I want there to be some part of this that is only about us."

She pulled his shirt up and pressed her breasts and belly against his skin. Her cool flesh and hard nipples demanded his attention. His body reacted, scorning his anger, ignoring the lack of instruction from his troubled, suspicious mind. Fotis' words came back to him. Who knew what her own secrets were? At this moment, who cared? Her tongue found his; he remembered the night they had spent together. He wanted more of that, wanted to lose himself in her. The Mother of Christ receded, but did not disappear from his thoughts.

9

The priest sat in a low chair in the corner, yet seemed to command the room. In the few minutes of small talk that accompanied everyone's getting settled, Matthew learned that Father Tomas was Greek-born but ordained in the American branch of the church, and served Bishop Makarios in New Jersey. He had arrived alone, no aide accompanying him. Fifty-something, gray temples and curly black hair, a lined, trustworthy face, and kind eyes. Little was said at first about his purpose here, but he produced documents from the Holy Synod in Athens that seemed to satisfy Ana's lawyer, Wallace.

In the only bright corner of the dark study sat the Holy Mother, on an aluminum easel, staring out at all of them. Matthew had looked at her a long time before the priest came, while Ana and the lawyer conferred, but now he turned his chair away and tried to clear his mind. Tomas had examined the icon when he arrived, but since then had mostly ignored it, his eyes instead roaming over the massive oak bookcases, hardly settling anywhere but taking in a good deal.

"Your grandfather collected more than paintings, I see."

"Yes," Ana responded. "He was very proud of his book collection. Maybe even more than he was of the paintings. I think he felt closer to them."

"Of course," the priest agreed. "One can be more intimate with a book, hold it, turn its pages. A book is a friend. A painting simply hangs there, aloof." He glanced upward again. "I see some friends of my own on these shelves. Dostoyevsky. Flaubert. Kazantzakis. And some rare titles. Maybe we can talk books after we talk art."

"How about we take one transaction at a time," Wallace cut in. Late sixties, gray-haired and rheumy-eyed, a gravelly voice and a hacking cough that bespoke a lifelong cigarette habit, recently kicked, judging by his fidgety fingers. Nothing in his slumped posture, shifty gaze, or false-friendly delivery conveyed trustworthiness to Matthew, but Ana seemed to rely on and defer to him.

"Indeed," Father Tomas said.

"Now," Wallace shuffled his notes to no purpose, "I assume we can take your satisfaction with the work as a given."

"If you refer to its artistic quality, I am hardly the proper judge, yet I pronounce myself well pleased. Of course, it's suffered much wear."

"Over the centuries," Matthew said. "Not in the last sixty years."

"In any case," the priest continued, "while this might put off a collector, for my purposes it merely helps to establish the work's age. And adds to its mystery."

The lawyer cleared his throat, seemed to want to spit.

"And you're satisfied that this is indeed the icon you've been pursuing."

"The Holy Mother of Katarini. Again, I am not an art historian, but it conforms in every way to the description. Some of my brothers in Greece know the work firsthand, and will be able to identify it. What does your own expert say?"

All three of them looked at Matthew. Though he had resisted pushing Ana toward a decision, he'd been aggressive in his support once she made it, fearing that the lawyer might change her mind. He had even asked to be present for these negotiations. It hadn't occurred to him that anyone would be asking him questions.

"Well, it matches everything I know about the Katarini icon. Of course, I haven't tested it for miraculous powers." Only the priest laughed. "I can say with confidence that it's pre-iconoclastic, which alone makes it extremely rare, and that it's a work of high artistic achievement."

"In your opinion," quipped Tomas.

"And according to the standards for religious art of that time."

"You are Greek?"

A harmless question, but Matthew hesitated. "Yes, I am."

"Then I shall consider your opinion doubly valuable."

"So we're agreed on those points," the lawyer insisted.

"Indeed, Mr. Wallace," sighed Tomas, with a long-suffering smile. "We can move on to the financials, as I can see you're eager to do."

"We discussed a figure a few days ago."

The priest created a dramatic pause by sipping from his water glass, staring hard once more at the object of his affection.

"Hardly a discussion. You simply named a figure. A very high figure."

"We don't think so."

"Perhaps a million and a half dollars is a modest sum by your own standards. The church of Greece is a small church in a small country, and I understood this was to be taken into account. We have never heard of any icon selling for such a price."

"I doubt that an icon this rare has been offered for sale in any of our memories."

"Fair enough. Yet an icon of considerable reputation was sold a few years ago for less than a third of the sum you name. That is the highest price we know of. It is perhaps lamentable that these items which we revere are not held in the same regard by the art community as certain secular masterpieces, but there it is. No one pays such prices for icons."

"I have to tell you, Father, that we have already received an unsolicited offer of that much from a private buyer." Wallace clearly enjoyed the silence which followed his little bombshell.

Matthew was as stunned as the priest, and wondered if it was true. "Mind you," the lawyer continued, "we haven't pursued it, and it is not our desire to go private with this thing, but a number like that commands respect. Look, the Russian market is drying up. They've stolen everything they can out of that country. The price for all icons will rise, but for an extraordinary one like this . . ."

"Of course, one cannot account for the eccentricity of collectors," Tomas said, recovering his composure. "I was under the impression that our only competition was institutional. Tell me, was the Metropolitan Museum prepared to pay anything close to this price?"

The priest was not looking at him, but Matthew wondered if he was supposed to respond. Instead, Wallace jumped in once more.

"We never got to that stage. For all I know, they might."

"Even if it turned out the work was stolen?"

"You know," Wallace said, lowering his voice threateningly, "you are the only source for that rumor we've heard from." His eyes went absolutely flat.

"It is a fact, sir, not a rumor," the priest answered coldly.

"I've never seen evidence. And it's an awfully convenient tool for driving down the price."

"We can provide the evidence, I assure you."

"You'll forgive me if I remain dubious. In any event, the estate has certain minimum financial requirements, and if we have to turn to private buyers to fulfill those, so be it. I don't think the collector we heard from would be troubled by this issue."

"You would seriously consider such a move?" Tomas' indignation filled the room.

"We are earnestly trying to avoid it. We are giving you the opportunity to keep the work available to the public and return it to its native soil, but you have to work with us, Father. Ms. Kessler has obligations to her grandfather's estate which she must meet."

Matthew realized that most of this was simply negotiating hardball, but the alternative which the lawyer threatened was exactly the one he feared, and he had to work hard not to convey his panic to Ana. Tomas became quiet again. Then the beatific smile returned.

"Let me, as they say, put my cards on the table. I have clearance to offer up to seven hundred thousand U.S. dollars. I am reasonably confident that with a telephone call to Bishop Makarios here and a few others in Athens, I could get that number to something very near one million. Beyond that, they will not go."

Wallace readjusted his glasses and sat up in his chair.

"Well, that's movement. We'll take that as an encouraging step, Father."

"Please do not misunderstand, Mr. Wallace. I have been straight with you; do not abuse me for it now. I have given you our best offer."

"It's enough." Ana's voice surprised them all. "Arthur, I think it's enough."

Nobody spoke for a moment.

"My client and I need to talk," Wallace finally said. The priest shrugged.

"No," Ana said quietly. "I don't think that's necessary. I know my mind here."

"There is absolutely no reason for haste. We have some options to weigh."

"I understand, someone else might pay more. It's not important."

"There are other issues."

She looked at Matthew. "What do you think?"

He took a deep breath and made himself block out his fears, ignore the heat on the back of his skull from that ancient painted gaze across the room.

"Mr. Wallace is right. If you're satisfied on the price, fine, but there are additional things you need to know."

"Such as?" queried Tomas.

"What will her access to the work be after the sale? Will it be available for possible exhibitions of her grandfather's collection?"

"Yes, I have those points here," said the lawyer, tapping his legal pad.

"Where will the work be displayed?" Matthew continued. "What sort of access to it will the general public have? What steps will you take for its protection and preservation?"

"Excellent points." The priest nodded. "None of which I can answer definitively at this moment, except to say that I suspect we can satisfy you on most of them."

"Let's run through them anyway," the lawyer grumbled, reasserting himself.

"Certainly any request by Ms. Kessler for a private viewing would be favorably heard. As for loaning the piece for an exhibition, I doubt the Synod would commit to such a thing."

"I don't care about that," said Ana.

"The icon would likely hang in the cathedral in Athens. Wherever it is, it would be on display to the faithful. It is not our intention to hide it, that would contradict its purpose. Yet we will need to take measures to safeguard it, so that we do not again suffer its loss."

"Of course," Wallace answered mechanically. "I can put all the details into a draft of the contract."

"Leaving us sufficient latitude, I trust. I am already agreeing to more conditions than most buyers would permit."

"That's part of the compromise," the lawyer said evenly. "These are the conditions we're demanding in return for giving you a bargain price."

"A bargain," the priest scoffed. "Mr. Wallace, you could sell rugs in a Turkish bazaar."

"You flatter me."

"Not a bit. Do I take it we have an agreement?"

"There is no agreement until you see the terms, and your superiors approve the money. But I'd say we have an understanding. Ana?"

"Yes. Absolutely."

The priest checked his watch. "I do not know if I can reach my people this evening."

"See what you can do," the lawyer said. "I'll draft the paperwork, and we'll wrap this up in the next few days."

"Very good. I am most pleased by this. Most pleased."

The priest smiled at all of them. If he was stunned by the speed of the negotiation, or his supposed good fortune, he was doing a good job of concealing it. Everyone stood to shake hands, and Matthew relaxed somewhat. It was happening. Now he had to keep his eye on the old men until the icon hung in the Athens cathedral. Then he could truly let it all go.

"I'm sorry," Ana said.

The lawyer looked up from packing his briefcase, then gave her his most paternal smile.

"Nothing to be sorry for. I wish that we had been a little clearer on strategy beforehand, but no matter. As long as you're happy with the result."

"I'm happy to have it over with. I couldn't stand squeezing him, he's a priest."

"I wouldn't worry about that," Matthew said, gently placing a drop cloth over the icon. There was an immediate sense of relief as the image vanished. "The Greek church is rich. Maybe not cash-rich, but certainly rich in holdings. They can afford it."

"He just seemed so vulnerable, all by himself."

"Vulnerable," laughed Wallace. "Vulnerable as an iron safe."

"Yeah, I agree," said Matthew. "Vulnerable is not the word I would use, but I was surprised by the lack of advisers. I thought there would be a whole entourage."

"Didn't need them." Wallace snapped his case shut. "He'll have their lawyers vet the agreement before he signs, you can be sure. Meantime, he's trusting his own judgment. I think they wanted to get this done quickly, and involve as few people as possible." He wrestled himself into a tired green overcoat, coughing furiously. Then he patted Ana on the shoulder. "I'll have a draft of the paperwork for you to look over soon. Take care, dear."

She saw him to the door. Matthew wanted to walk out with the lawyer and ask a few more questions, but a look from Ana made him remain where he was.

"Thanks for being here," she said when they were alone. "Those were good questions."

"Wallace had them covered."

"I just needed you around." She reached for his hand and he stepped closer to her. "Are you going to be in trouble with the museum?"

"Don't worry about that." In fact, if his role in this became public he could be in trouble with all sorts of people, but Matthew had put that thought aside whenever it came up. His work had suffered terribly in the last ten days, and he'd come to believe that he would never be able to focus on it again until this matter with the icon was settled, in a way which left his mind at peace.

"Stay awhile," she said.

He'd had no intention of doing so. This business was eating up his life; he'd stolen time to be here, was behind on everything. The pressure of her hand held him. He could not leave her alone now, and he knew that in a few moments he would no longer wish to.

The connecting flight in Frankfurt had been delayed, and Father Ioannes arrived at JFK hours later than expected. Makarios was supposed to send a driver to get him, but Ioannes did not know where they were to meet and had not been able to find a working telephone. His baggage was lost briefly, then found on the wrong carousel. Leaving the men's room, he became disoriented and could not find the Arrivals area. This is what hell must be like, he mused. This is when he needed the patience they had taught him on the mountain, but it came less and less easily as time passed. He would pray for peace of mind as soon as he was done silently cursing.

On the mountain they had taught him of a God very different from the one the village priests knew. The old priest's God had been sad and angry in turn, like the man himself. The young priest also had preached a God of his own fiber, a passionate spirit who spoke to the needs of the moment, the need to resist, to survive. These deities fulfilled a purpose generated by man; they did what was required of them. On the mountain, they were not above invoking the angry God, to frighten the novices. Fear was known to sharpen the senses, and fear kept a boy in line until

the mind, fed on incense and sacred visions, had grown sufficiently to accept the full depth and breadth of the true God, in all
his glory. Ioannes had needed more time than most to achieve
this readiness but had absorbed the lessons deeply. The terrors
which defined his youth, which had initially held him back,
became his sustenance once the path was discovered, became the
fuel for the fire lit in his mind. Darkness was banished, and a
door opened in his soul directly into the world of spirit. He
would have been more than content to spend his life in isolation
and explore the way.

The squat, balding young man in the leather jacket did not
inspire confidence, but he knew the priest on sight, took his luggage, and guided him out to the parking garage.

"I'm Demetrios, by the way," he said.

"I bet they all call you Jimmy here."

"Yes. I know why you've come, I know what's going on."

"Indeed?"

"I work very closely with Bishop Makarios. I'm not just a
driver."

"I see."

It was somehow appropriate that his masters would wrench
him from his solace at the moment he had fully embraced it, and
reintroduce him to the world. Ioannes hated them for it at first,
yet came to know after many years that it was consistent with
their message, consistent with the way. The world of spirit must
reside within him; he must take it with him into the world of
flesh and allow it to inform his decisions. Anyone could maintain
faith within the quiet of sanctuary walls. The flock lived outside
the walls, and the Word must go to them.

"You're here to check up on Tomas," Jimmy persisted as the
luggage went in the trunk and they settled into the needlessly
large black vehicle; the American bishops always had cars like
this. "Forgive me for saying that you're a little late."

"What do you mean?"

"No one has been able to reach him for a few days. It could
mean nothing, of course," the burly driver added, unconvinc-
ingly.

The difficulty arose when the old masters died, and instruction now came from men younger than himself, men who did not have the inner fire in their eyes. What was required of a man when the inner voices no longer matched the commands of the outer voices? Ioannes had been feeling his way along for years now, but he sensed that this latest assignment would challenge his entire way of being. Maybe it was time.

"I have an appointment with Tomas tomorrow," the old priest said.

Jimmy shrugged as the car made its way down the dim, winding ramp of the concrete garage.

"I hope he shows."

Ioannes fought down a rising unease. Everything happened for a reason, and in any case he should not be trusting the word of this twitchy little fellow.

"Father Makarios and I will sort the matter out, I trust."

"Makarios," Jimmy snorted. "No offense, I love the bishop. But I'll tell you right now, *I'm* the guy you're going to need on this matter."

"I'll keep that in mind."

10

He should have known better. The whole thing had felt wrong from the start, but Matthew had plowed mulishly ahead, needing to justify his actions to himself. The trouble had begun with the phone call the day before, Fotis suddenly skittish.

"The girl has spoken to you."

"She says the contract was signed yesterday," Matthew confirmed. "Tomas and someone else picked up the work last night. And deposited it with you, I assume."

"All has proceeded as arranged, praise God."

"That's almost twenty-four hours. I really would have expected to hear."

"My apologies. You are eager to examine it again. We must arrange a time."

He'd had to force out the next words. "We had talked about someone else seeing it."

"Yes." A nervous whisper. "Do you think he is up to it?"

"I don't know; he's not up to much of anything. I thought that was the point."

"I would not wish to cause him any unnecessary anxiety during his recovery."

"It's not a recovery, it's a remission. *Theio*, this was your idea. What are you trying to tell me now? I've got to make an appointment, and my father is not welcome?"

"I am simply being careful. How will you persuade him to come?"

"Leave that to me. When should I bring him?"

"Tomorrow. It's a Saturday, and I think you were to pay him a visit anyway."

It was unnerving the way he knew everyone else's schedule.

"Yeah, we even talked about a drive. I don't think he had Queens in mind."

"I will be here all day. And my boy, forgive this advice. Do not tell your father some foolish story. He will see through it and you will only make him angry."

"You're saying I'm not a good liar."

"Tell him I've asked you to come and look at some art. It's the truth. Tell him you want his company, his support. Let him feel he is doing something for you."

His father had not objected but had agreed to the visit like a man condemned, sitting grim-faced and silent for most of the drive. At the house in Queens, Fotis greeted them with barely veiled agitation, working his green worry beads nervously. Canvases hung about the study, and Fotis and Matthew discussed a recently acquired Dutch landscape. Alex seemed to relax, and scanned the bookshelves around him. His wheelchair was positioned by the window, weak sun spilling over his strong shoulders, a fresh stubble forming an aura of gray light about his head. Six feet in front of him, beneath a white cloth, a medium-sized square panel sat on an easel, and Matthew could not keep his gaze from swinging constantly back to it, drawn by a special energy. Suddenly the whole production filled him with dread. Catching Fotis' wet, round eyes, he saw that the old man shared his unease. Before he lost his nerve completely, Matthew stood up and stepped over to the easel.

"Dad," he said, pulling the cloth from the work, half expecting something else to be beneath it until the eyes caught him once more, nearly stealing his voice. "This is the piece I've been consulting on. Fotis is holding it for a buyer in Greece."

Alex turned his head to the panel only very slowly. There was a determined expression of resistance on his face, which loosened at once when his gaze met the image, and a true look of wonder seemed to play about his eyes. Matthew's spirit fed off that look.

"I know you don't have much use for religious art, but I find this one particularly affecting, and I really wanted you to see it."

He took advantage of his father's trancelike state to step behind the wheelchair and move it closer to the easel, close enough that Alex could reach out and touch the icon, if he wanted.

"Isn't it beautiful?"

He could no longer see his father's face, and there was no immediate reply. Then the large head seemed to nod, almost imperceptibly, and indeed the right hand reached up and outward. Did he actually touch it?

A spontaneous moan escaped Fotis at that moment. Alekos' hand recoiled from the painting, and his head swiveled to stare at the old man. Matthew squeezed the handgrips of the wheelchair in frustration and also looked at Fotis. The schemer wore an expression closer to naked terror than Matthew had ever expected to see on that calculating face, and the young man could not tell whether the old one's eyes were focused on Alex, or on the door behind them. No one said a word for several seconds. Then Alex shook his head slowly, as if clearing his mind of a dream, and when he spoke his voice was tight with disgust.

"Get me away from this thing."

Most of the return drive passed in embarrassed silence. There was nothing angry or accusing in Aleko's manner; more confusion, mixed with fatigue. For long minutes he seemed about to speak, and finally did.

"I don't know what you intended by all this. Maybe you're proud of the work and wanted to share it with me."

"Something like that," Matthew managed, eyes glued to the damp road.

"I know some things about that icon, some things your *Yiayia* told me, years ago. I don't know the whole story, but both of those bastards have blood on their hands over that painting. I thought your *Papou* was going to tell you about it."

"No. Fotis told me something. It was pretty awful."

His father grabbed Matthew's forearm.

"Listen to me," Alex said firmly. "Are you listening to me?"

"I'm listening."

"I mean *listen* to me."

"Dad, I'm listening, for chrissake." He fought the pressure on his arm to keep control of the wheel.

"Believe nothing Fotis tells you. Until you hear it from someone you trust, believe nothing. Do you understand me?"

"I hear you."

"But you don't believe." Alex released him. "After all, what could your idiot father know?"

"That's not what I'm thinking."

"No? What are you thinking?"

Matthew grasped after his own thoughts, then shifted lanes quickly to make the exit off the expressway, which he hadn't noticed coming up.

"I'm thinking that I'm hearing an awful lot of shit from everyone, and I don't know what to believe."

"Why would I lie to you?"

"I don't think you're lying, you're just not saying anything useful. It's this vague, angry ranting against those two that I've been hearing my whole life. What did they do?"

"They made a devil's bargain with the Germans."

"That much I know."

"Talk to your grandfather."

"He won't tell me. I've tried."

"Did you tell him whatever Fotis told you? Did you? No? Oh, that one has you wrapped around his finger. Ask your *Papou.*"

"I'm telling you he won't speak to me."

"He'll speak to you. I'll see to it."

They sat idling at a stop sign, though there was no traffic in sight. Matthew pulled the shift arm toward him once and the wipers made a quick arc across the rain-speckled windshield.

"Why do you hate them so much?"

"I don't hate them," Alex said, "Any more than I hate a dog that's been trained to kill; but I don't trust them. They're creatures of their time, and it was an ugly time. Greece suffered terribly during the war. Then the civil war, troubles with Turkey, Cyprus, all the changes in government, all corrupt. The politicians had a siege mentality. They were fighting to keep Greece free, so anything was allowed. Your *Papou* and godfather were government men, loyal soldiers. I don't know the details, but I know they participated in some terrible things. You can see it in their faces. And it started during the war, with that damn icon. They took the first step from being freedom fighters to being political operatives right then. Trading with the enemy for guns to use on their brothers."

"The communist threat was real," Matthew insisted, accelerating away from the stop, surprised by his own defensiveness. "They could easily have taken over Greece."

"I don't deny that, but it was a bad war that followed. Thousands were rounded up, tortured, locked away without charges. Some executed. Even the men who fought that war have trouble defending it. They just don't talk about it at all."

Matthew slowed the car as they neared the house. His father's inarticulate rage toward the old men had been a feature of the family dynamics for so long that no one inquired into it any longer. But Alex had revealed more of his feelings in the last few minutes than in all the years preceding, and despite how angry some of it made him, Matthew was loath to let the moment pass.

"Is it impossible for you to accept that they did what they thought was necessary? That it's in the past now and they're old men?"

"Would you accept that argument for the Nazis in South America? For Milosevic or Karadzic?"

"Come on, you can't put them in the same category."

"My point is that their actions do not disappear because they've become old men. They did what they did. And they still have their hands in it. Don't believe for a moment that they've given up those ways."

"This is where you lose me. Fotis has been in this country for decades. *Papou* spends his time in his garden. What would the Greek government need with a couple of guys that old?"

"I'm not speaking of whom they work for, I'm talking about their *ways*. They've been bred in the ways of manipulation and double-dealing. It's become instinct with Fotis. He has to have some scheme going at all times, business schemes, spy schemes, it doesn't matter. He's like a shark, in constant motion. If he stops plotting, he'll die."

"And Papou?"

"He's subtler. I don't think he takes the same pleasure in his work as your godfather, but he still takes orders from the Greek government, or some part of it. He keeps an eye on Fotis, and performs other jobs as well. Don't believe that he came here just to see me."

"I do not buy this stuff."

"I know. I don't know how to make you believe."

They pulled into the driveway and Matthew killed the engine, yet neither made a move to get out of the car. Rain built up slowly on the windshield, obscuring the details of the house, but a warm yellow light shone clearly in the kitchen window.

"Why does Fotis have the icon?" Alex asked at last. "What happened with the museum?"

"The seller changed her mind. The Greek church approached her about the work, and she decided that they should have it."

"How does that involve him?"

"They approached Fotis also, to try and influence the deal, I guess. He knows the estate lawyer. And to help arrange transport, so he got to hold on to the icon for a little while."

"To what purpose?"

"For him? So that he could pray before it. It's a very holy icon. It's supposed to have miraculous curative powers."

"The old bastard. Does he think he's found a way to live forever?" Alex seemed halfway between rage and laughter.

"He'll only have it a week or two, then it goes to the church."

"How did you end up in the middle of this? You were supposed to be appraising the work for the museum."

"I did. I really thought that would be the end of it. But Ana, Ana Kessler, the seller, she wanted me to advise her."

"And Fotis encouraged this?"

"Yes."

"So you talked her into the deal."

"No, it's what she wanted to do. I didn't talk her out of it, though. I didn't tell her about Fotis' involvement."

"You didn't influence her at all?"

"If I did, it's because I thought it was right, not because of him."

"Are you sleeping with this girl?"

Matthew only sighed and leaned back in the seat. The air in the car was cooling, and the house suddenly beckoned.

"I see," Alekos nodded. "He's teaching you well."

Matthew slammed the dashboard with his fists, startling both of them.

"Do you really think so little of me? That I don't have any ideas of my own, that I don't believe in anything of my own? Are you so consumed by this hate for them that you need to reduce everything to that level?"

Alex shook his head slowly, but he seemed more distressed at having upset his son than bruised by his words, making Matthew feel impotent in his anger.

"You shouldn't take it personally. They're masters. They've done it to me my whole life. If you can take a lesson from this, you can avoid some future pain."

"What in God's name do you think they've done to you?"

A figure appeared in the kitchen window, blocking most of the light.

"They've orchestrated my life. I'm a chemical engineer because my father wanted me to be. I live in America because he sent me here. Even marrying your mother . . ."

"What?"

"I shouldn't speak to you about this."

"You knew she was Fotis' niece, that's how you met her."

"I knew she was his niece, but I didn't yet understand who he was. He even pretended to disapprove, just to tempt me, knowing she and I would fight him."

"And why exactly did he do that?"

"Who knows? Maybe he thought it was a way to steal me from his old pal Andreas, turn me into the son he never had. God knows he tried, but I saw through him soon enough."

"This is bullshit."

"You don't know, you weren't around."

"I don't need to have been around. I don't even have to be your son to see through this, because either you loved her, so nothing he did mattered, and it was right. Or you didn't, and it was wrong. Either way it's on you, nobody else. So don't try to feed me this garbage. And by the way, I know we're having this heart-to-heart, but I don't want to know the answer to that, OK? She's my mother, so keep it to yourself."

The figure had vanished from the window, and the rain increased. Matthew breathed deeply in an effort to calm himself. He could not have imagined, even minutes before, being so angry with his father. Yet it was a pure, righteous, cleansing anger, and he could not wish it away, even knowing the guilt he would feel later.

"Of course, that's true." Alex seemed deflated, yet his face still had a warm flush of color, unseen there for weeks. "I'm sorry I spoke of this. Please don't ignore everything I've said. Please take warning."

"Let's go inside, you must be getting cold."

"No. I don't feel anything."

Ioannes was sitting quietly at the kitchen table in the bishop's small but ornate guesthouse when Jimmy entered without so much as a knock.

"Good morning, Father."

"And to you, my son."

"So, Tomas is gone. Vanished."

"It would appear."

"Left a whole congregation sitting in their pews last night, waiting on the word of God." The little man paced the room restlessly, checking his pockets, pulling out a small pistol to caress it. "Poor bastards."

"Father Makarios told me."

"Did he also tell you that half a million dollars of church funds disappeared with him?"

"I didn't know the amount, but it was clear there had been a major embezzlement."

"He's the one you should be looking for."

"I assumed that you and Makarios were doing that. Unless you are depending upon the police."

"Hah. Makarios can't even bring himself to tell the police, thinks the little devil will repent, show up with a good explanation. They hate a scandal. Anyway, I've got some people looking."

"I suspect he took that money for himself, to go underground." Ioannes spoke slowly, measuring his words. "I don't believe he has the icon. He was fronting for a buyer. A donor, he called him, in his communications, who was supposed to give the work to the church."

"But you never found out who the donor was."

"He didn't tell us."

"He could have invented the donor."

"Yes, he could have."

"So who is this man you're going to visit? Andreas Spyridis?"

Ioannes sighed. There were clearly no secrets within these walls.

"Someone who came here from Greece around the same time all this business started. Who has a history with the icon."

"Not from the church?"

"No, a government man. Retired, but he still checks in, or they check on him, or maybe the Americans do. Anyway, we were able to locate him. I don't know that he's involved, but it's a fair guess. I wish you would put that gun away."

"You say government. You mean intelligence, state security, something like that?"

"Yes, but he's old. Even older than me."

"Old or not, we may need this," Jimmy said, brandishing the pistol. "I'm not going unarmed."

"I'm not asking you to go at all."

"I think you will find that Father Makarios insists upon my involvement."

"Yes." Ioannes looked more closely at the younger man's eyes and nose, the shape of his head. "You know, you look like him. The bishop. Don't tell me you're related."

The little man did not like being identified.

"I'm his nephew. That's not important."

"And you are some sort of civilian detective?"

"Private investigator, we call it. But I work mostly for the church."

"Ah, a knight of Christ. How unfortunate that they have enough work to keep you busy."

"Why don't we go see this man right now?"

"Because he's not there. He left the city for a few days."

"So we sit?"

"I'm sure there are other things you could be investigating. Do not let me hold you."

"You know more than you're telling. I'm not letting you out of my sight."

"I need to emphasize that if you are going to follow me, you must do exactly as I instruct. I will not tolerate interference, whatever Makarios says."

"All of you are the same," the little man whined. "Think you know another man's business better than he does. Why? Because a divine light leads you? Priests should not lead investigations."

"Tell it to God, brother."

The Connecticut coast sped by outside the scratched, dirty train window. Deep coves and marsh grass, still going from dead beige to pale green. White egrets wading about or lifting slowly into flight. Marinas, empty beaches, the bare gray outline of islands. Then dense stretches of wood, trees mostly bare but acquiring bright green or red halos of tiny leaves about them. The world returning to life. Andreas looked away from the window.

The trip to Boston had been a waste of time. He had seen the widow of one of his operatives. The man had done good and unrewarding intelligence work for twenty years and lost his pension when he came to live in America, rather than return to a Greece run by the colonels, a place he no longer recognized.

Andreas had been unable to help him then, and could do very little now but pay respects. He had made dozens of such visits in recent years. They did not get easier. The American contact he'd met in Cambridge was an old friend, but he was at a lower level than Morrison, semiretired and teaching college, and could be of no help. It had sickened Andreas to sit there, trying to remember what a good man this was, how important human contact was for any soul, yet only be able to think in terms of the utility of the meeting. Information gained versus time lost. Had the ability to think in any other manner slipped away from him forever? He had even resented the widow, a woman of great kindness and courage, whom he would never see again. Disgraceful.

He was eager to get back to Alekos. That was certainly part of it, but his son was probably grateful for the break. The two could not spend much time in each other's presence, whatever degree of underlying love there might be. Andreas would have to return to Athens soon, unless Alex took a turn for the worse. The hotel bill grew unwieldy, and there was a claustrophobia about New York he could not tolerate. The main thing was to make sure that Matthew had not gotten himself involved in any serious way with Fotis' scheming. That was where his primary energy should have been focused all along, but he had gotten Müller's scent in his nose again. Best to let that go. In any case, Benny had found nothing so far.

He had resisted acquiring one of those portable telephones that everyone carried, and he deeply resented the seven meaningless phone conversations that went on simultaneously in the seats around him. Yet he could see how they were useful; they might have been indispensable to his kind of work, in fact, if they had existed twenty years before. Being without one, however, he waited for the ten-minute break in New Haven to go down into the dank, silent tunnels beneath the tracks and place a call by public telephone. He began dialing Matthew's number, almost by instinct, but hung up and then dialed Benny's instead.

"Where the hell have you been?"

"I'm on the train. What is it?"

"I've found him."

Andreas exhaled and closed his eyes.

"Are you certain?"

"Ninety-five percent. You'll have to fill in the rest. When are you back?"

"Two hours."

"Tonight isn't good. Too much activity. Tomorrow, first thing, we'll pay him a visit."

11

It had been his intention to go back into Manhattan that same evening, but his mother had convinced Matthew to stay the night. Early Sunday morning he called his grandfather's hotel but could get no answer in the room. Then he visited briefly with his father. Alex was too tired to rise, and Matthew settled for squeezing his hand, hoping that his expression would make the apology which his lips could not seem to issue. He took the train into Grand Central and walked to the hotel. It was Easter Sunday for the Western church, Palm Sunday for the Orthodox. Matthew had thought of going to services, but his mind would not be at ease while matters remained so confused, and he was certain that his grandfather would not be at church.

In the cramped lobby, the concierge took his name and telephoned the room.

"You can go ahead up."

"He's back?"

"He returned with another gentleman twenty minutes ago. Room 511. The elevators are to your right."

Matthew had been ready to wait a good deal longer, and now

he felt unprepared. It was difficult to maintain his anger, and his grandfather could use many means to deflect him. He must be firm, speak all that he knew, and demand answers.

A hard rap on the door brought footsteps and a muffled greeting.

"It's Matthew."

The door swung open, and a man stood there, tall, gray, and smiling.

"You are Andreas' grandson?"

"That's right."

"Yes, yes, come in."

The older man stepped aside, and Matthew entered. The room was not large. A double bed, television, desk, and two chairs, with a muted floral theme on the walls, cushions, and bedspread. Andreas was not to be seen, but there was someone clattering around in the bathroom.

"Sit," said the man, placing himself in the chair closest to the door. Matthew remained standing, but wandered over to look down at the concrete courtyard below. He had learned not to ask questions of his grandfather's business associates. The man's presence was frustrating, as Matthew intended to press Andreas hard, but he was determined not to be run off. He would wait it out. The click of the bathroom light switch made him turn.

A short, thick, nearly bald man with deep-set eyes stood there, draped in a leather jacket two sizes too big for him. The light was off in the bathroom, and there was really nowhere else that Andreas might be. He was not here, and the two men were between Matthew and the door. Panic took the form of a blurry numbness, and he did not trust his voice to speak.

"Please sit," said the older man again. "We should know each other."

Matthew sat gingerly on the edge of the mattress. The bald one remained standing, patting his pockets distractedly, an annoyed expression on his face.

"You came looking for your *Papou*," said the gray-haired man. "So did we. As you can see, he is not here."

The man was about Andreas' height and weight, and the face

had the same rectangular shape. Even similar features. Add the dark suit and shirt buttoned to the collar, and Matthew could see how the concierge might be fooled at a glance. Yet the man was a good ten years younger than Andreas, and far more kindly in his expression.

"What are you doing in his room?"

"Waiting. We are waiting, like you."

"I think you were doing more than waiting before I came in."

"Yes, well, we did avail ourselves of his absence to look around. I assure you that we have taken nothing."

"You shouldn't be in here at all."

"By law, you are correct. But extralegal imperatives are sometimes stronger. In any case, we did not break down the door. We were given the key."

"Is there any point in asking what you were looking for?"

"We're not precisely certain. Maybe something that would give us a clue to where the icon is now. Yes, the icon, *paidemou,* don't look surprised. What did you think this was about?"

"He knows," said the bald one, in an irritated voice. "He knows where it is. Don't you?"

Matthew processed answers, true, false, and in between. Which would protect him? Which would endanger someone else? Fear paralyzed his thinking. Could he simply get up and leave?

"You are in no danger," the older man said gently. "But we must learn where the icon is. It is terribly important."

"Why?"

"A fair question, and the answer is complicated. I believe that several people involved with the icon's sale, including perhaps yourself, are operating under a misunderstanding. Truly, a deliberate deception. Tell me, have you met a priest named Tomas?"

After pausing too long to deny it, Matthew nodded his head.

"And he put himself forward as a representative of the Greek church?"

"Yes," Matthew said, concern for his safety giving way to a deeper fear. "He's not?"

"He is, or was. He is a priest of the church in America, but Tomas has occasionally done business on our behalf. He was pursuing an opportunity to acquire the icon for us. In the last week or so, however, he allowed his own interests to overcome his spiritual obligation. I believe. Truly, we do not know where Tomas is right now, so we cannot say exactly what has happened. I am being very honest with you, more than I should be, perhaps. In any case, we do not believe he is in possession of the icon."

Which question to ask first?

"I'm sorry, but who are you?"

"The apology should be mine. Ioannes is my name. Father John, if you prefer. Many of my American friends call me that."

"I'm Greek."

"Of course you are."

"So you're from the church in Greece?"

"Yes."

"And you came here to check up on the deal?"

"Tomas' actions bred suspicion. Unfortunately, his superiors did not oversee him carefully, and we did not follow up with them until it was too late. I am here to see what can be rescued. The icon is of enormous importance to us. The joy at its discovery when Tomas contacted us was great, I assure you."

"Wait. You didn't know about Kessler having the icon already?"

"There were rumors, Kessler's ownership among them. Most people thought it was in a vault in Switzerland. I had assumed it was destroyed."

"So Tomas came to you."

"That's right."

"You never contacted anyone here to act on your behalf? Someone outside the church, I mean."

"Who did you have in mind?"

Matthew's thoughts lost their grounding. The entire business was beyond his grasp, and a sickening realization loomed. And yet, having been fooled so easily up to now, how could he simply accept what he was hearing? Should he abandon his faith in Fotis so quickly?

"You know, I have to say, Tomas was at least as credible as you guys. He went through all the proper motions. He put down a lot of money. Where did that come from?"

Baldy spoke sharply in Greek, something to the effect that they were wasting time. Father John answered him quietly: where were they going in such a hurry? Then the older man leaned forward and stared earnestly at Matthew.

"Obviously, Tomas had a backer. The person who was really after the work all along. Perhaps you know who that person is."

Matthew shook his head, in resistance rather than denial.

"You have no reason to trust me," the priest continued, "but I am asking you to do so. For the good of the church, for the good of others who have been deceived, and in memory of those who have died for the work, I ask your assistance. Please, tell me where the icon is."

Matthew's inclination to trust was enormous, but he was coming to see it as a character flaw.

"I have to go to the bathroom."

The bald one cursed, and Matthew stepped into the relative safety of the blue-tiled fluorescent chamber. Cold water on his face felt good but did not clear his mind. This priest was convincing. He exuded compassion and honesty to a degree that was nearly hypnotic. Could he be believed? Was it more complicated? A church faction fight, perhaps? The conclusion he kept returning to was the same one that had made him hold his tongue before: he could not turn his godfather over on such a slender thread of trust. He would have to investigate the matter himself, quickly, as he had been intending to do by coming here. That meant losing these two. Would they let him walk out? Did they have the means of following him without his realizing? There wasn't time to lie low for a day or two, every hour might count.

Through the door he could hear a cell phone ringing. When he composed himself and stepped out, Matthew saw the bald one just putting his phone away as he jabbered excitedly to Father John. The swift, heavily accented Greek mostly eluded him, but through the buzz of words he clearly heard a familiar name. The priest looked up.

"Are you unwell?"

"I'm fine. I have to leave."

"An associate of my friend here has made a discovery among

Father Tomas' abandoned possessions. A name, known to us. Fotis Dragoumis. I think he is related to you?"

Matthew nodded.

"You are close to him?"

"Yes, I am."

"He is, perhaps, a dangerous man to deal with?"

"I don't think of him that way. It might be dangerous for you."

"Nevertheless, we must see him. I think you should come with us. What do you think?"

"I don't know."

"We will not force you. It is completely your decision. Somehow I feel your presence will make things less hazardous for both sides."

Matthew absorbed the import of those words. The urge to be included in whatever fell out was overwhelming other considerations.

"I need to call him."

"I cannot stop you. But if you do, he will be gone when we arrive, and neither you nor I will see that icon again. I think you know this."

Still he hesitated. The priest was guessing; he couldn't know for sure that Fotis had the icon.

"*Scatá,*" spat Baldy, bolting forward. Instinctively, Matthew's arms shot out, the heels of his hands catching the other man hard in the chest, staggering him so that he grabbed at the mattress to keep from falling. Meaning to rush for the door, Matthew instead found himself advancing, a sudden unexpected rage replacing his fear in an instant, filling him. He hadn't thrown a fist since adolescence, but he wanted to beat the stocky little man senseless. Baldy recovered swiftly and sprang at him, his heavy fist catching Matthew in the stomach, awkwardly, but hard enough to bend him double with a deep, nauseating pain. He braced for another blow, but then the priest was between them.

"*Stamáta!* Stop it, both of you." Father John helped him to a chair, but Matthew would not sit, merely leaned on the pale wooden arm, pulling hard for breath. Baldy straightened his jacket, a combination of rage and surprise distorting his features.

"Demetrios was not after you," the priest said firmly, "he was headed for the door."

Matthew had realized that a moment after he struck, and yet the anger remained, barely under control. And wholly misdirected, he now understood. His hands shook. The floor seemed to drop away, like the shaky scaffolding that Fotis had built beneath him. A lie; he had built it himself, using the shoddy materials his godfather supplied, the half-truths and flimsy reasoning. Ignoring every sign, letting the worthy goal justify all. He had been played. It was just as his father had warned him, he could keep the truth at bay no longer.

"OK," Matthew said, once his breath returned. "I'll go with you. But we do this my way. Fotis is very sharp, and he's well protected."

The priest smiled.

"Then we shall count on you to protect us."

It was cold. Andreas had not been on the streets this early in a long time, and he was surprised at how the predawn chill penetrated him. He walked swiftly to get the blood flowing in his stiff limbs, knowing that he could not afford to be slow in the minutes or hours to come. Vigorous action might be required. He felt a tremor of unease rise up. He had poked and poked, expecting nothing, and suddenly he had stirred up the hornets' nest. Things could easily get out of hand now, and he would have no one to blame but himself. Yet he couldn't wish it were not happening. If it was Müller, well, a reckoning was required. Time did not wash away crimes, and instinct continued to tell him that the threat to anyone involved with the icon was real. He only hoped that Benny would be punctual, because it was very cold.

Shadows hung thickly in the narrow canyons of side streets, but the sky was slowly brightening over Queens. Some people were out already, solitary specters appearing not quite aware or awake. Taxis rocketed up Third Avenue. A silver-gray sedan sat before a brick bank on the northeast corner of an intersection. A small Japanese car, good for parking. The passenger door was unlocked, and Andreas slipped gratefully into the warm compartment. Benny was already smoking, and two cups of deli coffee were jammed into a plastic holder between them. The man's demeanor was relaxed this morning, and he allowed the thin stream of traffic to pass completely before pulling onto the avenue.

"Where are we going," Andreas asked.

"Not far. Yorkville. Germantown, they call it, but it's really more Hungarian. Hungarian churches, restaurants, clubs."

"I know the neighborhood."

"There's a kind of boardinghouse, run by a Hungarian woman. I didn't know about it before, but someone put me on to it a few days ago."

"And you sent one of the girls over with brochures?"

"Got in through the cleaning service, not that it's any of your business. Anyway, he's not staying in the boardinghouse proper, but in an apartment this woman owns, a few blocks away. Under the name Peter Miller."

"Miller," Andreas mused, skeptically. "That's an old one. He hasn't used that in years."

"Maybe that's why he chose it."

"Benny, are you sure of this? Peter Miller is a very common name."

"I saw him go in last night. Quite old, short legs, long torso, a slight limp."

It sounded right, but it could be coincidence.

"How many apartments in the building?"

"You really have no faith in me, do you, my friend?"

"I am asking a few questions."

"You are asking," the younger man said sharply, "how I know the man was even this Miller, let alone Müller, and not one of ten thousand old men who live on the upper East Side. It's a small building, eight apartments, two unoccupied. Four people went in who look like residents, younger people, briefcases, dry cleaning. That doesn't cover the whole building, but it narrows it considerably."

"Yes. It sounds promising."

"I think we have your man. If I'm wrong, I'll buy you breakfast."

"What is the plan?"

"He went in late last night. I don't think he will have left again. We park and wait. It's a quiet street, we could pick him up, take him to a secure location. I have two in mind. Or we could do the business right there, but I wouldn't recommend it."

"Then why mention it?"

"In case it would be easier for you."

In other words, thought Andreas, in case sitting in a car for an hour with a terrified old bastard who knows we're going to kill him makes me lose my nerve. He had never actually agreed to Benny's condition, but his failure to object had made the plan concrete. The moral issues did not trouble him; they simply weren't set up for an operation like this. It was just the two of them, no other support was possible. No matter how well Benny thought it out, it was bound to be messy, with the risk of failure or discovery very high.

"I'm prepared to do it quietly," Benny continued. "Sit him down on a stoop or against a car. It would take a few minutes, at least, for anyone to notice. It's far from ideal."

"It's impossible," Andreas snapped. "We haven't even identified him yet."

"You won't know him on sight?"

"I think I will, but I will need to be very close."

"So we pick him up."

"What if there are too many people on the street?"

"Then we follow him. See what he's up to. Wait for the next opportunity."

They turned east on Eighty-fourth Street and headed toward the brightening sky. Andreas hated being so close to the target with only the vaguest sketch of a plan. In truth, he had participated in numerous ill-advised operations for the Greek security forces, but they went against his nature, and his fears were usually proved correct by some blunder. He liked to run a tighter ship. The English, and later the Americans, had been his models. Mostly he envied their resources: secure apartments, high-powered surveillance, teams of trackers. His own former agency now employed all these methods, but it no longer employed him. He was on his own, at the mercy of this skilled but lunatic Jew. Andreas reminded himself that the consequences did not greatly matter. Sloppiness insulted his professionalism, but it was the result that counted. He was no longer responsible for anyone but himself. To get Müller, after all these years, would be worth something. A service rendered, and a debt paid. Let them do to him what they wanted after that. He began to feel calmer, surveying each tree-lined block, checking the pedestrian traffic at each intersection. Things would go as they went, and he was prepared for whatever happened.

Benny pointed out the building, an old brownstone with a tall, worn set of stairs. Second floor, front right, was where he had seen a light go on a minute after Miller entered. There was no place to park, so they circled the block until a space opened up near the avenue, beneath a leaning plane tree, still mostly bare. In summer the street would be shrouded in leafy shadow, but at the moment Andreas felt completely exposed.

"Relax," said Benny.

"We drove by the damn place three times."

"Looking for parking. Everyone does it. Remember that he's avoided detection for fifty years. Not everyone is like you, examining the stall for microphones before he shits."

"There."

A man came out the heavy wooden door of the brownstone and trudged wearily down the steps. In his sixties, dressed casually but carrying a briefcase.

"He doesn't want to go to work," Benny said, sipping coffee.

Andreas studied the man as he passed. Lanky, carrying a little extra weight. Exactly the right build for Müller, but too young, and the pink, freshly scrubbed face was not familiar. No one else emerged from the building for the next hour, while the sky grew brighter, and Andreas could feel Benny shifting restlessly in his seat.

"For all you know," the older man said, "he may have left an hour after he entered."

"I realize that."

"To do this properly you must be prepared to wait hours. All day."

"I'm aware of the procedure. I simply don't like it."

"That's because you're an analyst at heart."

"I've done my share of fieldwork."

And got expelled for overaggressiveness, thought Andreas, but it would not be the thing to say. A lot of good operatives got labeled overzealous by their uncreative handlers. It was the switch from analyst to operative that troubled Andreas. The skills were totally separate. For all their sharing of information, the two had never conducted an operation together. Yet Benny had been quite successful since going freelance, and had never steered the older man wrong.

Another forty minutes passed. Andreas nearly nodded off twice, and his legs were going to sleep. Benny continued to fidget and check his watch, finally popping his door open.

"Follow me in a few minutes," he said, then was out and walking briskly before Andreas had time to object. An unpleasant surge of adrenaline coursed through him as he watched Benny move down the street, pass the target house on the opposite side, cross over at the far intersection, and turn back. Without deliberation, Benny bounded up the stairs of the brownstone and disappeared into the vestibule. Andreas swung his door open and got out.

Cool air struck him at once, and he felt his stiff legs shake as he maneuvered his way across the broken sidewalk to the steps. Benny's large frame crowded the vestibule, but Andreas could see that the big man had already opened the inner door. They slid into the stairwell. Steam heat clanged in the pipes and fluorescent light flickered. The floor was black-and-white tile; battered mailboxes lined one wall and a steep flight of steps went up the other. Andreas left about ten feet between them as they ascended, and was surprised by the other man's speed. Neither of them made a noise.

The apartment door was steel-encased and painted brown. Benny ignored the mirrored peephole and put his ear to the door. The pipes continued to clank and bang, but Andreas heard nothing else in the building, no stirring of the occupants. After a minute, Benny took a razor-thin, flexible plastic card and wedged it into the seam between door and frame, taking a full minute to explore from top to bottom. Searching for a deadbolt, Andreas understood, but what would he do if he found one? Was there a hacksaw or drill in that capacious jacket as well?

Benny stood, holding up one finger: only the single, visible lock. Next he drew out a set of master keys and began trying one after another, making unavoidable noise now. Either he's not in there, thought Andreas, or he'll be waiting to blow our brains out. Then another thought struck him. No anti-crowbar flange, one lock. Would Müller stay in a place like this? Trapped in an apartment was trapped, of course, whether there was one lock on the door or ten. The trick was avoiding discovery at all. Still, it was troubling.

The moment the lock clicked, Benny pushed the door open and slid in, free hand stuffed inside his jacket. Andreas waited two or three seconds, then followed. It was a typical railroad flat—a long, narrow strip of rooms—and the men had entered at the kitchen. The place was dark and they heard nothing. Benny went right, toward the muted light from the street windows; Andreas, left, into the empty bedroom. There were gray curtains blocking the dim light from the alley, a small bed near the window, and a single scarred bureau. A lonely landscape print hung on one wall, but the others were bare, the green carpet was thin and stained, and the whole room gave off an air of barrenness and transience. No one lived here; no one stayed here long. No one seemed to be staying here at all, though the bed looked slept in, then badly made up.

A closed door faced him. Andreas considered whether anyone would be stupid enough to trap himself in the bathroom like that, then remembered that he was not carrying a weapon and Benny was three rooms away. He sighed at the idiocy of the whole undertaking, then yanked the stiff door open. The place was tiny, large enough to shit, shave, and shower, and not a spare inch more. No old Nazi cowering behind the shower curtain. Andreas caught sight of himself in the mirror, his ridiculous old man's face, pinched and lined and soured by decades of suspicion. He was a pragmatic man, an attentive man, and not particularly vain, and yet he often forgot that he was old. Mirrors always took him up short.

He looked away from the unpleasant visage, and his gaze fell to the sink. The porcelain was damp, and a thin film hung around the drain. He rubbed at it a bit, rolled the pasty matter between thumb and finger. It was the sort of residue one found often when there was a woman in the house. Foundation, makeup, exfoliate, any of the dozens of powders necessary to the maintenance of the public face. Of course, men used these things also. Possibly hair dye was included in the mix. Andreas closed his eyes, pictured the man with the briefcase who had left the building earlier. Add a few lines to the face, white hair, glasses. The limp would be easy enough to fake. And voilà, the ghost of Müller. The weight of it made him grip the low sink with both hands, nearly ill. Fool, he cursed himself silently.

Benny could be heard wandering back through the apartment, no longer trying to move quietly. Andreas went over and sat on the bed as the big man filled the door frame.

"No one."

"So it would appear."

"You were right," Benny said in disgust, "he must have gone out again last night."

"I think not. I believe that we actually saw him leave."

Benny ignored the comment, went to the bureau, and began pulling drawers open.

"Have you checked this?"

"You will find nothing there. No coats in the closet. No toothbrush in the bathroom."

His companion slammed closed the empty drawers, then wheeled on him.

"He's gone, then?"

The older man's mind had already begun to drift out over the city, across the East River into Queens. He'd had only Fotis' word to go by on Müller. That, and his own desperation for it to be true, a desperation the schemer could smell on him all these years later. It was the most obvious ploy imaginable. What were you distracting me from, he wondered. Why am I always so many steps behind you? Nearly sixty years and still the student. Poor Andreou, indeed.

"No, Benny. He was never here."

12

No activity was visible around his godfather's house, and Matthew climbed the steps with an awful sense of foreboding. Father Ioannes followed a step behind, glancing at the flower beds, while bald Jimmy waited in the car, an arrangement of which he had strongly disapproved. Matthew rapped hard on the door, reminding himself that he had the right of anger here. He had been deceived, or so it now appeared. There was no movement within. He knocked again, harder.

"Try the door," the priest suggested.

It seemed to surprise neither man when it opened, but Matthew's sense of dread became a black hole, swallowing all constructive thought. He stepped into the house. The parlor was empty but caught the day's weak light through its windows. A recent history of the Byzantine Empire lay on a chair by the door, a bookmark at page ninety-one. A half-filled water glass was on the table. Through the gauzy curtains Matthew watched Jimmy quickstepping down the sidewalk, disappearing into the alley between house and warehouse. The situation was getting away from him. Where were Nicholas and Anton? Where was Fotis?

Back in the corridor, Father John stood by the stairs, and Matthew was tempted to try that way, but the study beckoned more insistently. He turned the knob and the heavy door opened. It was too dark to see much. Unsure where a light switch might be, Matthew shuffled toward the lamp on the big desk. His foot struck something soft and giving at the same moment a voice spoke, an old man's voice, but not the one he was expecting.

"Stand still, my boy," his grandfather said. Light instantly filled the room from a lamp near the far door, and there Andreas stood, raincoat, gloves, hat, piercing stare. Tall and still. "Watch your feet."

Matthew looked down. The object he had kicked was a man. Nicholas, one of Fotis' Russians, lay pale and seemingly lifeless at his feet. The eyes were closed, the mouth grimaced, and as Matthew's vision continued to adjust, he could see that the oriental carpet was stained in a great, dark patch. A tangy, almost sweet odor hit his nose, and he stepped back instinctively, colliding with Father John.

"Merciful God," the priest whispered, then began a scattered prayer in Greek.

"Do not touch anything," Andreas instructed. Matthew ignored him and crouched down over Nicholas, steeling himself, feeling the cool neck, the lips. Was that breath he felt?

"I think he's alive."

The Russian's right hand was clutched upon the side of his stomach, completely encased in blood, and holding a soaked-through handkerchief against where his wound must be. Andreas was suddenly standing over Matthew, pulling a fresh handkerchief from his own coat and beginning to wrap it about his hand.

"Give it to me," said Matthew, possessive of the wounded man, determined to do one useful thing this day. Andreas handed him the handkerchief without debate.

"Yes, like that. You must hold it hard against the wound. I will try to find you a towel. Is it just the two of you?"

Matthew waited a fruitless moment for Ioannes to speak, then did so himself.

"There's a guy in the warehouse. Jimmy, I think his name is. He has a gun."

"I will call for an ambulance. Both of you stay here."

The old man vanished so swiftly and silently that it was as if he had never been there.

"I hope they will not harm each other," said the priest, kneeling now.

"Is your man dangerous?" Matthew tried not to look at his hand, to ignore the warm wetness beginning to cover it. The smell of blood was making him dizzy.

"He would like you to think so, but it is your *Papou* who is the dangerous one."

"You know him?"

"Only a little, a long time ago. He will not remember me."

Matthew looked around. The easel where the icon had sat twenty hours before was gone; the painting was nowhere to be seen. Some works had vanished from the walls as well. Which ones? Who else might have been hurt, killed? He should check the house, but he could not abandon his present task. Anyway, his grandfather would have done that already, unless he had just arrived. Or unless—

There was a noise in the kitchen and Jimmy appeared through the rear door, hands free of any weapon, Andreas a few steps behind. Both men seemed calm, if a bit flushed.

"Do we have everyone now?" Andreas asked.

"Where is Fotis?" Matthew shot back.

"Gone."

"Gone where?"

"We will discuss it. Who are these men?"

"They're from the church, in Greece. They say."

"Mr. Spyridis," said Ioannes evenly, "we must talk."

"Yes?" Andreas eyed the priest keenly. "Perhaps, but this is not the time."

"If not now, when?"

The wail of sirens filled the brief silence that followed. Far off, but getting closer.

"Maybe tomorrow."

"You do not think the police will have need of you tomorrow?" The priest stood to face him. "I should think they would find your being here, alone, suspicious."

Matthew awaited some convincing denial from his grandfather, but Andreas only stared.

"We shall see, Father. Perhaps they will look at the matter differently."

Andreas placed a hand on Matthew's shoulder and all of them became quiet as the sirens grew louder. Then Jimmy sidled up to the old man, desperation trumping embarrassment.

"Can I have my gun back?"

They were alone on the sidewalk. The ambulance had already pulled away, and police officers were going into and out of the house. Matthew did not know where the priest and Jimmy had gone, did not know what to say or not to say to the police when they questioned him. His grandfather stood beside him, staring down the empty avenue, deep in thought.

"I am sorry you had to see this," the old man spoke quietly. "You have never seen a wounded man, I think."

"*Papou,* do you know what's going on?"

"You ask me that? I had hoped that you might tell me."

"The only thing I know is that nobody has been telling me the truth."

"That is all?" Andreas gave him a hard look. "So you played no part in helping Fotis get the icon?"

"I'm not sure what part I played anymore. Fotis was supposed to be the middleman. He was assisting some people from the Greek church."

"These men?"

"No, another priest, who represented the synod in Athens. Except now it seems he didn't."

"Who was the other priest?"

"This Father Tomas Zacharios."

Andreas nodded. "I see."

"You know who he is, don't you?" Matthew struggled to keep a handle on his emotions, failed. "All of you know each other somehow, and I don't know a goddamn thing. You're messing with me the way you messed with my father."

"Do not speak nonsense, and do not blame others for your own foolishness."

The truth stung. He had been a complete ass, and it was time to face up to it.

"I have kept things from you," Andreas continued. "I was trying to protect you, not hurt you. I would never try to hurt you. I do not know this Father Tomas, but I have heard of him. He is well educated and well liked, and has been a liaison between the Greek and American churches. He is also thought to be a swindler, blackmailer, and thief. Not to mention a friend of your godfather. He disappeared with a large amount of church funds within the last few days."

"So it's like Father John said, he and Fotis were in it together." Of course, it could be another lie, but it made sense. There were no coincidences. Everything was connected.

"It seems likely."

For no logical reason, Matthew's mind veered away.

"Ana Kessler. Could she be in any danger?"

"I do not see why, her part in the matter is over. Do you have some reason for believing she might be in danger?"

"No, I just . . . No. I need to speak to her. I misled her. She never knew about Fotis' involvement."

"Tell me, why was he involved? Why was there a middleman at all?"

"He arranged it that way. The whole deal was his doing. He must have gone to Zacharios and had him contact the church, so there would be a gloss of truth to the thing. Where is Fotis now, *Papou?*"

"In Greece. Or on the way."

"He went today?"

"Very early this morning. For Easter."

"He never goes this early."

"This year he decided to spend all of Holy Week. Phillip, his restaurant manager, just told me."

"He told me a few days ago that he wasn't leaving until Wednesday."

"He changed his plans. Yesterday, Phillip said, right after you and your father visited with him." The old man paused, awaiting some reaction. "Do you know why?"

Matthew tried to keep his body from shaking, his mind focused.

"No idea, but he did seem agitated. I think Dad's being there made him nervous."

"Why did you bring your father?"

The shaking grew so intense that Matthew had to clench his jaw to stop it.

"We must get you inside," said Andreas.

"No, I need the air. I need to talk."

"Why did you help Fotis?"

"I thought the church should have the icon. Ana wanted it that way, too."

"But why allow it to pass through his hands?"

"I told you, he arranged that. I guess I could have prevented it, but it seemed so important to him to have it in his hands for a while. You know he's ill."

Andreas shook his head. "I wondered, but I did not know for certain."

"He doesn't talk about it. Anyway, the icon is supposed to have curative powers. The owners live long lives, the sick are cured by a touch, as if Mary or Jesus himself had touched them." He looked the old man in the eye again. "But you know all that."

Andreas grimaced. "Poor old fool." Then his expression changed, and Matthew knew what was coming. His grandfather stepped closer and placed a strong hand on the younger man's shoulder. "Is that why you went there with your father?"

Matthew did not answer.

"There is no judgment here," Andreas continued, gently, shaking the shoulder now. "This is a piece of the puzzle. Do you believe in these things?"

"Of course not," he said weakly.

The old man stared at him a moment longer, released him, and walked a few steps away.

"And I call *him* the fool. Your helping him made no sense to me. Now I see. It was not for Fotis', not for yourself, even."

"It's not that simple."

"No. It was a missing piece, the piece that fits the others together. It was in front of me and I did not see it. There is no shame, my boy, or the shame is mine."

"Why do you think he left so suddenly?"

Andreas scanned the street as he considered the question.

"Possibly so that he would not be here when the action unfolded."

"What do you mean? That he knew someone was going to rob him?"

"Not just knew. Planned it himself."

"He stole the icon from himself? Why?"

"I am not saying he did, but there are many reasons, if you would consider the chain of events. How could he keep it when he was only supposed to be the middleman?"

"And you think he had Nicholas shot?"

"It cannot be ruled out. Or perhaps his scheming collided with someone else's."

"What else do you know that you're not telling me?"

"In time, Matthew. I do not even know these things, I only surmise them. I realize that you mistrust me, and that I am to blame for that. It will take time to rebuild that trust. Just as understanding will take time."

The shaking in Matthew's limbs was diminishing, and with it the shock and confusion, replaced by something else. A cool resolve. Trust. It would be a long time indeed before he trusted again, and that was not a bad thing. He needed to stop answering so many questions and start asking a few himself. He needed to clean up this mess he'd made.

"Fotis told me some things."

"I am sure that he told you many things. Some may even be true."

"He told me you killed a priest."

Andreas appeared perplexed by this.

"During the war," Matthew coaxed, heart pounding. "He told me you were called the Snake, and that you killed a priest to get the icon."

The old man's face became an angry mask as understanding slowly sunk in. The transformation was so extreme that Matthew became alarmed, but he held his ground.

"Oh, he wants this thing badly," Andreas whispered. "He must want it very badly indeed to tell you such a story."

"Then it's not true."

"The priest's death is on my conscience, and always will be. But I did not kill him."

"And why should I believe that?"

The old man eyed him carefully. "He was my brother."

"Your brother."

"The Snake," Andreas continued, the hard look slowly passing from his face, the hard edge from his words, "was what we all called Fotis, behind his back."

Everything was turned around again. "And what did they call you?"

"My name, in those days, was Elias."

PART
TWO

The crypt beneath the church was many years older than the structure above, and housed the bones of countless village ancestors. Some old men claimed to know which shelf of skulls, shards, and powder belonged to which family, but most agreed that such arrangements had become confused generations ago, and the bones went wherever they fit. During times of persecution the crypt had been a sanctuary for prayer, and a refuge for wanted men, it was said; but the same claim was made for every crypt, cave, and cellar in the region. More recently, the dank, tangled passages of the ossuary had become a place to avoid for anyone who had sampled even a taste of his own mortality, but they continued to hold a fascination for the young.

As a boy, Andreas had shown no interest in the church, but the crypt was another matter. He would take whichever brave souls who would accompany him, even his gloomy half brother, on after-dark tours of the chamber, scaring the other boys senseless with made-up tales. Mikalis, bred on his mother's grisly Bible stories, scared least easily. Decades later, Andreas could still call forth the image of his runtish sibling, at the edge of the lantern's light, staring transfixed at a broken skull in a dark crevice. A disturbing memory. It would take until Mikalis went to the seminary for Andreas to understand what he had seen in his nine-year-old brother's face: not ghoulishness, but reverence.

A shot sounded nearby, a German Mauser, and the captain crouched among the spindly trees behind his cousin Glykeria's house. Were more *andartes* about; the communists perhaps? More likely a soldier's nervousness. A dangerous thing. All it would take was one frightened eighteen-year-old Austrian conscript to shoot a villager, and the whole company would empty their rifles at anything that moved. By morning the place would be a smoking ruin, women and children dead in the streets, another Koméno or Klisoúra. Andreas, who now went by the name Elias, would have to prevent that, but first he must get to the crypt. It was the most likely route of escape from the burning church.

Germans were scattered about the roads, and the captain moved cautiously. Fotis had called him Elias, herald of the Messiah, some bad joke, but the name had stuck. Most of the guerrillas took aliases so that the enemy could not trace them to a family or village which would pay the price for their actions. Who knew that the Germans would not care, that they would simply kill any random fifty or hundred civilians in the area? Tonight, the captain could call himself Elias or Fritz from Berlin, but if they caught him with a pistol in his belt, he would be shot, along with half the village.

The crypt entry was more or less an open secret. Every child knew of the low path that split off of the road to the churchyard. Beyond the last houses—shacks, really, for squatters or monks— at the edge of the wood line, a passage appeared in the earth at the steep bottom of the slope. Tall weeds and wildflowers abounded there, but the entrance was not hard to find. Most men had to duck to enter, and Captain Elias more than most, being tall. He would have to make his way by feel until he reached the place where a lantern was stowed. The walls were earth for the first twenty meters, uneven, liable to collapse. When his toes kicked the little step up, and he felt cool stone beneath his hand, he knew he'd found the ossuary.

The roar of the fire was audible, but no heat penetrated the crypt—just a thin smell of smoke. He made his way clockwise to the niche where the lantern was stored, found it: one panel of glass was broken, the candle a mere stub, but it would serve if he could find his matchbox. Yes, there. The spark of the match head was like lightning in that space. Slowly, an illuminating glow grew, and the shelves of yellow bones were before him. Beyond them was the stairway that led behind the flaming altar above. The bones were watchful, unmoved by recent events. They seemed saintly in their lifelessness, purified by death. Yet their owners were just dogs like me, thought Elias: selfish, angry, ignorant fools; breeding, feeding, boasting, stealing, killing, dying, generation after generation. They were not good souls simply because they had perished. Just wreckage. Just bones.

At the far end of the aisle, the sound of the fire grew louder, and he could see black smoke rolling down the stairway. The door above was open. Thrown aside by someone making an escape? Covering his mouth, the captain approached more closely, bent nearly to the ground: blood, dark pools in the shadowy lantern light, on several of the worn steps. The acrid smell was thickening. He would not be able to stay long. Elias searched the other aisles as swiftly as he could, and quickly found what he'd most feared.

In the space nearest the south wall, where the oldest bones lay, he saw a bunched black cassock on the floor. He put the lantern down carefully, his movements slowed, breathing the poisonous air freely now, and knelt beside his brother. He rolled the body over, and his right hand came away wet with blood from a wound in the back. The face, as the light found it, was far too pale, the eyes glazed, the mouth a pained rictus, and Elias reflexively covered it with his free hand. It required a long, deep breath before he could look again. There, an awful, jagged wound in the throat, around the larynx. Designed not necessarily to kill, but to silence the victim instantly. The captain knew that particular wound well. He had inflicted it a few times himself, had taught its use to his young disciple. He thought again of the strange look Kosta had given him earlier, and read new possibilities into it.

The aching grief welling up within him felt all out of proportion to the affection he had shown Mikalis in life. They had different mothers, had chosen different paths, believed different things. They were not close, except in the instinctive way that blood sometimes demanded. Elias would have died to protect Mikalis, yet could not swear that he loved him. Died to protect him; yet had he not let him escape his grasp, race to his death? The captain closed his eyes, tried to steady himself once more. Knife was better than fire, surely. The job had been mishandled, though; he'd not died at once but managed to crawl down here. Bled to death, a martyr to a painting.

His hands shook with rage, but the rage only masked a withering self-judgment. He could blame the Snake and Müller for dreaming up the trade, but he could not blame them for his part in it. The actual plan was his alone. The icon meant nothing to him, weapons were what mattered; but it had all gone wrong now. One life had been lost already, and more would follow if he could not discover who exactly had betrayed the dirty scheme, if he could not find a way to sew this ugly business back together. If he could blame Müller, there might be a righteousness to his anger. Yet he knew that the Prince had been as surprised as himself to find the church ablaze, and he certainly would not have stayed around to engage the *andartes* if he had the icon—he'd be back in Ioannina by now, with his loot. The captain looked at his brother's face once more. It wasn't a German who had stabbed Mikalis. No, the betrayal lay much closer.

Elias slipped the small gold cross and chain from around the priest's neck and placed them in his pocket. There was nothing else of value on the body. Grabbing hold under the armpits, pillowing the limp head against his leg, the captain dragged Mikalis to a corner of the crypt, nearer the tunnel exit. There, he arranged the body as respectfully as possible, placing his kerchief over the face, only noticing now the dark blisters on the hands, the burned and frayed bottom of the cassock. The priest had fought both flame and wounds to crawl down here and die among his ancestors. The captain placed two fingers on the cold forehead in a sort of benediction, but no words came. Next, he retrieved the lantern, doused the flame, and returned it to its place. Then, dizzy from the invisible fumes, twice as blind as when he had entered, Elias made his way back out into the night.

The glow from the church lit the valley, the fire reaching its apex. Elias stuffed his hands in his pockets, chin down, eyes alert, and slipped into the village. A small crowd had gathered at the base of the lane to the churchyard, women and children, buckets in hand. Four German soldiers prevented their progress. Light from the flames above caught the sentries' helmets and young faces, and Elias could see that they were edgy and ready to shoot the first fool bold enough to step forward. Müller would not want the *andartes* to escape by slipping into the crowd, pretending to be part of the fire brigade, and he would let the house of God burn to its foundation. Was that a clue? If there was a chance the icon was still in the church, would the German not have every adult and child, even his own men, throwing water on the flames? What had he seen before the smoke drove him out of the sanctuary? Had the Holy Mother been removed before the fire, and did the Prince know it? If Müller thought the icon was still intact, somewhere, then anything was possible.

Elias slid around the group unnoticed. His only clue was Kosta, and he had to make a choice now: the house or the shop? If the boy had escaped the fire, and if the captain's fears were true, then Kosta would not lead pursuers to his own home. The shop, then. Elias pushed on toward the heart of the village, using the crooked back streets. At the top of a lane the square came into sight, where another crowd was gathered. This one seemed dominated by helmeted figures and shouted commands. A number of people stood together by Tzamakis' tavern, under guard. Village elders. Glykeria's father was there, but Elias did not see Kosta's father, Stamatis Mavroudas, among them.

The Mavroudas shop faced the square, but the captain had no intention of trying the front door. Instead, he slid into an alley just wide enough for a man, invisible in the night shadows. Within a few yards the space widened into a small court, four meters square, and he was before the back door. The curtains were drawn on a tiny window, but Elias could make out candlelight behind them. He slipped his pistol from his belt and gently pressed his ear to the door. Only silence at first, but a minute's patience was rewarded by a raised voice, questioning, angry. Elias knew the voice.

Stepping to the side of the door, he rapped hard upon it. Silence once more.

"Who's there?" a weak voice asked, finally. The old man, Stamatis.

Elias merely rapped again.

The bolt slid aside within, and the door opened a hand's breadth. Mavroudas looked flushed and frightened. "What do you want?"

Elias looked the man in the eye but directed his words past him, into the room.

"Fotis, it's me."

There was a telling pause. Then the candle was covered, the door pulled wider, and Elias stepped inside. The door thumped shut behind him, the candle leaped back to life as a large bowl was lifted up, and the familiar figure of his commander stood by the table. Huge black mustache, hawklike nose, somber eyes in a long, sloping forehead. Fotis always conveyed a sense of calm, but the captain could see tension etched in the forehead and the jawline. The Snake was angry.

"You shouldn't use my name."

Elias ignored the comment. Stamatis knew them both.

"What are you doing here?" Elias demanded. It was not the tone to take with a superior, but he didn't care. Fotis should have been with the team sent to retrieve the guns, simultaneously with Müller's removing the icon. Elias, the only one among the guerrillas who knew where the Mother was hidden, had insisted on assigning roles. He'd never forgotten the covetous way Fotis had admired the work years before, stroking the cypress panels as he would a lover. He wanted the Snake nowhere near the church when the confiscation occurred, and leading the team that seized the guns was an honor Fotis could not refuse without revealing some ulterior motive for the whole scheme. The captain had thought it all through. A false message would get

Mikalis out of the church; the Germans guarding the wrecked villa where the weapons were stored—three or four men in Müller's pay—would fire some rounds at the *andartes* and withdraw. Each side would get what it wanted, and only the Prince, the Snake, and the captain would know what happened.

"Interrogating this son of a whore," Fotis answered him.

Mavroudas had used Elias' entry to shuffle across the small storeroom—now empty of the barrels of olives, figs, and cheese that used to crowd it—toward the front of the shop. Fotis covered the distance in two strides and flung the cowering merchant back into the old chair, which groaned beneath his sudden weight. Coiled rope and a six-inch blade sat on the table, on either side of the fat candle. Fotis had placed them carefully, to give Stamatis something to think about.

"Why aren't you with the men I sent?"

"They are safe," the Snake answered casually.

"What happened up there?"

Dragoumis looked at him hard.

"What do you think happened? The Prince didn't get his gift, so he didn't call off the men guarding the house."

"You couldn't overrun them?"

"We could have. There were only a few, but they had a machine gun, and it would have cost many men. God knows they were eager, but they were not my men to spend that way."

We're all your men, thought Elias, and you spend us in whatever manner suits you.

"So why are you here?" he pressed.

"The same reason as you. To find out what the hell happened."

"You seem to know already."

"I could say the same." Fotis circled the table like a shark. "Here we both are."

"Kosta went into the church during the shooting. I don't know why he went in or if he got out." Elias could not mention Mikalis. It was too new, too raw.

"The son, yes, he is part of it."

"And this one?" Elias kicked the chair leg and Stamatis flinched.

"This one," Fotis answered evenly, a hand upon the merchant's shoulder, "was seen leaving the church, with another man. And something wrapped in a bundle."

"Before the fire?"

"*During* the fire."

"Seen by whom?"

"It's a lie," hissed the old thief. "It's a lie. They all hate me. Peasants. They would lie for a crust of bread. Captain Elias—"

"Enough of that."

Dragoumis slapped the merchant's face to quiet him, and Elias became aware that the old man's desperate words were directed at him alone. Some tacit, if hostile, understanding already existed between the other two men. They were beyond petty issues like guilt or innocence, and bargained now for other lives, and the style of necessary deaths. Elias stepped closer to the table. Sweat glistened on Stamatis' forehead. His clothes were clean, probably freshly put on before Fotis' arrival, yet the bottom of his large beard was distinctly singed, and his matted gray hair smelled of smoke. The captain leaned over the shaking man.

"Where is Kosta?" he asked.

"Yes, where?" Fotis seconded. "You've sent him away with your prize, haven't you? Where do you think he can go? You know we control all the countryside around here. Where will he go that I can't find him?"

Stamatis shook his head vigorously, though what it was he denied was unclear. The whole pathetic situation, perhaps. A schemer snared in his own scheme. Intolerable. What the hell had he intended? Elias wondered. Not to get caught, first of all, but he must have known he would be suspected. To leave the village quickly? To sell the icon? To whom? To keep it until after the war? How to get answers from him? They could pretend to negotiate, but he would never believe them. Not now, not with the knife on the table. Besides, there was no time.

"I want to write a confession," the merchant announced.

Fotis drew a deep, explosive breath, then let it out. His voice stayed calm.

"Listen to me. I am going to take your fingers off one by one until you tell me where your bastard boy is, and what you have done with the icon."

"I want to write a confession," Stamatis insisted, voice quavering. "I'll tell you everything, but I want it on paper. And the captain must keep it, so one honest man will know the truth."

"I can know it just as easily if you speak," Elias answered, catching a withering look from the Snake for engaging in this dialogue at all.

"No, no, it must be on paper. So that you may prove I said these things. Men trust nothing spoken these days."

It was some game the old thief was playing. Simply buying time, perhaps, but Elias decided to call his bluff.

"So, write."

Fotis snorted in disgust but did not contradict his subordinate. Maybe he felt that the captain knew the merchant's ways better than himself. Perhaps he feared the things Mavroudas might say in Elias' presence, if pressed too hard. Elias knew that if he had not entered when he did, the interrogation would have reached the ugly stage by now, as it was still likely to do. And maybe that was the better course. Stamatis was stalling; Kosta— if Fotis was right about that—could not yet be far away.

The merchant snatched a stubby pencil from a cup, and a soiled sheet of brown paper from beneath the table, and began writing. Fotis risked a peek out the small window, and Elias slid over next to him.

"You got here quickly."

"Yes." Nothing more, of course. It was one of the Snake's rules never to explain, never to be placed on the defensive. It meant nothing either way. Yet it seemed only natural that fellow officers should discuss such a disastrous dissolution of their plans, not to mention forge a new strategy, and Elias could not help finding his chief's reticence disturbing.

"Where are my men now?" he asked.

"The little hill above the north road."

"So close? Müller has fifty soldiers."

"The church is south. For all he knows you're still there. He won't split up and strike north, not in the dark."

"He could call for reinforcements."

"He is not even supposed to be here," Fotis snapped. "Those troops are borrowed. He came for a trade, not a fight. Anyway, your men will know to scatter if there is trouble."

"Who did you leave in charge?"

"The one you picked, Giorgios. What happened at the church?" Fotis finally asked.

"I'll tell you later," Elias answered. Two could play the game. Besides, it would not do to say he wasn't precisely certain what had happened. "Are you sure this one has the icon?"

"You have another idea?"

"I only wonder how a man could escape that inferno. Or a painting. It may have simply burned."

"I don't think so. I think this bastard lit the fire behind him to cover his tracks."

"You said he came out during the fire."

"He lit it in front to keep Müller out. Then he escaped another way."

"How did he know Müller was coming?"

Fotis fixed him with a rare expression: incredulity bordering on disgust.

"How else? His son. Your trained dog, Kosta."

Of course. This conspiracy was not newly hatched; father and son had been in communication all along. Kosta had been with Elias when he told Müller the plan, and again when Elias gave Stefano the message that would flush Mikalis from the church and keep him from harm while Müller took the icon. Kosta, his most trusted man. The Snake saw understanding transform the captain's face.

"You were deceived, my friend. The boy was the old man's spy in your camp."

"You knew?"

"I just realized it tonight. And so have you, don't deny it."

A shout from the table startled them both.

"Damn it all to hell," Stamatis cried, tearing the page lengthwise. "Damn you both, I won't do it. I won't confess to what I haven't done." He tore the page to pieces.

Fotis moved quickly to the table, and the merchant threw the paper in his face, then sprang for the knife on the table. Dragoumis grabbed wildly and nearly caught the blade with his hand, then managed to snag the older man's wrist before the knife could find his throat. The table leaned and the guttering flame threw wild shadows about the room as the men struggled.

Elias first reached for his pistol, but that would make too much noise. Instead, he grabbed the rope and pulled it around the merchant's neck, yanking him back into the chair.

"Release the knife."

It clattered to the table, and Fotis quickly snatched it up, his wide eyes narrowing in rage.

"That's enough. Tie him there, with one hand free. We'll have answers now."

The captain had seen this before. Communists, collaborators, once even a German corporal, tied to a chair while Fotis worked on them with the knife. Torture had its uses. Time was wasting, and the fat thief was a likely candidate to break quickly. Still, Elias hesitated.

"Tie him," Dragoumis demanded, his composure gone, his face flushed with blood.

A hard rap at the door, followed quickly by two more. Fotis went to the window.

"It's Marko."

They covered the light again, and a thickset young man slipped in. He nodded to Elias who ignored him. Marko had a way of appearing when there was dirty work to do. He was a baker's son from a few villages away, but not with the captain's *andartes*. He worked directly for Dragoumis. Fotis had shaped him, or perhaps nature had. Nothing unsettled the boy, no order was too grim. Elias believed that he had found such a one in Kosta, but Marko was the genuine item. Perhaps a lack of cleverness was the key. Kosta was clever, damn him.

"What's happening out there?"

"They're gathering people in the square," Marko replied. "They started with the old men, but now they're grabbing anyone, even some women. I guess there aren't enough men left. I was lucky they didn't take me."

"Did you kill any Germans at the church?" Fotis asked.

"One," Elias answered.

"That's forty they'll shoot at sunrise. You'll be lucky if they don't burn the place."

"Bastards," said Marko.

Elias had let his grip relax, and Mavroudas slipped the noose, but only to fall like a heavy sack at the guerrilla leader's feet.

"Captain, for the love of Christ, spare me from these beasts. You're not like them, you're a good man, everyone respects you."

"Get up."

"No, please, I beg you. Show mercy, it is in your hands."

The merchant's face was damp with tears, his eyes wild. Elias knew that his terror was genuine, yet there was also a staged quality to the outburst. Stamatis seized the captain's right hand between his own in a prayerlike fashion, and fixed him with a meaningful stare. Even as he struggled to pull his hand free, Elias felt a scrap of paper being pressed against his palm.

The room's dynamics shifted invisibly. The old thief had made his choice; the rest was up to Elias. He felt the other men's eyes upon him and knew that Fotis rarely missed a trick.

"Let go of me, you pig."

"No, listen, I don't know where the boy is, I don't—"

He clouted the merchant across the face with his left hand, rotating his body in rhythm with the blow, stuffing the paper into his pocket while his right hand was obscured from view.

"You have no friends here, Mavroudas," Fotis said quietly, his calm restored. "Marko, put him in the chair and tie him, one hand free. Which hand do you want to lose first, Mavroudas, left or right? You see, you still have some choices."

Marko worked swiftly. Stamatis, his last card played, nothing to distract him from the horror to come, stared stony-faced at the wall, a whimper escaping him as the knots secured him in place. Elias would not watch. It was one thing to kill strangers in a fight, quite another to slowly drain the life from a man you had known since childhood. Yet the merchant's actions had caused Mikalis' death. It was right he should die. So let him; Elias had other work. He headed to the door as Fotis took up the knife.

"Where are you going?"

"To find my men on the north hill."

"Yes, good. If you must move, the old monastery, not the cave."

"I know my business," snapped Elias.

"Of course. Otherwise, stay on the hill and I will find you there."

"What is the plan if he talks?"

Fotis smiled unpleasantly. "He will talk. We will discuss it when I find you. Take care, my boy." The last words spoken in that urgent hush which convinced you of their sincerity.

Stamatis' whimpering reached a higher pitch, almost a scream, as Elias slipped out into the night. "Put something in his mouth" were the last words he heard.

Activity in the square continued. Scattered pairs of Germans were everywhere, pounding on doors, looking for something or someone. Müller probably had a dozen false leads to pursue, fed to him by panicked villagers trying to save themselves. Elias kept within the darkest shadows, thankful for the lack of moonlight, and slipped street to street between houses, stopping at a bend in an alleyway. He found the box in his vest pocket, with only a precious few matches remaining. Drawing out the little scrap of paper with one hand, he struck a match against the cold stone wall with the other.

St. Gregori's chapel. Spare the boy.

That was all. He touched the dying match to the paper, watched it flare brightly and vanish in ash. St. Gregori's. A good choice. It was not in regular use, and the captain had a hard time remembering just where it was. To the north somewhere, but well off of any road. Spare the boy? How could he be serious? Did Stamatis not know what Kosta had done to Mikalis? Did he think that Elias was unaware? Why should his mercy be greater than the Snake's, who had not lost a brother? The old thief had gone soft in his final minutes, but it did not matter.

How to proceed? He no longer trusted Fotis. It was best that he hadn't mentioned Mikalis, for then Fotis would not trust him to act rationally. The most important thing was to get to the chapel quickly. With the icon he had bargaining power, he could still make some kind of deal. Stamatis would talk; Fotis would be directly on Elias' heels.

The next few streets were clear of Germans, and this allowed freer movement. Stefano's tavern was closed, no light visible inside. The Germans might have the barkeep, but Elias doubted it. Not for nothing did he trust messages to Stefano. The man was a collector of secrets but never spoke them unless the price was right, and he was skilled at arriving and departing unnoticed. Where would he be now? Not at home. The wife and child were dead; only the mother-in-law was in the house, and Stefano would not care what happened to her. He would not be walking the streets with a roundup in progress. No, Elias guessed that Stefano was sitting in the darkened tavern, waiting for the danger to pass. The captain went to the back door. There was a bolt on the inside, but Elias remembered that the bracing screws were loose. A polite knock was not going to serve. Without deliberation, he stepped back and threw his left shoulder against the door, which leaped on its hinges, making a terrible noise, but did not give. So much for surprise. The captain stepped back again, shifting his right shoulder forward and placing the bottom of his left foot on the wall behind. Killed by a nervous tavern owner, he mused in disgust; and I gave him that damn pistol! Then he sprang forward with all his strength.

The door gave, just, but the shock of the impact staggered Elias and he stumbled to the floor. He stayed prone for several seconds but spoke at once, to identify himself.

"Stefano, it's me."

The tavern keeper would not have willingly let him in, but would not shoot him now that he was. Empty chairs and tables loomed in the faint light from the windows. The bar stood by the kitchen entry, and Elias crawled that way. Peering around the edge, he made out a figure peering over the top. He placed his pistol against the man's knee.

"I'm down here."

The tavern owner jumped in surprise.

"Easy," said the captain, rising to his feet. "Put your pistol down." He had not actually seen a weapon, but he heard the thunk of it being released. "Light a lantern."

"Who has oil, besides you and the Germans?"

"A candle, then."

The low, flickering light revealed a swollen bruise around Stefano's left eye, and his refusal to look at the captain made questions almost unnecessary, but Elias had to be certain.

"Did you deliver the message to Mikalis?" Elias asked.

"If you ask me, then you know I didn't."

"Who did that to your face?"

"Mavroudas. The old man."

"To learn the message?"

"He already knew that. To persuade me not to go, to let him go in my place."

"Beat you with one hand, paid you with the other."

"What does it matter?"

"You're very casual for a traitor."

Stefano's eye widened, the first sign of real alarm.

"I am no traitor. Did he not deliver the message?"

"You must have known that he intended more than that."

"How am I to know what he has in mind? He threatened to kill me if I crossed him."

"He delivered it. Then things went wrong. Mikalis is dead."

"No." The tavern keeper's face collapsed, and tears welled up in his eyes. Did he think that Elias was about to execute him, or was it real grief for the life of the popular priest? Who could say? The captain wanted to strike him, but might knock him senseless, which would not serve his purposes. He stepped in close and put the pistol to Stefano's throat.

"I should kill you, but I need you to do two things. You must not fail in either."

Stefano nodded.

"You will go to the German major, Müller," Elias continued. "You'll tell him that the business at the church was a mistake. The deal is still possible. I will bring him what he wants before sundown tomorrow, but he must not shoot anyone. If he does, everything is off. He must be alone when you tell him, and you must reach him before sunrise. Do you understand?"

Stefano paused only a moment, licking his dry lips.

"I will do it."

Elias stepped away and put the pistol back in his belt.

"If you do, you will save many lives. But you must be swift, and you must convince him. No one can know of this, ever. It is your death if you speak."

"Of course."

The tavern owner's eyes burned with sincerity, but that would pass. Such secrets got out. Someone would see Stefano and Müller together, maybe the communists would get hold of him. It was just the sort of story they wanted to hear, republicans and Germans in bed together. Stefano would say what he must to survive, or even sell the information. He was slippery, an unwise choice, but there was no one else. Kosta was gone. Elias' other men didn't know what he was doing, and they would never support it if they did. Every man in the village was compromised. Though who was he to judge, Elias wondered of himself; he, the most compromised man of all? All the good men were dead.

"After you see Müller, go to my father's widow." He would not call her his stepmother. "Tell her that her son's body lies in the northwest corner of the crypt. She may send a man there to find him. Go yourself if she asks."

Stefano seemed more daunted by this task than the previous one, but nodded his assent.

"Don't fail me, Stefano. Don't fail all of us."

They left by separate doors. Back on the dark streets, Elias made all possible speed toward the north hill. It was low, not heavily wooded, but on this moonless night it was merely a looming shadow, and he could make out no sign of his men. He still did not know what they might have heard, or guessed. Would they welcome his arrival, or stand him against a tree and shoot him? Pressed for time, he rushed up the slope, content for them to discover him. They did. Halfway up, young Panayiotis emerged out of the shadows.

"You're clumsy tonight, Captain. I almost thought you were a German."

"Take me to Giorgios."

Most of the men, twenty-five or so, were among the boulders near the summit, the rangy former infantry sergeant pacing fiercely among them. Giorgios was slightly ridiculous in his scraggly beard and soiled Italian colonel's uniform—booty from the Albanian campaign—but he was the best leader of men that Elias had.

"Mother of God, it's good you're here," said Giorgios when he saw the captain. "We needed you before. The damn Snake wouldn't let us attack."

So they were still blind to the subterfuge, thought Elias, with a strange sadness.

"Slowly."

"We found the villa where the weapons were stored, right where you said it would be."

"Yes."

"Just a few Germans guarding it, one light machine gun. We could have taken it, but when the shooting started at the church, the Snake sent word that we were not to try."

"Sent word? He wasn't with you?"

"The Snake? At first, but not then. He said he needed to watch the Germans in the village. He left me in charge. I should have ignored him, we wasted an opportunity."

"No, Giorgios, you did right. The men are more important than the weapons. Listen to me now, I need your help. Tell me how to find Gregori's chapel."

"Gregori's chapel? Why?"

"Kosta has betrayed me." He could not bring himself to say "us." "He has gone to this chapel to hide. I must seek him there."

It was still quite dark, but the sky was just beginning to pale in the east. Elias could not read Giorgios' reaction, except in his silence.

"The devil take him," Giorgios finally whispered. "Is the icon destroyed?"

"I do not know. Old Mavroudas meant to steal it. The Snake is dealing with him. I must find Kosta now."

"And Father Mikalis?"

The grief swelled again. When all this was over he would sleep for days, or perhaps forever, depending on how things fell out.

"Giorgios, the chapel. Help me."

"Down the other side of this hill, the path to the high meadow. Follow it to the end."

"That's Mary's chapel."

"Past that a kilometer, and up a rocky slope. You will be almost to Vrateni. It is a very desolate place. The chapel commands the ground. Be careful. Better still, take some men."

"No, I go alone. You must take charge here. Spiro and Leftheris are at the old monastery, the rest at the cave. Move to a safer place, if you can, and await word from me. Follow the Snake's commands if they seem wise to you, but protect the men. And Giorgios, do not tell him, or anyone, where I have gone."

The sky was just light enough now to read the confusion and unease on the *andarte*'s face. No one loved the Snake, but Giorgios was experienced enough to know that it was never a good thing to have commanders at odds with each other. Elias, with no words of comfort in his heart, turned away from the young soldier and the brightening eastern sky, and pushed north once more.

13

He had stood right there by the window, face in shadow, as befit his clouded intentions, perhaps. Ana couldn't say for sure. Outside it rained, and she had not turned on a lamp, so the room was dim—the long, cold dining room that they had not been in together before. Neutral ground. Matthew did not want to venture further into the house.

"I'm sorry I didn't come sooner," he'd said. "I couldn't speak to you until the police did."

"Did they tell you that?"

"No."

"You didn't want them to think you would influence my statement."

"I didn't want *you* to think that."

"OK."

"There are things you should know."

"I'm listening." But he couldn't seem to shape his thoughts, at least not swiftly enough to suit Ana, and like an idiot she had blundered on in a clipped, angry burst. "I didn't say anything that should implicate you, if that's what you came to find out. I told them that I knew your godfather was the buyer, that you had told me. I don't know why I did that. I don't even know if it will help you."

He shook his head, face twisted in frustration or disgust, and she thought she read him in that instant, thought that maybe he was not so far from being the man she felt she knew, despite the things he had kept from her.

"I didn't want you to do that," he had finally said. "I don't care what you tell the police. I came to tell you what I know."

It had all poured out of him then, his godfather's subtle guidance, Matthew's fixation on the work, his willful ignorance of the plot taking shape around him; and the more he spoke the more depressed and disengaged she had become. Questions banged at the door of her mind but could gain no entry. She was stuck on the one fact: he had come into her life to manipulate her. How then could she ever trust him? How could she know if anything that had passed between them was real? She could not, though she might yet try if he would even address the issue. But he would not, and she understood, with a keen sense of self-loathing, that without that question answered, the others—involving the full extent to which she had been played for a fool—were meaningless to her. She would not show it. Let her self-disgust seem like anger. He deserved her anger.

She had made him sit in one of the old, uncomfortable wing chairs, and eventually she began to analyze what he said, letting her thinking turn cold and clinical. Matthew had no doubt that the icon had been the reason for the theft, despite the other paintings taken. She decided to play along, to assume his innocence in anything beyond the initial manipulation.

"Has your godfather been questioned?"

"No. He's in Greece. He became suddenly ill right after he got there."

"You sound skeptical."

"He has been ill with something, but he's a trickster, that guy."

"You think he's behind the theft?"

"I don't want to, but it's a possibility."

"He put down almost a million dollars to steal it from himself?"

"From the church, to which he owed it by the conditions of the sale. You had a blind offer for almost twice that. He used the church to get his price, and to block other bidders. Theoretically, I mean; I hope I'm wrong. There may have been other reasons as well."

"Why didn't you tell me about him from the start?"

"He wasn't involved from the start," Matthew insisted. "Or he was, but I didn't . . . When the museum sent me over, I didn't know of any connection, except that he knew Wallace. Which you also knew," he reminded her, pointedly. "Later, he told me the church approached him, made it sound very casual. I should have spoken to you then. He asked me not to. He convinced me that it didn't change anything whether you knew or not, and knowing would only make you suspicious."

"And that didn't make *you* suspicious?"

"There was other stuff, too. I'm not going to lay it on you. I was stupid about the whole thing. I'm sorry, Ana. I truly felt the icon should go back to Greece."

"What if I had decided to go with a private buyer?"

"Then that would have been that."

"You wouldn't have tried to talk me out of it?"

"Not if your mind was made up."

"Bullshit."

"What could I have done? I couldn't make you choose against your will."

You could have made me do anything you wanted, Ana thought bitterly, but again the anger was directed mostly at herself.

"How can I believe anything you're telling me now?"

"That's a fair question. I can't answer it. You have every right to doubt me."

So calm and reasonable, even in his guilt.

"Fuck you, Matthew."

He had stood quite suddenly, as if she had thrown cold water in his lap. She struggled not to stand also, to keep her expression closed and ungiving. He could not stay, not now, yet she desperately did not want him to leave.

"Have you told the police all this?"

"They know the facts; the rest is hypothesis. I held back some of the history."

"What history?"

He'd hesitated, clearly not wanting to tell this part. "The icon comes from my grandfather's village. It turns out he and my godfather were involved in some scheme to trade it to the Germans, during the war."

More secrets. There was no bottom to them, apparently. The grandfather clock's metronomic click assaulted her thinking. Her great-great-uncle had built it; her grandfather had shipped it here with his other possessions fifty years before. Ana had loved the clock as a child, but at that moment she found herself wanting to toss it onto the street for the junk collectors.

"That would seem to be worth reporting," she had said coolly.

"The details aren't very clear."

"You came here to tell me everything, remember?"

"This isn't the sort of story you tell without knowing the truth behind it. It's pretty damning stuff, and everyone involved has a different version."

"How did my grandfather get the icon?"

"That I really don't know. But I'm going to try to get some answers, for both of us."

"How?"

Swaying where he stood, wanting to be gone, he had looked right at her for the first time.

"I'm going to see my godfather."

"They're going to let you leave the country while they're still investigating?"

"I don't plan on asking permission."

"Matthew," she began, rising to her feet, approaching him before she knew it. "You could get into serious trouble. It might look as though you're running." Was he? Were her instincts wrong? They had not been very dependable so far, but then why had he come at all?

"He's more likely to speak to me than to anyone else."

"He won't tell you the truth."

"He might. Or he might give something away."

"Look, if you're right, then he had his own man shot. He's dangerous."

"I don't think he planned that."

"Then he's not in control of the situation," she had insisted. Why was he not getting it? "Someone out there is willing to kill for this thing."

He'd opened his mouth to speak, but there was no easy answer to that ugly fact, and the truth of it settled around them quietly.

"Fotis is family," he finally mumbled. "Besides, I helped create this mess."

"Which is a stupid reason to make it worse now. Don't go."

She had tried awhile longer to dissuade him, knowing it was useless. For all his seeming rationality, he was actually incredibly stubborn. He left without touching her—sure he had forfeited that right, no doubt. She had given him no encouragement, had maintained her toughness to the end, but she fixed his dark head of hair and slouched, retreating back in her mind. Then she wandered into the dining room and sank into her hard chair, hollowed out. It was more than likely that she had seen him for the last time.

That had been two days earlier, and Ana sat now in the same empty dining room, shadows banished by the strong light through the windows, the warm sun of spring. Matthew would be in Greece. She expected no word, only hoped that he was safe, that he was not playing at some game that would prove too much for him. She had tried to put the matter of the icon out of her mind. After all, she had gotten money, gotten the thing out of her life, which was most of what she wanted. The police would take it from here. It was the Greek church's business to cry foul, not hers. She had fulfilled her side of the bargain. That oily Father Tomas had stood right there in the hall, watching his men carry the package out to the van. Let him explain what happened next, if they could find him.

And yet . . . Her intentions had been subverted; where was her anger? For that matter, where was her sense of responsibility? This had been no idle choice. The icon's provenance was sketchy, as with much of the other work her grandfather acquired just after the war. Her father had seemed embarrassed by it, and her grandfather's adoration had a covetous, unhealthy quality. Ana might never learn the details, but she had no doubt that the Greeks in that village of Matthew's ancestors had not parted with it willingly. It belonged back there. She didn't subscribe to family guilt as a concept, to the responsibility for old wrongs being passed down the generations. Yet she had long suspected that shady transactions lay behind many of the old man's acquisitions, and she had never raised the matter with him. Now she had the estate, and with it certain obligations. She didn't intend to make a life's work of seeking proper restitution for every painting on the walls around her, but the business of the icon had jumped to life on its own and could not now be ignored. There wasn't a lot she could do, but there were a few troubling details to ponder. One particular matter had bothered her all along, and set her wondering—not for the first time—about connections between these new events and things that had happened in the past. Don't start something you don't intend to finish, her dad had always said. Was that an argument for pushing forward, or for stopping now?

Ana strode down the hall to the kitchen. The place to start was Wallace. He knew things he wasn't sharing. She had always understood this about him, but had hoped her grandfather's death might cause him to drop his guard, release a few of those dusty family secrets. This hope had been disappointed; his armor remained in place. She'd had it in the back of her mind that testing the market for private bidders on the icon might bring forward someone who knew about its past, and her grandfather's. Possibly even someone with knowledge of what had happened that week her father went to Caracas. She hadn't shared these thoughts with Wallace, and he had kept his inquiries very much to himself, steering her dutifully toward the institutions. By then she had become too distracted by Matthew to press the wily lawyer.

She dropped into a chair at the kitchen table and lit a cigarette, her fifth of the morning. She would go through a dozen today. Eight yesterday, six the day before. Like quitting in reverse. She had been smoke-free almost four years. All it took was that first one, an hour after Matthew walked out the door, and she was back where she started. She drummed her fingers on the table. The kitchen now reminded her of Matthew, despite the fact that he had been here only half a dozen times. She exhaled the thought in a blue cloud of smoke. Never mind. The way to feel close to her runaway lover was to pursue the same mystery that he did. The thought stopped her. Was that all she was doing, trying to feel close to Matthew, to make his obsession hers? Were all those ideas about responsibility just flimsy justification? She inhaled the sweet poison, felt her body hum. Did it really matter?

Ana grabbed the telephone and dialed.

"Wallace and Warford."

"Hi, Millie, is he there?"

"Ana. He's in the middle of something. Can he call you back?"

"Tell him I'll wait as long as it takes for him to be free."

"It's really better if he calls you."

"I'll wait. Please tell him."

He let her hold for many minutes, as she knew he would, and her agitation grew exponentially over that time. Then that deep, gravelly voice was in her ear.

"My dear, sorry I haven't been in touch."

"We have business, Arthur. More paintings to sell."

"I know, I really do apologize. But look, we need to do this in person. Let me pass you back to Millie and we'll make a date."

"I have a question. The private buyer on the icon, the one ready to spend a million five. I want to know who that was."

He was quiet a few moments. "Why are you still thinking of that?"

"Because it strikes me as strange that anyone would offer that much."

"Who's to say if he would have paid in the end? I didn't find the approach very credible, or I would have pushed you harder to explore it."

"Yeah, well, look how credible the church deal turned out to be."

"The church is not responsible for what happened. And you got your money."

"Anyway, tell me who our spendthrift buyer was."

He sighed heavily, a disappointed sound, but she was not going to be deflected. He had played that long-suffering father game with her for too long.

"The approach was made via a dealer of rather dubious reputation, whom I would prefer not to name."

"Why? Did he ask to remain anonymous? A *dealer*? Come on, Arthur, whose lawyer are you?"

"Emil Rosenthal."

"You're kidding. That creep?"

"Now you know my reasoning in not pursuing it."

"But who would work through a guy like Rosenthal?"

"Who knows? Rich eccentrics use all sorts of unsavory middlemen. Someone's giving Emil business. Anyway, he's not going to tell you."

"And you have no idea who it was?"

"Of course not."

"Too bad."

"You're not thinking of speaking to him, I hope."

"No," she lied. "No, I don't see what purpose it would serve, and he's so slimy. I was really just curious."

"Best to let all that go. Let me give you to Millie now, and I'll see you very soon."

"Good. We have a lot to talk about."

14

For a long time after he woke, Fotis thought he might be dying, and the idea was not entirely unwelcome. Hot sweat was cooling on his wracked limbs, despite the heavy blankets, and he was having difficulty breathing. Water in the lungs. Sitting up would help, but he could not command his muscles. His mind was full of a thick muzziness, unable to hold a complex thought, and he imagined sinking deeper and deeper into this state, until there was no more awareness, no more pain, until he was released from the prison of his traitorous body. Then he remembered the dream.

It had not possessed the detail and time-suspended horror of earlier versions, but it had been a worthy echo. Those same shapeless, denuded hills, stretching to the horizon beneath a leaden sky. The same endless road twisting through them, his feet upon that road, walking but making no progress. Shuffling forms to his right and left, once human, he knew, all moving in the same direction. Someone waited for him; he knew that also. Someone or something that meant him harm waited for him, black arms outstretched, like vulture's wings, and the fact that he would never reach that fiend, but would be forever approaching it, did nothing to lessen the terror of its waiting. He had awakened then, but from the earlier visions he remembered that the hills turned to valleys, the valleys to tundra, impossibly flat and endless. Then he would pass the dark hill and empty crosses on his right, pass under the stone arch that marked the final stretch, pass into the tunnel, knowing he was near the end of the road, feeling it with every fiber of his being, yet knowing simultaneously that there was no end, that he would walk forever. This was what awaited him. This was the purgatory into which he was willingly sinking.

Fear coursed through him like cold liquid and he opened his eyes again. The ceiling seemed far above, his peripheral vision was gone. He tried to shout but heard only a weak gurgle. Gathering all his breath and strength he tried again, producing a long, weak moan, like a man crying out in his sleep, then fell silent, airless, lightless, awaiting the long descent.

Suddenly he felt strong hands upon his shoulders, felt himself pulled violently upright, saw the walls and the long slash of white light between the drawn curtains, wheeling about in his vision. His lungs convulsed. He heard a wheezing noise, then the agony of air rushing into his chest. In another moment sharp coughs shook his body, and a bitter, metallic taste was in his mouth.

At length, he slumped against whoever held him, spitting phlegmy gobs into a handkerchief held below his face. Disgusted with himself, with life. Pulling free, he swayed uncertainly as pillows were stacked behind him, then allowed himself to be pressed back, three-quarters propped up. Exhausted. Ready for sleep once more, but terrified by the prospect. At least he could breathe.

"Can I bring you anything?"

Fotis looked at the man. Not Nicholas. Nicholas was fighting for his life in a hospital in New York. This man was Taki, Fotis' nephew, who would do anything for him. Fotis was in Greece, at the big house he had built outside of Salonika. New York was 5,000 miles away, the theft had gone wrong, and he had no reliable source of information. A desperate plan. A mad chance he was taking, but all his reasons came back to him with that dream. God had a purpose for everything.

"A glass of water."

He sipped slowly. The water went down like mercury at first, heavy and unquenching, but eventually his throat felt somewhat soothed. His nephew stood attentively by his side. There was no love in the face of the ex-soldier and failed house-alarm salesman, but Taki was loyal, and eager for employment. And his black market connections were useful.

"Will you eat some breakfast?"

The idea sickened him, but some attempt was necessary.

"Coffee, and some bread."

"Your godson is downstairs."

"Matthew?" The old man was momentarily at a loss. "Matthew is here?" And yet, why was he surprised? It was only the timing that had caught him out. He had known there was a fair chance that the boy would come. "How long has he been here?"

"An hour. I tried to send him away, but he won't go. I didn't want to throw him out."

Of course you did, thought Fotis. Taki was Matthew's mother's first cousin, but the two men hardly knew each other. Taki had nothing against Matthew, but he would not like the boy claiming special status. He had been fending people off all week—friends, business associates, insurance investigators—and was clearly enjoying the role of gatekeeper.

"No, you did right. I will see him."

"After you eat."

"No," said Fotis, thoughts shaping themselves instantly. "Send him up with the food."

Taki seemed shocked. Fotis never met the world without being washed, dressed, and fed, but Matthew was a special case. His anger would need subduing, and the proper presentation was required. These considerations came to the old man unbidden, the product of sixty years of deception. The quick shift from the mortal terror of minutes before to these familiar tricks provided a superficial balm for his mind; and yet, deeper down, it oppressed him. He no longer knew what it was like not to plan every encounter in advance. He no longer had an honest relationship with any man. His instinct had become a thing apart from him, a trained animal, sometimes deadly, and only barely under his control. That the intrigues he engineered this time were at the service of his soul brought him some measure of peace. If the Holy Mother could heal him, all must be forgiven.

What would the boy know? The New York police were focused on Anton and his Russian connections, but they would be expanding their investigation. Fotis had worked hard on Father Tomas' credibility, having him secure the actual endorsement of the Greek church, paying him in small installments for his collaboration. And now the fool had vanished with half a million dollars of church funds, rendering all his recent actions suspicious. Of course, Fotis had known Tomas was a thief, but not that he was under investigation by his superiors and would choose this moment to go underground. Maybe it was best; maybe questioning would have broken him.

The out-of-work actor who had been checking in around Manhattan as Peter Miller knew nothing, not even the name of the man who had hired him. Fotis' file on Müller was thin. The man had ceased to be of interest as soon as it became clear that he'd sold the icon to Kessler. When Fotis had learned Andreas was coming to New York, however, he'd needed a ploy to distract him from the gambit being played with Matthew and the church. Something strong enough to skew the thinking of his keen-minded protégé. Only Müller would do, but the clues must be subtle, hard to find, or he would sense the ruse. By now Andreas had surely figured out the charade, but would he have shared it with his grandson?

"Kalimera," Matthew said without warmth, looking for a place to put the breakfast tray. Fotis nodded at the large footrest before him. Taki had wrapped him in his old blue robe and helped him to the chair by the bed before disappearing downstairs again.

"Bless you, my boy," he responded in English. "I don't know if I can eat, but Taki will have me try." Fotis took a drink of the bitter coffee before speaking again. "You've come a long way just to see me. Did you think I would die without consulting you?"

"I'm sorry to find you so unwell."

Surprised was more like it. No one was more surprised than Fotis himself when a feigned illness became a real one, but that was God again, still teaching him lessons after eighty-nine years. The pain in the bones he'd come to expect, but this fatigue and congestion were something new. He'd started to feel it right after Matthew and Alex left that day—a week ago, less? He had not expected Alex to know the icon; that had been the first shock. Perhaps Andreas had broken the pledge and said something, even years before. Who could say how much Alex knew or what he might say to Matthew? The fear of that, plus the news that this del Carros was speaking to the Russians, had been sufficient for Fotis to move up his plans a few days. And then, the figure. Even now he could not think of it without terror, like something from his dream, a strange, ghostly presence there in the doorway just as Alekos' hand touched the icon. For a moment he had thought it was that boy, Kosta. Then nothing, no one. The first signs of a fever, clearly, this present sickness, which would carry him off if he was not careful, or strong. At his age, life or death could be simple choices. Give in to the darkness, or fight it.

"Not so unwell. A slight cold, I think." The boy should have expected to find him ill, yet had not, which meant that he had worked things out. "Maybe something I picked up on the flight. Maybe just the emotions from this peculiar Holy Week."

"You look terrible; you shouldn't be up."

"I was told my godson must see me instantly." He smiled, but edged the words.

"I could have sat by the bed."

"That is not how I meet guests, or family. Anyway, you are here, and you are troubled."

"The icon is gone. Nicholas is in the hospital with a bullet in his back. The police think I'm keeping things from them. Nobody has been able to speak to you. It's a troubling situation, don't you think?"

"Indeed. How is your girl?"

"She's not my girl."

"I'm sorry to hear that."

"*Theio,* I want to know what the hell is going on."

"We would all like to know that. You think I have some special information?"

"You don't seem very upset about any of this."

"That is the sickness. I have only strength for the tasks I must perform, an old man's wisdom. I grieve for the icon's loss, and I have prayed every morning and evening for Nikos. There is nothing else I can do until I am well enough to return."

"Anton has vanished."

"The police told me."

"You've spoken to them."

"I accepted a telephone call. You see, I am trying to help."

"It doesn't look good, his disappearing like that."

"I agree."

"You think he was involved in the theft?"

"I fear we must assume it." Fotis sighed, expressing the effort this was costing him. "Of course, he might have other reasons. Some of these Russians have only a tenuous legal status in America."

"Anton's an illegal?"

"I do not say it is so, only that it might be. Yet in such a case, I would still expect him to contact me, which he has failed to do."

"He always struck me as very loyal," Matthew prodded, his steady gaze fixed on the old man's face. "And not very inventive."

"Ah, there is more to that one than meets the eye. He hides it well. But if he was involved, I doubt that it was his idea."

"Agreed. Whose, then?"

Fotis shrugged and reached for the heavy slab of bread.

"That's it," Matthew shot back. "A shrug? You have no theories?"

"What would you have me say?"

"You expect me to believe that you have no idea at all—"

"Spit it out, you pup." The old man dropped the bread, working himself up to a good, regal rage. "I won't be interrogated like this in my own home. You think I don't know about interrogations? I've conducted hundreds. You think I'm behind this."

There was a small flinch, far less than Fotis had anticipated.

"I do not say it is so," the boy mocked him quietly, "only that it might be."

Bravo. This was trouble, but Fotis could not help admiring the young man's cool. He was growing. He might prove good at this business, after all. The old man tacked again.

"Andreas."

"What about him?"

"Forgive me, it's only that I'm tired. I did not hear him speaking through you at first."

"You know, it's funny." Matthew picked the bread up off the footrest and put it back on the tray. "Whenever one of you gets into a tight spot, you always invoke the other. As if you're each other's evil twin. Nothing's ever your fault, nothing's ever his fault. It's always the other guy."

"Perhaps we've forgotten which of us is which."

"You've certainly forgotten which of you *did* what. Eat that bread, I don't want Taki angry with me."

The old man bent to obey, glad of the excuse to stay silent.

"These are my own questions," Matthew continued. "My grandfather has fed me a lot of stories, but no more than you. Maybe you both believe your own versions, I can't say. Right now, I don't trust either one of you."

Good, Fotis thought. He would accept even odds. The bread was soft and pleasant on his tongue. He placed it back on the dish, swallowing carefully.

"I do not know where Anton is, or what he is doing." That was more or less true. "With him missing, and with Nicholas in the hospital, I have no resources of the kind I can trust. I will have to see to it myself when I am more fully recovered."

"It doesn't sound like you could trust the resources you had. You're so damn careful, how could you hire a man so capable of betraying you?"

"Better to ask, how could I not? Men who will always be loyal are men who will never think for themselves. They are useful only up to a point." He took another sip of the cooling coffee. "Now, men who will expand upon your instructions, take risks, trust their own judgment, these are the truly useful men. And they are also, always, men of ambition, who will one day look out for themselves. This is natural."

"So how can you control them?"

"Limit their opportunities for mischief. Have other, less inventive men watch over them. Dismiss them, eventually. I was not careful enough with Anton. Too slow."

"You expected trouble."

"In time, my boy, I expect trouble from every man."

"Which kind of man is my *Papou*?"

"Andreas. The best. The best and the most rare, both loyal and ruthless, and more clever than the devil. Of course, even he proved untrustworthy in the end."

"Why did you tell me he was called the Snake?"

Fotis put his lips to the cup again, but there were only the muddy grounds remaining. No sense in denial, the boy knew too much. It only remained to learn just how much.

"That was unkind. Perhaps I was trying to punish him for giving that name to me."

"Maybe you didn't want to admit that it was your idea to trade the icon to the Germans."

"My idea? No, it was Müller's. A German officer. They were all thieves by the end, worse than the Italians. Müller's particular obsession was religious art, and he had somehow learned about the icon. Maybe he knew about it all along. The Nazis had a great fascination with the mystical, as I'm sure you know."

"Go on," Matthew said, impatient.

"I confess we had an open channel of communication with the Germans, even as we fought them. Müller approached me, suggested a trade. I was appalled, but we needed weapons, so I shared the idea with Andreas, my most trusted man. He convinced me we should do it. He came up with the plan. Can you imagine me burning a church, *paidemou*?"

Matthew said nothing, uncertainty clouding his expression. Fotis pressed on.

"No, it required an atheist to execute such a design. His brother died in that fire."

"That's not the same thing as his killing him."

"He let him run into a burning building, maybe even encouraged him. You know, they were only half brothers, they never liked each other."

"He grieves for that brother."

"The priest may have been collaborating with the Germans, and your grandfather was not a forgiving man. Not a man for half-measures, either."

"It doesn't wash, Fotis."

"I grow weary. Perhaps we can end the interrogation for today and let the prisoner rest."

"All your restitching now can't make truth out of the story you told me in New York," the boy insisted, real anger in his voice now. "It was an ugly story, and ten times uglier a lie."

"Not a lie, an exaggeration. A manipulation, I confess, but rooted in truth. You must see it. How could it have been my plan, to burn a church, to sell an object of such holy love and beauty to the enemy? That is not me. You do see it, I know that you do. The icon belonged back in Greece. You had the ability to influence that decision, but you needed a push. I gave it to you. In the process I oversimplified. I did wrong, but not the kind of wrong you accuse me of."

He sat back, exhausted by the volley of words. The boy was not convinced, he could see, but perhaps he had reintroduced some doubt.

"And I suppose," Matthew said slowly, "that the scheme with Father Tomas wasn't your idea either."

"Tomas is . . . a complicated fellow. But he has, in fact, represented the Greek church many times. I had no reason to doubt him."

"He didn't cough up nine hundred grand. That was your money."

"The church was to refund me."

"And you accepted that?"

"It's common practice. Their bureaucracy moves slowly; it requires committed souls to force the issue. Tomas clearly overstepped his authority, but the church would have made good on most of the cost. The rest would be my gift to them. It was a risk, but I was comfortable with it."

The words rolled smoothly off his tongue, bits of truth spread out to cover the lies. In fact, the Snake had half convinced himself, before it all fell out, that he *did* mean to give the icon to the church. Eventually, when he had derived whatever good from it there was to get. He'd had the fake theft in the back of his mind even then, but it was not until Nicholas—loyal boy—had told him about this collector del Carros that Fotis realized he must move. Del Carros was planning some action with Nicholas and Anton's former boss, a Russian named Karov. Anton and maybe Nicholas, too, were still in Karov's pocket, and if del Carros had enough money, the Russians would betray him. Fotis used their greed against them. He paid them to steal the icon from him before they did it anyway for the South American, adding a hidden twist or two of his own. Dangerous, but it had worked, all except the wound to poor Nicholas, whom Fotis had not quite trusted enough to let in on the plan. Anton and the others Karov supplied were supposed to be out of the house well before Nicholas returned from dropping Fotis at the airport, but they must have been slow, and the dear, stupid boy had obviously tried to stop them.

"That all sounds convincing," Matthew finally responded, pulling Fotis back to the present moment, "until Tomas and the icon vanish."

"Tomas was stealing funds. It's an unrelated matter." Strange that the truth should sound so suspect.

"Well, then I guess that leaves just you."

"You are forgetting Anton."

"Do you deny that you've wanted the icon for sixty years? Since my *Papou* showed it to you during the war, before his brother hid it away? An hour, a few minutes, is all it took, am I right? And you were hooked for life. You had to have it."

"Are you speaking of me," Fotis replied, the insight striking him at once, "or yourself?"

"Yes," Matthew nodded, undeterred, "I've felt it. That's how I know."

What was this? Was the boy a rival? Was this more serious than he had imagined, and could some use be made of it? But no, he mustn't think that way; this was Matthew.

"I am tired now. We should speak again tomorrow."

"What happened that night the church burned? Where were you? Why weren't you with the men Andreas sent to retrieve the weapons?"

"So he has finally spoken of it."

"Did you know Kosta would tell Stamatis where the icon was hidden, and that he would try to get it? Were you waiting for him to come out? Am I close?" Too damn close. The boy was relentless, never taking his eyes off Fotis. "Or maybe *you* sent Stamatis in yourself, and then he decided to double-cross you. Is that it?"

"You are growing disturbed, my child. You are creating fantasies. This business has become too much for you. It's time to let it go."

"Let it go?" With sudden, furious energy, Matthew swept the breakfast tray to the ground and leaned right over the other man. "Let it go? How the hell am I supposed to do that? I'm up to my neck it in, and you led me there. You owe me these answers, you old bastard."

Fotis became frightened; not of the boy, but of something, the broken fragments of truth beginning to reassemble. For a moment, he thought it was Andreas standing there above him.

"You all betrayed me," he whispered, "all of you."

"Who betrayed you? How?"

"One is going to trade it, the other sell it. Guns, money. Only I loved it for what it was, only I could keep it safe. You fool, don't you see?" He grabbed Matthew's shirt, and his face broke; the tears came. "Don't you see, *paidemou*? Only I can keep it safe. Won't you help me?"

The large silhouette of Taki appeared in the door, making them both turn, breaking the spell. Fotis shoved Matthew away weakly.

"I heard the noise," said Taki, both fierce and bashful, looking at the scattered plates and cup on the floor.

"He was just leaving," Fotis said hoarsely. "Show him out."

Matthew sized up the larger man for a moment, then relaxed. There would be no struggle. He gave Fotis a long look—was it confusion, compassion, or something else entirely?—and then started for the door.

"My boy, wait," said the Snake. The younger man stopped, Taki's hand on his shoulder, but he did not turn back to look. "Saturday night. The services at Saint Demetrios. You will accompany me? Please?"

Matthew glanced back at him briefly. "Sure," he said. "Why not?"

"We will speak further about all this."

But Matthew was already headed down the stairs.

15

The rain-dampened woods around the house produced a fine mist as the day warmed. The effect evoked a sense memory in Andreas that he could not quite grasp: a cove by the sea, a pale morning fog, and the desire to stay there upon that warm, wet ground where he'd slept—not pick up the rifle by his side, not rejoin his fellow soldiers, but simply stay there, disappear in the mist. When had it been, what had happened next? He could not say. Half a lifetime ago and more, before his brother died, before he'd met Maria, years before the son and grandson who so troubled him now had ever drawn their first breaths.

He had abandoned the heavy coat and hat and felt somehow exposed, even in the safety of his son's backyard. Alex leaned upon the fence beside him, shaky, but under his own power, and stared out at the shadowy trunks.

"You couldn't stop him from going?"

"I didn't know," Andreas answered. "He didn't tell me."

"The police will believe he's involved now."

"He is involved."

"You know what I mean. That he and Fotis dreamed it up together. Everything. The theft also."

"Let us hope they are wiser. His actions that day make no sense if he was an accomplice."

"Why haven't you gone after him?"

"He does not want my assistance."

"You're going to make him face the schemer alone?"

"He does not trust me, Aleko. You and Fotis have seen to that." The younger man looked as if he would protest, but held his peace. "I too am responsible, of course," Andreas amended.

"Did you speak to him?"

"About the icon, you mean? Yes. Too late, but we spoke."

"It should have perished in that church. It would have saved everyone a lot of pain."

"I have thought that before now."

Alex turned slightly to look at him.

"Does it trouble you? That you gave it to the Germans? Does that ever keep you awake at night?"

Andreas shook his head. He would be answering the question the rest of his life.

"I once watched Fotis cut the fingers off a German prisoner. A young man. He did not know the answers to Fotis' questions, but it didn't matter. Later, he cut the boy's throat." He moved some damp earth with his shoe. "Another time, I shot a communist guerrilla in the hills above Tsotili. I executed him. For spreading lies, and for being a communist. A good reason to kill a man, don't you think? Have you heard these things already?"

"Not from you."

"I saw an American reporter fished out of the harbor in Thessaloniki, hands tied, skull shot through, because he spoke to the wrong people. I watched dozens of men, young and old, beaten until they confessed to things they had not done. Once I even saw them take a woman—"

"Why are you telling me this now? I asked you questions for years and you never said a word, not a word."

"Why do you imagine I'm telling you?"

"I don't know. So I'll say it's all right, that I understand?"

"Your forgiveness," the old man spat bitterly, and Alex looked away. "Do you imagine your forgiveness could matter? You who have lived his whole adult life in this soft, fat country? There are things for which I would have your forgiveness, Aleko, many things, but not these. No one can pardon me, and I seek no pardon. But can you think, in the face of what I've seen, that a damned painting could mean anything? Do you really believe that is what keeps me awake?"

"All right, then. But here it is, back with us again. And it has its talons in my son now."

"I did not cause that."

"And you did not prevent it, either."

"What would you have me do?"

"Find it."

"Find it. Then what?"

"Burn it, bury it, give it back to the church, I don't care. Get it out of his life. It is a danger to him, missing or found."

"Finding it will not be so easy."

"Of course not. If it were easy, I would do it myself. It will take someone of your skills."

"Which skills? Killing, lying, planting tomatoes?"

"Hunting."

"I hunted men, not paintings."

"Hunt the men who have it."

"That is beyond what I can do. There are too many possibilities."

"Use your friends."

"You are as bad as Fotis, imagining I still have useful connections. My friends are few, and do not take instruction from an old man like me. The police investigation will be well ahead of us, and I have no influence there."

"So you'll do nothing."

"I did not say that."

Alex rocked on his heels impatiently, looking back toward the house.

"What then?"

"Matthew needs to stay clear of anyone who might believe he

knows the icon's location. He may be safer in Greece than he would be here. In any case, I have asked someone to look after him over there."

"One of these friends you don't have."

"This is a retired fellow, like myself, and Matthew may make it hard on him. But it's something."

Alex turned back to the woods again, squeezing the worn fencepost with one hand while he clenched and unclenched the other. "Thank you. Thank you for doing that."

"He's my grandchild. When he returns here, I will try to take him in hand, but it won't be easy. He is mistrustful and stubborn."

"Like his mother," Alex concurred.

"And his blood is up now. Hopefully, the matter will sort itself out swiftly."

"You don't care which way it goes? Whether Fotis is tied up in it, whether the icon ever appears again?"

"Stolen art is seldom recovered. I only want Matthew safe, and released from blame. I have business with Fotis, but I don't know that we shall ever resolve it."

"I'll kill that old bastard if I ever see him again."

"Yes, well, many have tried."

"He's like a disease. I'm surprised you didn't kill him years ago."

Andreas looked over at his son in some dismay, then nodded slowly.

"I was his creature. He looked after me long past the time he needed to. He was supposed to arrest me, you know, when the colonels were in power. Papadopoulis ordered it. Instead, he sent me out of the country."

"Very loyal of him."

"It was. And dangerous. There was no gain in it for him."

"He was banking your goodwill against the day that he was out and you were in."

"Perhaps. Perhaps that's what he told himself."

"You think he cares about you at all?"

"It's possible. Against his own will and understanding. Anyway, he's not a simple man, he keeps us all guessing."

"That's how he keeps control." Alex cleared his throat, working up his courage, Andreas could tell. "Why did you tell me those things just now? All those terrible things. It wasn't about the icon."

"I don't know. Maybe just to say them, to someone."

"Have you never spoken about them?"

"To your mother, a little. Only a little. Why should I burden someone else?"

"To ease your own burden."

"There is no ease in telling."

"How would you know?"

"These things have no meaning outside of the times and places where they happen, whatever the judges and moralists say. Much of the work, even the bad work, was necessary. No one can understand but the others who went through it, and we are too troubled to help one another. And now, too few."

"It's not my fault if I don't understand. You sent me here."

"I did not expect you to stay, to marry Irini—I thought you would come back to Greece. But it is much better that you did not. Much better."

"I probably would have become a communist, just to spite you. What are you smiling about, old man?"

"The idea of you taking any interest in politics at all."

"You don't make it sound like I've missed much."

"No, you were wise. It's a fool's game."

"It's good that you came here," the younger man said softly. "It's good that we've spoken."

Andreas breathed in the damp air, exhaled slowly. Such declarations from his son were the best he could hope for, and he tried to be grateful for them, grateful for this moment. Glancing over, he noticed that Alex no longer leaned upon the fence but merely touched it with one hand, swaying slightly, but standing on his own feet.

"You look good, Aleko," he said, against the dictates of ancient superstition. "You look strong."

Alex stared hard into the woods, searching, perplexed.

"Yes. I feel strong."

•   •   •

Sotir Plastiris lived in one of the many concrete apartment buildings that had come to deface the city of Salonika. Like most residents, he had filled his terrace with plants and bright flowers,
and the collective effect of all that living color somewhat amelio-
rated the gray, slapdash look of the buildings themselves. The
interior was furnished in the traditional bourgeois fashion: white
walls, dark wood, a hammered copperplate with Alexander's profile hanging in the living room, a figurine in gaudy peasant dress
in a glass cabinet. To the man's credit, there was no cheap icon in
the corner with a votive candle before it; this meant only that
Sotir had no wife to attend to such matters. Matthew might have
looked down upon the whole arrangement, but in truth the
apartment wasn't so different from his grandfather's in Athens,
and he felt comfortable in it.

"*Yiasou,*" said Sotir, handing Matthew a small glass of cognac,
then raising his own as he sat down in an easy chair opposite. He
turned his round face to the window, his expression slack, his
mind seemingly at rest, but his companion suspected otherwise.

"By plane, it would be difficult," Sotir said after a time, his
English precise, but heavily accented. All his grandfather's
cronies insisted on speaking English to him, Matthew mused.
Some matter of professional pride, no doubt. "They are careful at
the airports now. A ship would be easier. More private owners,
more space. You could hide a small piece within a large container.
Customs at the ports are overmatched by the volume, and also
corrupt. Mostly, they are afraid of what is being taken out, not
what is coming in."

"Piraeus, or here?"

"Piraeus would make more sense. More activity."

"It wouldn't have arrived yet."

"In a few days. It's more than a week from New York, depending on the stops."

Matthew nodded, sipped the cognac.

"Of course, it could be a plane. An isolated airstrip."

"Yes, and it may be coming by train from Paris." Plastiris
smiled with gray teeth. "It may not be coming at all. We are

speaking only about what is probable. It would be unwise to tire yourself with every possibility."

Instead of trying to duck his grandfather's watchdog, which would likely have been impossible in any case, Matthew decided to make use of him, and had to confess that he liked Plastiris' easy, Old World style. He also had to keep reminding himself that the man was one of the gang, an ex–freedom fighter, spy, assassin—who knew what?

"The main thing," Sotir continued, "is to keep your eye on Dragoumis, see what he does, who comes and goes. Which is difficult, since the house is on a hill and surrounded by trees."

"How was he able to buy that property? He was supposed to be in exile."

"Your grandfather opened the way. It was intended as a small favor. Visits, for Holy Week each year. He surely did not expect that Fotis would be allowed to build a fortress, or engage in his old activities."

"Why was he?"

"It's the way things are done. He was distrusted until the moment Andreas persuaded them to make a concession. Once they did, his file was downgraded, and they forgot all about him. Things must be black and white for bureaucrats. If he's allowed back in, well then, he must not be a real threat. Besides, he's old. It's all young men in there now. They don't remember the colonels. They don't remember anything."

"Do you have the means to watch the house? Because I sure as hell don't."

"Dragoumis is not my concern."

"No, apparently I am." He waited, but Plastiris gave nothing away. "And Fotis is *my* concern, so it all goes together."

"I am sorry, Matthew. I am retired. My nephews do favors for me sometimes, but I do not want them getting near your godfather. He is too unpredictable."

"Then I guess I'm on my own."

"Will you attempt to see him again?"

"We're supposed to meet tomorrow night. The Easter services at Saint Demetrios."

"Is he well enough?"

"If he decides he is, not much will stop him."

"Of course. And you will try to learn more of his plans."

Matthew massaged his temples with both hands.

"'Try' is the word. I pushed him pretty hard yesterday. Dredged up some stuff from the war, but nothing about what he's up to now."

"I think it unlikely he will tell you anything useful."

"I'll just have to stay nearby, look for him to make a mistake."

"You hope to catch him receiving the icon."

"That would be convenient."

"Why do you believe it will come at all? He does not live here. The chance of discovery and seizure is great. There is no logic to it."

"You're probably right, I don't know that it's coming. But the longer he stays, the more I think it must be for some reason."

"He is ill."

"Yes, but I wonder if that alone would stop him if he needed to be elsewhere. If the icon is in the possession of others in New York, even if they're in business with him, he's taking a big chance by being away for a week. They may get ideas. He's not that trusting."

"And what do you think he means to do with it?"

"Do with it?" Plastiris was younger than Andreas, Matthew figured, and measurably younger than Fotis. The story of the Holy Mother and what had happened during the war—to the extent that anyone really knew the true story—was an open secret in the Greek intelligence community, at least according to his grandfather. But it was a very old story now. Could it be that Sotir did not understand the icon's power? "I think he means to keep it."

"That's a lot of trouble, and a lot of expense he has gone to, just to keep it. Are you sure he doesn't intend to sell it?"

"He would never sell it."

"I am sorry, I know that he is your godfather, but I have always understood that Dragoumis would sell his own mother if he saw the profit in it."

"Not this. There's no price high enough. He believes in the icon's power."

"Yet he was willing to trade it once."

"I think," Matthew said carefully, recalling the shame that still attached itself to his grandfather over the incident, "had it been left to Fotis alone, he would not have gone through with it. I think he always meant to keep it."

"Yes," Plastiris said wistfully, and then again with sudden anger, "yes. It was up to your *Papou* to do the dirty work, and take the blame. You would think, with all the terrible things that happened later, the civil war and the communists, you know the history?" Matthew nodded, and Sotir plowed on. "You would think everyone would have forgotten, but it's not true. Friends, I call them friends, *ohee*, but men who know your *Papou* as well as any man could, who value his courage and intelligence, they still spit, you know, cross themselves, when this matter is mentioned. Many worked for the Germans. For profit, for safety, to sabotage the communists, that was allowed. But to turn over a religious treasure for guns was *véveelos*, how do you say, sacrilege. And Dragoumis, with his lies and his fatal interrogations, his friendship with the colonels, they never mention him. It was his idea, yes, but it was Captain Elias, and only Captain Elias, who handed over the icon. So that is it, your *Papou* will never live it down."

Better a thief than a heretic, thought Matthew. Strangely, and despite his own distrust, it pleased him to hear someone defending his grandfather. Andreas' stoicism, his refusal to explain, to defend himself, invited attack, but it wasn't right. They were both quiet for a few moments.

"How does the German fit into this?" Sotir asked.

"The German?"

"Your *Papou*'s German, the SS officer, from the war."

"Him, right. I don't think he does. Fotis just used his ghost to distract Andreas away from what he was actually doing. Even hired an actor to play him, I guess."

Plastiris shook his head and smiled grimly.

"He is a devil. So has Andreas given up on that, finally?"

"I don't know. I never knew until recently what an obsession it was for him. Nobody ever spoke about it."

"The trail was cold before you were born. He should forget it."

"I still don't have the whole story, but he says there are signs Müller is alive."

"What signs?"

"Some aliases have shown up on passports going into or out of Bulgaria, Turkey, other places. Some have appeared as the names of buyers in dubious art deals."

"He would be almost ninety."

"Well, so is Fotis."

"Ah," Plastiris smiled, "but he is Greek. Germans don't live so long."

"Some of these Nazis have."

"Yes. Sin would appear to be an excellent preserver of life. In which case, I expect to live forever." They raised their glasses in a salute and finished the cognac. "Sleep well tonight, Matthew. The Resurrection service does not finish until after midnight, and you shall need your wits about you for dealing with Dragoumis."

"Thanks for your help."

"I have done nothing. I hope that you will call upon me if you require true help."

"I'll keep it in mind."

"You have candles? For the service?"

"I'm sure there are a dozen places by my hotel to buy them."

"No, no, I have a box here. Come. This, at least, I will do for you."

16

Dark hair and eyes, olive skin, immaculately groomed and dressed in a black suit of Italian design. He would be handsome, thought Ana, if he were not so false and fawning in his manner. Across the gallery, he looked like a European movie star, but up close there was something about Emil Rosenthal that could only be described as sleazy.

"Ms. Kessler, I can't tell you what a pleasure this is. We have many friends in common, and I've been meaning to ring you for ages. It was such a wonderful surprise to get your call."

In fact, he had tried to reach her any number of ways, invitations to openings, messages passed through supposed mutual friends. Ana had acquired a reputation—unearned, she felt—for being a free spender. However, she bought contemporary work for the most part, and while Rosenthal had once dealt in modern, he had since inherited his father's gallery, specializing in early European: medieval and Renaissance art and artifacts. It was her grandfather's collection he was after, she was quite sure.

"Let me show you around. I know this stuff isn't your first love, but it might intrigue you."

The dark walls and soft lighting were comforting somehow, more like a museum than a gallery. There was little on display, so the tour was short. They looked at a fourteenth-century Spanish illuminated prayer book, moved on to a sixteenth-century Dutch portrait of a florid merchant, and finally moved to an older wooden sculpture of St. George on horseback, cracked, paint fading, but still glorious to behold with his golden armor and spear held high.

"From Syria," said Rosenthal. "I already have two buyers lined up."

"Two? How will they divide it? One gets the horse and the other the saint?"

The dealer laughed too loudly.

"No, no, I think that one will get both, certainly. Just a little healthy competition. Medieval art is still terribly undervalued. Sometimes we have to play little games. I have a bad habit of overpaying, so I have to make it up somehow. And of course, when I sell on commission, I owe it to my client to get the best price. We do very well for our clients here."

"I have no doubt you do."

"A little doubt, certainly. Our success in recent years has led to some unfortunate slanders. Which, in turn, have led to these absurd legal issues."

"I did read about an investigation."

"How could you not, it having been so well publicized? A nuisance only, I assure you. They have discovered nothing improper, and *will* discover nothing improper."

Which was not the same thing as saying that there was nothing to discover.

"Anyway," she said, "you're in good company."

A nervous smile appeared. "Excuse me?"

"Christie's, Sotheby's."

"Ah, well," he mumbled, "unlike many, I have no quarrel with the auction houses, but that is hardly the company I keep."

"And those investigations are equally foolish, don't you think? I mean, price-fixing is as old as time. What they really ought to investigate in the sale of looted art."

He was nodding furiously into the long pause that opened, obviously speechless at the idea of *her* raising the subject of stolen paintings. Yet he recovered swiftly.

"That, too, is as old as time, I fear. And if you head down that road too far you must drag in our friends at the museums, and that would be just too great an embarrassment for everyone. My God, MOMA would be renting empty wall space by the mile if they had to hand over every work of dubious provenance. Keith Haring would get a whole wing to himself."

They both laughed wickedly at the thought. Then the dealer fixed Ana with his brown, liquid gaze, as a lover would.

"Truly, I'd welcome the opportunity to eliminate all doubt about what we could do for you."

She maintained the eye contact.

"Your offer for my grandfather's icon was most generous."

"Alas, not generous enough, it appears."

"No, it wasn't that. I was attempting to do the right thing. Which, like most such attempts, went terribly wrong."

He shook his head in sympathy. Two scarred veterans of the art wars, ready to become soul mates. She could sense him moving in for the kill.

"Maybe we should talk in my office."

Ana looked about the room. There was only a pretty young intern, busily labeling boxes and answering the telephone.

"If you would be more comfortable."

"I think we both would."

The office was brighter than the other rooms, and furnished with plush beige chairs. Rosenthal closed the door and took a seat beside Ana, rather than behind the huge, empty desk.

"I was terribly sorry to hear about the theft," he said at once. "I hope you were paid."

"Yes. But the point was to return the work to the Greek church, so it's very upsetting."

"Of course, of course. And now there is some question of whether that fellow, the Greek philanthropist, was even working with the church, I understand."

How much did he know? About Matthew too? She had come

here not to answer his questions but to get answers of her own.

"There was a representative of the church involved. I met him. Unfortunately he's gone missing since the theft."

"And the businessman, Dragoumis, he is missing too, yes?"

"Not missing. Ill, I believe. Anyway, I'm leaving all that to the police."

He leaned back, crossing one leg over the other.

"Best thing to do. As you say, you were paid, so it's not really your affair anymore."

"Actually, it's not quite that simple. I trust we can speak in absolute confidence."

The sudden expression of sincerity that transformed his face nearly made her laugh, or applaud, but she contained the impulse. She thought for a moment that he would take her hand, but he settled for touching her knee.

"Your trust is well founded. Without extreme discretion, I would be out of business in a week."

"I accepted a good deal less for the icon than what you offered. I did so because I felt I was doing a good thing, the right thing, and I didn't want to put the squeeze on the church. Now . . ."

"You feel screwed."

"Precisely."

That sympathetic shake of the head again.

"May I say something? Never mind, I will. The matter was dreadfully mishandled. I don't blame you. Why should you not follow your lawyer's advice? And I'm sure he had your best interests at heart, but Mr. Wallace is not a young man anymore, and it's a new game out there in the art world. It's not a gentleman's game, I'm sorry to say. It takes contacts, savvy, and a certain fierceness. You needed an experienced dealer involved in that sale."

"That seems apparent now."

"I don't mean to scold. I would have offered my own services, but I was approached by a collector to act as buyer before I even knew the work was on the market."

"Yes, about that." Things were going so well that she decided to press her luck. "I'd like to know who that collector was. I don't suppose you could tell me. It would put me in your debt."

Rosenthal's face went blank, but Ana could feel the impulse to be agreeable, to purchase her loyalty, struggling mightily with his natural inclination toward suspicion. A moment later he chuckled nervously.

"Ms. Kessler, you would make a lie of my claim to discretion. And I don't see what good it would do you now, with the sale made."

"Please call me Ana."

"Gladly. And you must call me Emil."

"Emil. There are several issues here. The sale of the icon was made under certain conditions, which appear to have been violated. If it can be recovered, I would have a very good claim to it."

"I see."

"In which case I would need a new buyer. I also have a number of other medieval pieces which might be of interest to your collector."

"Ah, but those aren't reasons to contact the man directly. In fact, for your own sake, I would discourage it. Such transactions really do require an experienced go-between. For my part, it would be foolish to provide information which might remove me from the deal."

"There would be no question of that. We can make it a condition of your putting me in contact that you would handle any business between us."

"Alas, my first obligation is to the buyer. He may feel that I have compromised myself by associating too closely with you."

"Then you can represent my side of it. But you'll need to cooperate with Wallace."

"I do not think that Mr. Wallace would agree to such an arrangement."

"He'll do what I tell him to," Ana said. "My lawyers serve me, Emil, not vice versa."

Rosenthal smiled and clapped his hands together.

"Well said. I confess you do intrigue me. But look, I have to be honest, I don't think the man was interested in anything but the icon. And you and I both know the chances of it being recovered."

He was being far more careful than she had expected. Something more was required.

"OK. The reason I need direct access is a personal one. I have to ask this man some questions. I have reason to believe that he may have information about my grandfather. I can't say more than that." There, she'd thrown that little secret on the table, at last.

"Now I understand," answered the dealer, gently. "It seems like the best thing would be for me to contact him and see if he is willing to speak to you. How does that sound?"

"Reasonable. Except that if he refuses, then I'm nowhere. Whereas if I could speak to him directly, I think I could persuade him to open up."

"If anyone could make a man do more than he intended, I'm sure it's you, Ana."

She would need a shower when she got home. Meanwhile, she had come this far.

"You can't know what all this means to me, Emil, and I won't try to explain. So let me be more concrete. I'm going to have more work to sell to somebody, sometime. Maybe a lot of it. You've made an eloquent case for needing a dealer, and early European is your thing. I'm not going to make any promises . . ."

"Please don't. Before you parade more riches across my greedy vision, let me make a confession. The information I have for this man is very thin. Just a name and a voice-mail number. Mostly, he contacts me. I'm not even sure if the name is real."

Ana tried not to reveal her disappointment.

"Well, then. There can be no breach of trust in your giving me that information. If he doesn't want to speak to me, he simply won't call back. Either way, I'll remain grateful to you."

Rosenthal relaxed. Then went around the desk and took a card from the center drawer.

"I'm glad you see things that way. I happen to agree. Mr. del Carros has taken his own precautions, so I needn't worry too much about protecting him. And perhaps he will be pleased to hear from you. You have a pen?"

She took down the information on a small pad she kept in her purse, but there was a sudden disquiet in her mind. Del Carros. Where did she know the name from? Had her grandfather mentioned him?

"Thank you for this. I have to ask one more thing, at the risk of being rude."

"Let us not stand on ceremony, Ana. We're friends now."

"That was a hell of a lot of money your Mr. del Carros was willing to spend. The icon is rare, but there isn't anyone who would assess it at anything near a million and a half dollars."

"I did not inquire into the gentleman's motives. I did inform him that the offer was well above market value, but he pressed me to proceed. Religious art can have a strange effect on people. There are those who would not part with it for any price, those who would pay any price to have it. I believe he would have gone higher still."

"But look, you've got a name and a phone number. How do you know this guy is on the level? How do you know he won't vanish and embarrass you when it's time to pay up?"

Rosenthal leaned back and smiled once more.

"I can assure you that Mr. del Carros is absolutely trustworthy. I give you my personal guarantee that he will meet his obligations. You see, he and I have done business before."

"Coffee? Water? We'll have brandy afterward, to celebrate."

"Take the cloth off, let's see it."

"Patience, my friend. We still have business to discuss."

The thick, steel-haired Russian smiled pleasantly, but the old man calling himself del Carros was not in a patient mood. Were he dealing with gentlemen, he would make a greater effort at civility, but these thugs with artistic pretensions disgusted him. Still, they had what he wanted, and he must not seem overeager. They must be made to believe that he would walk away if the conditions were not acceptable.

"Business has already been discussed, Mr. Karov. That's the only reason I am sitting here."

"Circumstances have changed since we talked. There have been complications. Surely you heard that one of my men was shot."

"I understood him to be one of Dragoumis' men, and one of your own people shot him."

"Dragoumis has no men. Cooks and managers. I supply him with his bodyguards. Unfortunately, this one returned before my boys were out of the house, and there was an accident."

"Bad planning, I would say."

Karov shrugged.

"Things happen. Anyway, it's an extra expense."

In truth, del Carros had expected something like this. There was an additional hundred thousand above the agreed price in the case on his lap. Cash. The idiot had demanded cash, as if he had learned thievery from the cinema. As if he were still rooting around in the shattered landscape of Mother Russia, stealing cars and kidnapping bureaucrats. Here was his big payday, and the greedy pig would try to wring every penny he could from the exchange, maybe even call off the deal and make del Carros come crawling back. That must be avoided, but it didn't mean he intended to surrender easily.

"The expense is due to your own mistake."

"The price is too low," Karov insisted, losing his smile. No sparring, no shift in reasoning. Advance one argument until it failed, then move to another. Open, simple, crude. The Russian style.

"Then why did you agree to it?"

"Because I didn't know that you had offered three times as much to the Kessler woman."

Del Carros sighed and looked to his slouched blond companion. Jan Van Meer was silent. In contrast to Karov's two fidgety associates, del Carros' supposed artistic consultant—slender, bespectacled, utterly innocuous—seemed painfully at ease, bored even. The old collector appreciated Jan's performance but wondered now if a more obvious show of strength wouldn't have been a wiser decision.

"A million five," Karov continued. "That was the price. I am sorry to learn that your opinion of its worth has fallen so far since then."

This is what came of dealing with men like Rosenthal.

"That would have been a legal purchase, Mr. Karov. Without complications. Now, I too may be beset with the sort of expenses you have incurred. There are those who will pursue this work relentlessly. I will have to take precautionary measures, possibly expensive."

Van Meer had already informed him that removing Dragoumis would cost 250,000 euros. A bargain, he assured del Carros, because they were friends.

"We discussed this problem before, you will remember," said Karov. "You will be happy to know that I have already taken measures myself."

Indeed, this was nearly the last thing del Carros wanted to hear.

"When?"

Karov consulted the huge silver Rolex on his beefy wrist. "Now, more or less."

"While he is still in Greece?"

"Much better in Greece," the Russian insisted. "He has a hundred enemies there. It will seem the most natural thing in the world." Which was true, but if they bungled it, and Dragoumis went underground . . . Nothing to be done about it now. The main thing was the icon.

"So," Karov picked up again, "you can simply add whatever sum you had set aside for that business onto the price previously discussed. I ask you, is this not reasonable? After the trouble I have taken on your behalf?"

"It would be rash to assume success before hearing from your people in Greece. He has survived several such attempts in the past. Indeed, I think the whole undertaking was rash. You were to leave that part to me."

"You were unclear on whether you intended to act or not."

"I was being considerate." You ass. "The less you knew, the better."

"I am not such a subtle man," Karov sneered. "I like to be certain of important matters. The Greek is old, but he is still a viper. He knows by now that I crossed him. He will hurt me if he can. I did not hesitate to protect myself, and I offer no apology."

"Very well." Del Carros cleared his dry throat, sorry now that he had refused the water offered him, but he did not trust Russian hospitality. "Let us conclude this."

"Excellent. I despise drawn-out negotiations. So, in light of the losses I have suffered, and the efforts taken for our mutual protection, the price is now one million dollars."

Which meant he would take less.

"Jan, what do you think?"

Van Meer sat up abruptly, like a student caught daydreaming.

"I don't pretend to understand this action you are discussing," he mumbled in his vague Dutch accent, playing the willfully ignorant art expert to perfection, "but it's quite clear, Mr. Karov, that you have undertaken it for your own purposes, and against my client's wishes. There can be no reason to expect an increase in the price on these grounds. Half a million U.S. dollars was the figure agreed upon, and I must say it is generous."

The Russian looked as if he would snap the little Dutchman in half.

"I tell you it's not enough."

"More than enough," Van Meer prodded. "Too much."

"Listen to me," del Carros said, in a soft voice that quieted the room. "You need to understand, Mr. Karov, that market value is not driving this sale. Personal reasons, which are not transferable, support my interest. If I fail to purchase this work, you will have to sell it at a fraction of the price we are discussing. Given your means of acquiring it, you may not be able to sell it at all."

"My means of acquiring it! Listen to you. You are the cause of my acquiring it. I stole it for you; you cannot back out of this arrangement."

"You stole it at Dragoumis' instruction."

"And crossed him to sell it to you. We have a deal."

"Which you are attempting to breach by raising the price. I understand, you are a businessman. Very well. In this briefcase there is exactly six hundred thousand dollars. One hundred thousand more than the agreed price. Jan will object, but I am willing to go this far to meet your concerns. This far and no further. If I leave this room without the icon you will not see me again. My final word, Mr. Karov."

The Russian looked as if he would speak several times, but quieted himself, his black leather coat creaking about him as he shifted restlessly in his chair. Calculating. No doubt he felt he could simply take the case and keep the icon. Two bodies to dispose of, no big deal. Del Carros knew well that if he tried it there would be three bodies, and they would be the Russians, but Karov did not comprehend how dangerous Van Meer was. However, del Carros had previously hinted at future transactions, a new market in South America, drugs, emeralds, Incan artifacts. All smoke, but that was another thing Karov didn't know, and he clearly preferred the role of businessman to that of thug. At last his big, watery eyes focused on the briefcase and a thin smile returned.

"Who will say that Vasili Karov is not a reasonable man? I accept your offer. You," he snapped at Van Meer, "take a lesson from your employer. This is how reasonable men do business. Compromise. Anton, get the brandy."

"The icon," Jan interrupted, enjoying his role as spoiler. Was he disappointed that the deal was working itself out, that he would not be allowed to use his special talents? Surely he was too smart for that. "We have not seen the icon."

"Anton." Karov waved his arm and the blackbeard changed direction midway to the liquor cabinet, went to the easel, and unceremoniously dragged off the drop cloth.

Gold leaf, faded yet still brilliant. The graceful, oval curve of the Virgin's half-turned head. Large, expressive eyes, underlined with dark patches, a downturned mouth. A sad Mary. The deep blue of her robes was almost black, tinged green here and there by age or damage. The fingers were unnaturally long, pressed together in prayer, yet also pointing outside the frame to where the inevitable accompanying Christ would have hung. The traditional *Hagiasoritissa*. Skilled work, not masterful perhaps, but painted with feeling. And in remarkably good condition. The room was silent for many moments.

"Beautiful," breathed Karov.

"Yes," del Carros agreed, disappointment crushing the anger out of his voice. "It's the wrong work."

The Russian did not appear to understand him at first.

"What are you talking about?"

"You must call off the action on Dragoumis."

"What the hell are you talking about?"

"*Look* at it," del Carros insisted, but that was pointless, like asking a dog to look at it. An icon was an icon to this fool. The Greek had chosen his mark well. "It's all wrong. The style is wrong. It's late work, fifteenth or sixteenth century, probably Russian. The icon we're seeking is eighth century or older, and damaged. I specified that it was damaged."

"You prefer it to be damaged?"

It was intolerable. He would kill the idiot, he would strangle the life out of that fat, baffled face.

"I prefer it to be the right one, the only one I am looking for. This is not it."

"This was the one on his easel," Anton now spoke. "He was showing it to his godson the day before. It was right where he told me to find it."

"Then he switched it for another. Did you ever actually see it before you took it?"

"No. It stayed locked in his study."

"Why would he switch it?" Karov demanded.

"Because he knew you would betray him," del Carros replied, the matter becoming clear. Dragoumis knew that stealing the icon from himself would not be sufficient. The Russians would know he had it, and others would guess, so he needed a second feint. Give the Russians the wrong painting to steal. If Karov keeps the replacement, he has no idea what he possesses. If he sells it, the buyer will probably not have seen the original, and del Carros knew that most people—even collectors—could not easily place the age and origin of Orthodox icons. Either way, the replacement vanishes, and who can say that it was not the original? It was a clever plan, if flawed, one flaw being that the Greek had not anticipated a buyer who knew the real work very well. Still, he had bought himself time, and who knew where the icon was now? "You must call off the action."

"Why? Goddamn that Greek to hell, I'll hang him by his balls."

"If you kill him before we determine the location of the real icon, we may never find it."

"What do I care about that? Shit on your icon. If you are telling the truth, I want the bastard dead. Besides, it's too late."

The old man felt his eighty-six years like a weight on his shoulders, pressing down upon him. He had been young and strong when this chase began, but it had dragged on far too long, and he was tired. With all his other successes, why did he continue with this losing struggle? Because his spirit knew nothing else at this point. Once possessed, the icon lived within him, and he felt as though a part of his body were missing. More than fifty years now. There was really no choice. The tiredness was good, he decided. It hid his desperation.

"What must I do to convince you?"

Karov gazed at him carefully, trying to determine if this was a threat or opportunity. Van Meer was paying close attention also. They were beyond the possibilities they had mapped before the meeting, into tangled, dangerous territory. The Dutchman was freshly energized.

"You could give me that briefcase," the Russian answered after a long pause. Jan had a good laugh at that.

"I think not," del Carros responded.

"You owe me something for my trouble, damn it."

"I owe you nothing. Dragoumis was toying with you. You were never in a position to deliver what I wanted, but I am willing to make some effort to maintain our cooperation."

"What do you suggest?"

The Russian was an ass, but he would have to be given something or this would end badly. And he must be persuaded to call off the action.

"This isn't the icon I wanted," the old man mused, "but it is good work, and I am feeling generous. I'll give you a hundred thousand for it."

"That doesn't even cover my expenses."

"And fifty more when I know that Dragoumis is safe. A hundred more if you can deliver him to me, alive."

Karov's agitation had settled somewhat. He kept eye contact with del Carros as he slipped a bulky international cell phone from his jacket.

"If I can take him alive, we'll talk then about what he's worth. Let's see your money."

"Make the call. Time is precious."

17

Matthew had been awake most of the night, and the few hours of sleep he'd stolen before dawn were troubled. Shreds of dreams still floated past his mind's eye: a darkened city, that other New York of his sleep, full of narrow, poorly lit streets, twisting unexpectedly, a dangerous encounter around every corner. He knew the place, had visited its docks, parks, and alleys across a hundred nights, always pursued, always seeking the safe corridor, the straight way home. This night he had been the pursuer, chasing the Holy Mother down dark passages, around treacherous corners, without hesitation or fear, fearing only the loss of it. Logic dictated that someone carried the icon, but he saw just the image itself, a face more like the Mona Lisa than a Greek saint, smiling at his desperation as it vanished through doorways, up staircases, into shadow. In the end, the black eyes alone bore through the total darkness around him, close enough to touch, but he could not grasp her, never would.

Half a day later, an unsettled feeling still enveloped him. He wandered through the great church of Saint Demetrios like a ghost, cut off from the other souls around him, mourning the

Mother while they mourned the Son and looked forward to his resurrection. Huge chandeliers illuminated the place. The gold base painting of the rear wall and domed ceiling of the sanctuary, richly spotted with saints and angels, dazzled the eye, contrasting with the cool gray-white stone and marble of the interior colonnades. Matthew visited Ephthimious' chapel, with its red-haloed saints and ghostly, hooded figures. Time had not been kind to the frescoes, but their washed-out quality lent an air of mystery that appealed to him at the moment. He lingered, the cold leaching out sleepiness, forcing his blood and muscle to motion, his mind to consciousness. He had an hour or so before Fotis was to meet him, but he intended to be on watch before that. Who knew what surprises the old man had in mind tonight?

A service—the latest in an endless procession this Holy Week—had begun in the main body of the church, so Matthew took the side aisles around to the saint's tomb, a tomb only in name. The body was supposed to have been stolen by the Crusaders. Something had been returned from Italy twenty years before and now resided in a silver reliquary in the nave. The so-called tomb was merely an empty marble coffin with an icon placed on top. He didn't know why he always came here, except that the room was peaceful and contemplative. The fact that it was older than the earliest Christian construction, part of the Roman baths, and that the saint's remains had rested here for 900 years gave the chamber a gravity missing from the rest of the church, reconstructed in the 1920s after a great fire. Matthew didn't think that Demetrios would like his new digs; surely he would prefer to be back in this quiet place.

He crouched down next to the marble box, unwilling to place his knees on the cold floor, to assume the position of supplication. Prayer, for him, could never be so intentional or so self-surrendering. He closed his eyes and remembered the basilica from a child's perspective, remembered the seeming vastness of it, and the grand old man, his *Papou*, tall as a god, showing him everything. The tale of each saint was recounted with a skeptical smile. Andreas had no use for religion, but he wanted Matthew to understand the culture from which he sprang, and his admiration for and explanation of the extraordinary, painstaking work of inserting thousands of tesserae to create a mosaic, of how certain pigments in the frescoes were achieved, even of the warped perspective necessary to make a curved dome painting look natural, was mesmerizing for a child. It would take years for Matthew to understand half of what he'd been told, but the seed was planted in early youth, and he had never escaped the intense fascination of this art.

Yet it was not the same. His memory of standing before these images twenty years earlier carried more emotional power than actually standing before them now. Something had changed within him. Why, and when? It could have been his father's illness; so much had gone astray since then, his interest in his work, his relationship with Robin, his faith in the old men who had taught him so much. But blaming the illness seemed a poor excuse, and not even convincing, because two strong passions had come upon him in the meantime: Ana, and the damn icon. Crouching in the cold, Matthew felt it more likely that those new passions had blotted out the old, had become everything to him, and this sickness of the soul came from being separated from both. He did not know where the icon was; he could not go back to Ana without finding it. Yet the odds of that were very remote. Opening his eyes to make sure he was alone, Matthew began to quietly recite some words of Greek, a prayer perhaps, to the saint, the Son, the Mother, whoever was on duty at the moment. Let the icon be found. Let it be returned to its rightful place, wherever that was. Let troubled spirits, including his own, be at rest. The Greek served him as he imagined Latin did others, giving the words mystery and power, and creating a sense of ritual that removed the individual from the process. Using such words, one stepped into the ever-running river of the holy, and was submerged.

After some minutes he rose, went up the worn marble steps through heavy red draperies to the narthex and out into the cool dusk. The church's facade stood in shadow, but sunset touched the square tower with orange light, bringing out the red of the roof tiles and making the tall cross glow. The chanting of the priest and *psáltees* within was audible. The congregants were few in number so far, exhausted no doubt from the emotional exertions of the last two nights. On Thursday, the plaster Christ nailed to the cross. On Friday, taken down, draped in cloth, and carried about the church three times under a hail of carnations and the weeping of the old women. Tonight, they would stagger in by twos and threes until midnight, when a vast horde would be gathered on the broad plaza before the church. *Come, receive the light,* and candles would ignite in every hand. *Christos Anesti,* the priest would call, *Christ is risen,* and the crowd would echo it back. Stirring stuff. The mass hysteria of the Easter service was not Matthew's preferred time of worship, but when participating it was easy to get sucked in, to feel one with the blind, passionate spiritual community. Reason was chased off for a few hours; faith and brotherhood ruled.

Of course, the congregants then rushed home or to some restaurant to gorge themselves. But that was natural enough as well: celebrating after grief; food and drink as physical symbols of rebirth. Back in New York, he rarely partook of the whole ritual, but tonight Matthew wished he could feel part of it, wished that some table of food and candlelight and friends awaited him, wanted it in a way that only one certain of his alienation from the human tribe could want such a thing. He jammed his hands into his jacket pockets and patrolled the church doors like a sentry, ready to bring down a curse on his whole clan, damning their treachery and arrogance, their rationalism and cold, analytical worldview. Damning himself for being a product of his lineage and not his own man, not the engaged, spontaneous, alive crea-ture he wished to be. The curse died on his tongue. Actions, not words, were required. He needed to remember why he was here.

The figure in the long coat with the quick, confident stride did not fit naturally with this crowd, Matthew noticed, well before the man reached him. Graying hair, a square, strong face, and a smile of the kind normally reserved for an old friend.

"Matthew. You are Matthew, yes?"

"Who are you?"

"Your godfather sent me." The man held out his hand. "You can call me Risto."

"Sent you to do what?"

He did not take the offered hand, and Risto withdrew it slowly, his smile wavering.

"To take you back to his house. He is too ill for the ceremony, but he very much wants your company tonight."

"Why didn't he call me?"

"He had hoped until the last moment to attend, but it has proved too much. You cannot be surprised at that if you have seen him recently."

"What's your connection?"

"Just a friend."

"I see. Why don't we call Fotis and discuss this?"

"He may not be well enough to do so."

"He's too ill to speak on the telephone?"

"We can try, of course." Risto turned and looked out across the plaza with some consternation, and Matthew followed his gaze. Then the man's strong arm was around Matthew's shoulder and something dug hard into his ribs. "No trouble, please. The car is just this way."

"What the fuck," Matthew spat in English.

"Walk. You are quite safe, but you must come along."

In fact they were already moving, Risto's power propelling both of them toward the broad staircase down to the street. Matthew fell into step so as not to tumble down the stairs and breathed deeply to calm himself. Things were moving too fast once more. He needed to think clearly and act quickly, and he must by no means allow himself to be put into a car. As Risto looked up and down the avenue, Matthew dared a glance downward, and realized that it was a fair-sized candle being stuck into his rib cage.

They reached the sidewalk and moved toward the curb, where a small blue compact sat idling, a man at the wheel. Matthew pretended to stumble, and as he was pulled upright again, drove his elbow backward at Risto's solar plexus. The hard resistance of bone on bone told him he had missed the target, but the bigger man grunted and his grip relaxed briefly.

Matthew broke free and wheeled about, swinging wildly, his

fist catching the side of Risto's head. He turned to move away, figures scattering on the sidewalk before him, but felt a hand on his jacket collar, then a fierce blow to his lower back, stunning his spine and kidneys. He began to slide to his knees, but in a moment Risto had him firmly around the shoulders again, forcing him painfully into the car's backseat.

Face mashed against vinyl, Matthew could make no sense of the shouting that followed, nor of Risto's sudden weight on top of him, driving the air from his lungs. A new voice gave sharp, clipped commands, the car lurched into motion. Then there was silence, except for some heavy breathing. As the weight shifted off him, Matthew squirmed up into a sitting position, flushed and disoriented, blood roaring in his ears. Risto was pushed up against him, leaning forward with his head on the back of the driver's seat. Sotir Plastiris sat on the other side of him with a small pistol against Risto's right temple. In front, a younger man in the passenger seat had a larger pistol up against the driver's head, and the car raced and wove through the thin traffic on the avenue.

"Matthew, you are well?" Sotir asked with that odd mix of genuine concern and fierce insistence so peculiar to the native Greek.

"Yes." His tight throat barely released the word, and he did not trust himself to say more without his voice cracking.

"Here," Sotir said to the front seat, and his companion communicated a left turn to the driver, who obeyed. The car bottomed out on a narrow, cobbled lane and immediately reduced speed. They were in a rabbit's warren of small streets and after several turns stopped dead in a short alley. The silence was even more intense with the engine off. Matthew's senses, emerging from a thick gauze of fear, now seemed suddenly sharp, almost unbearable. He was aware of each man's scent, every movement in the car, throats clearing, mouths exhaling short breaths. The driver was young and very frightened, sweat staining his collar. The passenger with the large pistol was young also, slightly bored-looking, with curly black hair and handsome features not unlike Sotir's. One of the nephews, presumably, and they had been watching Matthew without his knowing it, probably the entire day. Andreas' hand was in this, but Matthew could not bring himself to be offended.

Sotir reached inside Risto's coat and after some fumbling around removed a small pistol, placing it inside his own jacket.

"Who?" he asked quietly. When there was no answer after several seconds, he struck Risto sharply on the head with his pistol, drawing blood, and Matthew reflexively looked away. "Who?" Plastiris demanded a second time.

"Livanos," Risto said.

"Taki Livanos?" Matthew asked, suddenly finding his voice.

"Yes."

"Fotis' nephew," he explained to Sotir, who nodded.

"And what do you want with the boy here?"

"Just to bring him to the house," Risto answered.

"You need a gun for that?"

"I always carry it."

"You need to hit him and push him just to bring him to the house?"

"They said he would be suspicious, but I must get him there anyway."

"Why?"

"How the hell should I know?"

Sotir struck him again, and Matthew bit down on his protest.

"Where is Livanos?"

"Gone. Into the mountains, I think, with the old man."

"So what happens at the house?"

"We keep him there for a day or two. I don't know why, they didn't tell me." Risto braced for another blow.

"That's all?" Matthew asked. "And then you just let me go?"

"Yes," Risto insisted, and Matthew believed him. Fotis merely wanted enough time to disappear. Evidently Sotir believed it too, because he did not strike the man again.

"The boy is protected. Don't come near him. Tell Livanos."

"I don't intend to speak to that bastard again," Risto sighed.

Matthew, Sotir, and his nephew got out of the car slowly and carefully, but the bewildered occupants clearly intended no more trouble. The nephew snapped open a ridiculously large knife and methodically punctured a tire, just to be on the safe side. Then the three of them made their way through the narrow lanes to Plastiris' own vehicle. Matthew's legs struggled to hold him up. Two knuckles were swollen on his right hand, and his lower back ached badly. The taste of fear would be in his mouth for days, yet he felt grateful to have escaped with so little harm, and stupid for not realizing how far above his abilities this game was being played. The nephew smiled at him with condescending sympathy.

"That was good, pretending to fall. But next time, hit him in the balls, not the chest."

"I'll remember that."

"We'll call your grandfather now," Sotir said. "He will be worried."

"Thank you. For looking after me like that."

Plastiris waved the comment off.

"We were slow, but it is good we were there. Do you know where your godfather is?"

"No. Not at the moment, anyway. But I have a fair guess where he's going."

On the switchback road that climbed to Veria, Fotis was sure they were being followed. Taki laughed. This isn't America, Uncle, there is only one road. Which was true, more or less; only one major road—narrow and winding—penetrated the mountainous heart of Macedonia. Yet something about the white Peugeot troubled the old man, the half-obscured license plate, the way it kept a perfect distance, even when Fotis made Taki slow down. Greeks did not drive so carefully.

He had Taki pull the black Mercury over at his favorite chapel, first making sure that two other cars were parked by the food stand across the long bend of road, beyond which the ground fell away to a landscape of beige hills spotted with dark vegetation. Hot and barren as Lebanon; not like the green hills of Epiros. From its little rise, creamy white in the dying sun, the chapel looked out over everything, a rocky cliff rising steeply behind it. The Peugeot stopped also. The driver bought a stick of *souvlaki* and a beer for himself, but nothing for the older man with him. The driver ate slowly, wandering back and forth from the cliff edge to the car, never once looking in Fotis' direction, yet tarrying.

The Snake seemed not to be looking either, but saw all in his usual sidelong fashion. He spent a full ten minutes examining the small church, shut up at the moment, standing inside the tiny vestibule, out of the sun, while Taki paced like a panther and checked his watch. The road could be dangerous after dark, but Fotis had his mind on other dangers. At length, the young driver got back into the white car and sped quickly out of sight. Perhaps a coincidence after all, Fotis thought, but he made Taki wait another ten minutes before proceeding.

In the backseat, feet set widely to brace himself against the endless turns, Fotis reviewed his documents. Three passports, Greek, Turkish, American. He had not traveled under a false passport in many years and probably did not need to now. He could have been out of the country hours ago on a commercial flight from Athens or Salonika, instead of getting carsick in these wretched hills. Yet there was too great a chance of being picked up by impatient American investigators in New York, or by their counterparts here. The fake ID might get him through, but his face was on file with every security bureau on both sides of the water, and if he was caught with a bad passport, his troubles would increase immeasurably. The Greeks especially would welcome a reason to prosecute him. Fotis sighed, then shook his head at the image of such an unlikely security net waiting to catch this tired old thief. The Greeks were too sloppy, and the Americans far too preoccupied with larger threats. Nevertheless, his caution had saved him more than once, and he did not see abandoning it this late in life.

The sun was low, and he regretted the delay, which would force Taki to navigate the winding road into the Kozani valley in twilight. Fotis would take a small plane from the airstrip outside Kozani, to Montenegro, or direct to Brindisi in Italy, whichever Taki's friend Captain Herakles thought best. Then a commercial flight from Rome, on some unlikely airline, under the guise of a Turkish businessman. That should do the trick. It was about getting to Rome. He would have to trust the brave Captain Herakles, who probably had never been more than a sergeant. Herakles, how sweet. These poor fellows, in their forties or fifties now, with their secret codes and brotherhoods and their heroic *noms de guerre,* they longed for the old days. The days when their brigandage might have had a patriotic justification, fighting Turkish overlords or the German occupation or even the communists. Instead they had the black market, smuggling goods and people, bribing officials, stockpiling weapons—for what? The closest to war they had come was Cyprus, when the idiot colonels had utterly failed to act. How Fotis could have fallen in with that group he no longer understood, and it had cost him his homeland. Andreas had been wiser than he on that matter.

He was drawn out of his reverie by the Mercury's steady acceleration, dangerous in these turns, and he noted Taki's tense hands on the wheel, his eyes shifting constantly to the rearview mirror.

"What?" Fotis demanded, twisting about in his seat.

"Motorcycle. Coming up quick."

The old man heard the engine now—a deep, shifting growl—and just caught sight of a vehicle disappearing into the car's blind spot. Then the road uncurled into a rare straightaway and they were suddenly *there,* right outside Fotis' window, two helmeted figures pressed together on a large motorbike, the one in back pointing something.

The doors of the Mercury were steel-plated, thanks to Taki's diligence. Bulletproof glass was harder to come by, and tinted glass only drew attention, so they were quite exposed. Instinct said to dive away from the window, but even across the seat he could be seen. Instead, Fotis moved the opposite way, sliding half into the footwell and pressing himself against the door, fedora knocked astray.

Both rear windows exploded together, the shot passing straight through, and the car lurched wildly as Taki ducked behind the wheel. A rain of glass fell on Fotis' hat and coat. Large caliber, .45 maybe. Motorcycle. Was it *November 17,* a political assassination? It fit their style precisely, but they were a long way from Athens.

The motorcycle roared ahead to avoid getting squeezed in a turn, and Fotis could see no more, but imagined the passenger twisting about on the seat, trying to get off another shot. He heard Taki fumbling with the glove box, swearing under his breath. Wind whipped through the car. Fotis was calm. Later, if he lived, he would be frightened, but he was calm now.

"Taki," he tried to shout, his lungs compressed by his contorted position. "Pull over, make them come back at us." His nephew would have a clear shot from a stationary position then, and the steel door for cover. If the idiot could get the damn glove box open.

The wind swept his words away, and Taki accelerated. Trying to run them down, which would not work. Fotis struggled to get back up in the seat, while the muffled ring of shots sounded ahead of them. One, two, three. There was the punching crack of safety glass as the windshield turned white, and Taki's head snapped back, spraying the roof with blood.

Fotis grabbed the headrest before him as the car decelerated rapidly, and used the sudden shift in momentum to launch himself between the front seats. He could see nothing, but pulled the wheel right, away from the hundred-foot drop to boulders and the rusted remains of carelessly piloted vehicles, and toward the upward slope of the hill. The lesser of two evils. A slight uphill grade slowed the car's motion further before it left the road, banging hard into a shallow culvert and coming up immediately against the slope. Loose dirt and rocks rattled down over the hood and roof. The engine died.

Fotis found himself looking up at the blood-spattered roof, his torso crammed beneath the dashboard, feet sprawled across the passenger seat, with no memory of how he had arrived there. The left side of his face stung, and there was a ringing in his ear, as if he had been slapped hard. He could not feel his left arm. The right one seemed to be working. His feet moved, but there was pain somewhere in his legs, or—God forbid it—his hip. None of it mattered greatly, as he was sure to be shot where he lay. He could make out Taki's still form draped over the steering wheel, could smell blood and the sharp stink of frightened men.

Strangely, nothing happened at once. It was a full minute before he heard a car engine, and dared to hope that a passerby might have run off the assassins. Generally, these fellows were not well paid enough to make it worth killing bystanders. Then he remembered the Peugeot. Voices approached, loud and nervous. Fotis felt their anxiety in his fingertips. Despite the late hour, another car might come by at any moment. It had been unsporting of him not to go over the cliff, to make their job harder like this. They half-circled the Mercury as if it might bite them, unable to get at the passenger door because of the slope, unable to see through the splintered windows. On impulse, Fotis reached up and popped the glove compartment. The nine-millimeter tumbled out and struck him in the head. He cursed, but gripped the pistol firmly and felt the annoying adrenal rush of returning hope. He had been ready to give it all up a few moments before. What was wrong with that? Why must he fight so hard to keep hold of this miserable, threadbare life? It was not a question for the moment. Without his left hand free, he could not make sure that the first round was chambered, so he would have to go on faith.

Someone pulled at the driver's door, finally wrenching it open a few feet. Fotis could not see clearly, but could sense whoever it was checking on Taki, noting the upside-down form in the passenger seat.

"Dead?" a voice asked from several meters away.

"Very close," returned a younger voice, halfway inside the car. Tight, barely controlled, had never seen a head wound before, no doubt. "Now what the hell are we going to tell them?"

"What about the other one?"

"I can't see, he's on the floor. There's blood everywhere. Holy Mother, what a mess."

"Pull the driver out." The older voice was close at hand now.

"He's wedged in pretty tight."

"Get out of the way, I'll do it. Go in the back, and over the seat."

Now the older one was wrestling with Taki's bulky frame while the younger one fought with the rear door. Fotis shifted his torso and realized that some feeling had come back into the left arm. With great discomfort, he pulled himself partway back onto the passenger seat, just as Taki was dragged out into the road, and as the younger one freed the back door. The Peugeot driver, definitely. He saw Fotis now, oddly arranged across both seats, bent over the gun as if he were holding his ribs. The Snake let out a pitiful moan, only half faked.

"He's alive," the young one shouted, leaning forward between the seats.

Closer. There. Fotis swung the pistol up as fast and hard as he could manage, catching the young man beneath the chin with a tooth-snapping blow, sending him reeling onto the backseat. Then he shifted his attention to the open driver's door.

The older man, a hollow-eyed, mustachioed brute in a dark suit, dropped Taki's body and reached inside his jacket.

"Do not," Fotis commanded, the nine-millimeter leveled at him. He would have shot both of them without warning but for the fact that they had not tried to kill him at once. They might be government, Andreas' men, anyone. Too slowly, the big oaf pulled a blocky .45 from his shoulder holster and took aim. Fotis fired twice, then a third time as the man fell, every shot hitting. The sound was less deafening than he expected. Nice weapon; easy trigger, very little recoil. He had not used a gun in years, had thought himself beyond that place in his life. Mustache rolled heavily into the culvert and was still. The smell of cordite filled the car.

Fotis returned his attention to the driver. He was sitting up in the backseat, holding his bloody chin, his free hand extended like a shield. He spoke quickly.

"Wait, it's a mistake. We tried to call them off."

"Who sent you?"

"I work for him." He gestured toward the dead man in the culvert.

Fotis leaned into the soft leather, reached his right hand between the seats, and placed the gun muzzle against the driver's knee. The young man flinched and moved his leg.

"Be still," Fotis said, gently. "First one knee, then the other, then I kill you. I won't even ask you any more questions, so answer this one. Who sent you?"

"I don't know." The driver was shaking, from shock or fear, Fotis didn't care which. He took none of the satisfaction in this he once might have. "I only overheard a few things. Someone in New York, some Russian. I don't know his name. I don't even know your name."

"You don't know anything, do you boy?"

"That's right."

It might even be true. Anyway, the information was sufficient. Of course, he had known that Karov might come after him. He just hadn't expected it so soon, or on Greek soil.

"Why do you say it was a mistake?"

"The Russian, or whoever it was. He called it off half an hour ago. We couldn't contact the others in time."

"The motorcycle men. Where are they?"

"They were supposed to make sure someone saw them. Some cars coming the other way. Then vanish."

"So it would look like a *November 17* assassination."

"I didn't know the reason. I guess that's right. Yes, of course that's it."

Once, he would have devoted all his efforts to finding those men and punishing them. Now, it would have to wait, maybe forever. He did not even know if he had escaped this encounter yet. How badly was he hurt? How dangerous was the boy? Could he drive the Peugeot himself, or did he need the little bastard?

"Where is your weapon?"

"I don't have one. I'm just the driver. All I was supposed to do is follow you." The young man shook badly, teeth clattering, sure he was about to die. Fotis had seen older men expire from heart attacks in the same situation. A nice, clean death, especially useful in political executions. The boy's heart was probably too strong for that. And too much fear would make him desperate.

"I should kill you. I will not hesitate to do so if you make trouble, but I require your assistance. I need you to deliver a message to the man who ordered this. Do you understand?"

"Yes."

"Good. Stay there."

It was impossible for Fotis not to expose himself to a swift blow as he crawled across the driver's seat and out into the cool dusk, but the young man never stirred. The old man stood, slowly. Pain shot down his left leg, but it did not buckle. The left arm was largely numb. A sticky bulge arose just above his left eye, but his vision was only slightly impaired. One rib could be cracked. All in all, it was miraculous. He might be able to avoid a hospital completely. He let the cool mountain breeze wash him, and tried to keep from vomiting.

The sun had gone behind the hills; the sky was still bright in a shallow arc to the west and blue, deepening to indigo, in the east. Captain Herakles would not wait forever. They must be fast. Fotis had the driver try to start the battered Mercury, and the engine turned over on the fourth attempt, coughing and sputtering miserably. Shocks gone, tires flat, it hammered and scraped its way across the road in reverse until it sat idling by the far ledge. Then Fotis made the young man load the bodies in: Taki behind the wheel, Mustache in back. Grisly work, covering the driver's hands and jacket with blood and road grit. He washed his hands with a water bottle and threw the jacket over the ledge.

Fotis leaned into the car and removed Mustache's wallet, then placed his own bent fedora on the dead man's head. Unwilling to part with a passport, he settled for tucking his box of Turkish cigarettes in the bloodied suit jacket. The gray mustache contributed nicely to the effect. Of course, the man was thirty years younger at least, but who knew, after the effects of a hundred-foot fall, it might fool someone, even briefly. He would take any small advantage he could get. Simple confusion would suffice.

A moment's hesitation as full dark took hold. Taki had not been quite dead when the driver checked on him before. What if he lived yet? His troubled sister's only child. Fotis had never really liked the boy, but he had been loyal, and now the old man was gripped by a deep and unfamiliar sorrow. Something like loneliness. He knew that this feeling, like the fear, would thicken with time, but he had no energy for either emotion right now. There was just enough to do what must be done. If Taki was not dead he would be an empty husk, no good to anyone. Probably he was dead. Let it be so. Fotis signaled the driver.

The young man grabbed the open door for balance, reached in, put the car in drive, hit the gas pedal with his right foot, and pivoted away on his left. The Mercury lurched, rolled, then teetered on the worn, dusty ledge, before tipping like a toy car. Then it was gone in a cloud of loose soil. They heard a thump, followed by a more decisive crunch far below. Fotis shuffled to the ledge and peered down into darkness. He could barely make out the car's scraped, oily underside, like an exposed insect. There was no smoke and the gas tank had not ignited. Only at that moment did he see lights approaching from the west.

He waved the driver into the Peugeot and got into the back himself.

"Pull into that little lay-by ahead. No lights."

The car from the west passed a few moments later, slowed somewhat where the Mercury had gone over, but then continued on. Fotis waited, and the wait nearly undid him. His aches reached him all at once, taking his breath away. Fatigue stunned his brain, he could think of nothing. He almost believed that none of it had happened, that the shaggy head before him was his nephew, and the Snake had merely been sleeping. A terrible, terrible dream. His hands shook, dampness was on his cheeks.

"What now?" asked the young man quietly.

The old man drew a wet, heavy breath.

"You're the driver. So drive."

PART
THREE

EPIROS, 1944

The trail was hard-packed earth, turning to stone, and Captain Elias could not locate footprints or other signs of recent use. He passed the tiny, burned-out village of Nikolaos, no more than a dozen scorched stone walls, on the largest of which some communist *andarte* had painted in large white letters: *What have you done for the struggle today, Patriot?* At Mary's chapel, still well maintained, the path seemed to end, but the captain was able to pick it up again on the far side. It was indeed desolate ground, as Giorgios had said. High and rocky, no good for goats or planting. Only for God. The religious always claimed this sort of place.

Gregori's chapel was easily visible a hundred meters above, although at first Elias had mistaken it for a boulder. It was the color of the gray stones surrounding it, walls and dome having faded years ago. Only the dark rectangle of the entry gave the place away. A nearly indecipherable path ran up to it. There were no trees, just a large rock or two, very little cover. The slope fell away sharply to the left and right, so it was straight up. The captain's only advantage was that the doorway faced directly into the just-risen sun, and the little dell in which he stood was still in shadow.

Anger and the heedlessness of exhaustion drove him up the hill. He ignored the trail, using the rocks as he could, sliding left and right in no definite rhythm so as to make a poor target. Halfway up he heard a sharp crack, and a small stone jumped three meters to his left. Elias darted behind the last rock of any size between himself and the chapel. A wide miss; either Kosta was warning him, or something impaired his aim—perhaps he was injured? Elias drew his own pistol, rolled right and risked slipping down the steep slope, then scrambled toward the domed cell from a more oblique angle. He reached the structure's northeast corner without drawing more fire. Now what? He could race in, shooting, but that would deprive him of the answers he sought. He could try to bargain, but Kosta would never believe that he would spare his life. The pistol shot was his only clue. Some hesitation there.

"Kosta, put down the gun, I'm coming in."

To his surprise, the captain heard two voices within, arguing softly but urgently. It might be his only opportunity. Three quick strides and in the door. He saw the figure in back first, a cringing monk in a cassock, then someone just inside the entry, crouched in the shadows, head turned away. Elias struck hard with the pistol butt, and the crouching figure dropped as the monk cried out.

"Don't hurt him, Captain, please."

Elias looked about as his eyes adjusted to the shadows. The chamber was small, no hiding places. It was just these two. The one at his feet now appeared to be a boy, ten or eleven, a pistol loosely clasped in his limp fingers. Ioannes, Kosta's younger brother. Then the voice of the monk registered with him and Elias looked hard at the man.

"Kosta."

He sat behind a small, crooked table. The cassock was really a long, loose shirt, beneath which stained, hasty bandages were visible. A pink discoloration ran up his neck and disfigured part of his face in a ghoulish whorl. The right eye was squeezed shut and leaking fluid, and much of his hair was gone. Only the left side of the face preserved that handsomeness that had so charmed women and men alike, until just a few hours before. An empty wine bottle was on the table before him, the last of its contents in the cup Kosta gripped with his left hand, while tiny bits of something, paper or cloth, were by his right.

The icon leaned against the wall beside him, the two panels slightly split, but otherwise undamaged. Mother Mary's eyes stared at the captain, seizing him with that dual power of judgment and forgiveness which Mikalis had always spoken of. It had soothed the priest. The captain felt only anger. All this for you, he thought, returning the painted stare. My brother, the old man, this young one, how many more over the years? A pagan goddess is all you are, demanding blood sacrifice. You should have burned. He lifted the pistol, as if to put out those damning eyes, but leveled it instead at his traitorous protégé.

"Wait," Kosta said quietly, his tone resigned. He placed one of the little scraps near his right hand in his mouth, took a gulp of wine. Administering his own sacrament. When he had swallowed, he leaned back in the chair and nodded. Elias resisted the impulse to simply squeeze the trigger. "Please don't kill my brother," Kosta added then. "He doesn't know what is happening."

Elias glanced again at the prone child and Stamatis' note suddenly made sense. *Spare the boy.* Not Kosta—he knew that life was forfeit—but the little one. How badly had he hurt him, Elias wondered. Why should he care? The boy had shot at him. The whole family was rotten.

"Why is he here?"

"I could not walk and carry the Holy Mother also."

"So your father sent the boy along. Why not your sister, too? Why not the whole family, if the prize is rich enough?"

The other man said nothing.

"You betrayed me," Elias continued, without heat, as if discussing the weather. "Not a man trusted you but me."

"You sent me to do your dirty work, and I did it well."

There was a new defiance in the voice—or had it been there all along, buried, released now by the flames that had burned the body?

"Of course you did. Thieving and killing are in your blood. I gave you a purpose, and you betrayed me."

"Maybe I was being loyal to my family."

"A pig like your father cannot command loyalty. Loyalty! You bastard, why did you do that to Mikalis?"

"He caught us with the icon."

"Your father was still in the church."

"He had trouble with the false wall."

"You told him where to find to it."

"Yes."

"Because you heard me give Müller the instructions."

"Yes, but they weren't easy to follow. Then it took him time just to make a small hole. He thought he heard the Germans coming, so he started the fire, in front. The whole place was burning before he got at the Holy Mother."

"How did he get out?"

"He meant to go by the rear door, but you and I and the others were already outside it by then. He heard the priest making noise, or else he would have run right into us."

"Why not use the crypt?"

The burned face seemed to size the captain up, weighing words.

"He tried. There was someone waiting there."

"Germans?"

"No."

"Who?"

"Can't you guess?" Shifting in his chair, Kosta grimaced painfully. Whatever relief the wine had provided was fading. There was no morphine or anything else within reach that would stem the hurt of such burns. Then a lifetime of disfigurement. I will be doing him a favor, thought Elias.

"Why did you have to kill him?"

"I didn't want to. I nearly had him turned around when my father came out of the crypt, with the painting. Mikalis understood at once. He fought my father for the icon. I tried to drag him off, but he began to shout. You must have heard him."

"We were shooting; we heard nothing. But that didn't matter. He had seen what you were up to, so you had to kill him."

"The first blow was only to silence him."

"It is a vicious kind of wound, usually fatal."

"I had no time to think. Even then, he kept fighting. The flames were all around us. I had to strike him again. He fell down the stairs to the crypt, still cursing us." Kosta's gaze was almost reverent with the memory. "I thought he might live."

"He did not."

Kosta nodded, his expression as sad as if his own brother had died. What strange animals we are, thought Elias.

"How did you get out?"

"The fire was mostly out in front by then. We made a run for it, through the burning."

Images came to the captain, less like conjuration than memory. He saw the wall of flame, death on this side, survival on the other, but at a cost.

"I pulled the counterpane off the altar and wrapped it around me," Kosta continued. "Then I went first, my father just behind. There was a charred timber, and I fell." His voice cracked. "My father . . ."

"Left you."

"No, he tried to help me."

"He left you." The scene unspooled in Elias' mind, a vision, clear and absolute. "Worse. He ran over your fallen body to safety."

"No." But the young man was overcome, shaking in grief and pain.

"He is a dog, Kosta, who would kill his own child for gold."

"He pulled me from the flames."

"After. After he had placed the icon away from the fire."

"You saw?"

"No. Who tended your burns?"

"My aunt. She is a poor nurse, I think. The balm does no good. My flesh is fire."

"She had no time. Your father sent you away, so that he might stay behind and bargain. But he miscalculated."

"How is my father?"

"Such burns take long to heal, Kosta. May never heal. Have you seen yourself?"

"I have not tried to. I must be hideous. Ioannes will not look at me."

The boy groaned at the mention of his name, tried to sit up, bent, and vomited. Only then did Elias snatch up the heavy pistol by the child's side. He was growing forgetful; he would soon make a serious mistake.

"Look, my friend, your brother lives. For how long, I wonder?"

"That is in your hands, Captain. I know how you and your master like to play God."

"What is between Dragoumis and your father?"

Kosta only smiled, a lopsided leer with no heart in it.

"Come now," scoffed Elias. "Your father, at least, I understand. You have no reason to protect Dragoumis. Every reason to tell me the truth."

"That is so, I suppose. Except for the pleasure of seeing you struggle in the dark. You two spend more time keeping secrets from one another than fighting. You are feeble men."

"You want to watch the boy die before you?"

The burned man rocked in his chair, the agony of his dead flesh relentless now.

"You will not kill him, I know you."

Elias looked at the child, who looked back with a stunned incomprehension. He would not kill Ioannes, though he had not been certain of that until Kosta spoke.

"How is my father?"

"Why should you care?"

"He is still my father."

Perhaps this was the way. Kosta should have known that his father was dead by now, but every man had his blind spot. Elias looked for a place to sit, but there was no place.

"The Snake has him. He will die, unless I intervene. Which I will not do unless you tell me precisely what happened back there."

"You know what happened. What do the details matter?"

"What part did Dragoumis play?"

"And how will that help my father? You would believe anything I told you now, me, a dying man. I could set the two of you against each other. To what end? What do I care?"

"The men follow me. I can protect your father."

"They follow you, but they fear the Snake. They will not cross him. I do not think that you will cross him either."

"You think I fear him?"

"No, my captain knows no fear. You are a slave to duty." Kosta began to laugh, then flinched. "My God, it hurts. Why do you not shoot?"

"Tell me what I ask, damn you, or I will make it hurt worse."

"The truth, yes, I will tell you the truth. Listen to me. Everything was my idea. The Snake knew nothing. My father cooperated only because I threatened him. I threatened to tell you all of his dark schemes. No, wait, this is better. He stole the icon to keep you from giving it to the Germans. He is a patriot, a hero even, my father. What do you think of that? Tell your master that story."

The boy was only taunting him. He had pushed him in the wrong direction. Now Elias would have to use other methods, and his spirit sickened at the thought.

"Kosta, I will make you speak to me."

"I have told you everything. I did it all, stole the icon, killed your hypocrite brother."

"What did you say?"

"All priests are hypocrites, liars. Religion is a lie. You have told me so yourself." The false smile was now pinned solidly on the burned mask. "I did not think you even liked your brother."

"Bastard."

"Truly. I thought you might be happy that I killed him."

"Be silent, you bastard." The captain squeezed the words out, barely able to speak, his entire body a clenched muscle.

"Why should I be? I am beyond the commands of men. I have nothing to fear, or to hide." He took a deep breath. "I am damned, and I will see your bastard brother in hell, where he burns right now."

The action was involuntary, instantaneous. The roar and flash filled the small chamber. Kosta's head flew back and a bright mist sprayed the ancient wall behind him, like an abstract gloss to the three-quarters vanished image of the saint painted there. The ringing persisted long afterward in Elias' ears. Days and weeks. The arm holding the hot pistol dropped to his side. He understood immediately that he had been played, had probably understood it before he fired. The two of them had conspired in this ritual of provocation and reaction, so that they each might avoid what must otherwise follow. Yet Elias could not help feeling made a fool of. He had learned little. Kosta died protecting a father who was already dead, and Fotis kept his secrets.

The captain lifted up the icon, too small and light to support its reputation, it seemed to him. A stream of daylight through the door struck the surface, setting the gold leaf ablaze. Out of the shadows, the eyes no longer accused but seemed more frightened or sad. Like a mother who knew her son was doomed. The two panels were indeed out of alignment, looking as if someone had dug at the seams on one side.

Was he really going to give it to Müller? His brother had died trying to save it; should he not try to honor that brave, futile action? What then, keep it? Fotis or Müller would pursue it wherever it went. And forty villagers would be shot. Then Mikalis truly would have died for nothing. No, the last good thing Elias could do was trade the work for those lives. And the guns, he must not forget the guns, the original purpose behind this madness.

A small scrabbling sound caught his attention: the little one, Ioannes, with his bruised head and eyes wide as plates, staring not at his murdered brother but at Elias. There was no determining how much he had seen and heard, and he was now a problem. A witness against the captain, to any number of parties. The last male of his family, and thus the certain carrier of a blood feud. Logic dictated an obvious course. Fotis would not hesitate, but he was not Fotis.

He ushered the child out into the sunlight, where he began shivering uncontrollably. Then Elias went back inside and wrapped the painting in the old sheepskin jacket in which it had been carried to this place. Kosta stared blindly at heaven. The captain settled for closing the dead man's eyes.

"I will come back for your brother," Elias told the boy when he stepped back outside, the parcel under his arm. "I will not leave him here."

The boy said nothing, stared off into space, though the shivering had receded somewhat.

"Walk," said the captain, and they started down the hillside together. When they reached the trail, Elias looked south. He would have to go that way soon, but one more detour detained him. The boy must be put somewhere, and he thought he knew the place. Still, he lingered a moment, staring south, his mind traveling to Katarini. His village. Some way or another word would get out of what he and Fotis had done, and it would be his village no longer. He would have to leave then, and probably never return. It made no difference. His life would be in Athens after they drove the Germans out, provided the communists did not get it. He could not expect others to see the necessity of what he did. The world was full of small men, and yet it made him sad. Generations of his ancestors had lived here. His father's bones lay in that village, and now his brother's would as well. But not his own, never his own.

Captain Elias shook these thoughts from his mind, took the boy by the shoulders, and turned him north.

18

The tables around them in the cramped airport bar were empty. No one would know what to make of such an odd tale in any case, Matthew figured. He had not wasted the opportunity of Andreas' coming to Kennedy to meet his flight, but had dragged the old man to the nearest quiet spot available and demanded whatever part of the story he was still missing.

"The exchange went off?"

Andreas sipped his ginger ale before answering.

"Yes. Stefano delivered the message. Müller was willing to make the deal, even then. The soldier we killed at the church meant nothing to him, he was gathering his riches. Many of the German officers were doing the same. Merten, the one in charge of Salonika, sank fifty cases of stolen Jewish gold off Kalamata, thinking he would retrieve it after the war."

"I read about that."

"Müller wasn't after gold. Art, especially religious art, was his calling. He had heard about the icon somewhere, from his father most likely. Art theft was a family tradition. I learned this later, when I was hunting him. He had himself stationed in Greece just to find it. Between Göring, the art lover, and the Nazi obsession with the occult, I imagine the story of a painting with supernatural powers got him some attention. Maybe one of them even sent him to retrieve it, a birthday present for the Führer, what do you think?"

The old man's tone was cynical, but Matthew felt the depth of his suspicion and disgust, felt a chill enter his own body. Was such a guess really so outlandish?

"Epiros was in the Italian occupation zone," Andreas continued, "so Müller had to bide his time. Even once the Germans came in, there were all those villages in all those hills. Needle in a haystack, you say, yes? Greeks love to gossip, but no one could tell him the truth about the Holy Mother. Many villages had old icons, all of them liked to claim theirs was the famous one. Nobody knew where our icon had gone. After we beat back the Italians, before the Germans attacked, my brother had it walled up in a secret space near the altar, behind the *iconostásis*. A good spot. Only Mikalis, the carpenter, and I knew where it was."

"Not Fotis?"

"No. That is why he had to come to me. Müller understood the political split among the guerrillas. The communists were strongest, so contacts developed between the Germans and the other groups. We were fighting them, too, especially in Epiros where that fat-assed Zervas commanded the republicans. But mostly Zervas was watching the communists, watching the royalists, whom he hated even more, until he made peace with them. As the war went on, and we knew the Germans would leave soon, everyone started to think about postwar politics."

"Including you."

"Yes. I was a republican at heart, didn't give a damn about the king. I wanted a president, like in America. But your godfather and I served the government-in-exile, and that made us royalists. Better royalists, better anyone than the communists. Fotis and I agreed on that, and at a certain point it became the focus of our thinking. We fought the Germans, though, killed many, lost good men. Watched villages burn. My people fought."

The old man sipped at his small glass again and seemed to go far away.

"So Müller came to you."

"To Fotis. Fotis was our regional commander. He is from Epiros, too, from Ioannina, and went to Athens for training years before me. He was already an instructor when I got there. A very clever fellow, and strong, hardened in some way, as I wanted to be. We were *Patriótis,* so of course we became friends. I'm sorry, you know all of this already?"

"Most, but go ahead."

"After the Germans cut off our army, we volunteered to go back to Epiros. The government was leaving Athens, and men were going out to every region to organize. Most never made it. The resistance sprang up locally, on its own, and the communists did the best job. Fotis and I worked with the British, brought letters and gold to Zervas. Can you believe it, they had to pay him to fight? Even then he delayed. Fotis was patient, but I needed something to do. The men from my area had formed a guerrilla group, and I joined. They lost their captain, and chose me to lead them."

"You were very young for that."

"Older than most. I had been in the army, and my father led guerrillas against the Turks, years before. That meant a lot to them, fathers, grandfathers. As if a hero could not father a drunken sot, or the other way around. Anyway, Müller contacted Fotis. Two men of the world. The icon for guns. Fotis persuaded me to go along with it. We needed weapons, ours were old and poor. Zervas was stockpiling what the English gave him, and we didn't even know whose side he would be on in the end. The icon had vanished as far as anyone knew. To me, it already seemed a sort of . . . mythological creature. I was a modern man."

Andreas' words were sour, and Fotis' defense echoed in Matthew's mind. *How could it have been my plan? To burn a church? To trade a work of such holy love and beauty?* His godfather always told a lie with a piece of the truth. It was how he managed to be so convincing.

"Burning the church was Stamatis' idea," said Matthew.

"Yes."

"And Fotis never meant to give the icon to the German." He spoke the thoughts as soon as they came to him, as if translating for his unconscious. "The whole thing was an excuse for him to find out where it was. To get you to tell him. For all you know, it was he who approached Müller, and not the other way around."

Andreas was silent a long time, staring past Matthew to the streaked glass wall and busy runways beyond.

"I have thought about those things all these years," he said at last. "I had suspicions from the start. It was why I made the plan myself, which went all to hell. It was why I kept Stamatis' note to myself, made the final exchange myself. I wanted to know what Fotis' game was, but we killed the two men who could have told me. He, the father; me, the son. And as time passed I became less certain that I wanted to know. Because to know the truth might put my brother's death on his head, as well as my villagers. And then I would have to decide what to do about that."

"What about the villagers?"

Andreas clenched his teeth once or twice, the false ones clicking.

"Müller shot them."

"What, after you gave him the icon?"

"The next morning. He took the icon and let me walk away, and we retrieved the guns that night. A good take, fifty rifles, a few machine guns, crates of ammunition. Fotis knew nothing until it was over. I made up a story about someone seeing Kosta, tracking him down, how I had to act swiftly to save my villagers. He was angry, deeply angry, but made a show of congratulating me. We still had to work together. The next morning Müller shot twenty people. He had been able to delay a day, but his men could not accept that there would be no retribution. It was part of their system; I should have anticipated that. He probably thought he was being generous, twenty instead of forty or fifty. Two of them were cousins of mine, one a woman, I would call her girl today. Glykeria. Her parents wanted me to marry her. She was shot with her father. Another was my messenger, Stefano."

Matthew thought of photographs he'd seen, fallen, twisted figures in an olive grove, the entire male population of a village, lined up and shot; a German officer walked among them with a pistol, finishing off the wounded. It was Crete, he remembered, but it could have been anywhere in Greece. The death of Mikalis the priest became absorbed in those other deaths, like a drop of water in the sea.

"That's why you hunted Müller all those years. It had nothing to do with the icon."

"It had everything to do with it, but I was not looking for it, if that's what you mean. The painting is bad luck. When I heard the shots fired that morning, I would have destroyed the thing if it had been in front of me. I wish it had burned in the fire."

Matthew took a deep drink of his beer and imagined the icon, the chipped paint, the haunting eyes, enshrouded in flame. Blackening and peeling away to ash. If it had burned fifty years ago there would be no cause for this present strife. His godfather and grandfather might not be at odds. He himself would have been saved this troubling obsession. And yet who could say how many lives it had touched for the good? Between Andreas' contempt—a kind of reverse superstition—and Fotis' perverted reverence, Matthew had come to see only the negative effects, which had more to do with the men involved than the work. Was his own desire so impure? He wanted it, yes, but only to study, to sit in contemplation within its calming radius. Others must feel the same. The church had used the icon as a force of good for centuries without any legend of death or discord growing up around it. It was a matter of putting it back in the right hands.

"That's a terrible story. I'm sorry."

"Just one of many from those times."

"There were lots of executions, weren't there? They made the people pay every time you resisted them."

"Yes."

"But you didn't stop fighting because of that. The icon was incidental." Matthew hated the tone of his own voice. "Anyway, you needed the guns, right?"

"Oh, yes, the guns proved very useful later, for killing our countrymen."

"Müller would have killed more people if you hadn't bargained."

"All my life," Andreas said quietly, "I have been able to see through men. Not all the time, but often enough that I have come to depend upon it. Some fool will be telling me a lie and the truth will appear before me clearly, as if I am watching it. Like a film. I uncovered many secrets this way, saved myself from bad mistakes. Yet in every piece of business involving this icon I have behaved like a blind man. I see only part of the truth, and my decisions are always bad ones. Every step of the way I have made the wrong move."

"*Papou,* you're being too hard on yourself."

"Not too hard, I think. The signs were there, a wiser man would have read them properly. I knew enough to keep Fotis out of the exchange, but I made a terrible mistake trusting Kosta. And it cost my brother his life. I made a bargain with Müller that anyone should have seen he could not keep. Twenty more died."

"You couldn't have saved them."

"I chased a phantom all over New York while Fotis was making mischief right under my nose, using you."

"You could not have known any of those things. And you're not responsible for me. I've been a bigger idiot than anyone."

"You were lacking information. And you have a weakness for this thing. There, again, he saw what I did not. He has been one step ahead of me all along. He still is."

"If he's not dead."

"I would not wager on it."

"You don't think that was him in the car with Taki?"

"I have only secondhand reports, but the description, presumed age, everything I've been told sounds wrong."

"I should have gone out there to identify him. Sotir hustled me onto the plane, didn't want me mixed up with any investigation."

"He was right. They might have held you for days, weeks."

"At least we'd know."

"Perhaps not, the body was badly damaged. I am glad you were spared viewing it. They will know for certain in a day or so—teeth, fingerprints. But it is not him."

Andreas closed his eyes, pursuing his own thoughts. Matthew took another long swallow. *He saw what I did not.* What did Fotis see? What did Andreas imagine he saw? That Matthew could be coerced, or inspired, by faith? Was it true? Could one call these half-formed gropings, these awkward manifestations of awe, faith? Should he be ashamed of that? He was embarrassed now to think of his father before the icon. What had he expected, that the Holy Mother would reach out of the wood and smite him on the forehead, *You are healed!* Maybe only that the man would feel some of the mystery and joy that his son felt before the image. That the two would join in some silent communion there on the spot. Ridiculous.

"I wish I knew what the hell to do next," Matthew said.

The old man looked him in the eye for the first time in many minutes.

"I have not dissuaded you from this hunt at any point. I have assisted you to the degree that I was able. True?"

"Sure. I was a little upset about Sotir, but he saved my ass, so I'm grateful."

"Then what I must tell you now is to let this go. Two men are dead. Another in the hospital, another missing. This has become far too dangerous a pursuit, with far too small a reward. What would you do with the icon anyway?"

"Give it to the Greek church, as Ana Kessler intended."

"Not good enough. Not a reason to die, or to put others at risk. She received money, and she is safer without the work. If she does not reverse herself, her story should protect you from prosecution. There is no reason to continue. Not to mention that the trail is cold."

"What about the Russians?"

Andreas sighed.

"They are dangerous people. Information would not come easily. Chances are, they disposed of the icon days ago, if they ever had it."

"What do you mean? Where did it go if they didn't take it?"

"All I mean is that we have been underestimating Fotis." Andreas looked hard at him. "I see I have made no impression on you. Does this mean you do not intend to give up the search?"

Matthew felt trapped, then suddenly angry, even furious,

absurdly so. He wanted nothing more than to let this all go. It had frightened and sickened him. Why did it provoke him so to be asked to say it? I will let it go. Just say it.

"So the risk was worthwhile when you thought you might find your Nazi," he said instead. "But now that there is no Müller, it isn't. Is that about the shape of things?"

"The risk was never worthwhile, especially for you."

"You're asking me what I'm going to do. What about you? Are you going to let it go?"

"I want to know what happened to Fotis. If I can find him, I must persuade him to talk to me about old matters. I see now that this should have been my priority all along." Andreas cleared his throat. "When I ask you to let this matter go, I do not speak merely of the physical search. I would like you to let it go in your mind, in your heart."

A flight attendant marched past them to the bar, tall, blond, her professional smile replaced by an acute weariness about the mouth and eyes. She reminded Matthew of Ana.

"The police will be ahead of us with the Russians," Andreas pressed. "That is where they have focused their efforts. I will make inquiries, and let you know what I learn. Would that help? Or would it help you more if I let everything go? There is your father to think of. The woman. These are more worthy objects of your attention."

A hint of desperation had crawled into the old man's speech. Matthew made fists with his hands, aware of his grandfather watching him. Why not just say it?

"The icon is poison," Andreas whispered, hoarse with emotion, a tone so unlike him that it paralyzed Matthew's anger. "It's poison in your blood. Over and over this has happened; you're not the first. You must cure yourself of it."

"I need to go to the bathroom."

Matthew stood quickly and left the table. Instinctively, he headed toward the rear of the bar, having no idea where the bathrooms were. He might well be going in the wrong direction. Let it go, give it up. Magic words. Why could he not bring himself to say them?

19

This was a bad idea, Ana thought. She had thought it from the moment the man on the telephone suggested the place, but it was only now, standing in the dim, cavernous nave of the cathedral, that it struck her just how foolish she was being. These underworld dealers were an eccentric lot, always concerned about safe locations. Her grandfather had dealt with a number of them, perhaps with this very one she awaited. That was the reason she was here. But they were not making an exchange; there was no reason for secrecy, for this Gothic, out-of-the-way location. Wouldn't a coffee shop have done just as well?

The Cathedral of St. John the Divine was a lovely mess. No one would expect to find the world's largest Christian church—short of St. Peter's at the Vatican—on Morningside Heights between Harlem and the Hudson River. In true medieval fashion, work had been proceeding on it for a hundred years, was still not complete, and probably never would be. Ana couldn't imagine the square towers ever outreaching Notre Dame, yet what had been achieved so far was remarkable. She always went the long way around in order to approach from the west. As she climbed the hill from Riverside Park on 112th Street, the massive, looming facade filled up the view, sunlight catching the fifty-foot rose window and every curve and adornment, the rows of larger-than-life saints made miniature by the whole. It might, as many right-minded people claimed, be a waste of money, but Ana understood the impulse to create on such a scale, to overwhelm the eye, to touch the soul with grandeur. It was a substitute for the pure spirituality that few could muster on a regular basis. It was made for people like her.

The broad, empty nave was large enough to seat an army. The aisles were lit by hundreds of yards of stained glass and lined with displays. As directed, Ana stood before the Holocaust Memorial, a fallen, skeletal figure stretched taut upon the ground. It was powerful but ghoulish, and after some minutes she felt a growing embarrassment at being made to stand there so long, as if del Carros were stirring up the darker rumors of her grandfather's past by suggesting it. Simple paranoia on her part, no doubt. It was cold in the place, and Ana felt alone, more alone than she ever had before, and that was saying something. The emptiness of the church served to echo and enhance a hollowness inside herself. There were, in fact, a number of other people in the place, but the cathedral's vastness swallowed them. She saw only tiny figures at a distance.

One of those figures was making his way toward her from the direction of the altar. Tall, or his leanness made him appear so, with short blond hair and spectacles over transparent blue eyes. Bland features, but a winning smile, which did not leave his face from the time he spotted Ana until the moment he stood before her.

"Ms. Kessler."

"That's right."

"Jan Klee." He put out his hand, which she took. A soft, European handshake. "I work with Mr. del Carros. Who is awaiting you, this way, if you would come along please?"

She followed him, trying to identify the accent. Must be Dutch, with that name. He walked with a casual stroll, yet covered ground with deceptive speed. Ana strode quickly to keep pace.

"I hope I haven't kept him waiting long. I believe I was on time."

"You are perfectly punctual, not to worry. Mr. del Carros is always early. And very patient."

"How good of him. I'm always late, and impatient."

Jan chuckled agreeably.

"I am also that way. Patience comes with age, I am told. Though you might expect the reverse to be true."

"What do you do for Mr. del Carros?"

"Many things. Mostly I help him get around. He's quite old, you know."

"Right, of course."

They passed through the broad crossing. Far above was the immense inverted bowl of the dome. Rust-colored and unornamented. Both of them stopped and stared a moment.

"One hundred and sixty-two feet," Jan pronounced, "from floor to dome."

"Wow," Ana said, stupidly. "I couldn't have told you that. You must know a lot about this place."

"No. I just read it in that brochure." He started off again. She was starting to like this guy. Anyway, she was pleased that del Carros had a studious assistant; it made all this feel more normal.

The name had troubled her from the moment it left Emil Rosenthal's mouth, and she had racked her brain to think why. Her grandfather did not keep a diary, as far as she knew, but his calendars were large, leather-cased volumes in which he recorded a good deal of information. She had found the long line of black books a few days after his death, on a shelf in his study, fifty of them, numbered and dated. She'd meant to look through them then, but there had not been time, until yesterday. On impulse, she had turned to 1984, and found what she was looking for instantly. June 16 was circled, with departure and arrival times for a Pan Am flight to Caracas, a flight her grandfather never took, because of illness. Her father went instead, in his own jet, and presumably met with the man whose name was written below: Roberto del Karos. Two days later her father's jet crashed in the mountains. The names were close, but close enough? And how common a name was either?

They went up a few steps into the south ambulatory, part of the semicircular corridor surrounding the choir and altar, and opening onto seven chapels. Jan stopped before an entry in the stone wall to their right. Unlike those further on, fronted by decorative iron gates that made them fully visible to the passage, St. James' chapel was hidden away. Ana glanced at Jan and thought she found something challenging in his smile, saw an unnerving flatness in his eyes that was visible only close up, and he stood very close to her now. She was breathing too quickly; her pulse throbbed in her neck. This was ridiculous, the collector was only being careful.

"Just inside here," Jan instructed, pleasantly.

Ana stepped through the archway. The chapel was deceptively large, big enough to be a small church, spare in its adornments, except for the highly detailed windows and a carved stone altar, four saints flanking a cross. A shrunken old man sat several chairs into one aisle, draped in a black raincoat with a gray hat in his lap. He was round-faced with a head of pure white hair and watery blue eyes, and his gaze never shifted from the altar, even as Ana slid into the aisle beside him. She left one chair between them. Jan had vanished.

"Thank you for coming, my dear."

He looked at her now, one shy glance before shifting his eyes downward.

"Thank *you*. This was my idea."

"But I've taken you out of your way."

"It's fine. I love this place."

"Do you? It's rather freakish, but I like it too. And it has these discreet corners."

"Are you hiding from someone?"

"Oh, yes." He grinned mischievously. "Many people. Does that surprise you?"

"Not at all. I know a bit about the complications that afflict collectors' lives."

"Of course, you are one yourself. And a dealer too, yes?"

Had she told him that? Anyway, Rosenthal could have; it wasn't a secret.

"Strictly an amateur, on both counts."

"But your grandfather was a great collector."

"You knew my grandfather."

"Not well. We did some business a long time ago."

"Would it be too rude to ask what that business was?"

"Not too rude." He was looking down again, shifting the hat about in his lap with his long, withered hands. "It's simply that business is so boring. Especially old business, and I've forgotten the details. If I'm not mistaken, we are here to speak of more recent business. True?"

What was the accent? Certainly there was a Spanish lilt, but it overlaid something else. He didn't look Spanish. She was getting distracted.

"You know, I sort of had a deal in mind," she answered. "An exchange of information. I don't want to sound mercenary. I'd like this to stay friendly."

"No need to apologize. I understood the conditions. I was to explain my willingness to pay so much for your fine icon. You were to give me your best guess at its present location. I imagined that trading stories about your grandpa was something extra, just friendly conversation. Have I misunderstood?"

He was not a doddering old man, she must get rid of that idea at once. He had thought this through more carefully than she had.

"Let's make this simple," he continued, leaning in her direction. "We shall each take turns speaking, until we run out of things to say. I'll go first." He faced the altar once more. "There is no good reason I should have offered so much for the icon. It is a personal matter. My father was also a collector, and an art historian. Byzantine art was his special love. He had heard and read what little there was on the Holy Mother of Katarini, and then, between the wars, he went to Greece to see it. It was not easy. The icon had moved over the years, and there were several villages which claimed theirs as the true one. Maybe they believed it. The Greeks are not a people careful about history. My father bribed a priest, and was able to see the real icon, the genuine Mother of Katarini. And he became so entranced by it that he made the priest an offer to buy it. A generous offer, I believe, but it was no use. The Greek would not part with it for any price."

"What was your father's name?"

"William. It would have been William in English. In any case, years later, I went to see the icon myself. I was trying to be a collector also, though I had to do other things to live. My family was not rich, despite my father's indulgence in art. I too fell in love with the work. It was . . . well, I need not describe it to you. You have had years to admire it. I envy you that."

"I seem to have been less affected than others. Maybe I didn't spend enough time looking closely."

"Perhaps, but the effect is usually immediate, in my experience. Can I ask you, do you believe that Jesus Christ is your savior?"

"My goodness, there's a question. I'm not sure that I do, to tell you the truth. Is that necessary to the proper appreciation of the work?"

"We are not speaking of appreciation, but something deeper. The work's ability to move one, yes? To heal, to comfort, to teach, even. Is belief necessary? No, probably not. Not as a precondition, in any case, but one is unlikely to feel that caress of the spirit and be unchanged. Conversion goes hand in hand with the healing."

He had a schoolteacher's manner, this del Carros. There was no evangelical thunder in his speech, yet a certain quality of hushed awe had crept into these last words. Ana felt alien, isolated, denied something that all these men around her had been able to access.

"You really believe this?"

"I believe in my own experience. I am not a man given to fanciful thoughts, I assure you. My life has not been an easy one. I have seen much cruelty, and my sins are great. My sins are great," he said a second time, as if hearing himself for the first time. The hands worked the crumpled hat furiously now. He had lost his way a little. "In some degree this belief is a burden to me, but inescapable. For the brief time that I held the icon, I felt a calm, and a love, that have lived within me always. I long for that feeling again. That is why I made the offer I did."

He had said more than he intended, that was clear, and a poignancy like truth had infused his words. She believed in his reasons. And yet so much had been left out of the tale.

"Do you know how the icon made its way to my grandfather?"

He smiled sadly.

"You are hungry for the past. Me, for the future. I think it is your turn to speak now."

He would tell her what she wanted if she could only keep him talking. How much truth did she owe him, after his little unburdening? How much did he already know?

"My grandfather had his own theories about the icon," she began, for no reason in particular. "He thought it was a lot older than anyone guessed. That it had been made in Constantinople in the fourth or fifth century. Even that St. Helena commissioned it herself."

"Indeed?"

Ana had expected scorn, or amusement, but in fact her words seemed to unsettle the old man. His watery eyes fixed upon her, no longer shy, and a stillness came over him.

"I suppose that's ridiculous," she added quickly. "I mean, all those really old works were destroyed, right? By fire, or the iconoclasts, or the Turks, or somebody."

"Undoubtedly. But I wonder where he arrived at such a theory. Do you know?"

"Not really. Something he read, I suppose. Maybe something in the work itself."

"I see." His body language expressed terrible agitation, though his voice remained calm. "Did he have experts examine the work?"

"Not that I was ever aware of. He was very protective of it. A few friends saw it. It's possible that one of them was an art historian."

"But there was no close examination, no testing paint, playing with the frame, and so on."

"Nothing like that, I'm sure."

"I am relieved to hear it. You know, those people have no reverence for sacred art. Sometimes they do great damage in the course of examining. Your own expert, Mr. Spear, was also careful with the work, I trust."

Again, Matthew's involvement was no secret, yet del Carros' speaking his name made her uneasy. There was nothing about this encounter, it seemed, that did not make her uneasy.

"He was very gentle. He only looked at it."

"And what useful analysis did he provide you?"

None of your damn business, she wanted say, but restrained herself. There was more to learn here. Her real annoyance came from not being able to figure out what he was after. She no longer had the icon, so what she might have learned could be of little importance. Unless he felt that certain information held value, or threat, quite apart from ownership.

"Mr. Spear works for the Metropolitan Museum, not for me. He confirmed that the work was old, possibly as old as the St. Catherine's group. That was about it."

"Yet he has taken a very personal interest in the work's recovery, has he not?"

"You would have to speak to him about that."

"Very well. To the point. Where is the icon now, Ms. Kessler?"

"I never claimed to know exactly where it was."

"Your educated guess, then. Whatever it was you came here to tell me."

She stared at the altar, picking through the scattered facts in her brain for an answer that might halfway satisfy him.

"There's a man named Dragoumis. A businessman, who was the intermediary for the church, or claimed to be."

"I know who he is."

"The police think that he might have stolen the icon from himself. The Russian mob was in on it with him. He used the church to get the price down, then had it stolen to avoid turning it over."

He nodded slowly, but without satisfaction.

"Someone reading the newspapers closely could have discerned that much. Though I thank you for confirming it. Is there anything else?"

"The icon may be in Greece now."

"Why do you say that?"

"Why else would Dragoumis have gone there?"

"I can think of a number of reasons. Do I take it, then, that you have no reliable information that the icon is in Greece?"

Ana prided herself on quick thinking. Even now, she could dredge up numerous tidbits of fact to support her assertion, but they would all be known to him, she felt sure. She remained silent. Del Carros nodded again and slumped back in the hard wooden chair, disappointed less with her, it seemed, than with the world in general. They both faced forward. A burly, bearded sightseer entered the chapel from the far door and began carefully examining the altar.

"Tell me, Ms. Kessler," del Carros said finally, "why your continued interest in the work? You did receive a tidy sum."

"I'm not interested in it," she answered.

"I find that hard to believe. Could it be that you have found parting with it more difficult than you expected?"

"You find it hard to believe because you're obsessed, so you think everyone else must be. It's a bit egocentric, if you'll forgive my saying so." Her words carried more edge than she intended. Must be careful. "I truly don't care about the icon. I'm only here because I hoped to learn some things about my grandfather. I guess I should have been clearer about that."

"Then we have both been disappointed," the old man said, empathetically. "And sadly, I now lack any incentive to speak to you on that subject. Though I could not have told you much in any case. So I must apologize once more for taking you out of your way."

She was being dismissed. Just like that. As she had been her whole life, whenever she pressed too hard, whenever the questions got sticky. These men. Her father, her grandfather, Wallace, her miserable ex, Paul. Even Matthew. Push them at all and they clammed up, shut down, sent her packing, their precious mysteries preserved.

"I think you're being a little unfair," she said, trying to control her anger.

"Oh?" He seemed amused.

"I've tried to be straight with you. And you've really told me nothing useful. I don't have the information you want, but I feel that if we shared ideas, we could help each other."

"So, I am egocentric and unfair." He was ignoring her overture. "Is there anything else?"

"OK. You're dishonest."

"And a liar also."

"Don't put words in my mouth."

"And how do you believe that I have been *dishonest* with you?"

"You tease me with these hints about my grandfather, then tell me that you know nothing. And you left an awful lot out of that story you told."

"Is that being dishonest? In my business we call that being careful. And you have been careful today also, though you are being rather careless now."

"When were you in Greece to see the icon?"

"What does it matter?"

"Maybe it was during the war? And maybe you were there without an invitation? And maybe you had more in mind than looking?"

He no longer appeared to be amused, and she knew she had gone too far, knew it even as she was saying it. She was terrible at games. Quick to catch on, but impatient.

"Someone has been telling you stories," the old man said slowly, studying Ana.

"No. Just some thinking on my own." Too much thinking was a bad thing, she had heard. Too much talking about what you thought was worse. "Why don't you set me straight?"

"Tell me what you've been told, and I will fill in the details."

"I haven't been told anything. That's the problem, do you see? I'll just keep getting things wrong until someone tells me the truth. Meantime, God knows what I'll come up with."

She had struck a nerve. He felt threatened by her. This was

risky, and she must be careful not to overplay her hand. In the end, she was holding no cards.

"You think I was some wartime profiteer, yes? Because I did business with your grandfather." He lowered his voice as the bearded man wandered closer, but his whisper was harsh, unpleasant. "Doing business with a thief does not make you one. We were very different men, I assure you."

"Are you calling my grandfather a thief?"

"I have told you that my sins are heavy, but at least I know what they are. I was forthright in my actions, and I believed certain things, right or wrong. Your grandfather believed in nothing, had no scruples, played every angle. All from his fat, easy perch of neutrality."

"Hang on now." It was one thing to have your own suspicions, another to have a stranger attack what was yours. "I didn't come here to listen to you insult my family."

"Did you not?" He was clearly warming to his subject. His round, wrinkled face was flushed pink. "You came to learn about your grandpa, no? It's what you have been begging me to speak of. What did you expect to hear? Does my opinion of him surprise you?"

Jan had appeared in the far door, shadowing the bearded man about thirty feet behind.

"I know he was involved in some shady deals," Ana responded. "And he felt bad about those. But he truly believed he was saving works that would have vanished otherwise."

"Child, you have no idea. The museums would not take work from him, and they will not take it from you, because they know it is tainted. Your legacy is dirty money. You sleep among pilfered treasures. I am sorry if I am the first to tell you this, but somehow I doubt that."

Ana was too shaken to think clearly. She had broken his shell but had not found what she wanted inside. The bearded man wandered out the near door, and Jan doubled back to the far one. When she glanced at del Carros again, his face was placid once more.

"You know," he said, in a very different tone, warm, surprised,

"I now begin to think that I am the foolish one, and that you are a clever girl."

"I don't know what you mean."

"I think you do. You are too wise a woman not to know about your grandfather. You have deliberately provoked me, and I have reacted. And now, perhaps, you think that you have learned something. The question remains, why?"

"I haven't learned anything, except that you hate my grandfather."

"Is it for yourself or someone else? Come now, speak to me, do not be afraid. We are exchanging information, that is all, and it is clear that we have both been holding back."

Two middle-aged women entered the chapel at the far end, gabbling happily, but their presence only slightly alleviated Ana's rising panic. *Do not be afraid.* There were no more frightening words he could have spoken to her.

"I think I have to leave."

He reached over and touched her arm.

"We should both leave. We require more privacy, I think. I intend to reward your cleverness with answers, but I will require some in return."

"I really have to be someplace soon."

He took gentle hold of her forearm.

"Ms. Kessler. I may have to insist."

She bolted. His grip was just tightening as she slipped it, stood quickly, rattling the old chairs, and raced out through the near stone arch. Instinctively, she turned left, toward the front of the church. There was no danger that del Carros would catch her, but she remembered Jan's coiled energy and watchfulness. Nothing could happen here, surely, with all these other people around, yet it was hard to be certain and she walked as quickly as she could without running. Down the steps into the open space of the crossing, past the roped-off section before the choir, and toward the central aisle of the nave. Halfway there, the bearded man appeared before her suddenly.

"Ms. Kessler," he said, "wait."

She reversed and immediately noted the side exit, simultane-

ously seeing Jan bouncing down the steps from the direction of
the chapel. They nearly had her boxed. Ana ran now, pure adrenaline guiding her toward the daylight beyond the exit.

A steel staircase led down into the front end of a dirty, empty
cul-de-sac between the cathedral and the sacristy. She turned right
at the bottom and scampered toward the narrow parking strip that
led out to the avenue. There was no one in the security guard's
box, damn it, just a square young man in a suit jacket standing in
the middle of the lane, smoking a cigarette and looking hard at
her. How many of them were there? This was ridiculous, what was
going on, why the hell had she come here at all? And alone.

Again, she wheeled and went the other way. Five Asian
tourists stared in wonder at one of the dazzling blue-and-green
peacocks that roamed the grounds. Cameras whirred; a little girl
shrieked with pleasure. Ana saw no safety among them and
pushed on. To her right, steps and a broad path dropped away to
a lower lane that led back to the avenue, but it was roundabout
and she would be visible the whole way. She risked a look back
and immediately felt like a fool. The square young man was
embracing a woman and walking off arm in arm with her. Panic
had sent her the wrong way. Jan emerged from around the corner
of the sacristy a moment later, smiling and waving, like a friend
asking her to wait up. Ana paused in confusion. She was jumpy
as hell, had been since she arrived. Had she gotten it all wrong?
Would Jan apologize now for the old man's impertinence? Had
she misread the whole situation? Too flustered to reason, she
simply stood there as he drew closer.

The bearded man appeared behind Jan, and he did not smile or
wave but bore down on them with a fierce energy. Released from
her daze, Ana turned and moved off again, to the end of the lane:
enclosed gardens on the left and right, the stone Cathedral
School before her, and between the school and gardens a narrow
path that seemed as if it must run out to Morningside Drive in
either direction. She turned left instinctively, down the passage
between walls.

Clearing the corner of the building, she saw her mistake. The
greensward between the school and the rear of the cathedral was

closed off from the street by a high chain-link fence; she would never get over it. There was no time to reverse. Like a child, she looked for a place to hide among the dense bushes. No, that wouldn't do. Letting herself be trapped in an empty corner of the grounds would be exactly what they wanted. Meeting them in the open was her best chance. She raced back up the path.

Jan leaned casually against the stone wall of the north garden, smoking. He stood away from the wall as she approached, but made no move toward her.

"Ms. Kessler, you will exhaust both of us. I think there has been a misunderstanding."

There was room to get past him, but she somehow knew he would be fast. An old woman's hat bobbed in the garden. The Asian family had gone.

"Whose misunderstanding? Your boss threatened me." She could not keep a slight quaver out of her voice.

"Threatened you?" Jan seemed amused by the idea. "With what, death by boredom? He only wants to talk."

"Yes, by force if necessary. He's got some wrong idea that he wants me to confirm. And he wouldn't take no for an answer."

"He has become quite a difficult fellow, it's true. Stubborn, and his manners are appalling. We have discussed this, he and I. I'm sorry if he frightened you. I really don't mean to make light of it, but he is just a harmless old man. Please come back and speak to him. I'm sure that he feels terrible."

He had moved closer to her, without seeming to move at all, and she began to make a slow half-circle around him.

"I'm not going anywhere with him."

"Of course not. We simply don't want to part on bad terms."

They walked parallel now, back the way they had come. Ana let herself relax a little.

"I'm going down to the street. If he wants to come out to the sidewalk and say good-bye, that's fine."

"The sidewalk will do. I'll bring him by in the car and you can speak through the window."

Jan was interrupted by a large figure lumbering out of the garden and colliding with him. The bearded man. Words were spoken, quickly, softly. The two did a little dance, and Jan swung his arm to fend the other off. There was a heavy clatter and the large man sank to his knees.

Ana took a step or two back, grasping at comprehension. There had been some swift, violent exchange right in front of her, too fast to see. The bearded man gripped his left forearm with his right hand, dark blood staining the sleeve of his jacket and welling up between his fingers. On the pavement before him lay a large black pistol, a little closer to him than it was to the still-standing Jan. Neither man moved for a few seconds.

"Ms. Kessler," said the man on his knees, never taking his eyes off the Dutchman. "Please step away."

Ana's legs felt as heavy as lead. She tried to take in what was happening. Jan's expression remained placid, but she could see his eyes gauging the distance to the weapon, the man, her. She also saw several inches of steel blade protruding from his right hand, held close against his leg.

"You will note," Jan countered, "that this man assaulted me. I merely protected myself."

"Ana," said the bearded man, urgently, "Matthew asked me to watch you. Do as I say. Step well away from us."

She stepped back several yards. She had the impression that the man on the ground, though pained by his wound, was not distracted by it. That he had sunk to his knees only to get closer to his fallen weapon. Now it was a standoff. Neither could reach the gun without exposing himself to a blow by the other, yet neither could withdraw and give up the gun to his opponent. Ana looked around for some figure of authority to break this up.

Then Jan was backing off, not down the lane but up the garden path, his free hand held close to his chest, as if ready to reach inside his jacket, but not doing so. The other man shifted closer to the pistol, even stretched his hand out, but made an equal show of doing no more.

"Ms. Kessler," Jan said. "I'm sorry to see our business concluded this way. Please keep an open mind. And be careful of this man, he is clearly dangerous. In fact, I will wait a bit if you would like to leave now unhindered."

How nice of both of them to worry so much about her.

"I think you better go, Jan. Before something worse happens."

"Very well." He smiled at her. "Do take care."

He did not go right, into the garden, but continued up the path and through an archway in the brick wall that Ana had not even realized was there. Vanished, God knew where.

The bearded one was on his feet with the gun instantly, staring long at the archway, then all around them, ignoring Ana.

"You're bleeding pretty badly," she said.

He glanced at his soaked sleeve and nodded.

"Stupid. I didn't know he would be so quick."

"Were you trying to kill him?"

"No. That would have been easy, he was completely focused on you. I was trying to take him, but he was too fast. Lucky he didn't kill me. I'm Benny, by the way. Sorry about this."

He still barely looked at her. She realized that she should fear him, but did not, whether from instinct or from emotional exhaustion, she couldn't say.

"Did Matthew really send you?"

"No, his grandfather, but on Matthew's behalf. I guess the boy loves you or something."

Ana felt dizzy, then nauseated. The shock hitting her, no doubt. She wanted to sit down on the pavement and cry.

"We should go," Benny advised. "We can get a cab at a Hundred-tenth."

"Where are we going?"

"To a hospital, first. Then someplace where we can keep you safe. You've stirred up some unfortunate interest."

20

The platform was emptier than he would have liked. Matthew made it a point not to take the subway late at night, but getting a cab near Grand Central had become impossible, and his feet naturally guided him down the long staircase and through the turnstile. A smattering of people were on the upper level, coming up from the trains or heading west down the wide passage to the Times Square shuttle. He descended to the uptown platform, to find almost no one there. Just a very large homeless man in a filthy red bandanna, muttering to himself. Anxious and sleep-deprived, Matthew wandered north along the dirty concrete.

You must cure yourself.

He had let everything go for days now but the all-consuming chase. Thoughts of his father and Ana had broken through, but not sufficiently to distract him. He had not checked his answering machine until getting back from Greece, and he was stung to find two messages from his mother, angry that he had not called. There was one from Ana also. She was doing some research; they could compare notes when he returned. There was no warmth in her words—she was all business—but he took comfort in the fact that she had called at all. He went straight to his parents' house, before even going to his apartment, and tried her from there this morning, but there was no answer.

Despite his mother's protests to the contrary, his father looked stronger. He had more color and energy, and felt good enough to give Matthew hell about vanishing. The visit had been tense, but they both felt better by the end of it. Needing to be at work the next day, without fail, Matthew had taken the train back into the city after dinner. His body clock, which had barely adjusted to Greek time, had not yet reset for New York, and exhaustion, combined with travel and emotional stress, had kicked him into a strange, nearly surreal state. His eyes drooped, but his heart hammered. A certain color, or the shape of a face, would leap out at him from the blurry details of a crowd. He needed sleep badly.

A bunch of kids with an angry boom box shuffled down the steps, posing and cursing in their droopy jeans and baseball caps, displaying all the artificial, late-night animation of intoxicated young men. Matthew moved away from them. From far down the tunnel came the sound of the number six train.

You must cure yourself.

He almost felt he had. Those haunting eyes, that layered mystery, had been left somewhere behind, in some dream life he'd briefly passed through. The icon was not in Greece, he knew, yet he felt he had left it back there. It was part of that culture; its beauty and otherness had no place in this city without history. Past and present fused in Salonika. The past was crushed by New York, even the personal past, his own past. It was lost, left somewhere on a baggage carousel. It had never happened to him. Such magic did not exist.

His mind whirling, he sat down on a wooden bench to still himself. These were fatigue thoughts, delusional riffs from a traumatized brain. He could not get his hands around them. He was trying to free himself from an emotional condition by force of will, and in this delicate and overreceptive state of mind he almost believed he had succeeded. But it was white noise, sound and fury, meaningless. It would all be clearer in the morning.

He glanced up, and a huge figure loomed over him.

"Jesus knows your sins. You can't lie to him."

Matthew flinched, knocking his bruised spine against the bench. Mad, bloodshot eyes stared through him and body stink stunned his senses. The mutterer had become a shouter.

"I'm sure you're right."

"Your Father knows when you're lying. He sees into your heart."

A roar filled the station now, the uptown local hurtling out of the tunnel. There was no getting past the homeless evangelist in any conventional way, so Matthew swung his feet over the low bench back, and staggered across the gum-sticky platform to the yellow line. Reflected light climbed the broken white wall tiles, then the square front of the train rushed by him. The preacher's voice bellowed from behind.

"He has spoken to me of you. You are one of the lost ones. Your sins are deep, but in Jesus all things are possible. Repent, and be one with the Lord."

Several silver cars swept by, scratched windows, fluorescent light, very few people in the orange seats. The train slowed and Matthew's eyes locked with those of a figure, or maybe a face only in a door window, quickly gone. Wide eyes of the deepest brown, alarmed or saddened, half the face discolored. There and gone in a moment, but Matthew's body was electrified to his fingertips. He had seen that face before, those eyes. In a dream, perhaps.

The train stopped and a door opened before him. He stepped through but did not sit, looking back at the platform. The homeless giant was still by the bench, no longer looking at Matthew, muttering once more. Somehow his familiar insanity seemed less threatening than the face in the window, and Matthew had nearly decided to step off again when the doors closed and the train lurched forward. He grabbed a pole to avoid falling.

There was nobody in the car, and there were only two old women in the one ahead. Matthew held the steel pole fiercely, gazing down a vanishing series of windows in the doors connecting the cars, waiting for the specter to reappear. Or some new threat. He regretted all of it now—every incident and decision that had drawn him deeper into this bloodstained chase and further from his dull, comfortable life. Let him go back to worrying about staff politics, or some troubled girlfriend. He could not take this enervating obsession, this fear, this miserable paranoia. Nothing had happened. He had, perhaps, seen a face. He had been harassed by a homeless man. So what? Every encounter had become heavy with hidden meaning.

A few others got off with him at Seventy-seventh Street. Matthew rushed up the stairs and into the streetlit night as if pursued by demons. Lexington Avenue, lined with florists, coffee shops, and copiers, was dead at one o'clock in the morning. A banging grate beneath his feet startled him; a cab turning onto Eightieth Street nearly ran him down. The empty side streets were worse. It had been a warm day, but he felt chilled. Perhaps he was sick. Restaurants and twenty-four-hour delis created more human traffic on Second Avenue, and he relaxed somewhat. Entering his building, he dropped his keys on the black-and-white tiles, picked them up quickly and dropped them again, cursing loudly in the echoing stairwell. Waking the neighbors, if any of them were home. He barely knew the other people in the building. There was no one here he would go to for help.

Two flights up, he turned both locks and stepped into his cramped kitchen. It took him several seconds to realize that something was wrong. There were lights on. Then he heard movement somewhere, the quietest shuffle of feet, a creaking floorboard. He was looking about for something to use as a weapon when she called to him.

"Matthew."

Ana appeared in the bedroom doorway, looking the way he felt. Her hair was wild, dark shadows hung under her eyes, her clothes appeared slept in. He thought she looked beautiful.

"How did you get in?"

"Benny let me in."

"Benny."

"Ezraki. Don't tell me that you don't know Benny."

The name came back to him. An Israeli friend of his grandfather, did marketing research or something. Ex-Mossad, as if any of them were really ex-anything.

"Yeah, I know him. But I never gave him my keys."

"He's got this big set of skeleton keys, says he can open eighty percent of the ordinary locks in the city."

"That's comforting. Why did he bring you here?"

"I got myself into some trouble." She tried to sound flip, but her voice broke. "He didn't think I should go back to my place right away."

Matthew turned swiftly to bolt the useless locks, and turned back just as she rushed into him, knocking her forehead against his chin.

"Sorry."

"It's OK."

He held her for several minutes, arms wrapped tightly, fingers digging into her ribs. Strange to feel such comfort, to be able to give such comfort in the midst of such distress. He had not expected to hold her again. His mind had been packed with all the explanations, justifications, pleas with which he might win back her trust, all of them insufficient and unconvincing even to his own ears. Yet here she was. No explanations, no excuses. Warm breath on his neck, the aloe scent of her shampoo.

"I feel so stupid," she said into his collar. "And frightened."

"Tell me what happened."

She released him slowly, sat down at the little kitchen table. He boiled water for tea they would not drink while she told him of Rosenthal, del Carros, and the encounter at the cathedral. By the time he told her of his misadventures in Greece it was three o'clock in the morning. He held her hands across the table, shaking from fatigue.

"I can't believe you went hunting for that guy after the speech you gave me last week."

"I assumed he was just some old collector," she answered. "It didn't seem dangerous. I thought I might learn a few things."

"You did that, all right," he laughed.

"Well, I was told some things, anyway. You have to consider

the source. Then I had to open my big mouth, pretend to know secrets. I wonder if they'll come looking for me."

"I doubt it. Now that they know people are protecting you."

"Maybe they believe I know where the icon is."

"What does Benny think?"

"What you said. They were willing to grab me while they had the chance, but they won't try again. They just want the icon. I can't get that fucking thing out of my life even when I give it away."

That's because you let me *into* your life, he almost answered, but thought better of it. They were silent for some moments.

"So they're gone, right?" Ana spoke again. "The icon, and your godfather."

"It looks that way. Actually, I have a wild guess where he is."

"Really, where? No, don't tell me."

"I have no intention of telling you. In fact, I'm trying hard to let all this go."

She squeezed his hands firmly.

"That's exactly what we need to do."

"I'm so tired."

"You should sleep. I can go now."

"What are you talking about?"

"I'm sure it's safe. You need time to get your head together."

"You're not going anywhere. You are not leaving my sight."

"OK." She smiled at him. "But I'm not sure I can sleep. I'm afraid I'll have nightmares of people chasing me."

"I felt like someone was chasing me tonight."

"When?"

"Earlier. In the subway, all the way home. Don't worry, it wasn't anyone. Just paranoia, but it really felt like someone, or something, was after me."

"This thing is eating you alive. Please tell me you'll let it go."

"I will," he said, in a tone that sounded convincing even to himself. "I have to, I'm not cut out for this."

She came around the table and held him again. "Promise me."

"I promise myself. I want out." He closed his eyes. "I just pray that they leave us alone."

•　　•　　•

"It could have been him. It could very well have been him."

They had retreated from the coffee shop to the car so that Benny could smoke. In any case, it afforded a better view of Matthew's street. Neither the boy nor Ana had emerged yet, which Andreas took as a likely sign of reconciliation.

"But you can't be sure," said Andreas.

"How can I be sure?" Benny slammed his door and lit up immediately. A heavy white bandage covered his left forearm and made some actions clumsy. "I've never seen him, just photographs. All old men look alike."

"So what makes you think it might be him?"

"The face was close enough. And he would have someone like that Dutchman around him. Why does a simple collector need someone like that?"

"He is no simple collector. A dangerous man, certainly. That doesn't mean he's Müller."

"The Kessler woman thinks he is."

"What are her reasons?"

"Female intuition? I don't know; she was too shaken for me to debrief her properly. But apparently he admitted seeing the icon years before. More than seeing it. She had the impression that he had spent time with it, maybe owned it. Then, when he was about to get rid of her, she accused him of stealing it. Just to get a reaction."

"Which she did, it would seem."

"Oh, yes. His interest in continuing the conversation grew immeasurably after that. He managed to frighten her out of her wits. I can only assume that she had done the same to him, somehow."

"I didn't realize she even knew Müller existed."

"She may not, by name, anyway. But she isn't stupid, she's heard rumors. Her grandfather got the icon as loot from a Nazi officer. She doesn't have to know his name to guess that this might be the guy."

"Of course. Damned foolish of her to taunt him with that."

"She didn't know what she was dealing with."

"It's good you were there."

"It's good that you put me on to watching her. Now we may have Müller in our sights again. Then all of us doubters will owe you an apology." Benny shook his head in a bemused fashion, sucking on his cigarette. There was a look in the big man's dark eyes that made Andreas uncomfortable.

"You would have executed him," Andreas stated, more than asked. "Right there in the church. If you could have been sure it was Müller."

"What should I care for churches? That place is more like a museum, anyway."

"So the answer is yes."

"If I could have been certain, why not? It would have been risky. I would have had to take out the Dutchman as well, and there were a lot of people around. Then again, how many opportunities can one expect?"

"This recklessness of yours is disturbing. You make me question involving you."

"What recklessness?" Benny barked smoke into the old man's face. "It's all been talk so far. Raiding empty rooms. Bad information. The only reckless thing I've done is get that girl out of danger."

"Forgive me, you did well there. It is only that I take you at your word, and your words have been disturbing."

"I don't know why. We both know the man needs to die. Anyway, it doesn't matter, because I lost him and who the hell knows if we'll ever find him again."

"You didn't lose him, you took care of Ms. Kessler. That was the correct thing to do. Now you are wounded, and I can be of little help in a fight. And he has this bodyguard. The business has become too dangerous."

Benny stared at him for several seconds.

"You're saying we should give up."

"Turn it over to the authorities. It's what I was telling Matthew. The odds are not in our favor, and the goal is insufficient to the risk."

"The goals are different for each of us. Your boy is an innocent, chasing a painting that will only bring him grief whether he finds it or not. You are right to tell him to stay out of it. Our goal is much simpler."

"Your goal."

"My goal, then. Simple, direct, well justified, and I am capable of carrying it out."

"Yet your arm is bandaged, and we still do not know if we are even chasing the right man."

"Damn you," Benny said, mashing out the cigarette in the filthy ashtray. "We've just been through this. I got cut doing what you asked me to do. It would have been much easier just to eliminate those two."

"It won't be easy the next time. They will know you now."

"Are you trying to convince me or yourself? Finding Müller was your idea. Now we are close and you want to give it up. What the hell have you been after all this time?"

There must be something in his face, Andreas decided, that kept inviting the question. And no matter how many times he recounted the arc of this journey in his own mind, it yielded no obvious answer. The dream of confronting Müller had lived within him for more than fifty years. It lived still, an unconscious reflex, like breathing. Yet something had changed. There were times when he could recall his brother Mikalis, the child Mikalis, so clearly that it was as if he had just seen him days before, scampering across the square toward him: round, dark eyes; stick-figure arms and legs; tousled hair; a small scar on his forehead from an errant rock thrown by Andreas himself. The fiery Mikalis from the war years, however, the young man martyred in the church, had achieved the murky indistinctiveness of myth. The same was true for all of them. Stefano, Glykeria, brave Giorgios, poor unfortunate Kosta—all the dead had become vague memories. The events remained etched firmly in his mind, and he knew they were real, but the players had become ghosts, as if such courage, treachery, grief could never have been the stuff of true lives. Even that hardened killer Captain Elias seemed insubstantial, a role he had once played and then put away. Which was more or less the case.

What was real to him now was his son's illness-ravaged body, his grandson's dangerous predicament. The young, ruthless Fotis was a shadow; the old, scheming Fotis—kind, cantankerous, desperate for life—was the man he contended with now. It was hard to keep the desire for revenge hot for decades. Who knew when a word, a scent, would transport him back to those bad days? It still happened, but less frequently, and more of his time and energy went to the living, as was only right. He wanted to protect each of these people from harm, from the past, and from each other, and it seemed an impossible but worthy task, sufficient in itself.

"I do not want to see the boy hurt, Benny. And I don't want you hurt any further."

"You are not considering that the other side will not let this go, whatever we do. They are still searching. Meeting with the girl shows how reckless *they've* become. She doesn't know anything, but they were willing to seize her on an innuendo. Who will they try next?"

"They know we are on to them now. They will be more careful."

"Don't depend on it. These old men do not behave logically about this painting."

It was true, of course. With death so near, they felt they had nothing to lose, and immortality, real or spiritual, to gain. They were capable of anything.

"Then we must be on guard. And seek further protection from the police."

"Our best defense is to hunt down the threat ourselves."

"My friend," Andreas spoke gently, unsure for a moment what he wanted to say. "Do you have anyone you are close to now? A wife, a lover?"

"What the hell does that have to do with anything?"

"Where is your son?"

"In Israel. With his mother. Like good Jews should be."

"Why aren't you with them?"

"We're divorced, years ago. You knew that. Anyway, I can't live in that country anymore. It's all factions and I'm still considered an unstable fellow. I can't even bear to visit."

"Does the boy come here?"

"Yes. Sometimes he sees me and sometimes he doesn't. What are you getting at, Spyridis? That I need love?"

"A man's family steadies him. Risks are considered in proportion to what might be lost. A man who feels he has nothing to lose is a strong weapon, but a dangerous one. I was feeling that way when I came to you two weeks ago. I no longer do."

They were quiet for a time while Benny smoked a third Gauloise. Andreas regretted the personal questions, the lecturing tone. Benny was too old to be treated that way. The mood had come upon the old man without warning.

"What do we do with these two?" the big man asked, pointing his chin down the street toward Matthew's apartment. "I can't keep playing bodyguard, I've got better things to do."

"Ms. Kessler should report yesterday's incident. It might gain her some protection. The police might even be able to find del Carros."

"Why? He didn't actually do anything. His man cut me when I stuck a gun in his ribs."

"We can ask her to leave your name out of the report, if that is what bothers you."

"It's nothing to me. I'm a licensed investigator, the gun is registered. But it may look bad for all of you. Why is the girl talking to buyers after she has sold the piece? Why is a suspect's grandfather putting an investigator on his girlfriend? Anyway, I wouldn't count on police protection. They're very stingy about handing that out."

"Matthew can go to my son's house for a while. The woman can go with him, if she likes. They should be safer out there."

"Will you call your man back? Morrison."

"Yes. It was too late last night when I got the message. I will call him this morning."

"And you will tell me if he has discovered anything of interest?"

"Perhaps."

Benny exhaled furiously.

"Don't play with me, Spyridis, or I'll wash my hands of you."

"That would be tragic."

21

This time it was Morrison who wanted to meet. Andreas joined him at the corner of Fiftieth Street and Fifth Avenue, beneath the looming facade of St. Patrick's Cathedral, and they walked east toward Morrison's next appointment.

"How's your son?"

"I think he has improved," Andreas replied. "I cannot explain it."

"Don't try. That's good news."

"We shall see."

"And how was your grandson's trip to Salonika?"

"Robert, please, we have only a few blocks."

"You think this is chitchat? He's in deep, my friend. There are two people dead in Greece, and your buddy Dragoumis is AWOL."

"Are you part of the investigation now?"

"No. Just curious."

"You are, as they say, covering your ass."

"You bet I am. I'm the one who gave clearance for your grandson to leave the country. Now it appears that the matter has escalated. You don't think you owe me some answers?"

"So you have no information for me?"

"I have information. I believe in sharing. I'm a sharing kind of guy. Share with me, Andy."

Very well, then. Andreas considered what to say.

"Matthew was nowhere near where the incident took place. Someone tried to assassinate Dragoumis in the mountains. At least two were killed, one of them his nephew. The authorities there suspect *November 17,* which means that no one will be caught. Myself, I am skeptical."

"Why?"

They stopped at a streetlight on Park Avenue. A tattooed bike messenger zipped down Fiftieth Street, crossed himself, then pedaled furiously into traffic, just ahead of a roaring Brinks truck. Andreas found Morrison's questions tiresome.

"The nephew was shot by a forty-five, and there was a motor-cycle, which all sounds correct for *17.* But Dragoumis is too old and obscure a target for them, and it happened too far from Athens."

"Who do you suspect?"

"Everyone. Fotis has many enemies. Anyway, you are bound to know more than I do, so why not simply tell me?"

"I don't know that much," Morrison claimed as they crossed the avenue. "They identified the second man. Serious prison time for everything from extortion to weapons sales. He was so mangled they thought he might be your friend at first. Now they think the hat and cigarettes were a kind of calling card from Dragoumis, letting whoever ordered the hit know that he had gotten the better of them."

"How did Fotis escape the scene?"

"Not sure. They did find an abandoned car near a small airport in Kozani."

"He's back here," Andreas said with certainty.

"Could be. I assumed he'd go into hiding."

"He will, but he came back here first. I tell you, Robert, I do not believe that icon ever left New York."

"You're right about that."

"Ah, now we come to your information."

"The NYPD has been looking into Dragoumis' employees, especially the one who disappeared after the theft. Anton Marcus, aka, Marchevsky. They picked him up at Kennedy the night before last. False passport, ten thousand in cash on his person. He's actually a tough cookie, wouldn't tell them anything. But there's a guy he used to work for, Vasili Karov, liquor wholesaler, Russian mob. Apparently Dragoumis gets a lot of his boys from Karov, and there is some question whether they ever really leave Karov's orbit. You following me?"

"I am not yet senile."

"So anyway, they figure Karov may be mixed up in this. They shook him down once before but got nothing. This time, they tell him that Anton squealed, which is bullshit, but they must have made some good guesses. Two lawyers and eight hours later he cuts a deal, tells them everything. It's pretty much what you guessed. Dragoumis and Karov cooked it up between them. The other Russian wasn't supposed to get shot, but no one told him the plan and he put up too much of a fight. The icon gets put aside for Dragoumis. The Russians get three other paintings which they take at the same time. Except that Karov says Dragoumis tricked him, left the wrong painting for him to steal. Anyway, Karov figures that was his excuse to shaft the Greek and sell the switched painting to a new buyer."

"You don't believe that."

"Why would Dragoumis go to the trouble of setting this up just to leave the wrong painting? And why does Karov care, when the painting isn't his in the deal? He's making an excuse for double-crossing your pal."

"What was the name of the new buyer?"

"Del Rios? Something like that. Probably a false name. Cops are looking for him now."

"Did Karov say how much he paid?"

"A hundred and fifty, I think."

Not enough. The Russian might be bending the truth, but there was truth there. Del Carros—surely the name Morrison was fumbling for—had been willing to pay Ana Kessler a million and a half. Unless he was a complete fool, Karov would not settle for so little.

"When did this exchange take place?"

"Four days ago."

Before del Carros cornered Ana. Yet it was obvious from that meeting that he was still hunting for the icon. He had purchased the fake knowing it was fake. Why? To put Fotis off his guard? So Fotis still had the icon, had never parted with it. Andreas felt certain.

They crossed Second Avenue and walked a little way without speaking. The old man understood that now was the time to pass on what he knew about del Carros, and what he guessed about Dragoumis. To let go of these last bits of secret information and be truly done with it. Still, he hesitated. Morrison touched him on the shoulder.

"One more thing. A Felix Martín flew into Newark from Mexico City five days ago. Argentine citizen. Probably means nothing. There must be a hundred guys in Buenos Aires alone with that name, but it is one of the aliases your German used to use. Just thought I'd mention it."

Andreas said nothing. He had resisted Benny's words the day before, and even now he wished that he was a man who believed in coincidence. Morrison began walking again, and Andreas fell into step behind him. They emerged onto First Avenue with a brilliant afternoon light striking the white-and-black tower of the UN, and a huge gray freighter moving down the East River.

"There's a great Greek restaurant just one block up. We'll go there sometime. So, Andy, you got anything else to tell me? You sure do seem to be thinking hard about something."

"Trying to put some things together."

"You let me know if you do. I have to run."

"Thank you, Robert. I will keep you informed."

"That would be a first."

  . . . brought back from the Holy Land by Helena, the mother of Constantine. Upon the robe were stains of sacred blood from the

wounds of our Savior as he lay in his mother's arms, fallen but soon to rise. From the robe, a section was cut bearing these stains, and sealed between two panels of cypress. Upon these Matthias, a monk of the Studium, created the image of the Holy Mother as she appeared to him in a vision, so that all who looked upon it knew this to be her true face. The image was then placed in the church of the Blachernae, above the silver casket which held the robe itself, and there it performed many miracles, especially curing the ill among the family and followers of the Emperor. From that church, the image would be brought forth in time of need and carried in procession around the walls to instill courage in the hearts of the city's defenders. . . .

When, on that evil day in the year of our Lord 1453, the infidel Turks, by benefit of the weariness of the defenders and the faithlessness of their allies, laid low the great city of Constantinople, the church of the Blachernae was defiled, and the holy objects within it were destroyed. Then it was that a monk named Lazarus risked death to enter the church and take the Holy Mother created by Matthias from its golden frame upon the wall. Protected by the Virgin's power, Lazarus walked through fire and devastation to leave the fallen city of Constantine and carry the holy image west. Thereafter he was seen throughout the lands of the vanished Empire for many years beyond the normal life of men, preserved by the Virgin above for the protection of the Living Presence below, and wherever he passed, the sick were healed, and the troubled in spirit were made calm. Some say he went to Thessalonica, and some say to Ioannina in Epiros, but to this day no one knows for sure what was the fate of Holy Mother.

Ioannes folded the pages carefully and placed them in the envelope. They would open the way for him, he had to believe. In the beginning was the word. In what direction these words of Theodoros would push the boy, he could not guess, but something must be attempted. One voice had now separated itself from the rest, and it had become more and more adamant about the need for decisive action. He had decided to surrender to that voice.

After studying the map, he took the PATH train in from New Jersey, became lost in the bright tunnels and plazas beneath Penn Station, but finally found the platform for the number one train, which carried him to Columbus Circle. From there, he walked diagonally through Central Park toward his destination. He got lost here too, on the twisting paths and roadways, but he did not mind so much. The park was alive with growth this early May, faded yellow daffodils, just-blooming red tulips, sweet white and pink apple blossoms, cherry trees, lilac. He had not known the place could be so beautiful. And he understood that he was meant to appreciate it, even now, especially now, in this time of turmoil. It was always this way, moments of great beauty accompanying darkness of the soul. It was a gift not to be despised or ignored, and Ioannes drew breath deeply and smiled at everything around him.

He had dismissed the useless investigator Jimmy, had stopped taking calls from Bishop Makarios. He had even left a call from the secretary of the Holy Synod in Greece unreturned. They had all made a mess of things. All those involved in the matter had been thinking only about themselves—small, mean plans. A bolder vision was required, and Ioannes had some sense of what he must do, though very little sense at all of how to accomplish it. He only knew that the boy was the key.

The broad stairs of the museum were thronged with the usual students, tourists, homeless people, smoking and drinking soda and enjoying the day. Ioannes weaved through them and passed in the central door, through the grand hall of a foyer and over to a little alcove he had spied out on his last visit. The elevator was at the end. A key or card would be required to operate it, and so the priest merely waited by the doors, as if he were precisely where he ought to be. Within ten minutes a woman appeared beside him, trim, middle-aged, with glasses and a name tag hanging about her neck: Carol Voss. She smiled at Ioannes.

"You realize that this is a staff elevator?"

"Yes." A whole world of corridors and rooms existed behind, beneath, between what the common visitor saw, he knew. As in a cathedral or monastery. The inner sanctum. "I am meeting one of the curators."

"They're supposed to come down here and escort you in. Who are you meeting?"

"Matthew Spear."

"Oh, Matthew's a friend of mine. We're in the same department. But I'm sorry to say that he isn't here today. In fact, I'm not sure exactly when he returns."

"Really. How unfortunate. You say you are a friend of his?"

"That's right."

He had cut himself off from all investigative assistance. He could not hope to find the boy on his own, and must depend now on the greater design. There would be a purpose to whatever happened. The voice spoke quietly but firmly: *trust her.* Ioannes reached inside his jacket pocket and withdrew the envelope, held it out to her.

"You will give this to him when you see him, please?"

"Um, sure, I don't see why not." She took the envelope.

"It is extremely important that he receive it. As soon as possible. And also very important that no one but Matthew should see it. I pray that you understand me."

She was a quiet soul, like him, and she sensed his urgency in his stillness.

"I promise to keep it private. I don't know when I'll see Matthew, though."

"I am confident that he will return here soon. I place my hopes in that, and in you. Bless you." He turned and moved away before she could say anything in return, but he had made his impression. She was not the kind of woman to shirk the duty he had placed upon her.

The sky above the avenue had grown strange. Still blue to the south, fierce gray clouds to the north. Ioannes could not tell which way the clouds were moving, or what the evening's weather held. It did not matter greatly. He would walk in the park once more, extract some sweetness while he still might, before the terrible task beckoned again.

There was something both touchingly intimate and maddeningly claustrophobic about her forced captivity with his family. His father was ill, though less so than she had expected, and still quite handsome, in a harsher way than Matthew. He stayed in his study, reading or sleeping, accepting the occasional visit. The mother had left Ana alone at first, when they arrived the night before, but had been at her all this next day. Trying to feed her every ninety minutes. Asking all sorts of questions about Matthew, as if Ana were a wife or girlfriend of long standing, instead of someone who had met her son only a few weeks before, someone who felt that she might already love him without really knowing him at all.

"She likes you," Matthew said, when they were alone for a while, his mother shopping, his father asleep.

"Is that why she keeps scowling at me?"

"That's just her normal expression. She likes talking to you."

"She's plying me for information about what's going on."

"Don't worry, she doesn't really want to know."

"Anyway, what difference does it make if she likes me?"

"None at all, but she does. Trust me."

"Would I be sitting here in your parents' kitchen, after everything that's happened, if I didn't trust you?"

He put his lips to hers and her body responded immediately, despite their exertions during the last two nights. They barely made it upstairs to the guest room, his old bedroom. There was something vaguely taboo about doing it in the afternoon in his parents' house, with his father asleep below. She understood very well that there was a good deal of seeking for relief and comfort mixed in with the lust, but it didn't make the sex any less intense or satisfying.

Matthew fell asleep minutes after they finished, still making up for lost time. Ana waited a little while, watching his chest rise and fall, stroking his arm, and breathing in his scent. Her friend Edith insisted that you could forget about good looks, intelligence, and all the rest; attraction was about scent. Ana wondered if it wasn't true. Then she crawled from the bed to her travel bag, digging out a box of Marlboros and a lighter. Sitting in the window seat, she pulled up the sash several inches, lit a cigarette, blew smoke into the breezy air and tried to set her mind in order.

What she really needed was a day or two alone, away from everyone, including Matthew, to think all this through. They had promised each other to let the icon go, yet details had nagged at her for days. The name in the diary, del Carros' hints, his fear of her knowledge, which made him say more then he should. Eight years earlier, during another terrible illness of her grandfather's, he had raged semiconsciously about being responsible for her father's death. This was not a new thing, and she had tried to calm him, but he had been inconsolable. It was supposed to be me, he had insisted over and over. As if the death had not been random, but that someone was meant to die. She had chalked it up to guilt and the delusions of fever, but like these later details, it had stayed with her.

What to do about it? She could try to set up another meeting with del Carros, but that would be madness, and he would surely never go for it. She could leave it alone and hope that he would be caught, that the truth would come out some other way. Was she prepared for whatever the truth might be? Would it be better if he just vanished again, if it all remained a mystery?

"What are you doing?" Matthew spoke from the bed. His voice was more alert than she would have expected.

"Oh, just making myself crazy."

"You're supposed to leave that to me."

"I was crazy long before I met you, sweetheart."

"Why don't you come back over here?"

Why not, indeed? Yet she sat there several moments longer, finishing the cigarette, wondering now about Matthew and herself, and if whatever was between them could survive beyond the elevated emotions of the current crisis. Would they still care for each other when all the excitement was over, when dull, humdrum daily life returned? When the icon was well and truly put to rest? Was she really so eager to know? Better to enjoy it while it lasted. She stubbed the butt out on the exterior sill, closed the window, then rose and went to him.

22

The hospital in Queens was not as impressive as the one in Manhattan. Older, dingier, even less well organized, if that was possible. Andreas rode up to the eighth floor in an elevator that vibrated alarmingly underfoot. The tired Jamaican nurse beside him took no notice of it.

His thinking had become confused once more. Morrison's news echoed in his mind, testing his will. It was easy to tell himself that nothing had changed, that this visit was simply a last convulsion, a necessary act for purging his conscience and satisfying his curiosity. Easy to tell himself, but hard to believe. The important thing was not to involve Benny and Matthew any further. That much he was determined upon.

The gray-green corridor was suffused with the universal smell of institutional sickness. Stale air, urine, cleaning fluid; the memory-scent of a hundred visits to men now dead. Andreas found the room easily enough. There had been a police guard for the first few days, he'd heard, but since the patient had become well enough to question, that had been dispensed with. It was his information they had been protecting, not this life. Nicholas

looked up at him as he entered, face thin and pale, dark eyes wide
with concern. Andreas understood that the wounded man might
still not know what exactly had happened, and that his visit could
hardly be welcome.

"Peace, Nicky," he said in Russian, taking a chair by the bed.
The other man shifted under the white sheets, but the IV in his
left arm limited his motion. Thick bandaging on his chest was
visible beneath the flimsy blue hospital gown. Someone had
placed a vase of yellow tulips on the rolling table beside him. A
screen pulled halfway across the room separated his bed from the
one by the window, where another patient watched a game show
on television. Nicholas nodded, but spoke no reply.

"I'm here on my own." Andreas reverted to English. "I wanted
to see how you were doing."

"I'm alive." His voice barely above a whisper.

"Yes. My grandson had a hand in that." Nicholas looked at
him blankly. "Matthew. He went to see his godfather that morning, and he found you instead, bleeding on the floor. He held a
towel against your wound until the ambulance arrived. Has no
one told you?"

"The police asked questions. They didn't tell me much."

"No one has visited? No one from Fotis' operation has
checked up on you?"

"Phillip, you know, who runs the restaurant. He's the only
one."

"Did he bring the flowers?"

"No." Nicholas smiled just a little. "My girlfriend."

"Good. I'm happy you are not alone."

"She's working now. She'll come by soon."

"I won't stay long."

Nicholas cleared his throat and shifted again, obviously still in
some pain.

"I didn't know that about Matthew, what he did. I'm grateful."

"He's in trouble. Matthew is, with the police. They think he
might have had something to do with the robbery."

"Has he been arrested?"

"No. They have nothing to hold him on. With Fotis gone,

though, they may become frustrated and decide that someone else must take the fall."

"I don't understand. They've already arrested Anton and Karov. My girlfriend told me. Why are they looking for anyone else?"

"Come now, Nicky, we both know there was more to it than that. And the police know it also. Fotis put Karov up to it. They were all in it together, Anton, Karov, Dragoumis. Everyone but you. You were left to take the bullet."

Nicholas made a sour face and grabbed a fistful of sheet with his right hand.

"Everyone, eh? Why not your grandson, too? Why not you?"

Andreas nodded diplomatically.

"I don't blame you for suspecting me. You know very well that Fotis and I are at odds. Maybe you think I have some plan. But surely you know better than to suspect Matthew."

"I don't know anything. How can I know anything lying here?"

"Do you know who shot you?"

"They were wearing masks. I couldn't tell."

"*Bravosou!*" Andreas laughed derisively. "They try to kill you, and you are still keeping their secrets. That is what you were trained to do, yes? Keep secrets. You're a good soldier, Nicky. They will say that about you when you're dead. He was a good soldier, a useful tool. He kept the secrets."

"Go to hell."

"At least you'll have the woman to mourn you."

"What is any of it to you, anyway?"

"I told you. The boy."

"Yes, well, your boy was with Dragoumis all the damn time, talking about that icon. So maybe the police are right. Maybe I should tell them so."

Andreas leaned forward and made his voice quiet. "Fotis used the boy. As he used you, as he has used me a dozen times. It is what he does. You know this. The time is long passed for defending him, you must look to yourself. They have all betrayed you. You are the only friend you have left, unless you choose to trust me, even a little."

"You think I'm a fool? I *am* looking out for myself. I don't care about protecting them, I want to stay alive, that's all."

"But your silence is no protection. You did nothing wrong, and they tried to kill you anyway. Now they are on the run. Dragoumis is in hiding. Karov is in custody, and his operation is shut down."

"Someone will replace him. You don't know how it works in my neighborhood. If I testify against any of them I won't be forgiven."

"I wonder if you are right. Karov has plea-bargained, there is no testimony necessary. And I don't think anyone would blame you about Anton, after he shot you. But let that go. I'm not asking you to testify against anyone."

"What, then?"

"Very simple. I want to know what Fotis was up to before you put him on the airplane that morning. Anything you can tell me. You see, not a dangerous question."

"Talking to you at all may be dangerous."

"Well, it's too late to protect against that. It was you who drove him to the airport, yes?"

Nicholas considered him carefully.

"Yes. I drove him everywhere. Anton is a terrible driver."

"Early in the morning."

"Before early. It was a seven-thirty flight, we left at four. I've told the police this."

"I'm not with the police, Nicky. Why so early? It's twenty minutes to Kennedy at that hour."

"He likes to be early for things."

"Did he have a lot of luggage? Anything bulky?"

"No, just a small bag and a suitcase."

Andreas paused, looked carefully at the younger man's face. Circle back.

"Why so early?"

"I told you."

"You went somewhere else first. You made another stop before the airport."

The Russian grew more agitated. Because he could not lie with ease, Nicholas could only choose between withholding information or speaking truth, and he clearly did not like his choices.

"We went into the city first. Into Manhattan."

"Why did you go there?"

"He has a few apartments. People stay sometimes, or he does business there with people who won't come to Queens. We stopped by one of those. He needed to drop off something."

"What?"

"A painting he sold. A big abstract. I helped him wrap it the night before. He was leaving it in the apartment for the buyer to pick up."

"How big?"

"I don't know. Big enough to break my back getting it up those stairs. Maybe four or five feet square."

"And you were with him the whole time? In the apartment?"

"No, he had to make some calls or something, I don't remember. I went back to the car."

"I see. Now tell me, where is this apartment?"

As the old man had anticipated, this was the question Nicholas balked at. He did not outright refuse to answer but simply stayed quiet a long time, glancing at the door. Andreas knew that the moment the nurse arrived, or the girlfriend, that would be the end of the conversation.

"Nicky. Matthew wants the icon returned to Greece, to the church. That is all he has been working for. All I want is to help him. He has done you a kindness. These others have left you to die, you owe them nothing. Your silence benefits you nothing. You could be of great help to us. You could do a service to the church. Which will you choose?"

"Damn you," whispered the wounded man. "You talk like Dragoumis. I don't believe either of you. For the boy, for Matthew, I will tell you. Twenty-eighth Street, near Third Avenue. The gray building one in from the northwest corner. I don't remember the number. The third floor, in back."

"Thank you."

"Please leave now, Mr. Spyridis. I don't want you here when the girl comes."

"Of course. Did you tell the police about the apartment?"

"No."

"I wonder why not?"

"I don't know. Something in my head said don't talk about it."

"I am grateful, Nicky, and I will keep your trust. Be well, my boy."

"We should not even be here. We should have left the country yesterday."

Van Meer's voice carried the calm, lazy tone he always affected, as if nothing really mattered to him, but the fact that he had repeated the thought twice in the last twenty-four hours underscored his disapproval. Del Carros had no real fear of Jan's backing out, yet some attempt to mollify him must be made, to ease the younger man's professional conscience. Jan thought of himself as someone who did things by the book, but del Carros knew him better. The Dutchman throve on chaos, ever since his violent youth in Amsterdam. The professional polish had come later, and it was a thin coat.

"There is no immediate danger."

"You cannot know that," Jan insisted, scanning the street through the windshield. "You don't know their resources. And there is the police to consider as well."

"They will be looking for del Carros. They will not find me under that name."

"It was unwise meeting the woman."

"We've discussed that."

He would be damned if he would take a scolding from Van Meer, but he had also come to feel that the business with the woman had been handled poorly. She knew some things, yes, but not where the icon was, so what the hell did the rest matter? He kept making mistakes with that family, letting his rage at the dead old man who had robbed him cloud his thinking. He had done the same thing with the son, Richard, the girl's father, when he had come to Caracas in his father's place. The banker had a good eye and saw right through the scheme: he knew that the icon they offered him was a fake, that the one on his father's wall was, in fact, genuine. Del Carros had not really intended to fool anyone in the end, wanting only to get the elder Kessler in his clutches. His son replacing him spoiled that, and the conditions set on the meeting made hostage-taking impossible.

In frustration, del Carros had done the same thing then that he had done all these years later with the daughter. Taunt the banker, insult his father, drop hints about the work, failing to either anger him or draw him out; giving him, instead, the knowledge to piece together things that he should never know. After the meeting, del Carros panicked and called in a large favor. At the time it had felt necessary—the banker knew too much—but del Carros could not lie to himself now as he did then. He had, at that moment, temporarily lost hope of getting the icon, and the action was intended solely to punish the elder Kessler. An act of pure cruelty. Bad enough to have wasted life and energy that way. To repeat the same mistakes with the girl two decades later was unforgivable.

"We've discussed it twice," he said again. "She requested the meeting. I could not rule out her knowing something useful."

"Spear is the key," Jan insisted. "He is the one who is close to Dragoumis."

"So where is he?"

"Did you expect me to get on the train and follow them? The woman knows my face, and there is no escape off a train. That's why I followed this one instead." He nodded his head at the hotel down the block.

"And you are certain he did not spot you? He is good, you know."

"If he's that good, then I can't be certain. But I do not think he did."

"And he went out this morning?"

"Yes, for a few hours."

"Why didn't you follow him?"

"I was waiting for you to arrive, as agreed."

"But he is in there now?"

"Unless there is a way into the alley from the kitchen."

"There may be."

Jan showed him the most condescending smile possible.

"You would have me be everywhere at once? Perhaps you should overcome your cheapness and hire more men. Or otherwise trust to reason. He has used the main entrance every time. You worry too much about the wrong things."

With great difficulty, del Carros held his tongue. It was completely unacceptable that he should be spoken to like this, but Jan ignored the niceties of the employer-employee relationship. And the old man could not rule out that his own anxiety was getting the better of him.

"Let's hope you are correct. He is the last thread we have to follow."

Paranoia was a common condition for anyone who had been in the game too long, and Andreas was not immune. The man who stepped out of the double-parked vehicle fifty yards behind the spot where Andreas left the taxi may have been nobody. However, paranoia could also save a man's life, and so the old Greek passed by the doorway he'd meant to enter, and continued around the corner to Third Avenue.

An odd neighborhood. Indian restaurants, cheap diners, at least one obvious welfare hotel. Neither a good nor a bad part of town, but a passing-through kind of place—a good neighborhood to hide in. Andreas crossed the avenue suddenly and glanced behind as he looked south for traffic. The man from the car had also turned north on Third, but he continued on his way without looking back.

Andreas went down Twenty-ninth Street to Second Avenue as the light grew lower and paler, wasting time, but wanting to be certain. The fact that he was more vulnerable than usual—no Benny and no gun—fed his suspicion. The best thing would be to return to his hotel, but time seemed precious, and he had come all the way down here. He didn't want to be defeated by irrational fear. *Find it,* Alekos had commanded him, *get it out of Matthew's life.* Turning on Twenty-seventh Street, he headed back to Third, walked the block north, and crossed Twenty-eighth to the gray building he'd passed earlier. The double-parked car was gone. Andreas had still not made up his mind on a course of action when a man emerged from the building in question: squat, heavily whiskered, and sucking hard on a cigarette. When he tossed the butt aside and began shoving the plastic trash barrels into line, Andreas took it as a sign, and knew he had his man.

"Excuse me, sir."

"What?" The unappealing fellow was immediately suspicious.

"I need to look at an apartment here."

"No apartments. Everything is rented."

"I understand. I need to look at one of the rented apartments. As part of an investigation."

The man pulled himself up straight, but this accomplished little.

"Yeah? And who the hell are you?"

Andreas realized that a police officer would have shown a badge at once. Still, the man seemed movable, if he could find the lever.

"The third floor, apartment in the rear. The one who rents it is a countryman of mine." Andreas reached into his coat for his old Foreign Service ID. It was an impressive item, small as a passport with gold-embossed leather and an official stamp next to his ten-year-old photograph. He gave the surly superindendent several moments to scrutinize it, trusting that the man could not read Greek. "Fotis Dragoumis. He is being investigated by my government."

"What do I care? We're not in your country. Here you need a warrant, from a judge."

"We are obtaining one. It is a slow process in this city. I would rather move more swiftly. It is very important."

"To you. Not to me." The man pursed his fat lips, then lit another cigarette. "Come back when you have a warrant." He blew smoke in Andreas' direction and turned to his work.

"I may lose an opportunity by waiting. You may lose an opportunity also."

"For what?"

"For profit."

The words had an immediate effect, and the super shuffled his barrels distractedly.

"What profit?"

"Do you want to discuss this out here?"

They retreated into the vestibule, though the bulky super would not open the inside door. Andreas was acutely aware of his exposed back facing the big glass pane of the outer door as he slipped his wallet from his coat. He slid out five twenty-dollar bills, then hesitated.

"You *do* have keys?"

The man shrugged.

"Yes? No?" Andreas' voice became sharp.

"I'm not supposed to, but these damn absentee tenants. You have to check a leak, you have to be able to get in, you know?"

"I know." Andreas handed over the money. The super stared at the tiled floor for too long. The old man slid five more twenties out.

"You're not taking anything," the stocky fellow insisted. "You're just looking, right?"

"That is correct." If he found anything worth taking, he would worry about it then.

The apartment was small. Only two rooms, the second a bedroom with a chipped bureau and a narrow bed that clearly got no use. The larger room had a good-sized painting on each wall, a landscape and three abstracts. A large, narrow cardboard packing case leaned against the small sofa, one end open and bubble wrap spilling out. It cost Andreas another fifty dollars to persuade the super to wait in the corridor. Then he went immediately to the open container. Inside was a green-and-blue abstract painting, as big as the box and still wrapped. Reaching his arm in as far as it would go, Andreas felt around behind the canvas, where the frame would have provided more than sufficient depth to hide a smallish, flat object. Nothing. Yet a great deal of the bubble wrap seemed to have been pulled out. Had the Snake retrieved the icon in the last day or so? Had he trusted it to be safe for a week before that, sitting in a packing crate in the middle of the room? Knowing, as he must, that the super was not trustworthy? It did not seem like Fotis.

Andreas turned a tight circle in the middle of the room, surveying walls, floor, ceiling in the dying light from the narrow, dust-streaked windows. What else? He explored the small closet containing nothing but wire hangers, testing its walls and floors for hidden panels. He slid painfully to his knees to search beneath the sofa, pulled up the cushions, opened all the cabinets in the tiny kitchenette, feeling more foolish by the moment. The super would expel him in a few minutes. Something was amiss here, something was slightly off, and it would come to him if he had enough time. Chair, coffee table, sofa, closet, paintings.

Paintings. The landscape did not go with the abstracts. That was nothing, Fotis collected both. It was smaller than the other paintings. Smaller, but with a large, deep frame that raised it a few inches from the wall. He stepped onto the sofa, balancing carefully on a spongy cushion, and lifted the painting from its hanger. Then stepped down and flipped it. He had been so certain of success that the empty space in the frame confused him. It was precisely the right size. He could even detect spots where the inside wooden frame had been rubbed against something. It had been here. Or something had been, and what else but the icon?

Andreas rehung the landscape. Tiredness took him and he sat down. He almost felt he could sleep; just put his head back on the striped cushions and fade into oblivion. Another one of Fotis' abandoned items. Once more, too slow. He would never catch the Snake.

The super spoke to someone in the corridor, and Andreas struggled to his feet again. Quickly, he lifted each of the other canvases a few inches from its perch, just far enough to see that there was nothing behind it, then moved toward the door. It occurred to him at the last moment that he should have defied the super's instructions and turned the locks.

A youngish, blond man wearing a leather jacket and tinted spectacles entered the apartment, smiling. The same man who had seemed to be following him earlier. And quite likely, Andreas intuited with resigned dread, the Dutchman who had slashed Benny. There was no way out of the place but through him, and the man would be quick.

"Mr. Spyridis, sorry we are late. You have probably examined the place already, but I need to beg your indulgence while we do so again. Turn around, please."

Andreas easily batted away the hand that reached for his shoulder, but he was too slow to stop the fist that struck his stomach. Not a hard punch, or he would have ended up on the floor, gaping like a caught fish. In fact, the gentleness of the blow was almost an insult, customized as it was for an old man, yet sufficient to send Andreas to his knees, gasping softly. Black patches danced before his eyes while the other man's expert hands searched him for weapons, finding none.

"We are very confident, I see," the blond assailant murmured, standing up straight. He pulled Andreas gently to his feet. "Listen, please. It will take nothing for me to harm you. And I know your qualities, so I will be prepared for whatever you do. Sit here and catch your breath."

It took several moments after he sat down for Andreas to notice that someone else had entered the apartment. A man older than himself, in a heavy coat like his own. Thin lips and protruding blue eyes. It was at moments like this that time became compressed, years fell away like dead skin, age was no more than the wrinkled casings that covered the young men they had been, and in some ways still were. It didn't matter that he had seen this man only three or four times up close, fifty-six years before. Andreas recognized Müller instantly. The old German stared back at him, expressionless.

"Del Carros," Andreas said for no reason.

"If you prefer," the other man responded, in a voice different from the one remembered, in an accent warped by time and travel. "I hope Jan was not too rough with you."

Andreas thought of saying something snide, but shortness of breath prevented him. He knew that fear would come next, once he got over the shock, but hoped to maintain a clear head and an attitude of calm. He understood that the Dutchman could hurt him easily, and would probably do so eventually. Andreas was afraid, not of the pain, but of shaming himself. Silence was his friend now. He must neither provoke nor cajole, but bide his time and hope for an opportunity.

Jan conducted his search swiftly, hitting all the same spots Andreas already had checked, begging his pardon as he stepped next to him to remove the landscape from the wall. He and Müller then examined the interior frame for a minute or two.

"It was here," the German said, looking up at Andreas. "I wonder where it is now."

Their two expectant faces irritated him unreasonably.

"What the hell would I be doing here if I knew that?"

The German nodded agreeably.

"I thought you might be in it together, you and Dragoumis, but now I see differently. He has betrayed you again, yes?"

The fool saw nothing, Andreas realized, but good, let him pursue that line of thinking.

"Still," Müller continued, "you must know him better than anyone. You can probably guess what his next step will be, where he is now."

Andreas shook his head noncommittally. Müller would think whatever he wanted, and whatever he thought might be put to use. Müller. Incredible that he now stood before him. Unreal somehow.

"And if not you," the German went on, "then perhaps your grandson. Maybe he is the one who knows. Maybe he and the girlfriend have kept some secrets from you. What do you think? Still nothing to say? Why do I believe that the three of you together could connect all the pieces?"

Careful now, thought Andreas. This was just the terrain he feared treading on. Show nothing. Jan whispered some words.

"Yes," Müller agreed. "Time to go. Nothing more we can accomplish here. You will come with us, Captain. We'll give you a little time to decide how you can best assist us."

There was nothing to do but go. At least he would have the advantage of knowing where they were. The Dutchman helped him to his feet once more, then took up position behind him. Müller started out the door first.

"Look out for that superintendent," said Andreas. "He's a thief."

Jan laughed.

23

We need to talk, Mr. Spear. Matthew. There can be no further delay."

Ana had argued strenuously against his going into the city. Even his parents, who were mostly ignorant of what was happening, tried to forbid him. Yet his work wouldn't wait forever. His department chief, Nevins, had shown enormous patience with Matthew's continual absences, but the senior legal counsel wanted a meeting about the icon business, from which a probation or suspension could easily follow. He promised Ana that he would go straight from the train to the museum, stay out of sight, and return as soon as possible. After he read the pages that Carol had left in an envelope on his desk, however, his mind could not focus on his work, and the odd looks and probing questions of colleagues finally drove him out of his office and into the relative quiet of the Islamic wing. There, before the blue brilliance of the wall-sized *mihrab* from Iran, the priest found him.

"Father John."

"Ioannes, please. You told me you were Greek."

The light reflected off a thousand turquoise tiles gave the man a sickly pallor. There was no smile this time, only intense concern, and a brave attempt to restrain it.

"That's right, I did," Matthew confessed. "I wonder why. I'm American, of course. Someone told you to find me here?"

"One of your associates. Don't be upset, people will tell a priest anything. Apparently you come to this room often. I can see why; it's quite beautiful."

"And quiet. I'm sorry the Byzantine rooms aren't finished yet. Meantime, I slip over borders and religions."

"The Orthodox and Muslims have much in common. Only a fool would deny it. Did you read the material I left you?"

"Yes."

"And?"

"I've removed myself from the situation. It's too dangerous for amateurs. People have been hurt."

"People have been killed. More will be."

"Perhaps, but I can't do anything about that. I only risk becoming one of them. You too, Father. These guys don't care who they hurt. Priests have died before."

"I'm not concerned with that. And I do not ask you to put yourself in danger, only talk to me. Do you know where your godfather is now?"

"No."

Ioannes regarded him for several long seconds. Despite the literal truth of his reply, Matthew felt uneasy in the priest's gaze.

"You have no idea?"

"Look. What is it that you think you can do? Do you think you can keep it safe? Do you think you can get it back to Greece without being intercepted? Do you think your corrupt church can really protect it?"

The calm face registered no offense at the hard words.

"I am uncertain about the answers to those questions, but my fears are similar to your own. That is why I feel a more permanent solution is necessary. Shall we go on discussing this here, or find a more private place?"

Matthew looked around, seeing nothing. Something in the priest's words had gotten to him, and he knew that they must go on with this. Where? What coffee shop would be quiet enough and private enough? What place was safe any longer?

"I need to do a few things. Then we'll go talk."

Matthew spent another half hour finishing an acquisitions memo and reviewing the growing mountain of reports and phone calls he would have to return to another day. The cardboard model of the new Byzantine rooms sat on a table just outside the door of his cramped, airless office, and he stared at it a moment as he passed. The proudest achievement of his time here; work was already proceeding in the chambers beside and directly below the great staircase. He could not bring himself to care about any of it. He could not even fake it anymore. Nevins gave him a sour look as he left. Surely they would fire him.

Father John wandered the great expanse of the Medieval Hall until Matthew came to collect him. The priest asked no questions as Matthew led him through the busy streets of Yorkville to his apartment. No better location had occurred to the younger man, and he could at least lock himself in and keep the telephone ready at hand. He had memorized Andreas' and Benny's numbers.

Surprisingly, the priest accepted a beer, which he sipped slowly from a water glass. Matthew left the shades down and lit a short, fat emergency candle to minimize the light any window-watcher might spy. The effect was more gloomily atmospheric than he would have liked.

"You are convinced, then?" Father Ioannes nodded at the pages spread across the wooden kitchen table. "That it is the same icon."

"I wouldn't say I'm convinced. It's quite possible."

"And this means nothing to you?"

"It doesn't change the nature of the work, or what it was intended to do. Heal. Engender faith. I suppose what it does is explain why people who know of its genesis would be willing to kill for it. It's exceptionally old, and built around an artifact even older and more precious."

"The swatch of robe."

"Yes."

"Soaked in the blood of Christ."

The quiet awe in the words, spoken by the old priest across a flickering candle, first chilled, then annoyed Matthew.

"If you choose to believe that."

"Why not believe it?"

"Because there are countless claims of such things, pieces of the true cross, finger bones of saints, the crown of thorns, the spear of Longinus."

"Undoubtedly many are false. And very likely some are true. The icon has power; you have felt that yourself. The power comes from somewhere."

"Faith," Matthew insisted, "does it not? The image inspires faith, and the power is granted by God. The image holds no power by itself. Any more than Peter's skull or Paul's thumb knuckle. It seems to me you people had a big fight about this a thousand-odd years ago. Iconoclasm. The destruction of images. I'm no supporter, but they had a point, and they forced a distinction. *Proskynesis,* the kind of veneration you could show an image, versus *latreía,* the true worship due to God alone. Yes?"

Ioannes put down the beer glass.

"The lesson was not necessary. Your point is understood, but your reasoning is false. Of course an icon is only wood and paint, worthless by itself. You cannot compare *that* to the blood of the Savior. Not even the bones of a holy man compare. A line is crossed when dealing with the very substance of the Christ himself. There is nothing more precious, nothing more terrible."

"My mistake. But why believe it's genuine? There are at least two famous icons associated with the clothing Mary wore, both lost. This one doesn't seem to match what I've read about either, so now we have a third one that nobody knows of?"

"It was known. The fragment of Theodoros I left you. The knowledge was lost."

"Why does Theodoros the Blind know this story that nobody else does? Why does it not appear in other histories?"

"There are few histories for those times. Very often we must trust a single source."

"And for that matter, why have I never read that passage before, when I've read Theodoros inside out?"

"It does not appear in the standard translations. It was found eighty years ago in a very old manuscript copy, somewhere in central Europe. Vienna, I think. By a man named Müller. He went to Greece a few years later to take the icon, but was unsuccessful. The priest with whom he tried to negotiate became suspicious of his motives and shared his concern with others in the village, including a curious, and larcenous, altar boy. The boy stole the papers from Müller and gave them to the priest, who delivered them to a nearby monastery for safekeeping. Müller's son, who became a Nazi officer, also had a copy of the pages, or knew their content. Later, he too came to Greece. I think you know that story."

Matthew nodded. The priest knew everything he did and a good deal more.

"And you read the pages at the monastery."

"Yes."

"OK. Let's assume Theodoros was writing the truth as far as he knew it. This found piece of robe really is in the icon. We still have to trust that what Helena brought back from Jerusalem was the robe of Mary. There's more than a three-hundred-year lapse. Who has been holding the robe all that time? Who can authenticate it? Who, having held it so long, is willing to surrender it to the mother of a pagan emperor?"

"The Arabs. What do they care for it?"

"Why would they have it?"

"They had the cross, which they did give to her."

"If you choose to believe *that* story."

The candle flickered wildly, and Matthew realized that it was his breathing causing it to do so. Ioannes stared into the darting flame and raised his hands in a gesture of surrender.

"We go in circles. This argument begins to resemble a more basic one. The man of reason demands proof in exchange for his faith. The man of God may believe in reason also, but knows that it will only take him so far, that there will come a stepping-off point into the unknown. He thinks with his mind until he reaches that ineffable place of mystery. Then he thinks with his heart, pushing forward or retreating. You are a man of reason.

Good. But tell me, when you stood before that image, when you touched that wood, did you not feel a special power? Speak the truth."

Matthew had nearly suppressed the mesmerizing experience of being before the panel. There was art to it—the sad eyes, the dusky shadows—but with the image as damaged as it was, artistry alone could not explain his response. And he had known nothing of the robe or the history when he first encountered the work.

"I felt something. It's difficult to describe, or to say what it means."

"You need not try. I have felt it also."

"You've seen the icon."

"Yes, I know it very well."

"How?"

"I grew up in the village where it lived. Just like your *Papou,* though I was much younger."

"Then you knew him."

"I thought I had said as much. Not well, he went to Athens when I was still a boy, and only returned to join the guerrillas after the Germans came. In fact, I don't ever remember meeting him until the morning he caught my brother and me in the abandoned chapel."

"Christ," whispered Matthew, understanding coming at once, "you're Kosta's brother."

"So you know about that."

"I know what my grandfather told me."

"I would like to hear what he said. Please."

"Your father burned the church and took the icon. Kosta killed Mikalis, the priest, when he tried to intervene. Then your father sent you and your brother to hide in the chapel while he . . . I don't know what he intended to do. Make a deal for it, or sell it later when things died down. He told my grandfather where to find you once he realized that my godfather was going to get the truth out of him sooner or later. Assuming Andreas would spare you. Fotis killed your dad. My grandfather tracked you to the chapel, shot your brother, and retrieved the icon."

The priest was silent as Matthew spoke, his large hands gripping the table edge. It occurred to Matthew that the older man might be hearing some of these things for the first time.

"I don't know," Ioannes began slowly, "about everything you say. It was years before I heard the whole story, and then just little pieces from different people. The fire in the church was a mystery. No one knew for certain who started it. Many said the Germans did. Some accused the *andartes* instead. Your grandfather's was the name on many people's lips."

"The atheist. Of course they would blame him."

"Yes. I cannot rule out that Andreas speaks true, that my father did do it. I was too young to understand what was happening. I remember firing that big pistol at your grandfather, half praying to kill him and half praying to miss. Kosta told me to stop, but I was only following my father's instructions. Protect my brother. Ten years old, I could barely hold the gun. Your grandfather was like a ghost. It was said he could vanish at will, and I believe he does have that power. He vanished from that rocky hillside, then suddenly he was coming through the door, bigger than life, an avenging angel. He must have struck me. I don't remember. I do remember waking up. They were arguing, cursing each other, and Andreas stepped over and shot Kosta in the head. Just shot him."

"That must have been terrible to see."

The priest nodded vigorously.

"I had seen the Germans shoot people, people I knew. And I was aware of the communists, the black marketeers, like my father, the collaborators, so I knew that our own people killed one another, but I had never seen that. Watching my brother die was, yes, it was terrible, but strange too. I had been hit on the head and felt sick and dizzy, so I wasn't sure it was real at first. And then Kosta had been so badly burned, so badly, in the fire. He was in great pain. I don't know if he would have wanted to live like that. What your grandfather did was merciful, I believe. Maybe even intentionally so. Which did not keep me from hating him for years."

"It's amazing that your brother made it to the chapel at all in his condition. You must have half carried him there."

"No, I could not touch him because of the burns. But he leaned upon me with one hand, and carried a long stick, like a staff, in the other. Moaning with every step. What a sight we must have been. Some mad prophet and his disciple, though I don't believe anyone saw us. And I had the icon tucked under my arm, wrapped carefully. It was a clumsy bundle, and I carried it for hours, but it seemed to possess no weight. It was the lightest burden imaginable. I remember unwrapping it on the little altar table in the chapel, just after I lit the candle, and seeing those eyes, and falling into that space. I felt the strength in it then. Bigger than me by far, almost too great for man to experience. I was awed, frightened even. It was good preparation for what happened next."

"Andreas brought you to the monastery."

"Amusing, isn't it? The atheist was the instrument of my faith. He should have killed me, that would have been the sensible thing. Perhaps it was this bargain with my father that stayed him."

"Maybe he just couldn't do it."

"Yes, that's what I decided later, when I thought about it. But it is pleasant for me to know that my father bargained for my life. It is difficult to despise one's father, but more difficult to do otherwise with mine. The icon undid him. He was that altar boy who stole the papers from the elder Müller, and he remembered what was in them. I heard him speak of it to my brother, though the memory did not come back to me until I read the pages myself. He destroyed our family, destroyed himself. This information, that he pleaded for me before he died. It's a little gift. I thank you for it."

"And you stayed at the monastery," Matthew said, with some surprise, and some odd eagerness. "You became a priest, even after all that you saw."

"What else to do after all that I saw? Go mad or find God. I was still young enough to believe in a higher purpose behind the horror I had witnessed. I had lost my mother the year before, then my father and brother together. My sisters were married and gone, there was nothing for me to return to. My soul was desolate, but my heart and mind were open. I was ready for the Word.

I was very fortunate. A few years older and I would have turned to cynicism, cruelty. I would have turned my back on Christ, as your grandfather did, as many young men did during those years. By the time my sister found me in the monastery, two years later, I had no desire to leave. I was home."

"But you did leave. I don't know what your position is in the church, but you're fluent in English, you get sent on sensitive assignments. Not the life of a monk."

"More a politician, or a spy, yes? I assure you that I am ill-suited to it. I was fortunate also in my mentor. A monastery can be a hard place for a young boy, but the abbot was a kind man, and your grandfather must have told him my tale. There was no other reason he would have taken me in. He saw right away that I was unprepared for the rigors of religious discipline, and taught me slowly. I learned English, a little French. I was even allowed to read some religious philosophy when I was older. The Orthodox have always emphasized asceticism and prayer above learning. My abbot was more cosmopolitan, and must have known that monastic life was merely a stopping-off place for him. Perhaps he sensed that the same would be true for me. Or perhaps I give him too much credit. Maybe he simply needed a protégé, and there I was, clever, and young enough to be molded to his purposes."

"What happened to him?"

"He is dead now, but first he made his way up the church hierarchy to the Holy Synod itself. I think he hoped for me to replace him there, but I was too much of a dreamer, too little of a politician. Another of his protégés was elevated, and that is the man I now serve."

"The man who sent you here."

The priest's face grew troubled, and he broke eye contact with Matthew.

"He sent me, yes, because I could identify the icon, and because I have had dealings here in the past. But Tomas and your godfather were ahead of us, and more killings followed."

"More? You mean in addition to those during the war, or have there been others since?"

"I mean throughout its existence," hissed Ioannes, guttering the flame. "The icon carries death in its wake. We no longer know how to treat an object of such preciousness. The mind-set has been lost. It overwhelms us, possesses us, makes us mad with longing. These many days I have spent searching for it, searching for you, have given me time to think. I do believe that things happen for a reason, even terrible things. I was granted this time to know the teachings of my own spirit. My mission is no longer the one I was sent upon. Voices have spoken to me."

The awed tone had returned. The priest had two modes—man of the world and wild-eyed believer—and they were beginning to alternate with frightening swiftness. Matthew suddenly wondered if Ioannes was not a little unbalanced.

"What have the voices told you?"

"Many things. They must be interpreted."

"But you've arrived at some answer."

"Not an absolute one. Anyway, it is not a thing you will wish to hear."

"Tell me, Father." But even as he spoke, Matthew realized that he already knew what the priest would say.

"I believe in my heart that this struggle will go on, the killings will go on, as long as the icon exists to tempt the weak. And we are most of us weak creatures. This object was created for another time. It can no longer exist in ours. It is too strong for our modern, godless condition. It must be returned to the power that inspired it."

"You mean it must be destroyed."

"Yes."

They were both quiet while the idea took substance between them, a bridge or a barrier. Matthew wanted to remain reasonable, to assess the priest's suggestion with cool detachment, but it was impossible. The idea was monstrous, even sacrilegious.

"I think," he began slowly, "that you're forgetting all the good associated with the icon, and giving too much credit to a few greedy old men. Do you give no credence to all the miraculous healings reported over the years? And even if that turns out to be just mind over body, don't we have to respect the object which can inspire that?"

"No doubt healings have occurred. In my youth I saw women cured of their arthritis, and one man cured of his blindness, at a touch. These were mostly poor and doubting souls, always Christ's favorites, and their contact with the work was brief. Compare this with the few who possessed it for some length of time. Ali Pasha, Müller, Kessler. Covetous souls, who may have lived long lives, but not happy ones. Strife and illness plagued them, they watched their loved ones die young. Then look at all those who tried to possess it, who came to grief somehow. My father and brother are two. Look at the lives it has used up and twisted. Your own godfather. Look what it has begun to do to you."

"Don't put me in that group, Father. I've been trying to let it all go."

"And doing admirably, though I wonder if you can succeed. Müller and Dragoumis left the icon alone for years at a time but were always drawn back. I need someone like you, who has tasted the work's power, to be my ally in this, to understand me. The icon carries death."

"How can that be so if it carries the blood of Christ?"

"Where is the contradiction?" the priest demanded. "Christ was surrounded by death. Death pursued all his followers but the timid, and many millions have died in his name since then. The promise of Christ is salvation of the soul, not long life on earth."

Matthew tried to frame a response, but his mind was alive with fear and agitation, and no logical rebuttal would come to him. The priest's thinking was wrong. Not just wrong but dangerously simplistic, a product, no doubt, of his own brutal experience. Understandable, but somehow he had to set the man straight before Ioannes did something rash.

The telephone rang, startling them both. It seemed to Matthew that it must be late, yet the clock indicated it was not, even if full darkness had fallen outside. The candle had burned down; for short emergencies, clearly. He knew he should simply let the phone keep ringing, but some uncontrollable urge caused him to reach back to the counter and pick it up.

"Yes."

"Mr. Spear. I am pleased that you are finally at home." The voice was old and unfamiliar, and Matthew felt at once that he had made a mistake in answering. "We have some time to make up, so I will come to the point. Your grandfather is in our care, and it is necessary for you to speak to me about the icon. I understand that your knowledge of its present location may be imprecise, but I do require that you tell me all you can. Are we clear so far?"

"My grandfather." What the hell was this? A threat, certainly, but from whom?

"Yes, Andreas is with us. We are getting on famously, but such things seldom last."

"Listen. Who are you?" No, that was stupid. "Let me speak to Andreas."

"Of course. Briefly."

"*Paidemou.*" The old man's voice sounded sleepy. "Do nothing. I have explained to these princes that you know nothing, but they are both stubborn fellows. Tell—"

"Well," the first voice came back on the line, "that was not very constructive, but at least you can be satisfied that he is with us, and healthy. Now, Mr. Spear, I cannot stay on this call for long. Please speak to me."

"I don't know what to tell you." What a mess. They really had the old man. Were these the same people who had gone after Fotis, after Ana? He squeezed the receiver hard. "We should speak in person, shouldn't we? Someplace public. With my grandfather there."

"A meeting is an excellent idea, when I am convinced that you have something to share. You must convince me of that first."

"Why would I tell you anything over the phone? This has to be an exchange, right?"

"That depends upon the value of the information. Do you know where your godfather is now?"

"I have a pretty good guess. I know that's not enough. Let me check it out and contact you again tomorrow."

"He is within the greater New York vicinity?"

"If my guess is right. How can I reach you?"

"You cannot. I will telephone you tomorrow."

"I won't be here. Let me give you my cell phone number."

Matthew carefully recited the number, the digits swimming in his panicked brain.

"Very good. I need not mention, but I will, that you must not include the authorities or anyone else in your search. I am sure you understand."

"Look, my grandfather isn't really involved in any of this. My godfather and I dragged him into it. You should go easy on him."

"I have no wish to be hard. Until tomorrow, Mr. Spear."

Father John gazed at Matthew sympathetically after the younger man hung up the receiver.

"Do you know who it is?"

"No. It could be this del Carros. South American collector, tried to grab Ana Kessler a few days ago. Or it could be someone else."

"You should contact the police at once."

"Yes, I should. But he made it clear they would hurt Andreas if I did."

"They may do that anyway."

"I know. I have to try something. I have to go speak to someone." He struggled to assemble a map in his mind, the roads of northern Westchester, that day trip with Robin to find Fotis' house. The Snake's denial of purchasing the property he had coveted for so many months had not been convincing, even that day in the park; and alone in his Salonika hotel room weeks later, Matthew had guessed what the denial was all about. But could he find the house again, without Robin's assistance? Not in the dark, but first thing in the morning he must try.

"Let me help you," said the priest earnestly.

Matthew gave him a hard look.

"What, the kind of help you were just talking about? I can live without that, Father."

"Who else is there? All that I said before was intended only to convince you of what I believe. I will not force your hand. I want us to be allies."

Matthew exhaled. God knew, he needed friends. Ana had to be kept out of it. He would want Benny with him when he went up against del Carros, but Benny would be only a liability in speaking to Fotis. So he was down to the mad priest. Somehow, it seemed appropriate.

24

Steam heat clamoring to life awakened him. The room was dark, the shade on the west window half-raised, and orange light had broken across the crowded trees and white stucco mansion on the opposite hillside. For the several long moments required to reach full awareness, Fotis was treated to this warm and placid vision of dawn, budding branches sketched from shadow by the rising sun, the sky shifting from deep lavender to blue, the real or imagined trill of birdsong. Dawn was primal, and he might have been a hundred different places, or a hundred different men. He might have been young.

Then the pain arrived. Radiating from his lower back up the spine to his shoulder blades, and in pulsing waves through the center of his thighs. Acute discomfort returned him to himself, drew his boundaries, and cut him off. The quality of light outside ceased being a display of beauty and became a means of determining that it was six forty-five without consulting the clock on the night table. He pressed his fists into the mattress and pushed himself up to a sitting position. He hadn't the energy to go further right away, and fishing the square pillow from between his worn knees, he placed it behind his ruined spine and leaned back into the headboard. The pipes banged again, shaking the floor, and the valve on the bedside radiator began to hiss. The heat coming on had confused him. It was not winter but spring, early May. Yet the nights were still quite cool here, and he had set the thermostat up the previous evening. His bones had no tolerance for any cold whatsoever.

At these moments, thinking of the hot shower, the first pills after breakfast, the first drink after lunch made the pain seem bearable. When the time came that he could no longer subdue the agony by such simple means, he knew his days would begin in terror, end in despair. Perhaps it would never come to that. The degeneration had advanced quite slowly up to now. Maybe he would be carried off by something more dramatic before the illness reduced him to a groaning, bedridden ghost. Or perhaps the Mother would save him. He could not see her, but he felt her presence in the room. Yes, he felt her. The same warming, enveloping sensation of well-being that had possessed him when Tomas had arrived with the package nearly two weeks before. The very same feeling that had taken him, body and spirit, that had shaken him to the core sixty years ago, when Andreas had first shown him the work. He had not been the same man since. Certain preoccupations, certain necessities had ruled him from that time forward. Andreas had given him a great gift with that private showing in the empty, candlelit church. Yet in another sense he had troubled Fotis' spirit, unsettled his life, and the worst part had been that Andreas himself was utterly unmoved by his prize. The icon was a curiosity that he was happy to show his friend, but it meant nothing to him. Such love for his men, and later for his wife and children, but a heart of stone for his God. Andreas. They would never choose each other's friendship at this late date, but it was no matter; they were helplessly linked.

Fotis woke again with a start. He had sensed someone at the foot of the bed, but no, there was no one. Neither enemy nor friend. He was quite alone in the house, and had to force himself not to think about all the ways in which sick old men could die, alone in a house. Even getting out of bed was dangerous. The shower would be pure peril. Perhaps he should avoid it. The house was warm. He would dress and eat and see what strength he had after that.

It was a slow process. There was no longer anyone to help him. Roula had died before he had lost the strength he might have needed from her. It was too hard to think about her with him now, the years of contentment they might have had. And children, which she had desperately wanted, but God had willed otherwise. The young creature who had followed had been less than useless to him; only beautiful, what was that? She had expected to become his wife, but he had sent her away, grateful for the lesson in vanity, not repeating his mistake. His niece belonged to Alekos, who hated him. The men were more dependable, but he had lost them all. Phillip ran the restaurant and kept his distance, as had been arranged between them. Nicholas was in the hospital, the faithless Anton had run. Now Taki was dead, his sister's only child. He closed his eyes and tried to close his mind to the grief and guilt that rushed in upon him.

This resistance was critical. If he could not stem the tide of regret at once, the past would break over him in an irresistible wave, and all the dead would swirl about him together. Marko, strangled in an alley, staring bulge-eyed from the mortician's table; Roula coughing up her last bloody breaths; the young priest, burned and bleeding, writhing at his feet in the dark crypt. All of them with some claim upon him. And he, Fotis, old, broken, fearful as a child, damned, and yet still here. Ninety years of life and fighting for more. Ludicrous. Disgusting. He nearly reeled with bottomless self-loathing as he dropped the sweater with which he had been struggling and sat upon the bed once more.

Look to the Mother. That was the only way out of this. That was what all the pain and trouble had been about. He shifted around on the bed, and there she was. The light was not yet strong enough to strike her directly, but it had suffused the room in a warm orange glow that caught the brighter spots on her surface. The gold upper region and the yellowish parts where paint was missing created a contrast by which the maroon robe, the long brown hands, the enormous eyes came into focus. The eyes held the old man in their hypnotic, forgiving caress, and he could not help feeling that even there, where the paint had held, the painter's hand did not rule. Artifice had been stripped away, and these portals burned directly out of the heart of the wood. Their black depths sounded in a time before the artist's brief life, in the deep and sacred soul of the original. She was the first, even before the Son. She was the source, the life. Within the wood lay both. Her garments, his blood, her tears.

There was no way that a man could not be made small before this wonder. Fotis welcomed the smallness, his sins shrinking with the insignificance of his life, the lives he had helped, harmed, ended. Dust. A man had to live a very long time to feel it, to understand the lesson as well as he did now, and there was no teaching it to others. It took the transformative power of a sudden, burning clarity, lent by the Lord to the lucky few. Christ loved sinners. So there was yet hope.

Time lost meaning in the face of such contemplation, but a man was still a man, burdened with needs. Hunger brought the Snake back from the garden to the solitary room, now full of mid-morning light. He had no idea how much time had passed, but he forced himself to his feet, tugged on the gray cardigan, and went downstairs to the kitchen. Only after his coffee and oatmeal did he allow himself to consider his position once more. It was not an enviable one. Between the purchase and bribing Tomas, he had spent nearly everything to get the icon. Keeping it, and finding the means to live, would prove challenging. He had some cash, and disguised accounts in three countries. The house had been bought in Phillip's name, and he had told no one about it, except the boy, apparently. Why had he told him? A need to share his pleasure with someone? A simple slip of age? The reason did not matter, it was done. He had then told Matthew the purchase was off, and the boy didn't know precisely where the house was, did he? Troubling to be unsure of such details. In any case, Andreas could take what little Matthew knew and discover the rest. Others would be searching, too, even though Fotis' return to the country had been in secret. The house could not be considered secure. He had already tarried here three days, regathering his strength. A new short-term location must be found, and a long-term location finally decided upon. Someplace warm. Mexico, perhaps.

Fotis peered out the kitchen window at the narrow wooded dell to the east. He had determined weeks before that it provided the best covert approach to the house and had intended to place motion sensors there, but had not seen to it. There was as yet insufficient foliage to provide real cover, but his eyes were not good any longer, and he could certainly miss a man at this distance. A careful soul could reach the house unseen, but could not enter it unheard.

Between the kitchen and rear stairs was the converted pantry, which served as a security room. The house alarm was controlled from here, and it could be set to produce the terrible clamor typical of such devices, or only a low pinging coupled with a flashing light specifying the location of the break, on a panel in this room and another in the master bedroom. It was the second setting Fotis used while in the house. Why disturb the neighbors? Better to surprise uninvited guests. There were also eight video monitors for cameras placed on the house and about the grounds. Too few, but without someone to constantly monitor them, the whole array was useless anyway. He simply had not counted on losing everyone. The pilot, Captain Herakles, could not be bought for such menial work. The young Peugeot driver might have served but could never be trusted, and now rested beneath the Adriatic. That had cost him triple with Herakles. So many complications.

Just before leaving the room, he saw a movement on the monitor covering the gate. A dark sedan rolled between the big stone pillars and proceeded slowly up the drive. Fotis watched unblinking as the car slipped from the first screen to reappear moments later on the monitor near the front door. It looked to be the same car he'd seen Matthew driving twice before. Who else among those who sought him would be trusting enough to come straight up the driveway? Unless it was a diversion. Scanning all the monitors now, mind utterly clear, Fotis crouched to unlock a short gray filing cabinet and took a pouch from the bottom.

Inside was a small black pistol, an old Walther from a friend in MI6. Still operational as of a few months ago, and the right size and weight for his shaky hand. He snapped in a loaded clip and put a second in his cardigan pocket. For the moment, he did not brood over the pointlessness of a fight. He was unlikely to win, and even if he did, he would have to face the authorities. Still, he was a lucky man, and with survival came possibilities. He would fight for his prize.

The screens revealed no other activity. Nothing in the woods. No one on the little hillock behind the house. The car sat silently for a full minute before the driver's door opened and Matthew stepped out. Damn him, why had he come? Who was in the car with him? Surely not Andreas, who would never allow such a foolish approach. His godson headed for the front door, and Fotis forced down a rising panic. Why Matthew? And then again, who more likely? He desperately did not want to hurt the boy, but who knew what larger game was playing out here? He could simply refuse to answer the door. Would the young man try to force it? Could Fotis let Matthew walk away, having found the place? He fingered the smooth jade beads in his pocket. Instinct spoke. He deactivated the front door alarm. Then, without a plan, he went to face his godson.

The smile on his godfather's face was a surprise, but Matthew realized that it should not have been. Any reaction contrary to expectation was precisely what should be expected of the Snake. The smile did not disguise the fatigue and worry around the mouth and eyes, the enervating agitation that seemed to bend his whole form. Illness, or the demands of this lousy business, was clearly killing Fotis.

"Excellent, my boy. You must tell me how you found me, but come in, come in."

What else to do? The priest offered no actual protection, only the illusion of it, and that was better maintained by putting space between them. Matthew knew that Ioannes had no intention of driving away or phoning anyone if things went badly, but Fotis did not. Only after stepping inside did he see the pistol in his godfather's hand, but there was nothing odd in that. He was a hunted creature, and Matthew had seen too many guns in the past week to be startled.

"Who is in the car?"

"A friend. A priest, actually."

"He knows what is happening?"

"He knows some of it."

"He will not come inside?"

"No."

The old man seemed satisfied with this answer. He shut and locked the door, shuffled toward the staircase, paused, and then started up. The indecision and absence of courtesy were sufficiently out of character to disturb Matthew, but at the same time there was a satisfying sense of seeing behind the mask. He could do nothing but follow, first quietly unlocking the door again. The house resembled many he had seen in the area, a combination of stone and half-timber, slate-roofed and larger than it appeared to be. The interior walls were cream, scattered with bookcases and any number of impressionistic landscapes and religious works that had previously been in Fotis' storage. The heat was ridiculously high, and Matthew shed his jacket as he climbed.

"I must have been more specific about the location than I remember," Fotis posited.

"I would think you would be more interested in *why* I'm here."

Fotis whirled about at the top of the stairs, his wide-eyed amusement verging on madness. The light from a high window caught an ugly yellow bruise on his left temple.

"Why? Why else? There are no secrets with us. We share the same hunger, only I hope you will see that my need is greater."

The old man rushed off down the corridor, and Matthew could only yell at his back.

"You've got it wrong, *Theio*. It's not about that. Listen to me."

Following, Matthew entered a large bedroom near the back of the house. The blankets were still rumpled on the king-sized bed. Light poured in through three windows. A telephone and an odd console dominated the big oak desk, and his godfather sat in a leather chair in the corner, staring at the mantel. Leaning there, above an unused fireplace, was the icon. It was smaller than Matthew remembered. In fact, it seemed diminished in every way, unworthy of the blood and anguish spent on it. The eyes appeared to recognize this. They had lost their magnetic hold, their promise of mysteries to be revealed in time, and now looked only forlorn. Perversely, Matthew felt this new vision of the work begin to breed in him a feeling of protectiveness nearly as strong as the passion for revelation it had replaced. He became cognizant of the profound effect that the circumstances of his viewings were having upon his reaction. Ana's presence had provoked a sort of holy lust, his father's a deep fear and a need for healing. And now this appropriate sadness. Was it for Fotis? Was the painting no more than a conduit?

"She holds you still," Fotis whispered.

"No," Matthew answered, but it was not completely true. She held him differently now.

"Understand me, my child. I cannot live much longer. When I am gone she will be yours, but I need her with me if I am to die well. I have no other hope. If you had seen the things I have seen, you would not try to deny me."

"The things you've seen? Or the things you've done?"

"Who else knows you've come here?"

He would not follow the old man's lead. That was a tired routine.

"They have Andreas."

"Who has him?"

"I'm not sure. I think it's this del Carros. He tried to grab Ana Kessler a few days ago. I'm pretty certain he had a deal with your Russians to get the icon."

Fotis nodded. "You are sure they have him?"

"I spoke to him."

"What did he say? Precisely."

"Not much. I think he was drugged. He told me to do nothing, and he referred to 'both' of them, so I assume it's only two men who have him."

"Good. That's all?"

"He called them 'princes.' I figured he was being sarcastic."

Fotis' stare bored into the younger man for many long moments. Matthew knew he was being read, but he remained calm, in the knowledge that he was not hiding anything. "They're going to call me soon," he pressed. "They expect information on the icon's location."

"Did it not occur to you this could be a trick by your grandfather?"

"What, you think he's faking being held?"

Fotis nodded, still looking him hard in the face. It was a sure sign of how deeply the paranoia of the last few weeks had penetrated that Matthew seriously weighed the idea in his mind.

"No. You have no idea how badly he wants me out of all this. He would not invent some scheme that sent me after you alone. You must know that."

"Maybe you're in it together."

"That doesn't make sense, for the same reason. You're thinking out loud, you don't even believe what you're saying."

"Perhaps."

"We have to help him."

"Of course we do." But there was no heart behind the words. Fotis stared, unblinking, no longer seeing Matthew, but scheming again, stalling for time.

"So what does 'princes' mean?"

"The Prince," Fotis began slowly, "was what your grandfather and I called the German officer I told you about. Or sometimes the Pasha, because he liked to live well, and surround himself with stolen treasures. He is the man Andreas made the deal with, sending the Holy Mother into exile."

"Müller. The Nazi he was hunting all those years."

"The same."

"Del Carros is Müller."

"It may be so."

"What did he intend by telling me that?"

"Only that we should know. Or as a warning, perhaps, that we are dealing with someone far more dangerous than I had guessed. He is still a loyal fellow, your grandfather."

"Yeah, and how will you repay that loyalty?"

"I have not the means to help him. I can barely protect myself."

"You have the icon. It's not worth Andreas' life."

"His life is forfeit already. You did not tell him, or them, of this place?"

"Of course not."

"Then there is nothing they can get from him. Do you see? He has used his last opportunity to warn us. If you give them the information now, he still dies, and very likely you and I also. And they take our Lady. He would become the instrument of our deaths. Do you think he wants that? Do you think he wants Müller to have the chance to betray him again? For shame. They only win if they get the icon. We can prevent that. You must assist me."

"I know someone who can help us. He's ex-Mossad, a friend of Andreas. We can't give up on him, we have to try something."

"You understand *nothing*."

Fury shook his godfather's ill frame, and the hand gripping the pistol bounced on his leg. A dull trilling drew both sets of eyes to the desk, where a red light flashed on the console. Fotis jumped up and shuffled over to it.

"The priest has gotten curious, perhaps? No. Not the front door, the back, the back . . ."

He wheeled about and pointed the gun at Matthew's head. The body language was so threatening that Matthew found himself throwing his hands up and recoiling two steps.

"*Theio!*"

"Who have you led here? Speak the truth."

"No one. Just the priest."

Fotis dropped the gun to his side again, speaking more quietly as he marched past Matthew.

"No, you have brought them. Maybe unawares, but they followed you."

Recovering himself somewhat, Matthew followed the old man out of the room on shaky legs. Fotis turned once to put a finger to his lips, then started along the corridor, not the way they had come but in the opposite direction, turning once onto a shorter corridor. At the top of a steep, narrow staircase he gestured for Matthew to stay put, then started down. In moments, he had vanished around a turn and Matthew stood there, mute and help-less, staring at the place where he had gone. What should he do now? Who was down there? Should he go check on Ioannes? Indecision held him to the spot, and perhaps a minute later he heard a faint noise below. Then Fotis reappeared. The Snake struggled a bit on the ascent, but he gripped Matthew's shoulder with a strong hand and placed his lips right at the younger man's ear.

"I hear him but don't see him. There's another at the front door now. We'll hold the second floor against them. Can you use this?"

Fotis held out a large pistol, grip-first. Matthew nodded hesi-tantly. His godfather slid the carriage back and forth as quietly as possible, chambering the first round, then placed the gun in Matthew's hand.

"Squeeze the trigger hard. Stay right here and shoot anyone who comes up those stairs."

He pressed Matthew against the wall, then slipped the Walther from his sweater and headed toward the front of the house. Fear of whatever was about to happen battled with the anger that events had overrun his intentions, but Matthew did not take his eyes from the stairs. He did not wish to distract himself with thinking, but thoughts came unbidden. If it was del Carros or his companion down there, he would need to act without hesitation, as Fotis had instructed. But what if it was someone else? The FBI, or Benny, or even Ioannes? If he waited to identify the person, would he get the chance to react? Could he look some stranger in the eye and pull the trigger?

Or was it all some game that Fotis was playing with him, yet again? He backed up ten feet to the turn in the corridor to make sure the old bastard wasn't going down the front stairs with the icon. A faint noise from below made him quickly retrace his steps. Then all thought vanished as gunfire erupted from the front of the house.

25

Jan had not liked the plan one bit, but their options were few. They had drugged Spyridis, but he said little and clearly didn't know where to find Dragoumis. The boy was their best chance. Seizing him would have been the surest course, but Müller gauged the young man's tone and guessed that he did not precisely know his godfather's whereabouts. Yet he might find him if given free rein. Jan's trying to grab the boy and priest together could go terribly wrong, even leave Spear dead, and in any case three hostages would be a very clumsy business for two men. One was bad enough. The best plan was for Van Meer to trail the boy.

The Dutchman was annoyed, the closest he got to being angry. He'd been watching Spear's apartment on and off for days, and was amazed the boy had been stupid enough to return. Let me take him, he urged Müller, he's right here. Yet he had gone along in the end, and the trail had proved every bit as challenging as predicted. Müller drove the rental car while Jan followed on foot, and they had to scramble when they realized Spear was borrowing a friend's car and about to disappear. Jan took the wheel and managed to maintain the tail all the way out of the city, up the Bronx River Parkway, and along the winding back roads of northern Westchester. Jan was good, and the boy was not experienced, but over so great a distance there was a chance he had noticed the pursuit. This meant they might be walking into an ambush.

Müller looked at Spyridis in the backseat, still unconscious from his last injection. He would get another one when the car stopped, and in all probability would not wake up again in this world. The Greek's wrists were bound with a cord Jan carried for the purpose, and a blanket was thrown over his lap to hide them. Müller returned his eyes to the road, and realized he'd lost sight of Spear's vehicle.

"Where is he?"

"He just pulled in there, the gate in the brick wall."

"Then why are we driving past?"

Jan glanced over at him in mild disgust.

"We should go in behind him, you think? Invite ourselves in for drinks?"

They continued past the gate for a hundred yards but saw only trees and wall, then lost sight of the property. Jan turned around and doubled back, passing the gate again until he reached a wooded dell a few hundred yards on the far side, and parked among the weeds. He waved his cell phone, switched to walkie-talkie function, at Müller, then opened his door.

"Give me time to get in. Then you come in the front, as we planned."

"Yes, yes."

"About ten minutes should be sufficient. Remember that I may not be able to speak once I'm inside."

"We've been over everything. Just go."

"Don't be impatient. We're too close now."

No answer was required, and then Jan was gone, melting into the thicket of young oak and maple like a ghost. Müller took a deep breath and slid over to the driver's seat. He let five minutes elapse on his watch before he put the car in drive, looked for traffic on the empty road, pulled out slowly. Jan was correct—damn him, anyway—there was no need for haste, no need to panic.

They were closing the noose. Now was not the time for stupid mistakes.

As he shaped the turn and started up the incline, the brick wall came into view once more, old and moss-covered, and within a hundred feet the stone pillars appeared, bracketing the drive. He pulled over onto the grassy shoulder of the road, slipped out his cell phone, and settled in to wait for Jan's call, glancing once more at Spyridis. Had he moved, or was it simply the motion of the car? He checked the road, the trees, the wall itself. Then he noticed the tiny camera on the west pillar, pointing straight at him.

Damn it all, he should have seen it before; there must be cameras everywhere. On instinct, he put the car in gear again and pulled into the long gravel driveway. Why give Dragoumis any more time to think? With luck, only the old Greek would oppose them. The cell phone on the seat released a burst of static, indicating that Jan was inside but could not speak. Müller felt his heart beating dangerously and sucked hard at the stale air in the car. He parked at the most oblique angle possible from the windows of the house, then got out and rushed to the front door.

There was no one in Spear's car, so both he and the priest must be inside. Müller ignored the inevitable camera by the door and tested the large brass knob. It was unlocked. Either Jan had worked swiftly or it was a much too obvious trap. He slipped the pistol from inside his coat and pushed the door open with his free hand. Nothing happened immediately. He could see a handsome blue-and-red oriental carpet at the base of a staircase, and wide arches opening to sunlit rooms on either side of a hall. Müller stepped in quickly and made for the stairs. The first bang startled him, but by the second he was on the ground, rolling to his right, instinct overcoming age. There was at least one distinctive thump of a round striking wood. He bumped into the heavy leg of something and pulled himself to his knees, knocking his head against the bottom of a large dinner table. Through blurred vision he could see that he was in the dining room—out of the line of fire, he guessed.

He checked himself for damage but did not seem to be hit. The shots had come from the top of the stairs. Dragoumis—if that's who it was—had waited for him to get well inside before firing, but his aim was off badly. The German shook his head as his vision cleared. He had been lucky. Now he was on sore knees with a bruised skull and no way to get up those stairs. Never mind; at least he was inside the house. He glanced across the hall. There was a large, plush living room with light pouring in through French doors over a white sofa, glass table, and thick flokati rug. It reminded him of a room in a house he had once owned, a place where he had been almost content. Don't think of that now. There was a door at the back of the dining room, next to a tall, glass-fronted hutch. There must be a back stairway in a house like this. He had to find it, and find Jan. Müller stood slowly, painfully, and moved toward the narrow door.

The kitchen was large and gloomy, despite the white walls and blue curtains, and there was a faint smell of gas in the air. A bowl and a mug sat in the sink. There were two doors, in addition to the one from which he had entered. The one on the left appeared more promising, but no sooner had he thought that than a loud boom came from that direction. A larger-caliber gun than the one in front, so there were two holding the upper floor. Where was Jan? If the Dutchman was down, then this business was finished, and he would be lucky to get out with his life. Lucky. Hardly the correct word. There was no escape but one for a man his age. He was not leaving without the icon, whatever the consequences. He willed himself to move toward the sound of the shot.

A short corridor led into a small room full of filing cabinets and black-and-white monitors. He saw the cars parked in front, several empty views of the grounds, the front steps, the priest wandering aimlessly around the side of the house. There were no interior views. A moment later he glanced up to see Van Meer standing beside him. Jan smiled.

"You've lost your hat."

"Yes," whispered Müller, repressing his shock at being so easily surprised. "I guess I have. What about that shot?"

"A poor one. Missed me by half a meter, but someone is up there."

"In front also."

Jan nodded. "This is an unfavorable position. Two on two and they have the high ground. Wisdom says we should withdraw."

"Impossible. We'll never have this opportunity again."

Jan nodded once more, having expected this response. His eyes were directed over the German's shoulder at the kitchen door, and as they spoke his head made small adjustments to catch any stray sound. There were moments when Van Meer seemed pure mechanics, pure calculation, but Müller could tell that the gamesman in him had been aroused. He would not leave now.

"I expect a large bonus," Jan said.

"Done. The front stairs are long and straight. It's no good."

"There's an angle in back. Maybe four meters from the landing to the shooter."

"That's the way, then."

"Wait here."

Müller despised the tone of command from inferiors, but he was getting used to it with this one, and he watched the entry to the stairwell as Jan ducked into the kitchen. The younger man returned a minute later with a bundle of dishcloths tied together, stinking of something. Cleaning fluid, perhaps. In his other hand he held a wet towel.

They moved carefully into the stairwell, then up the narrow steps together. Jan pulled a silver lighter from his pocket and sparked the bundle, nodding to Müller. The old man slid along the outer wall, aware of the fist-sized crater in the plaster an arm's length away. Before he quite cleared the angle, he stuck out his shaking left hand and fired three quick bursts, the noise tremendous in that tight space, then withdrew. Jan stepped into the open spot and tossed his flaming bundle up the stairs.

The air smelled of acrid burning. Would they light up the whole house, Müller wondered, still shaking? Was it fear or anticipation? When had he become so nervous, so feeble? Jan stared at him with that damned serene expression. A scuffing noise came from above, a foot stomping the fiery bundle. Crouching, Jan slipped halfway around the angle, fired twice, and ducked back. There was a dull metal thud on the stairs above.

The Dutchman leaned out once more, then darted up out of sight. Müller took a deep breath and followed, picking up the wet towel on his way.

Two steps from the top a black nine-millimeter lay on the stair, and there was a smudge of blood on the corner of the wall. Jan stood in the smoky corridor, looking left and right. Müller tossed the wet towel over the burning pile of rags, stamped on it several times. The floor was scorched, but nothing seemed to have caught. Bullet holes were everywhere.

"You hit him," Müller whispered.

"In the hand," Jan said. "Spear. He's nearby."

"But disarmed."

Disarmed, wounded, surely terrified. The German mentally crossed the boy off. Now it was down to Dragoumis, and the odds were back in their favor. The icon was here, somewhere on the second floor, or the Greek would not have abandoned the first without a fight. The corridor they were in connected with another about four meters ahead, where a right turn would take them to the front of the house. Van Meer took a glance around the corner.

"Yes?" Müller prompted.

"Nothing. Lots of doors."

"Can you see the top of the front stairs?"

"Yes."

"Good. Then the Greek can't block them without getting hit from here. Circle back around and come up the front, and we'll move in from both sides."

"Spear is here somewhere."

"Never mind him. Dragoumis is the main thing."

The Dutchman looked dubious, but he nodded, slipped down the short corridor, and vanished noiselessly down the back stairs. Müller edged to the corner and glanced around, seeing only what Jan had described. This was it. They were closing in by the moment. The surrounding houses were probably too far away to hear the shots, and Dragoumis would never call the police. They had him, unless they committed some blunder. Like losing track of rounds. How many had he fired? Only three, he was fairly certain. He searched his coat for his spare clip and came up instead with a small leather case. The syringe and narcotic. He had neglected to give Spyridis another shot before leaving the car. It hardly mattered; the man was out cold and bound besides. Yet such errors reflected a state of mind. He must focus. He must do better if he was to survive this day. No more mistakes. Be like Jan, he told his shaking hands, a machine, until the business was finished.

Benny's silver Nissan came up the off-ramp at terrific speed, barely stopping for Ana to get in, and they were back on the curving parkway in under a minute. The first thing she'd done was call Benny. Matthew's message had given her very little to go on; he'd only wanted her to know what he was up to in case something happened. However, he'd already told her the story about searching for his godfather's house with the old girlfriend, who had grown up in that part of the world. Robin was the key. Benny went straight to Matthew's apartment and ransacked it for an address book, which he quickly located. Men were notoriously bad about actually recording anything in such books, but Benny had found a Robin Sprague with a phone number, and Ana had convinced him that the call was better off coming from her.

It was early, and she had caught the woman preparing for work. There was the expected resistance and annoyance, and Ana had to toss out a lot of personal information about Matthew in order to prove the close connection. Then she told Robin that he was in danger—something involving his godfather. Robin knew Fotis, and clearly did not find this too hard to believe. The details had gotten fuzzy in the intervening month or two, but as best she could, she reconstructed the route to the house. Ana would not tell Benny what she had learned, but insisted that he pick her up on the way. He was already driving north at that point, and her ploy infuriated him. You're putting Matthew at risk, he raged, but the delay would only be a few minutes, and the matter was too important for her to concede. She calmed Matthew's parents by telling them she was going to see him, which was true, she prayed. Then she hurried down the hill on foot to Fennimore

Road, and west a few hundred yards to the Bronx River Parkway exit.

"You see, no trouble at all," Ana said as Benny accelerated.

"The trouble is in front of us. Put on your seat belt, I'm not slowing down."

"You really think they followed him?"

"It's what I would do. Now tell me where we're going."

They passed the Kensico reservoir and turned off onto more winding secondary roads. It would have been a drive to enjoy on another day, lakes and forest and gorgeous vistas, but Ana was tight with tension, checking every landmark against Robin's vague instructions, trying to forget how much might depend upon her making the right choices. Before long they passed through a wooded dell, then came up a rise to the brick wall and pillared entry. Ana could just make out the slate roof beyond a screen of trees.

"This is it, this is the house."

"You're certain?"

"As certain as I can be, Benny. We're not going on much here."

Benny turned around out of sight of the house and returned to the wooded hollow, parking where the weeds had been crushed by the recent presence of another vehicle.

"Stay here," he commanded Ana, putting her behind the wheel and making her slide down in the seat. "Keep your eyes on the road and the woods, and if anyone looks curious, drive the hell out of here. Don't stop to talk. Don't get out of the car for any reason." He patted her shoulder. "You did right to call me." Then he vanished among the trees.

She waited five minutes, then followed. She was frightened, but more frightened at the idea of sitting in that car and wondering what was happening up in the house. And she was angry; a slow, smoldering rage had been growing for days. The image of del Carros' smirking face hung in her mind, taunting her. The trees had not yet acquired their full complement of leaves, but there was a distinct haze of green, and the small trunks were clustered closely enough that she could not see very far ahead. About thirty yards in she passed carefully through a great rip in

an old chain-link fence. A little gully rose swiftly to level out
behind a small stand of pine, beyond which she could make out
the house, about a hundred feet away. She flinched violently
when several sharp bangs issued from somewhere within the
walls. So much for everybody talking this through, but who was
shooting at whom?

Ana made her way behind the pines to the front of the house.
Two cars sat in the long drive, and the front door stood half open.
She moved quickly, in a long curve that would let her use the
vehicles as cover. As she went from one to the next, her eye
caught a figure slumped in the backseat of the black Marquis. An
old man in a raincoat, with a blanket across his lap and a fedora
pulled down over his eyes. His head lay still against the seat. Was
he dead? She lifted the silver handle and the door popped open.
Then she crawled over the seat to him. Ana had met Andreas
only once, but she recognized him easily as she slipped back the
fedora. Straight-nosed and sunken-eyed. Two days before he had
seemed too young to be Matthew's grandfather, but now he
looked very old indeed. His dark eyes opened slowly and tried to
take her in, but then closed again. He was ill, wounded, or
drugged. She pulled the blanket aside and saw that his hands
were bound, the fingers white from the loss of circulation. There
was no obvious sign of harm.

She needed to get inside and find Matthew but didn't feel she
could leave Andreas alone. On the car floor was a bottle of spring
water, and Ana snatched it up and wrenched off the white cap,
putting a few drops on Andreas' dry lips. His licked at them and
coughed.

"Mr. Spyridis, try to wake up."

She applied cool handfuls to both sides of his face, and he
murmured some complaint. She shook him gently, then more
vigorously. When she slapped his cheeks with more cool water,
his hands sprang up out of his lap, fingers laced together in one
strong fist, and just missed striking her under the chin. She slid
back several feet.

"Mr. Spyridis, listen to me. It's Ana, Matthew's Ana. Matthew
is in the house. Do you understand?"

He was looking at her now, confused and suspicious, but nearly awake.

"Matthew's in the house," she continued. "And Benny. There's been shooting. What? What did you say?"

"Where is Müller?" he rasped.

"I don't know who that is."

"Del Carros."

"I'm not sure. Did he bring you here? Is Jan with him?"

"Yes."

"Can you stand?"

Andreas shrugged. She moved swiftly around the car and dragged him out by the door facing the house. He could not keep his feet without assistance, and slumped against the vehicle. What the hell good was he in this condition? She grew impatient trying to understand him.

"What are you saying?"

"Weapons," he snapped.

"I don't have any."

The old man sighed, taking great mouthfuls of cool spring air, blinking.

"Search the car," he commanded.

But there was nothing to find, no gun under the seat or in the glove compartment, no keys to open the trunk. Ana worked for several minutes to free the cord from the old man's wrists, feeling fear claw its way back to the top of her emotional free-for-all.

Andreas massaged his liberated hands and looked to the open front door.

"Wait here," he whispered, then moved toward the steps, stumbling, ridiculous. She nearly let him go, then ran after him, sliding her shoulder under his left arm for support, and they went purposely toward the door, until their progress was abruptly halted.

Ioannes stood against a bank of budding mountain laurel at the rear of the house and watched the burly, surefooted man slip in the back door. He had seen the man come out of the tree line and move swiftly and silently across the lawn, looking in all directions and yet never seeing the priest. More men had pulled up in front of the house some minutes before, just as Ioannes had gotten out of the car to stretch, and he had thought it wise to get out of sight. How many were in the house now, or who they all were, he could not guess, though there were at least two factions, since they were shooting at each other. Either no one had seen him yet, or nobody cared that he was there. Just a priest, after all.

The boy had probably been killed, Ioannes considered, sadly. These were dangerous men, and young Matthew was an innocent. His chances in the midst of this deadly cross fire did not seem good. It was all happening again, yet again. Ioannes would have to pursue his own solution. As quietly as he was able, he followed the big man into the house.

Instantly, before he even passed through the kitchen door, he heard two more loud shots, close together, to his right. The big, bearded man backed into the room from that direction, looking before and behind in quick succession, a large pistol in his hand. His gaze fixed Ioannes for a moment, but then slid past. He turned quickly and moved across the large kitchen, slipping through another door and into the dining room beyond.

Ioannes considered whether he might have become invisible to his enemies. This had happened before, during times of great need, and it would seem to reaffirm the necessity of his mission. Such power was not granted for no reason, certainly not to preserve the life of a weak, sinning priest. No, he had been delivered to this place, quite unexpectedly, for some purpose. He was an instrument. They were all of them instruments, poor blind fools.

His mind and spirit began to hum in a sweet unison. His feet moved him across the kitchen, stopping before the huge gas range. There was a smell of gas in the air, and he noticed that one of the dials was not in the off position. This kind of carelessness offended his sense of order. The voice in his head spoke just as his hand reached the dial, and he paused a moment to absorb the message. Yet only a moment; thought was the destroyer of action. He turned the dial to the high setting, without igniting the gas. Then he turned the other three dials as well, all four silver burners throwing invisible fumes. He waited a minute or so until the odor was strong, then stepped back. Was it enough? He went around and squeezed his arm into the space behind the stove, pulling hard on the narrow tube he guessed was the gas line, loosening it—did it hiss?—but not breaking it clean. He removed his arm. By the sink was a large bottle of industrial cleaner, which Ioannes emptied over the counters and floor. The noxious smell was now making him quite dizzy. What next? On impulse he followed the bearded fellow into the dining room.

The man was crouched by the long, dark table, gazing fixedly into the hallway beyond. He had clearly been there for some time, listening, waiting. He must be warned of what was about to happen, and Ioannes took a step forward, the floor beneath him groaning softly. The big man came out of his crouch and turned, finger to his lips and gun hand fiercely gesturing the priest back into the kitchen.

The air exploded with the sound of gunfire. Blood erupted through the big man's jacket and Ioannes doubled over as something punched him in the stomach. They fell together, the bearded man twisting as he did to fire once at a thin figure standing in the hall.

The priest realized he had been shot as he hit the ground, and he waited for the pain to come. He rolled onto his side, looking to his unfortunate companion. The big man dragged himself into a sitting position against the wall, bleeding copiously through his shirt and jacket. He was angry.

"Son of a *bitch*," he hissed, fumbling at his shirt with one hand and lifting the pistol with the other. It roared twice more, blowing chunks of plaster out of the opposite wall. "Damn it all to hell." He looked at his oozing chest, then at Ioannes, shaking his head. "Fucking priests."

Ioannes attempted to reach out a comforting hand, but the arrival of the pain stopped him. A long shudder racked the bearded man's body and his wide eyes became fixed at a distant point. The pistol fell from his right hand. "Fucking priest," he whispered again, and then was still.

It grew silent once more. A circle of throbbing discomfort

was expanded from Ioannes' diaphragm to encompass his whole body, and he had to bite down against the agony, taking shallow breaths. The test was always more difficult than expected, he reminded himself, but the thought was hard to hold on to. He succeeded now in reaching a hand out to wrap around the ankle of the man whose death he had just caused. Give rest with thy saints, O Lord, to this thy servant . . . he didn't know the man's Christian name, or if he even was a Christian, but the matter would be sorted out above. Too damaged to indulge in scolding or grieving, he refocused his mind on the task. Everything happened for a reason. The wound replaced his agitation with a mind-cleansing pain, and removed the possibility of escape. Slowly, excruciatingly, Ioannes pulled himself up on his elbows and dragged his stricken body back into the kitchen.

The smell of gas was strong; not as strong as he would have liked, but then, he was on the floor. An alcove with drawers was beside the range, and he pulled himself over there, noting the snaking blood trail behind him as he rolled over. He coughed wetly, tasting iron. His limbs were almost too heavy to use, but he pulled open the drawers, searching for one thing. There was not much time. The man who had shot him was probably the same one the big man had faced in the rear corridor. They had each circled around the house to ambush the other, the thin man winning the game because of Ioannes' interference. Now he would circle back and find the bloody priest sprawled here. Very good, but let Ioannes find what he needed first.

"Father, forgive me," said an arch voice from the rear corridor. "You should not have stood so close to him. It was an accident."

There are no accidents, thought Ioannes, his hand finding, at last, the familiar cardboard box. Calmness swept over him, and the keen euphoria of great possibility. The fumes were so potent he could barely stay conscious.

"I have great respect for priests," the man spoke again, closer. "My uncle, you know . . ." The surly fellow caught the smell then, and rushed across the room to the gas range. Ioannes saw the blond hair and narrow face, just as the cool blue eyes saw him lying there in the alcove. The man's hand was upon the first dial, twisting it to OFF, but the eyes grew wide when they saw what it was the priest held.

"Don't," breathed the Dutchman.

"I forgive you," said Ioannes, striking the match.

26

The muffled boom reached Matthew through the cool tiles of the bathroom floor. He had been lying there with a blood-soaked towel wrapped around his right hand, greasy sweat covering his face and neck, legs vibrating uncontrollably. Fear or shock, he wasn't sure which. Whispered voices had come to him from the corridor, and several times a shadowy movement could be seen in the space under the closed door. They would find him. That seemed certain, and he would die like a wounded animal, quivering here on the floor. It was a sickening thought, but he had not been able to figure out any kind of plan.

The noise below filled him with a perverse sense of hope. It was possible that the attackers themselves had caused it, but to what purpose, especially downstairs? More likely someone else had joined the fray, or some device had detonated prematurely. Matthew had no idea, only a strong guess that chaos was his friend. He waited a few minutes to see what would follow. There was no sound in the corridor, but the smell of smoke began to reach him. He must get out.

Gently, Matthew pulled the bathroom door open with his

good hand. A few inches, then a few more. Still nothing. Finally, he shuffled out on his knees. Black smoke billowed up the back stairs and raced across the ceiling, and the thick snap of flames below was audible. Crawling with the injured hand was difficult, but the acrid fumes required that he stay low. As quickly as he could, Matthew scampered around the corner into the next corridor, then along the wall to Fotis' bedroom.

Just inside the door, two old men were wrestling on the rug. The one on top, in the gray suit, must be Müller, who was cuffing furiously at Fotis' head, but without sufficient force to do much harm. The Walther was half under the bed. There was no sign of Müller's gun. Matthew guessed that they must have surprised each other at the door and come to blows before either one could fire. He sensed rather than saw that there was someone else in the room, but he chose to ignore this for the moment.

Getting most of the way to his feet, Matthew attempted to drag Müller off using only his left hand, but a fierce wave of dizziness and nausea pushed him back to his knees. The old men ignored him. Fotis bit Müller's hand and the German howled, striking the Greek on the temple with real force. Fotis went slack, and Müller scrambled off him, sprawling on his face as Matthew punched him in the shin. Smoke hung thick on the ceiling. The light through the windows was becoming obscured, and the air was bad.

Matthew's gaze went to the mantel ,and the other figure was there, all in shadow. The burned man, standing by the icon. They were a pair, the burned man and the ruined Mary, now surrounded by a weird glow. The same eyes, the same color to their robes; they were a matching set. The man stood in for John the Baptist, the third member of the triumvirate, on the right. And there was Mary on the left, with Christ, the object of their veneration, invisible in the air between them. Of course it was not real. An illusion of smoke and light, the delusion of a shocked brain and troubled spirit. Indeed, when he tried to look straight at the figure it seemed to lose its substance. It was only when Matthew's hungry gaze fixed on the icon that the man grew strong again, great-eyed, solemn, waiting. There was a choice involved. Many before had faced it. The three living men in the room faced it now.

Müller was on his knees at the foot of the bed. He had retrieved his pistol and was searching his jacket for something, perhaps bullets, coughing hideously all the while. Fotis was shaking his head, attempting to rise. Matthew was watching them both, watching it all. The air was becoming poisonous, and he must do something at once. The icon called. He half stood, mind reeling, and imagined crossing the room, pushing Müller aside, seizing the Holy Mother, and rushing for the door. It would be easy, but his feet would not move. The burned man watched him. There was no judgment there, and no assistance. Ioannes' words came back to Matthew. The work's power was too strong, it bent intentions. Why had he come to this house? Remember. To save a life. Not for the icon, but to try to save a life.

The towel had come off somewhere, and his right hand bled freely from the bullet hole in his palm. Matthew ignored it, bent low to the dusty carpet to suck in a last breath of smokeless air, then proceeded to haul his struggling godfather onto his shoulder.

"What are you doing?" raged the Snake.

Legs shaking with the effort, Matthew rose to his feet, his head immediately shrouded in mist. Weak fists pounded on his back, old legs kicked the air.

"No, no, not me, boy. The Mother. Save the Mother."

Matthew shuffled out of the room without a backward glance. Fire had reached the back of the second floor, and the visibility was very poor. He found the railing without going over it, and slid along to the top of the front staircase. Whoever and whatever waited below could not be worse than the conditions upstairs had become. Fotis was frantic.

"You fool. Go back for the Mother. What do you think you are doing?"

Choosing the living, thought Matthew as he started down.

Andreas had traveled over great time and distance before the girl awakened him. Some places he did not know, others he remembered well. The crypt beneath the church, and the child Mikalis, staring at him with the eyes of an old man. Pretty Glykeria smiling as they passed on the village street. Young boys mixing clay and straw with their feet, to make the bricks that would rebuild their burned homes. The balcony of his old apartment, with Maria, young and dark-haired, and Alekos playing with toy soldiers at their feet, the sweet resiny smell of a summer dusk in Athens. He went back to the hillside chapel again, with Kosta and Ioannes, and he noticed something new this time, something he had to remember for Matthew. He went to Müller's well-guarded house at dawn; he watched the German's face as Müller promised there would be no executions. He sat among the old, twisted apple trees in the late morning, eating bread, exhausted by his night's work, and heard the ordered rattle of twenty rifles. The bread falling from his hands, the knowledge that he had been betrayed. All over again, though less intensely, he felt horror turn to rage, rage to sadness, sadness to resolve. He saw the hasty grave and the wooden cross in the Argentinean countryside, the end of the journey.

The anger was gone. In dreamtime, he could not maintain it. The white-haired specter who had walked into Fotis' apartment had Müller's eyes but was otherwise a pale imitation. A tired, desperate old man. Andreas could summon neither hate nor forgiveness; the fellow was simply pathetic. It would be best if he died, but Andreas doubted that he would be the man to kill him. In fact, he had no expectation of seeing the conscious world again until Ana Kessler woke him. And then, how hard it was to return. He had been light as a breath of air in his dreams, able to see and understand events that had been veiled in fear, rage, sorrow, lust the first time through. He had felt himself making the separation from petty concerns. How hard it was to return to the world, to this feeble aching form, to this weak and sluggish mind. Every bruise, every scar and strain, every insult to body and spirit over seventy-nine years was reintroduced to him in the space of a few moments. This brutal accumulation of experience was his life, and it was not done with him yet.

But Matthew's Ana was beautiful, and beauty was always worth waking up for. Matthew's Ana, that was what she called herself after he almost took her head off. The cold water on his face was effective, but it had felt cruel to him just then. Something bit at his wrists. He was surprised to be alive. He had no idea where Müller had gone, but it seemed logical that he was in the house, with Matthew, Fotis, and whomever else. Andreas' will leaped ahead, his body dragged after, and he did not fight the woman when she gave him her shoulder for support.

The sound of the blast deep within the house caused them to stop. They waited a minute before moving, to see what would follow. When nothing did, they again made for the open door, from which smoke had now begun to drift.

To the left was a handsomely furnished living room. Ahead, stairs went up to a corridor already filling with smoke. Smoke was also billowing in from the rear of this lower hall and gathering against the ceiling of all these front rooms. To the right a dark-paneled dining room was gathering smoke fastest, as actual flames spat from a doorway in back. A bloodied figure sat against the far wall, next to the French doors. Ana saw him just as Andreas did.

"Benny." She rushed toward him.

"Stay down," Andreas commanded, "stay below the smoke."

She slipped down and crawled the rest of the way. Very well, let her look to Benny; the stillness of the form told Andreas his friend was dead, but he put the thought aside. He went the opposite way, into the white living room, half walking, half crawling across the flokati rug, as far as the doorway into the study. Black fog filled that room, and there was no sound of activity, only the growing snap and sizzle of flames. Anyone in the rear of the house would be overcome by smoke already, and he was in no condition to help. He returned to the hall, the pungent reek beginning to burn his sinuses. Where was Matthew? His eyes drifted up the stairs. The air would be even worse up there, but there was no place left to search. He might last a few minutes. In any case, he could not face Alekos if he left without Matthew. Ana was now trying to drag Benny across the dining room.

"Ana," he shouted. "Leave him, get out of the house."

She seemed not to hear, and he realized that retrieving her

would mean losing his chance at the second floor. He trusted in her survival instinct and started up, being careful of his feet, aware of how easy it would be to fall in his current condition. Halfway up, Andreas stopped suddenly as a strange form emerged from the gray mist above. Bent over, moving a careful step at a time. Matthew, with Fotis kicking and raging on his shoulder. The younger man stopped a few steps from his grandfather.

"*Papou*. Thank God."

"Keep going, get out of the house."

"Don't go up there."

"No, no. Keep going now."

"Andreou," screamed Fotis, red-faced and bulging-eyed, grasping at his old comrade as he passed him. "Get the Mother. Mikalis would want you to save her. The bedroom. The Prince is there." The rest was lost in a wave of painful coughing, and Matthew moved on down the stairs, one hand bleeding badly.

Andreas looked up into the boiling maelstrom of smoke. Leave it. Let the fire do its work. There was no way out the back. The devil would come down these stairs, or not at all. No sooner had he thought it than another hacking cough sounded from above, and another form emerged from the smoke. Two legs with a square shape above them, white hands gripping the edges. Those eyes that Andreas had not seen in more than fifty years: dark, almond eyes on gold leaf, a maroon cowl of robe, rocking back and forth, moving down toward him, a painting with legs. Only gradually could Müller's face be glimpsed above the frame, blue eyes squinting, just noticing Andreas below. He stopped, but there was no way to go but forward. The German was nearly paralyzed with coughing, but one hand disappeared into his jacket and reemerged holding a pistol. The blue eyes sized him up coldly. A loud shot rang out, and Andreas flinched.

But the shot had come from behind, not in front, and a large hole had opened in the icon, just above the Mother of God's eyes. Müller reeled back violently, and fell across the upper landing, swallowed by the smoke, the icon vanishing with him. Andreas turned around to see Ana below, both hands gripping Benny's

.45, eyes wide with disbelief. He looked up again but could make out nothing. Suddenly, his lungs could not pull in air, only heat, and he moved down the stairs with all possible speed. Ana seized him at the bottom, dropping the pistol. Tears streaked her sooty face and her expression was wild.

"Matthew."

"He is already outside."

"Benny's dead."

"I know, child, we must go."

"We can't leave him here."

"We must. Quickly now, go."

They went as they had arrived, bent, stumbling, leaning heavily upon each other as they left the dying house.

Fotis lay on a damp patch of grass at the edge of the driveway. Andreas sat down beside him while Ana rushed past them to where Matthew knelt on the gravel, heaving and spitting. The Snake's body was slack, all tension gone, as if the cord of his life force had been cut. Only the blinking eyes showed that there was anyone inside. There were black streaks of ash in Fotis' hair, his left temple was bleeding, and there were bruises over the rest of his head. The thin, fragile limbs and gaunt face were the same as they had been at that troubling dinner a few weeks before, but the vibrant energy that had animated them then was utterly gone. He was not simply old but used up, dying. It might be tomorrow, thought Andreas, or a few months off, but it would be soon.

"Well," Fotis whispered.

"It's gone."

The eyes closed for several moments, then opened again, staring at the sky.

"You killed him?"

"No," Andreas answered, bemused. "The girl did."

"The girl?" In different circumstances, Fotis might have laughed. The best he could manage now was a grimace.

Behind them there was a roaring rush, windows shattered, and flames licked out of the empty frames. The entire house would be consumed shortly. Nothing would be left but the exterior stone wall of the ground floor. From where they sat the two old men could feel the heat.

"You've killed me also," Fotis continued. "All of you. You've taken what I needed to live. For what? To feed it to the flames? Better it should be destroyed than I should have it?" There was bitterness in his words, but little heat. "You've killed me."

The words made Andreas tired. He could not expect wisdom or peace to come to his friend so near the end, but still it made him sad. It was a painting, nothing more. Pigment on wood, no pumping heart, no ageless spirit, no soul. He had held it himself, and he knew. They were all mad.

"You are dying from the inside, Foti. No one can help you."

"You can help me. You can finish the job. You are the one who showed me the icon, made it necessary to my life. Then took it from me, twice. I do not understand why you have worked so hard to destroy me, but at least finish it."

Andreas looked to the two young people. Ana was attempting to bind Matthew's hand with her scarf.

"Send them away," whispered Fotis, "so they will not see. Then put my body in the burning house. I am not brave enough to do it myself, Andreou. You must help me."

"No."

"And what if I tell you I killed your bastard brother."

"I would not believe you."

"I let him die, then. I was in the crypt, waiting for that fat Mavroudas."

"But he got out through the flames, instead. So the plan was yours."

"You knew that before now."

"Including burning the church."

"No, that was Mavroudas' idea."

"But you went along. You agreed to it. Or else you would not have expected him to use the crypt for his escape."

"All right, then. I burned your brother's church. I watched him come down the steps and fall at my feet, bleeding. And I did nothing. I left him to die. How does a brother punish that?"

"There was nothing you could have done. The wounds were

too serious. It was evil to leave him like that, but you did not kill him. Your sins are heavy enough without borrowing others."

"Andreou." Fotis' voice became pleading. "Cancer is a terrible death. And I have had these dreams. I am afraid to do what I should. You must help me."

Nothing Andreas had just learned surprised him, yet it struck deeply. He had not wanted it to be true, had buried it in his heart, fastened upon the hunt for Müller as a means of leading himself away from the truth. His connection with Fotis could not survive this news. He had lost his friend already. And he could imagine no worse judgment than that which nature had already decreed. There was nothing for him to do.

"My punishment for Mikalis," he said, gripping his old friend's shoulder for the last time as he pulled himself to his feet, "is to let you live."

Andreas wandered over toward the younger people, hesitant to invade their intimacy, yet needing to speak to them. Sirens could be heard now, still far distant. A fragment from his dream, or memory, or whatever it had been, came back to the old man suddenly. Something he had not thought of in more than fifty years. He saw the icon there by the table near Kosta, the space between the two panels dug at with some tool. And then, after he had shot the boy, he noticed little scraps upon the table, paper-thin bits of beige cloth. And it had occurred to him that it was one of these which Kosta had placed upon his tongue to swallow with his wine. That last sacrament. He must tell Matthew, sometime. Or perhaps, in fact, he would not.

There was another rushing boom, and part of the roof collapsed, sending gouts of red sparks high into the air. Andreas watched intently. Nothing could have survived in there, and yet he would sift the ashes until he found Müller's bones. The icon would be only dust. There would be no evidence of its destruction. They would have to trust to logic. They would have to take it on faith.

T
he church of Katarini had been built over the ruins of its burned predecessor, and if he looked carefully, Matthew could see the places where the old stone met the new. He had been to this village and this church before, but not for years, and never with his grandfather's unearthed memories, or the image of the lost Holy Mother, so clearly in his mind. According to the priest, the new construction followed the destroyed original closely, and Matthew tried hard to imagine the past still present in this place that was both at once. Was this the window that the *andarte* captain Elias had looked through for signs of his brother? Was this the same stone floor that had bruised the knees of his pious great-grandmother while she prayed, and her mother before, and so on for generations? Was this the patch of wall behind the altar where the Holy Mother was hidden for three years? Then abducted, rescued from fire, only to perish in fire in the end. Was fire its fate all along? Matthew was not a strong believer in fate, but he was withholding judgment on a number of such matters at present.

The church was large for the village it dominated, but smaller than his imagination had made it, and sufficiently cluttered with the usual assortment of modern improvements to impede his experiment in conjuring up history. The priest flicked a switch behind him and the bright chandeliers, ubiquitous in any Greek church now, cleared every shadow of ghosts. The images in the iconostasis—John, wild and lean; Mary, gentle and sad; Christ dressed in the white robes and miter of a bishop—were expertly rendered, but without any age or mystery behind them. The nave was crowded with unadorned pews, where once there would have been only a few, for the old, while the rest of the congregation stood, for hours sometimes, swaying half asleep on their feet, drugged by incense and the priests' chanting. There was a big clock on the church tower, donated by an American businessman—village time eradicated, forced into hiding in the hills and caves, or down in the crypt.

The priest beckoned. Matthew followed him through the opening in the icon screen and around the altar to where a narrow passage ran back to the priest's chambers. There was an almost invisible door in the wall of the passage.

"You want to go down?" Father Isidoros asked.

Matthew placed a palm on the wooden door. "Yes, I do."

He turned and looked to where his father stood by the altar. Alex's hair had come back gray, still surprising Matthew every time he caught sight of it. Yet the leanness had vanished, and the older man carried himself with the upright posture and determined stride that had been his signature before the illness. He was trying to take an interest in the church for Matthew's sake, but he kept looking at his watch, as if he had an appointment somewhere else.

"Dad, we're going into the crypt. Are you coming?"

Alex shook his head.

"No. I was down there once, years ago, that was enough. Enjoy yourself. I'd better find your mother."

"She can't get lost in a village this size."

"Don't underestimate her."

The priest unlatched the door, switched on an electric lantern hanging from a peg within, and started down the narrow steps. A cool draft struck Matthew's face, a high, earthy smell, like a garden shed. He took a deep breath and started down.

They had buried Fotis in a cemetery outside Ioannina. The old man had made the arrangements years before, so the logistics were not difficult for his executor, Matthew Spear. At one point it had seemed that only Matthew, his mother, and the priest would be at the graveside, but Alex had agreed to accompany them at the last moment, and Andreas had come up from Athens. He would not follow them on to the village, though. He had not been back to Katarini in decades and did not intend to see the place again. He was an Athenian now, and would die there.

Ana had wanted to come with Matthew. Or she had offered, in any case—a significant gesture. The fire, the killings, the whole business of the icon had traumatized her deeply, and she'd needed a few weeks to be away from everything having to do with it, including him. Even once they had started to see each other again, del Carros, Benny Ezraki, and the Holy Mother of Katarini were off-limits for discussion. Fotis' death had opened something in Matthew, had freed him of some burden. Responding either to that or to her own heavy therapy, Ana seemed to be coming out the other side of her grief as well. In spite of this, Matthew had been slow to take up her offer. Perhaps intuiting that he needed to do this alone, she made plans to go to Rome with her friend Edith instead. Now he felt the separation keenly, and wondered if he had not made a mistake.

The bottom steps were deeply worn and polished by the passage of thousands. This was the old church. Father Isidoros moved slowly, holding the lantern up here and there. Matthew could feel the tightness of the chamber, the low ceiling, the narrow passages. So much history forced into this little space. There were fewer bones visible than he expected. The compartments mostly hid them, or maybe some had been moved elsewhere. Did they even use the ossuary anymore? In a far corner of the chamber, the priest stopped and looked back at Matthew.

"Here, this place here, is your family."

The younger man glanced at the shelves, but there were almost no bones to see, and those there looked no different from any others. The conformity of death. Yet those yellow shards were his ancestors, maybe souls his grandfather had known in life, not so long ago.

"There," Isidoros continued, pointing to the ground, "is where your great-uncle Mikalis died."

Matthew knelt then and put his hand on the dusty floor, feeling around a bit, as if there might still be a warm spot where the body had lain. Nothing. If he sensed a presence here below, it was not to be found in any one place but was everywhere at once, in the very air. Nevertheless, he knelt upon that sad spot for many minutes, and finally the priest moved away and left him to his meditation. Prayer was no more available to him now than it had ever been, and seemed less necessary. He had nothing to ask, only a last task to perform.

From his pocket he took the smooth jade beads that had spent so many hours in his godfather's hands. What worries had they absorbed, what secrets? What penance could they do now for a man damned by his own conscience before death took him? What was the life of one priest in the weighty scale of Fotis' sins? Mikalis had forgiven, or not, in his last moments, and nothing that Matthew did now mattered. He sighed. Such an evanescent faith was no faith at all. He squeezed the stones in his hand and thought of his grandfather. For Andreas? Could it be for him? But no, the old man would not care, the gesture would be lost upon him.

A memento, then. Like flowers upon a grave. That would have to be good enough. Abandoned by the priest's lantern, in darkness, Matthew placed the beads upon the stone floor and rose to his feet. A slight dizziness took him, and he leaned upon the cases of his ancestors' bones to steady himself. The air down here was too thin for the living; they must go. He wandered back toward the entry, looking about the chamber once more, fixing it in his mind. He wondered if he would return, or whether this might be the last time that a Spyridis visited this ancestral space. Did it matter that the connection would perish with him? Surely the dead did not care either way.

The priest waited for him by the stairs, and they went up.

After the crypt, the newness of the upper church struck Matthew more forcefully. The Holy Mother could never have come back here; it would not have belonged. The thought of the vanished icon opened that dark, aching place within him, as it had done a hundred times already in the past three months. Yet each time with less force. Deep breaths steadied him; he turned his face away from the priest. He would mourn its loss for a long time, the rest of his life, but perhaps Father Ioannes had been right. Perhaps there was no place for such a sacred work in such a compromised world. Except a monastery. Yes, that was the answer. Metéora, Mount Athos, Saint Catherine's in the Sinai. The world still did not know all the treasures hidden away in those places. The Holy Mother of Katarini would have been quite safe. Why had he and Ioannes not thought of that when they contemplated its fate? It hardly mattered now.

The afternoon sun had gone behind the mountains when they emerged into the courtyard, and Matthew could feel the day's heat dissipating, cool dusk coming on swiftly, as it did in these hills. Ana had given him the number of her hotel in Rome. She did not expect him to call, had encouraged him not to, in fact. But she had given him the number. Words were untrustworthy, false. The face spoke the truth. The eyes did not lie, if you knew how to read them. Remember her face, that day he had last seen her. What had it asked of him?

Orange light bathed the top of the distant hill called Adelphos, little brother to the mountains behind it. He would have liked to climb that hill with his grandfather, but he would do it on his own. Find the caves, maybe grow a beard and change his name, live like an *andarte* or a mad hermit. Matthew smiled at the thought. He would settle for climbing the hill, but not today, not just now. Now he had to find a telephone.